Oliver Jewett has reached his fifty-eighth year, an age that no longer accepts self-delusion or flattery. It is his time of truth, the time to reflect on the disappointments of his life with clear-eyed irony and scaled-down dreams. Jewett must come to grips with his acting career, which now hangs in perilous balance between stardom and oblivion. He must examine his past, the family he has fled from, and the men and women he has loved. He must face his present, the lover he feels himself losing, the young man who tempts him so dangerously. He must do what he has to to survive.

This wise and mature novel, by a writer at the peak of his craft, scrupulously lays bare the hidden workings of the human heart. By turns wry, witty, searching, and poignant, it is a brilliant study of a truly good man in a troubled territory familiar to us all.

JOB'S YEAR

JOSEPH HANSEN is the author of the acclaimed Dave Brandstetter mystery series, as well as poetry and stories published in leading magazines. He was founder of the pioneering homosexual journal *Tangents*, and in 1974 was awarded a grant by the National Endowment for the Arts. He currently teaches writing at U.C.L.A. and lives with his wife in a household of cats and dogs. His highly praised novel *A Smile in His Lifetime* is also available in a Plume edition.

ALSO BY JOSEPH HANSEN

Fiction

Fadeout
Death Claims
Troublemaker
The Man Everybody Was Afraid Of
Skinflick
The Dog & Other Stories
A Smile in His Lifetime
Gravedigger
Backtrack

Verse

One Foot in the Boat

JOB'S YEAR

Joseph Hansen

A PLUME BOOK

NEW AMERICAN LIBRARY

NEW YORK AND SCARBOROUGH, ONTARIO

PUBLISHER'S NOTE

This novel is a work of fiction. Names, characters, places, and incidents are either the product of the author's imagination or are used fictitiously, and any resemblance to actual persons, living or dead, events, or locales is entirely coincidental.

NAL BOOKS ARE AVAILABLE AT QUANTITY DISCOUNTS WHEN USED TO PROMOTE PRODUCTS OR SERVICES. FOR INFORMATION PLEASE WRITE TO PREMIUM MARKETING DIVISION, NEW AMERICAN LIBRARY, 1633 BROADWAY, NEW YORK, NEW YORK 10019.

Copyright © 1983 by Joseph Hansen

My thanks to Sid Spies, M.D., Charles Macaulay, and Ed Rucker for their advice on technical aspects of this story.   —J.H.

Grateful acknowledgement is made for permission to quote from the following: "The Mind is an Enchanting Thing," from *Collected Poems* by Marianne Moore. Copyright 1944, and renewed 1972, by Marianne Moore. By permission Macmillan Publishing Company.

Lyrics from "Indian Summer" by Al Dubin and Victor Herbert. © 1919, 1939 (Copyright Renewed) WARNER BROS. INC. All Rights Reserved. Used By Permission.

This is an authorized reprint of a hardcover edition published by Holt, Rinehart and Winston, published simultaneously in Canada by Holt, Rinehart and Winston of Canada, Limited.

Library of Congress Cataloging-in-Publication Data
Hansen, Joseph, 1923–
  Job's year.

  I. Title.
PS3558.A513J6 1985   813'.54   85-11070
ISBN 0-452-25754-9

 PLUME TRADEMARK REG. U.S. PAT. OFF. AND FOREIGN COUNTRIES
REG. TRADEMARK—MARCA REGISTRADA
HECHO EN FAIRFIELD, PA., U.S.A.

SIGNET, SIGNET CLASSIC, MENTOR, PLUME, MERIDIAN and NAL BOOKS are published in the United States by New American Library, 1633 Broadway, New York, New York 10019, in Canada by The New American Library of Canada Limited, 81 Mack Avenue, Scarborough, Ontario M1L 1M8.

First Plume Printing, November, 1985

1 2 3 4 5 6 7 8 9

PRINTED IN THE UNITED STATES OF AMERICA

For Leonard and Maxine Gerhart
and Marguerite Erchul

Walking is a series of coordinated falls.

—*Lewis Thomas*, M.D.

JOB'S
YEAR

January

HE HOPES his own death will take him somewhere
else, but the deaths of others always bring him back here. He
calls the place Perdidos, though that is not its true name. Its true
name sounds something like that. He stumbled on the similar-
ity in Spanish class after Richie Cowan died of a broken neck
practicing high-school football. Soon afterward, Joey Pfeffer
died in the war, and Perdidos stuck as the only right name in his
mind—losses. He has been back only on account of sicknesses,
deaths, funerals.

Tucked into the foothills of the brown Sierra Madres, streets
steep and crooked, trees old and shaggy and dark, the town has
changed in forty years. The houses he remembers had deep
eaves, long, low porches with square beams, and crouched cool
and dim under the trees. Whole streets of those houses have
been torn down. Apartment complexes of pale stucco, with
boxy balconies and sliding glass doors, loom up among the
treetops today.

Deodar Street, however, has not changed, is still wrapped in
the old hush, under its mournful, drooping, blue-green trees.
He leaves his car in front of the tongue-and-groove garage doors

that front the street, and climbs the cement steps that don't feel familiar to his feet anymore because they have cracked and shifted with time, with the swell of tree roots, with small quakings of the earth. The house is high up the slope. The steps ascend zigzag, and there are forty of them. Running up and down them as a kid gave him strong legs, but he thinks the steps killed his father, and has been angry about them ever since.

Halfway up the steps, he stops to catch his breath, and is struck by the sudden realization that he is as old now as his father was when his heart gave out. Today, his sister has told him on the telephone that she is dying, and she is only five years older than he. Have the steps done it to her too? They would be extra hard on her. He wonders for the thousandth time why she moved back here. He leans his butt against the cold cement retaining wall where moss grows coppery green, and he lights a cigarette. An instant later, shocked at himself, he drops the cigarette, crushes it with his shoe among the brown pine needles. He draws a deep breath to clear his lungs, and climbs the rest of the way to the porch.

It feels shaky underfoot—from dry rot, he wonders, or termites? With his father, he used to creep around under the house, painting the support beams with creosote to kill the termites or discourage them. Redwood was supposed to be termite-proof, but his father didn't trust it. Jewett hated the job, the spider webs, the dead rats, and the fear of meeting a live one in some dark crawlspace, so he told his father that he was being ridiculous. How right he had been about everything at seventeen! Is the house even redwood for sure? He gazes at the stained-glass water lily window of the golden oak door, wondering whether to ring the bell. How sick is she? He tries the brass latch. It drops under his thumb with a limp click. He pushes open the door and puts in his head. He calls:

"It's me—Oliver."

"Come in," she calls. Her voice sounds strong, even cheerful, which annoys him a little. If she is dying, she ought to sound as if she is dying. He steps inside and closes the door. For a second, he feels disoriented because small dogs, gray and woolly, don't come yapping and jumping noisily around him. But the small dogs are long dead. Lambert, her gangly, desperately cross-eyed husband, took them for a walk in the rain one night years ago. A car on a dark street hit and killed them all. She hasn't replaced the dogs. Dogs always frightened her. Other dogs.

The living room is paneled halfway up in golden oak. Above that, wallpapers of one pattern and another used to come and go. Now the many layers have been stripped and white paint applied. He guesses the room is a shade brighter than it used to be because of this innovation of hers, but it is still a gloomy room. Its sound is still gloomy—the solemn tick of a grand-father clock, brought by some forebear from Portsmouth, Eng-land, to Portsmouth, New Hampshire, in 1720. For a long time, it felt strange to Jewett to live without that sound in his ears.

Every now and then, to lift his spirits, his father used to call in antique dealers to admire the clock and to tell him how much it was worth. He wouldn't have considered selling it. He just enjoyed turning over in his mind the large sums of money they mentioned. When they had gone off empty-handed, he would stand in front of the clock, chuckling, wagging his head in amazement. "Can you beat that?" he would ask Jewett. "It's a fine old piece," Jewett would say. He said this because then his father would squeeze his young shoulders or ruffle his hair. He loved his father, but he never learned to love the clock.

A set of golden oak sliding doors separates the living room from the dining room. In his father's and mother's time these doors were rarely shut. Now they are open only a few inches. From beyond them he hears the wooden clacking that means she is weaving, sending the shuttle back and forth, trampling the long wooden beams under the loom with her one good leg and her one crippled leg. The shortness of that leg forces her to twist on the bench each time she uses it. The motion would startle a stranger. It looks as if something with sharp teeth is nipping her behind.

How can she be dying? He parts the doors and stands watching her in annoyance and admiration. She is very good at weaving. He wishes he were good at some basic craft like that, something that can be done alone and with the hands. It is an old wish of his that he can't shake off, no matter that it is beyond reach and getting farther beyond reach with every birthday. She works quickly but without seeming to hurry. The wools she uses are the colors of the sheep, goats, llamas they came from, browns, tans, muted yellows, grays, duns, blacks. The yarns, spun for her by Indians in Arizona to whom she sends the wool, are crude, thick, nubby. She is famous for the hangings she makes of these wools. Her hangings—no matter that she meant them to be rugs—drape the walls in the permanent collections of great museums.

"Shouldn't you be lying down?" he says.

"I'm not dead yet," she says, but she stops weaving, turns on the bench, gives him a smile. Her bad foot clunks against a strut under the bench. He is not startled by how homely she is. He spent too many years with her for that. But he has not seen her since Lambert was alive—can it really have been seven years?—and her homeliness impresses him anew, perhaps because he spends so much time with people whose good looks are all they have. She is pug-faced and dwarfish, and her mouth looks as if her teeth were crowding to get out of it. She wears glasses now almost as thick as those poor old Lambert wore toward the end in the frail hope of staving off blindness a little longer. Since their mother's death, Susan has kept her hair cropped short. It is almost white, though she is only sixty-two, and he finds it touching that a bald spot has started at the top of her skull at the back. As if she can read his thoughts, she says, "Handsomer than ever, aren't you? Tall and straight and trim. Beautiful Oliver."

"Your eyesight is playing tricks on you," he says. "I'm old, Susan."

"Distinguished, then," she says. "Is that better?"

"Your phone call was pretty frightening." He steps to the

loom and stands looking gravely down at her. The loom is large and high and takes up most of the dining room. A round golden oak table used to stand here, hedged by stiff, uncomfortable golden oak chairs. A Tiffany lamp hung on a chain over the table. That too is gone, but some stained glass in the same pattern still tops the wide windowpane at Susan's back. Big cardboard cartons are stacked high and untidily around the paneled walls. The cartons bulge with hanks of yarn and with bulky folds of woven stuff. Along the walls, high up, and from the plate rails where no plates stand anymore, hang lengths of hefty braiding and macrame work. These she sometimes weaves into her great panels, making of them bristly bas-reliefs. He says, "How do you feel? What does the doctor say?"

"I feel marvelous," she says brightly, "that's why I went to the doctor. Doesn't everyone?" She looks worried and touches his hand. "You're not really a numbskull, are you, Oliver? You just talk like one, sometimes, isn't that it? You pretend. Of course." She turns back and shoots the worn shuttle across the strings of the loom rapidly, two, three, four times, the treadles under the loom, the beams above, clattering, her squat body giving, each time, that jerk that seems to be from pain and is not. "You're an actor. Pretending to be someone else is your whole life. Isn't that what they say?"

"The numbskull part is genuine," he says. "It's me. Are you going to answer my numbskull question?"

She stops weaving, but does not look up at him, looks at her work, runs her stumpy hands on it. "I have what Mother had," she says quietly. "Leukemia. I had to check in at the hospital, waste ten days with doctors and machines. They had to have tests, the results of tests. I didn't. I knew. I watched her get sick." Her hazel eyes swim behind the thick lenses when she looks up at him. "I watched her die. We are simply not a long-lived family."

He says gently, "What can I do for you?"

"Nothing." She makes a deprecatory face. "I'm sorry I brought you all this way. As you can see, I'm all right. I'll be

making runs to the hospital. Every fourth week, every day of
that week. For chemotherapy."

"I'll drive you," he says. "Mother was weak. Are you weak?
You look strong. What about all the steps? Can you keep climbing all those damned steps?"

"They've never stopped me yet," she says, "game leg and all.
They won't tell you anymore how long you've got—but Mother
had more than a year, and I'm stronger than she was. It was
selfish of me to call you. I'm used to being on my own. It's just
that this—surprised me."

She chooses words oddly, always has. He doesn't know what
his word would be, but not surprised. "I imagine so," he says.
"Susan, I'm sorry. It's so terribly unfair."

As if he hadn't spoken, she goes on. "I don't get all feminine
and frantic as a rule. But suddenly I wanted Lambert. Suddenly
I needed him. And he isn't here. And Mother isn't here, Father
isn't here. I needed you. Or thought I did. You were the only one
I could think of that I wanted to tell my troubles to. And now I
don't know why, do I?" She smiles a crooked smile and pats his
hand again. "We're not what we used to be, are we? We've been
apart too long. We're strangers...."

They were in the back bedroom. She was twelve years old
and he was seven. She had had polio and had been in the
hospital where he could not see her for a long, lonely time. Now
she was at home again at last, in her bed, crutches leaning
against the wall by the head of the bed, steel brace with its
leather straps and many buckles lying on a chair beside the bed.
Sun streamed through the window. The window was open. A
warm breeze bellied the pale mesh curtains, and the wooden
strip of the half-raised roller shade tapped the window frame.

He kept trotting out and down the hall to their parents' bedroom, where he plundered the closet for dresses and shoes and
hats. He changed these with eager swiftness, tossing helter-
skelter the garments that smelled deliciously of his mother's
perfume. Everything was absurdly too big, and he cinched up
the dresses with scarves. He regarded his small, impudent self

in the oval pier glass, turning this way and that—lipstick, rouge, eyebrow pencil. He staggered and clunked in the loose high heels back to Susan's door. He had already done a song-and-dance number—*Around the cor-ner, and under the tree, a handsome ma-jor, he waits for me....* What should he do now?

He breathed deeply through his nose, puffed out his chest, stood straight and haughty, and simpered in, announcing, "I am Madame Letitia van Pumpernickel, very fashionable, just back from the Riviera. What a lovely holiday, my dear." He flourished a carved ivory cigarette holder he'd found in his father's cuff-link box. He batted his mascaraed lashes and twittered, "We caught ever so many goldfish." Susan burst out laughing, and this made him laugh. So hard that he fell in a heap of organdy on the floor and rolled about helplessly, breaking his mother's beads....

"You're not a stranger to me," he says now. "If I'm a stranger to you, it's because they've tampered with your blood. What we are to each other is in the blood, Susan. Absence can't change that, time can't change it. We are not strangers, and we never can be." He is moved by the speech. It brings tears to his eyes. To hide the tears from her, he turns and peers into the living room. He wipes away the tears with his fingers. The living room, he sees now, is dusty, neglected, the only spot of brightness a potted yellow chrysanthemum newly brought by some well-wisher. When Lambert was alive—Lambert who could see scarcely anything, who stalked lankily around indoors, even by daylight, following the beam of a powerful flashlight, bald head thrust out on skinny neck as he peered and squinted—when Lambert was alive, she had kept the house spruce, which the shedding of Lambert's beloved dogs couldn't have made easy. The place is scruffy now. He turns back. "I'm moved that you called me. I would have hated it if you hadn't called me."

"You'll get fed up when I repeat the process often enough," she says. "The first week of treatments starts soon. What a prospect. It makes you feel so sick."

"You told me she had her good weeks," he says.

Her laugh is faint and ironic. "Oh, yes. And for the time being, she'd forget. But she hated her hair falling out—that's a side effect of chemotherapy, you know. She loved to look pretty. I can't look pretty if I try. I don't care about my hair. It's the vomiting I hate. You remember how I hate it? You used to hold my head." She runs her hands on the weaving again and sighs. "Ah, it's not important. It'll give me time to get my work done." She peers up at him. "Will you come hold my head?" She adds quickly, "I can hire a nurse. I'm all right for money, and you have your life to live."

"I have time on my hands," he says. "The phone is not exactly jangling off the hook with offers of jobs." He strokes her hair. It is old-womanly soft and thin. "If that should miraculously change, we'll think about a nurse."

She takes his hand and lays it for a moment against her cheek, also soft and old-womanish. She kisses his hand and smiles at him. "I see you sometimes on the television. It makes me proud."

"You must not blink often," he says. "My bits tend to go past pretty briskly. I go into bookstores now and then to read the art magazines for free. You're in them more often than I'm on the tube. That makes me proud. When I was in London with that lousy musical, I went to the Tate and looked at your hanging there. I told everybody in the room you were my sister."

"They must have thought you were crazy," she says, but she is pleased. He can tell. She blushes.

He looks at his watch. "It's noonish. How about I fix us some lunch?"

She grimaces. "To feed those voracious white cells?"

"Oh, Susan. Come on, now." Her bitterness chills him.

"Sorry," she says. "I've stopped eating lunch. I've got too much work to get through." She begins to weave again. "I'm full of ideas. If I don't get cracking, I won't be able to use them up."

He heads for the kitchen, calling back, "If you're going to be an invalid, you've got to start letting people do things for you. I want to cook. Is that all right?"

"Thank you," she calls, and the loom keeps clattering.

The kitchen is a horror. The linoleum is a welter of grimy spots and smears. The pots on the stove are blackened, greasy, clotted with food. Dishes, glasses clutter the counter by the sink, unwashed. He opens the refrigerator, which hasn't been wiped of fingerprints in a long while. The light inside has gone out and there is a powerful smell of food gone bad. She has given up, hasn't she? She must have known what was happening to her long before she made herself see that doctor. He probes among bowls covered in furry mold, a transparent envelope of green bacon, plastic bags flaccid with vegetables turned to brown mush. He sniffs at the red and white milk carton. Sour. He regards three eggs in the rack on the door. Can they be fresh? The freezer is clotted with snow, and holds only a tray of ice cubes and the crystallized remains of a pint of chocolate ice cream. He closes the refrigerator and opens cupboards. A few cans, tops thick with dust, a collapsed box of cornflakes. Dog biscuits. Really? He returns to her. "When did you last eat?" he says.

"I don't seem hungry." The beams and treadles lift and fall, the shuttle runs like a rat across the strings and back. She throws him a little smile meant to reassure him. "I have toast and tea and maybe an egg. It's a bore, cooking for yourself. Look at me. Do I appear to be withering away? I eat when I think of it."

"Start thinking of it now." He digs his keys from his jacket pocket and heads for the front door, tossing the keys in his hand, jingling them. "I'll do some shopping. I'll be right back."

When he returns, she is not at the loom. She lies in her clothes on the bed in her childhood room asleep. The sheets and pillowcases of the bed are grubby. The air of the room is sour with the smell of unwashed clothes. These are strewn everywhere. The mirror over the handsome old chest of drawers hasn't been washed in years. In it, he appears to himself a ghost. He has bought detergent, spray cleaners, sponges, pot scrubbers, oven cleaner, paper towels, plastic trash bags at the supermarket. He scrubs the pots, washes the dishes, scours the sink, cleans grease and grime off the stove top. All that rots in the refrigerator he dumps into the big green bags, which he wires shut and sets at the foot of the back steps, because the rubber garbage can and galvanized trash barrels are overflowing.

"All I have time for," she says, by way of apology, "is my work. I didn't mean for you to have to clean and scrub." She is eating at the kitchen table, which he has sponged of years of accumulated food spills and whose white enamel does its aged best to shine. "I can hire someone to do that. I just keep putting it off." She regards him earnestly. "You mustn't think it's the neglect of despair."

"How's the omelet?" he says.

"Scrumptious," she says, though she has taken only a few small bites, quite plainly to oblige him. "Light as air. Delicious. You should open a restaurant."

"Should have," he says. "Too late now to change careers." He laughs at himself. "Career? That's quite a word for it, right?"

"You've lived," she says, "by doing what you wanted most to do. Very few people can say that. Me too. We've been lucky."

He nods at her plate. "Eat," he says, and, watching her, worriedly, "You were only sitting at that loom to impress me with how well you are, to show me that the phone call was exaggeration. You went to lie down as soon as I was out the door. You didn't mean for me to find you that way. You meant to be all perky and weaving away when I got back. Be honest, now."

"I get tired quickly," she says. "But an hour's nap and I can work again. It's just a question of pacing." She lays down her fork and her eyes beg him. "I'm sorry. I can't eat it all. It's not your fault. My stomach's shrunk. I does that, you know, when you don't keep stretching it. Ah, but it *was* good."

He smiles. "I'm glad," he says.

"You can put it in a plastic bag," she says, "in the icebox. I'll heat it and eat it for my supper."

"I'll cook Alfredo for our supper." He stands and takes away the plates. "It's the easiest thing I know on the stomach. Fettucini in butter and cream with parmesan."

"I didn't mean to make a servant of you."

"Don't talk nonsense." He scrapes her plate and his neatly into a new white plastic garbage bag. He washes and dries plates, knives, forks, and puts them away. Glasses—she agreed to a taste of white wine. He says, "You know I was meant to be a happy little housewife."

She says sharply, "That's not so. There was that Rita Lopez woman. I hate it when you talk like that."

"Sorry," he says. "It used to amuse you."

"A little boy dressed up in Mommy's clothes is one thing," she says. She doesn't say what the other thing is. She gets up from the table. Awkwardly. It tilts and rights itself with a bang. "I didn't know what it meant then."

Her harshness startles him. It is new and it is old. It began forty years ago. It didn't relent during his time with Rita— Rita scandalized Susan. It held on grimly until she married Lambert, when she began to send Jewett birthday cards, Christmas cards, even to phone him now and then. With the advent of Bill, she made sure to ask after him—coolly but dutifully, calling him Mr. Haycock. Then Lambert died, and Jewett was in Spain with a film and couldn't come to the funeral, and Susan became angry and silent.

Into a long, crisp, white paper bag marked Pfeffer's in red he slides the fresh loaf of crusty sourdough bread, and folds the end of the bag tight. He won't put it into the breadbox now. He hasn't investigated the breadbox, but he can guess what he will find. He lays the loaf in its sack on the sink counter. Maybe that she is dying has made her bitter all over again. She has time to think, hours of it every day, sitting at the loom, only her hands and feet occupied, no one to talk to. Has it come to her that there's no time left, no chance left to alter, amend, reverse the past? While we live most of us cling, against our common sense, to the hope that somehow we can.

Faced with final hopelessness, why wouldn't her old bitterness resurface? Lambert is gone. Why wouldn't she think again of Ungar and her loss of Ungar all those long years ago, and blame Jewett afresh in 1980 as she had blamed him in 1939? Maybe, after all, he is well off earning his sketchy living as he does. No time to think—not while he is working. Happily for him, acting doesn't take brains, or he'd have starved long ago. But it takes attention and a lot of other people. And since he can't forget anything, any more than she can, it was a lucky choice for him. And he is angry with himself now for having reminded her of something hateful to her....

It was raining. The long cement stairs up to the house had drains, but the fallen needles of the deodars clogged the small outlets. It was one of Jewett's chores to keep these clear, but he forgot when the weather was fine, only remembered too late. Now, for example, scrambling up the stairs two at a time because when he'd set off for school the sky was cloudless, and he hadn't taken his raincoat. The steps were little waterfalls, and the rain, which had already soaked his hair, his clothes, and, worst of all, his books, now seeped cold into his shoes. He splashed at a run around the side of the house and flapped in at the back porch screen door. He set the books down and stood miserably shaking his arms and plucking at his damp trouser legs. He teetered on one foot, then the other, prying off shoes, peeling off socks. He padded across the cold kitchen linoleum for a dish towel. The dyes of the book covers stained the towel red, blue, green. To hide the towel, to postpone hearing about it, he lifted the lid of the washing machine and dropped the towel inside. Also the socks. He wrapped each book in dry newspaper and left them on the porch, along with his shoes.

Ear cocked for Susan's voice, he made for the bathroom. She didn't call out, and he decided she must be asleep beyond her closed door. She had been sick with pneumonia—it was always something—and was only slowly getting well. He lowered the plug on its little soapy chain into the drain of the clawfooted tub, set the faucets so the water rushed hard into the tub, testing it with his hand to be sure it was on the temperate side of scalding, then, shivering, stripped off his wet clothes. He remembered that his mother would probably arrive home—she was a high-school teacher—before he finished his bath, and he trotted naked down the hall to get his bathrobe from the hook on the inside of his bedroom closet door. Dragging the robe behind him, he was trotting back up the hall, when a young man in a clerical collar stepped out of the door of Susan's room, saw him, and stopped dead in his tracks, staring.

This had to be Ungar, the new curate at St. Barnabas Episcopal Church. Jewett hadn't met him, but Susan had chattered about him, excitement in her voice, brightness in her eyes. Ungar had begun visiting her in the hospital, and had continued his visits here, sitting beside her bed for an hour every morning, reading to her. He had brought her gifts. A crucifix now hung over the carved head of her bed. A prayer book lay among the medicine bottles on the bedside table under the lamp. An odd, brown, medieval drawing of an immense St. Theresa, seated, leaning back against a tiny cathedral, adorned a wall. Stepping in to play chess with Susan, Jewett had caught her praying. It repelled him. To him, as to his father and mother, religion was all right, but you didn't let it show.

He had pictured this Ungar as a sickly runt. He looked like a Viking—six feet tall, blue-eyed, clear, healthy skin, a body obviously all trim, hard-packed muscle under that black suit. Jewett whipped the robe around to cover his nakedness, gave Ungar some kind of smile, gulped out "Bath," dodged into the steam, and shut and bolted the door. He washed, then lay stretched out in the soap-milky water, letting the heat soak the cold of the winter rain out of him. He thought about Ungar. The way the curate had looked at him made him uneasy. Ungar hadn't just been surprised. There'd been more to it. Jewett had seen that look once before. In the dog-brown eyes of John Le Clerc. Jewett sat up sharply, sloshing the bathwater. He didn't want to think about that. He yanked the plug, used a hand to wipe off the soap ring, climbed out of the tub, dried himself hurriedly, flapped into his robe, and knotted the sash tight.

Whenever he saw parked at the foot of the stairs Ungar's gray Plymouth with the St. Christopher medal hanging off a chain from the rearview mirror, Jewett veered away from the house. If Ungar showed up when Jewett was at home, Jewett closed the door to his room and stayed in there, doing homework, listening to records, reading, until Ungar had gone away again. When his mother told him Ungar was coming to dinner, Jewett made up urgent rehearsals of his little-theater group to keep himself away. His mother and father didn't notice, but Susan noticed. She wasn't sick anymore, but she stayed in bed a lot. She felt safe there. If she were up and dressed, she might have to go out, and she shrank from going out, hated people staring at her, dwarfish, limping along. She was in bed, holding a pulpy little brown playscript, cuing him in some silly lines in a childish play, when she closed the book and said:

"Oliver, what's the matter? He always asks about you. You're hurting his feelings. He doesn't understand. You don't like him, do you? The first man who's ever paid any attention to me in my life, and you don't like him. Why?"

Jewett felt his face grow hot. "I like him fine. Why wouldn't I like him? You're crazy. Come on, throw me the stupid cue."

He had never minded telling her the truth before—mostly anyway. But those words of hers, *The first man who's ever paid any attention to me in my life*, stopped his mouth. It had never made any difference to her, had it? Hadn't she run and hidden from boys? She was rarely sick in summer, only in winter, so she wouldn't have to hobble along the hallways of the school. Books were her life, drawing, painting, things she could do alone in her room, in her safe bed. And here she was suddenly talking like an ordinary woman. She was, for God's sake, in love with Ungar. It hit Jewett in the head, like the hammer they hit steers with at the slaughterhouse.

He was jerked up on a hook and swept along like a carcass through the slaughterhouse, gutted, hollow, stripped of his hide. All he had thought of was himself, keeping away from Ungar because he knew what Ungar was and what Ungar wanted of him, and it frightened the hell out of him. He hadn't thought what Ungar might mean to Susan. Not until this moment. He began to sweat. It was a bad situation—he could

see that much. But how did his seeing it help? He couldn't help.
He was sixteen years old, for God's sake. How could he help?
What would happen if he didn't help? For a week after that,
worry broke up his sleep. Once, he sat his father down to tell
him about Ungar, but he couldn't speak the words. Anyway,
maybe he was mistaken. He didn't have any proof, did he? If
Ungar was a queer, then why was he courting Susan?

St. Barnabas had a little radio station in its parish house, gray
carpet, gray, asbestos-sprayed walls, two or three shiny ribbon
microphones on iron pipe stands, a tiny control room with one
turntable and a double-paned window that peered out into the
studio. Once a week, the radio broadcasting class at the high
school got to use the place. A clever Jewett would have kept
away. But Jewett was beautiful, not clever. More than that, he
had a deep, pleasant voice, and read with ease and expressive-
ness. He was always given big parts to play in the lame dramati-
zations of the lives of scientists the high-school class was doing
that year. He had his heart set on a brilliant future as an actor.
He couldn't make himself stay away.

Naturally, Ungar saw him going in and out. Naturally, Ungar
began coming into the control room, standing back out of the
student engineer's way, listening to rehearsals, listening to
broadcasts. Pretending to. His eyes, blue as flowers, always
seemed to be on Jewett. Whenever Jewett caught him staring,
Ungar didn't turn his eyes away. He smiled. Jewett didn't know
how to cope with that, and foolishly smiled back. Then, one
night after a broadcast, when it had come on to rain, Ungar was
there to offer to drive home students who didn't have rides.
Smelling of wet wool, five youngsters crowded into the gray
Plymouth. To deliver them, Ungar twice had to pass Deodar
Street, yet Jewett somehow wound up alone with him. And
Ungar said the words and made the moves Jewett expected but
had fooled himself for weeks into thinking wouldn't be said,
wouldn't be made. He was cornered. He didn't know what to
do. He'd only worried, he hadn't planned. But he had to do
something, and he took Ungar's hand off him and said:

"What about my sister?"

"This was your idea," Ungar said, "from the start." They sat parked under dripping trees that cut off the light from the streetlamps. "Don't pretend to me. You're the same as I am. You've been waiting for this. You know it."

"No." Jewett found it hard to breathe. He put the hand away from him again. "I'm not the same as you. I'm not a queer." He couldn't look at Ungar. He looked straight ahead at the rain streaming down the windshield, and knew with a stab a grief and shame that he was lying. His voice sounded to him like a child's cry, afraid in the dark, not of a dream but of the truth, of the real terror standing tall and murderous at the foot of the bed. He had told himself that masturbating with Richie Cowan, naked in Richie's room, or up the canyons where they sometimes hiked, was just something boys did. For the fun of it, because it felt good. All boys did it. But he knew they didn't do it to each other, not most of them. He and Richie were the only ones he knew about for sure. What Richie was, was Richie's secret—but Jewett knew what Jewett was, and not facing up to it was lying. Still, it was different with John Le Clerc, with Ungar. They were men, grown men. There was something vile about that. It turned his stomach.

"What about my sister?" he said again, and groped for the door handle with a shaking hand. Ungar's fingers were warm on his fly again, gently squeezing. Jewett was getting an erection. Ungar chuckled softly.

"See?" he said. "I'm right about you."

"I can't help it," Jewett said, and found the handle, shouldered the door open, and fell out onto wet grass on his hands and knees. He scrambled to his feet and turned to face the car. Ungar was leaning across the seat, reaching out—for Jewett, or only for the door? Jewett caught the door to keep him from closing it. Jewett leaned down, wet hair streaming in his eyes, and shouted in a broken voice, "I don't have to help it. You have to help it. You're a minister, for God's sake. Now, are you going to tell her, or am I?" The door was wrenched out of his hand. It slammed loud in the rainy night silence. The car shot away, swerving, skidding on the wet pavement, Jewett shouting wildly after it, "What about Jesus? What about sin?" Somewhere inside a house down the street a dog barked at his shouting. He pushed his hands into his pockets, hunched his shoulders, and sloshed miserably home.

"He's quit his job. He's gone away." Susan's eyes were red and swollen with weeping, her knob of a nose was red with weeping, and her mouth was wet and ugly, crying at him. He'd rarely seen her weep. She had been through terrible times with disease and doctors but she'd rarely broken. It had taken Jewett to break her, hadn't it? He had to be the one. She stood in the doorway of his room. At his desk, he was cutting cardboard for a miniature set he was making for Our Town. He turned to stare at her, amazed and afraid. "And it's your fault," she cried. "If it hadn't been for you, he would have been all right. He told me all about it. You. You." She came lurching on her uneven legs to stand over him. Her spittle struck his eyes. "Traipsing naked through the house that day. You saw his car. You had to see it. You knew he was here. You did it on purpose."

"No." Her fury dazed him. "I didn't. Why would I?"

"You know why. Because you're beautiful, and you knew he'd see you naked, and then he couldn't help himself."

"It's not true," Jewett said. Hopelessly. Could it be true? Had he seen the car? He couldn't remember seeing the car. It had been raining terribly hard, and he had been running with his head down, only thinking of how to get in out of the rain, to get dry, to get warm. "I didn't know anything about him. I'd never seen him before. After it happened, I tried to stay away from him. You know that. You saw it. Remember, you even talked to me about it?"

"But you didn't answer," she said, "did you? You lied to me. Yes, you kept away from him when I could see, but you went to St. Barnabas, didn't you? Where I couldn't see. And where you knew he'd see you again." While she spoke, her eyes searched the disorderly desk top, the open copy of Theatre Arts, poster paints, sliced cardboard, brushes, masking tape. "And remember how beautiful you are naked. All that beauty in the house. And me. Something to scare children in a fairy tale. What would he want with me when he'd seen you? Ugly Susan. Ugly, ugly!" She lunged past him. Her hand scrabbled after something on the desk. He saw the dangerous glint of it in her stubby fingers—the single-edged razor blade he used for cutting. She tried to slash her throat. He caught at her, jumping up, the chair clattering on its back. He wrestled with her. She was a head shorter, but she was strong. They fell to the floor, struggling. Her cries were keenings of despair. A great smear of blood crossed her blouse suddenly. His hand had made that. The blade had slashed the palm of his hand. He didn't know when. She didn't have the blade. It lay small and harmless on the floor. He picked it up.

"I'm bleeding," he said stupidly, and laid the blade on the desk. He should go to the bathroom, wash the cut, put disinfectant on it, bandage it. He didn't go. He was afraid to leave her. She lay weeping, facedown on the oval braided rug, shaking with sobs, wailing. He held the bleeding hand with his other hand, standing over her. "I didn't mean it," he said, tears running down his face, the blood from his hand dripping in a quick patter on his shoes. "I didn't want it to happen. You have to believe me. I'm sorry, I'm sorry...."

He says now, reading the red lettering on the bread sack, "Joey Pfeffer's son wants to sell the bakery. Can you imagine that? How long had it been there? Fifty years I know about. I'd like to buy it. It was fun working there, getting up when the whole town was asleep. When was that? Nineteen-forty, 'forty-one? Summers." He smiles and is wryly surprised that he can smile, considering what Joey Pfeffer did to him. Poor Joey! "Good, honest work, baking. Something people need."

"Buy it," she says from the kitchen doorway.

"No money." He has glimpsed a green plastic bucket on the back porch. He goes to get it, and lifts down a dry, cobwebby mop from a rusty nail. He carries bucket and mop to the clean sink. "I thought that after I got enough lines in my face, enough gray in my hair"—he dumps detergent powder into the bucket—"they'd stop turning me down because I was too pretty. They still turn me down." He pours from a white plastic jug into the bucket bleach whose strong fumes make his eyes water. "I'll never get rich." He runs hot water hard into the bucket.

She says, "My work is bringing ridiculous prices. Has been for years. Armie makes me keep it off the market. Your old room is stuffed with it. Don't worry—you'll have plenty of money when I die. I promise."

"No more talk about dying, all right?" He turns off the water and lowers the heavy bucket to the floor. He plunges the stiff, matted strings of the mop into it.

"You don't have to mop," she says.

"Of course I don't have to." He pulls up the mop, bends, squeezes some of the soapy water out of it with his hand, the one with the long, white scar across the palm. He slaps the sopping strings down on the floor and begins to mop. He tosses her another smile. "I'll do it because I want to, all right?"

"Take off your shoes, then," she says, "and socks. Roll up your pants legs."

"Yes. Too right." He sits on a chair to do these things. "You going to weave? You going to lie down?" He sets the shoes on the table, tucks the socks into them. He picks up the four chairs and turns them, legs up, on the table. It reminds him of the café jobs he took when he was young and acting in hole-in-corner theaters that paid little or, more often, paid nothing at all.

"Work, I think," she says, and starts away, and then turns back. "Oliver, I'm sorry I snapped at you. I know—" She frowns, struggling to find words. "I know you can't help it. It's not your fault you're—the way you are. It was that miserable Le Clerc."

He is mopping again, his back to her. He shuts his eyes and says wearily, "That's not true, Susan. He wouldn't have done what he did if I hadn't already been—what did you say?—the way I am. I didn't know it, no. Not to put a name to. But Le Clerc knew. He could see it. So could Ungar, when he came along. It's a sixth sense."

"Rubbish," she says.

He looks at her. "Now you're forgetting the boy who got himself up in Mommy's dresses. And Mommy's makeup. Even Mommy's underwear. Ah, no, you didn't know about the underwear. That was a secret vice. But the rest? Didn't that strike you as a little odd for a boy?"

"It was playacting," she says dismissively. "You loved it from the start, and you still love it. Dressing up. Being someone else. The laughter, the applause." She stops and eyes him. "You don't wear women's clothes today?"

Jewett shakes his head, pads barefoot to the bucket to rinse out the mop, squeezing hard. "It wasn't Le Clerc's fault. It was mine." He lets the mop soak up the soapy water. "I led him on. I was flattered by all the attention he gave me, his smiles, the way he touched my hair, the little presents. But I sensed there was more." He lifts the streaming mop and slaps it down. Water runs across the filthy linoleum. He mops at it. The bright blue of the linoleum begins to show in streaks. "I played that poor man like a doomed fish, Susan."

"You didn't know what you were doing." She scoffs. "You didn't know he'd attack you sexually. You didn't know anything about such things. Surely not."

Mopping away, Jewett smiles crookedly, miserably. "Attack. What a word. He was gentle, he was tender. I remember how his hands trembled. Susan, there were tears in his eyes."

She snorts. "He was an easy weeper. I remember how he wept out there in the living room when Daddy confronted him with what he'd done to you."

"Done to me?" Jewett gives a bleak laugh. "Susan, I nearly destroyed that man. I'll never forget it, and I'll never forgive myself."

"Nonsense. If anyone tried to destroy John Le CLerc that day it was himself. He was a grown man, Oliver. He knew the chance he was taking. You were only a child."

"I was eleven years old," he says, "no baby."

"He disgusted and frightened you and you panicked."

"And ran in a sweat to tattle on him. It was a mean-spirited, vindictive, horrible thing to do." He wrings out the mop again, lets it sop up soapy water again, splats it down again in a new place on the linoleum. He shoves and pulls it with the gritty handle. "And I knew it. I knew he couldn't help himself. Don't ask me how I knew. There are some things that just can't be explained."

"Oliver, all the man lost was a pathetic job directing a tiny community theater. He didn't go to jail, didn't go to court. There wasn't a word in the newspapers. Not even a word of gossip. Daddy let him off to protect you. Do you suppose he starved to death?" Her laugh is brief and mocking. "He got another job in another little theater in another little town, didn't he? And lived happily ever after, I have no doubt, molesting little boys to his heart's content. You are such a fool, sometimes."

"Have to change the water," he says.

"I'm sorry to be disagreeable," she says. "I'm glad you came. I've missed you all these years. It never felt right, our being apart. I love having you here again—and not just for all this drudgery you're doing, either. I needed you, Oliver. I need you."

He dumps the water from the green bucket into the sink. More mud than water. He pours a new jolt of detergent into the bucket, more bleach. The sink stops draining, still half full. He pulls up his sleeve and plunges his hand in. The drain is clogged with what? He lifts out a greasy wad. Dog hair. She hasn't mopped since Lambert died. He slaps the clot of hair into the white garbage bag. The sink empties with a sucking sound. He holds the bucket under the tap and turns hot water into it hard. He glances at her in the doorway, in her misshapen blue jeans and chambray shirt stitched with flowers. Her clothes need washing too.

"Thank you," he says. "I've been waiting a long time for someone to say that to me. I'm glad it turned out to be you."

February

HE IS late and disgusted with himself about it. It is almost eight, and Bill will have left by now, sulky, resentful. Jewett unlocks the heavy plate-glass door and, keys in his hand, crosses the deep, not quite spotless carpet of a lobby jungly with vines and creepers. He turns a key in the brassy little tin door of the mailbox. Bill never checks it—not unless he has entered his name in a lottery that promises a house, an automobile, a television recorder, matched luggage—once even a purebred Jersey cow. The color photos of smiles, blue skies, shiny premiums, on heavy high-gloss paper lure him now and then. But not often. And not lately—not that Jewett knows of.

Jewett doesn't really believe there will be checks for him in the box. But he lives in hope. Occasionally, without his knowledge, some commercial is rerun in which he has smiled benignly upon a pretend grandchild and a box of cereal. Not today. Not tonight. Tonight, a single envelope leans in the box. He pulls it out, and pushes the little door so that its lock clicks. He drops his keys into his pocket and wearily mounts the steps from the patio by the pool of blue water to the second-tier gallery, staring at the envelope without a lot of interest.

He is too damned tired. He feels as if he has driven all over Southern California today. From here in Mar Vista near the beach, thirty miles north and inland to Perdidos, ten miles back to University Medical Center, because the hospital in Perdidos can't treat Susan's illness, back to Deodar Street, where he washed a week's dishes, cooked lunched, dusted and vacuumed, changed Susan's bed, cooked supper, washed up afterward, then fought traffic on three freeways back here, only in time to be too late.

The envelope is one of those with a hole cut in it to show the address, his name and Bill's typed by a computer. In the return-address corner in blue type is the name of the land management firm that collects the rent. But it is the wrong time of month for the rent bill. Besides, the envelope is too big. He slides it into his jacket pocket, takes out his keys again, and unlocks the door of the apartment. He will fix himself a stiff drink, set a record on the turntable, take off his shoes, sit down with his feet up, and maybe open the envelope and maybe not. Maybe he will let it go until tomorrow morning. His hand finds the wall switch, and lamplight blooms around the room.

He hangs his jacket in the closet, lays the envelope beside the brown velour wing chair he means to relax in, and heads for the bathroom. The coffee, and the wine in mismatched cheese-spread glasses that he shared with Susan at dinner, have been pressing for release. He empties his bladder, flushes the toilet, splashes his face with cold water, uses the towel, comes out of the bathroom, and, starting back to the living room, hears thumps beyond the closed door to the guest room, scufflings, agitated whispers. He stops. For a moment he is only puzzled. Then he is alarmed. Who the hell is in there? How did they get in there? It's not Bill—his car is missing from its slot in the underground garage. He is on his way to the Music Center. Alone. Which he hates.

Jewett goes into the kitchen because that telephone is nearest. He doesn't turn on the light. He lifts the receiver down and in its belly the transparent plastic pushbuttons glow. His hand is shaking. What numbers is he supposed to push for the police? He doesn't know. He punches 0. At the far end of the line, the telephone rings and rings and rings. Jewett hears footsteps behind him and turns. He is afraid. He feels old and unable to defend himself. But there is nothing to be afraid of. Dolan Haycock stands there, hardly more than a shadow, but unmistakable, pushing shirttails into his pants. He is Bill's father, small and trim like Bill, but seventeen years older, seventeen hard years. Jewett hangs up the phone.

"Jesus," Dolan says, "I'm sorry. Thought you was gonna be out." He squints and winces when Jewett turns on the kitchen lights. His shiny necktie is loose around his greasy open collar, his pants are rumpled and stained, like the jacket over his arm, though both are new, the whole ensemble cheap double knit in an unnameable shade of greenish tan. The cowboy boots into which the trousers are tucked are new also, but probably not cheap though their colors are lurid. His black hair stands up in stiff tufts. Jewett can smell him—dried sweat and stale booze. Dolan is a quick talker, jerky, one word tumbling over the next, a rapid-fire liar. "I was just grabbing forty winks." He glances nervously over his shoulder and moves closer to Jewett. Jewett has heard his self-effacing laugh before, never with pleasure. "Guess I put away a few too many this afternoon. Out at the Skipper's. The beach. You know?"

Jewett knows. It is a loosely joined straggle of shanties in faded barn red, situated on a headland with a fine view. Its two gaunt barrooms, with their wide, salt-fogged windows staring as if through cataracts at the sea, are inhabited by beery old boat bums and beach bums during the days. At night, its restaurant draws from Malibu and Beverly Hills picture people, music people, TV people, because the Skipper's has the best fish chef in a hundred miles, a squat, wicked-tempered old Portuguese woman whose sons and grandsons—maître d', waiters, busboys—scurry in fear of her bitter tongue. Dolan would never eat at the Skipper's. Dolan belongs, if he can be said to belong anywhere, among its daytime clientele. Yet Jewett is surprised and resentful that Dolan knows the place at all. Like all customers of the Skipper's, Jewett wants its existence kept secret. It is his place, his and Bill's. Can Bill have been so stupid as to tell his father about the place? Bill can.

Dolan is chattering on. "I wasn't driving too good. I seen this place, and I knew if Billy was here, he'd let me sleep it off. He says you two was going out tonight. You was gonna meet him downtown."

"He had that part wrong," Jewett says.

"I was gonna be gone when you got back, long gone," Dolan protests. He smiles with his brown teeth. The smile lights him up and makes him beautiful. It is from this creature that Bill gets his ravishing smile. Jewett hates for Dolan to smile. "Look," Dolan says, "you wouldn't want me out on the streets smashing into cars, would you? That would really mean trouble."

"You weren't sleeping," Jewett says coldly. "You weren't in there alone. I heard you talking. Where's your bimbo, Dolan? You may as well let her out. I'm not going anywhere tonight."

"Bimbo? Bimbo?" Dolan acts bewildered. Not convincingly. He glances over his shoulder again. And just as he does, a small bump and tinkle come from the living room. Jewett goes there, Dolan trailing him. "Now, listen, Mr. Jewett"—he speaks through stiff lips in an urgent undertone, not wanting to be overheard, and he calls Jewett mister because he is frightened—"this is no bimbo. This is a very high-class lady. She was in the Skipper's and—"

The high-class lady is a big woman, taller than most men. Jewett sees this as she gets to her feet. She has been crouching, picking up the contents of a vast handbag she has managed to drop right at the front door. The bag is of soft lavender leather. She wears a hand-loomed Scotch tweed suit, the color of heather, a green blouse of pure silk, handmade green shoes, a handsomely styled wig in sensible gray to frame a face that says she is sixty, though maybe it wouldn't say that with makeup. She hasn't taken the time now to make up. She says to Jewett:

"I'm terribly sorry. This is all a misunderstanding." She eyes Dolan with irony. "He said this was his apartment." She lets her glance travel the lamplit room where glow the handsome surfaces of antique pieces bought cheap and lovingly restored by Bill. As Jewett envies Susan her weaving, he envies Bill his woodcraft. The woman says, "I can see now that that was unlikely."

Her speech and taste are educated. Jewett can't think how such a woman could agree to go anywhere with Dolan, let alone to bed. But maybe Dolan smiled at her. Maybe hours ago in the forlorn silence, in the bleak sea sunglare of the Skipper's, he wasn't soiled and rumpled. Jewett has known Dolan to wreck new clothes, bought with winnings at Hollywood Park or Santa Anita, in a single day. And maybe the woman was drunk—tiny red veins thread her plump cheeks and meaty nose—drunk, lonely, and beyond giving a damn. And how must she feel now, sober, caught in a man's apartment where she doesn't belong, paired with smelly Dolan? Jewett tries to make her feel better by smiling.

"Mr. Haycock is not wedded to the truth," he says.

"Well, Haycock's on the mailbox," Dolan tells the woman. "It's my son's place as much as it's his. You met my son."

"Did I?" Her laugh is sorry and lost. "Maybe I did. Here? When?"

"When we got here, couple hours ago," Dolan says. "You remember, you got to remember." He peers up into her face for a worried second. He shakes his head. "Well, anyway, Mavis McWhirter, this here is Mr. Oliver Jewett."

They shake hands. Mavis McWhirter says, "I've seen you before, haven't I? On television. You're an actor."

"She's airfreight," Dolan says proudly. "McWhirter. You seen their ads. Great big company."

She makes a deprecatory face. "The discarded wife of a younger son," she says. "His father liked me better than he did. A little money comes down. A trickle. I always wanted to act. I do some little theater now. But it's not easy to find parts for anyone so tall. Any woman." She looks Jewett over thoughtfully. "I always wonder, when I see you, why you're not a star. You're terribly handsome."

"That's as useful to me," Jewett says, "as your height is to you."

"You ought to see her car," Dolan says. He has found the bar and is rattling bottles out of it. It is a beautiful nineteenth-century mahogany cabinet, top thickly coated in invisible plastic to prevent rings. "Shit. A trickle of money! A car like that? Excalibur." He adds, "I need a drink. All right if we have a drink?"

Mavis McWhirter says to Jewett, "A castoff, like its owner. A gift. I saw it at the estate and admired it and Dave left it to me in his will. An amusing gesture. To him. I could have done with a few more shares, instead."

Dolan brings three drinks on a small tray of Mexican embossed tin. He puts their glasses ceremoniously into their hands, takes his own, sets down the tray. "Here's to new friends," he says. He drinks. They drink.

Mavis McWhirter says, "It's not an antique, you understand. It's a modern replica."

"Man could live for years on what it cost," Dolan says.

"Or one day at the racetrack," Jewett says.

"Why don't we sit down?" Dolan says. "What are we standing up for?" He sits. "Sit down, Mavis."

Studying Jewett, Mavis says, "I somehow don't think Mr. Jewett wants us to sit down. I think Mr. Jewett would like us to leave." She sets her drink carefully on the Mexican tray. "I think we've imposed long enough. Why don't we go find some dinner? At the Skipper's." She hangs the big bag over her mighty shoulder. It seems heavy, the bag does. And Jewett wonders crazily whether there are gold ingots in it. Mavis McWhirter puts a hand on the doorknob. She wears three large rings, and Jewett is afraid the stones are real. She says, "We have to get you back to your own car, don't we?"

Dolan jumps up. "Have to use the bathroom first." He starts off, comes back, tilts up his glass and gulps its contents, sets it down with a bang on the tray, and goes off down the hallway. "Be back in a second."

Mavis McWhirter says to Jewett, "We could have lunch sometime." She digs in her bag and brings out a little linen-finished calling card, old-fashioned, her name in elegant embossed script, a phone number and address tiny in a corner. "I'd like to pick your brains about acting. Lunch would be my treat, of course."

Jewett studies the card, tugs his earlobe, looks at her expectant, her plainspoken blue eyes, draws a breath, and says, "Thank you, I'd like that, but there's something you'd better understand—I'm homosexual."

"Oh, Oliver!" She sags, playacting dejection. How has he suddenly become Oliver to her? Has she, in her mind, already tumbled him into bed? She looks strong enough. "You think I'm a gal with only one thing on her mind?"

"I didn't say that," Jewett says.

"No, of course not." She puts out the big, twinkling hand as if to touch him in apology, but draws the hand back before it touches him. "There had to be something, didn't there? Otherwise you'd be as perfect as you look." She tilts her head mournfully. "Only why couldn't it be booze or a wife who doesn't understand you? Those I can live with. I'm used to them. I've got all the skills."

"You've also got Dolan," Jewett says. "Why?"

"Is that his name?" she says, and Dolan comes back. He has slicked down his hair with water and combed it. Splashes of water darken the shoulders of the jacket that he has put on. He has also knotted his awful necktie. In his hand he carries a new roll-brim cowboy hat. "Let's haul anchor," he says, puts on the hat, pulls open the door. "See you later." He goes out onto the gallery.

Mavis McWhirter squeezes Jewett's hand. "We can still have lunch and talk about acting, can't we?"

"I'll be in touch," Jewett lies. "Good night."

They go off along the gallery. She looks big enough to put Dolan in her pocket.

He is watching pale John Hurt hack wrinkled Beatrix Lehmann to death with an ax in slow motion in a badly lighted nineteenth-century Moscow apartment when the telephone rings. The jerk of surprise he gives suggests that either he is immersed in the drama—unlikely, because he doesn't watch television that way: he watches television to study how well or badly actors, directors, cameramen, editors have done their work—or he is, was, almost asleep. If so, it is no reflection on Hurt or Lehmann. They are doing well. No, it simply means that he is an old man who has overtaxed himself today. He picks up the receiver and sighs hello.

"Is Billy there?" The voice is adolescent. Male.

"He's out. Can I take a message?"

"Is that you, Mr. Jewett? This is Larry." In the background a woman is shouting, and Jewett understands where the call is coming from. "You seen my old man?"

"What's he done this time?" Jewett says.

The telephone clatters as if dropped. Larry yelps, "Give that back, you punk." Into the phone, mouth close to the phone, a small child squeals, "Shit fuck piss damn!" There is a scream from the same small child. Larry has the phone back. "He ripped off Gramp and Gran." The sound of a slap is unmistakable, and the child shrieks in the background. The woman yells, "Now you get your ass back in that bed." A dog barks. A door slams. Sirens wail and tires squeal, sounds Jewett judges come from a television set but that may not—all things are possible at the Haycock house. Larry says, "They got their Social Security checks this morning, cashed them at the supermarket, and they didn't even have time to buy their food stamps. My old man is on the doorstep to rip them off."

"He was here," Jewett says. "I think you're too late. He was wearing new clothes."

"Wait a minute," Larry says, "hold on." He muffles the television noise with a hand over the mouthpiece. Then a different voice is on the phone. Cherry Lee, Dolan's wife of thirty-two years in spite of everything, or maybe because of everything, who married Dolan at thirteen because she was pregnant with Bill, and who has been pregnant every nine months and nine minutes since. Her voice is hoarse, Jewett believes, from yelling at her children. He has never known her to address them in any other way. She says:

"There was some woman with him, wasn't there? And he was drunk. You don't have to tell me. Did you see any money? He made Gramp and Gran turn loose of every nickel. Almost five hundred bucks."

"I didn't see any money," Jewett says. "But I wouldn't worry about the woman. She could pay her own way."

"What do you mean?" Cherry Lee says.

"I mean that she is what you might describe as a rich old broad. Dolan seems to have changed his M.O. He's become a gigolo."

Cherry Lee snorts. "She must be blind. She must not have no sense of smell. You putting me on, Mr. Jewett?"

"It's the truth," Jewett says. "He was here with her when I got home tonight. But he's gone now." Jewett reads his watch. "It's been two hours."

"I don't know what Gramp and Gran are gonna do. You know what he told them? That he was gonna double their money on some football game, basketball, something."

"Maybe he did," Jewett says hopefully.

"In a pig's ass," Cherry Lee says. "He lost it, that's what he did. And what he didn't lose he spent on them clothes and buying drinks for the boys."

"Not all boys," Jewett says.

"If Gramp and Gran get stuck," Cherry Lee says, "can you help out? Billy won't. He won't turn loose a dime to me. Not since Dolan skipped bail that time and he had to pay up. He don't want nothing to do with us. It ain't my fault, it ain't the kid's fault, but he won't help us." She begins to sniffle. Her voice wobbles. "But what's gonna happen to Gramp and Gran?"

Jewett has a vision of Gramp and Gran. They resemble plucked turkeys. He has never found out whether they are

Dolan's parents or Cherry Lee's—or anyone's, for that matter. They look too old. They look as if they have always been old. Like faded photographs of dust-bowl types in overalls and sunbonnets on unpainted farmhouse porches, or dangling stick legs from the backs of rickety trucks on the road to California in 1936. They are gnarled, wrinkled, skin and bone. He doesn't see how they can afford to miss a meal. He sees them turned to mummies on their sagging cots.

"Don't worry," he says, "if worst comes to worst, I won't let them starve."

"Oh, thank you, Mr. Jewett," Cherry Lee sobs. "You are the nicest, kindest man that ever walked this earth. Wait till I get my hands on that Dolan. I'll kill the son of a bitch for sure this time."

"Don't do that," Jewett says. She has tried to kill Dolan before. He has tried to kill her. Once she got hold of a gun but her aim was poor, though not so poor that it didn't bring on large hospital bills. Once Dolan had come home unexpectedly and found Cherry Lee entertaining a young fellow from the neighborhood in bed and had cut the boy badly with a butcher knife. These were exaggerated cases. Ordinarily there were only beatings. But always there were police, days in court, sometimes jail; there were foster homes for the kids, recriminations, divorce papers, reconciliations, jobs lost, houses and apartments lost, and always money to be paid. Oh, and cars smashed. When she lost her temper and couldn't get her hands on Dolan, Cherry Lee took vengeance on Dolan's cars, which rarely, except for down payments, actually belonged to Dolan.

Jewett says, "It will only cause a lot of trouble, and I don't want to pay for that and I won't pay for it. So please calm down, Cherry Lee. Just calm down. Maybe it will come out all right. Maybe he had the right number of points on that football game. Maybe he can give Gramp and Gran their money back and more."

Cherry Lee says thoughtfully, "You think he can get money out of that old rich bitch?"

"If he doesn't," Jewett says, "it won't be for lack of trying.

Now, listen to me. If he comes home broke, don't say anything, don't do anything. Beating him up won't get the money back, will it?"

"It'll teach him a lesson," Cherry Lee says ominously.

"He doesn't learn," Jewett says. "You know that."

"Where did Billy get his brains?" she asks. "Books and acting and antiques and going to the opera and all that? He sure as hell didn't get that from Dolan."

"Then he got it from you, didn't he?" Jewett says.

"If I'm so smart, " she says, "why am I still with Dolan? Why didn't I take the kids and get out of here years ago? I can support myself, I can support the kids. Shit, don't I have to do it most of the time, anyways?"

"I'd think about it seriously." Jewett has said it often before. This part of this conversation they have often had before. It has done no good and he doubts that it ever will. Cherry Lee is, as she calls it, a beautician, as Bill calls it, a hair bender. Evidently she is competent, but she and Dolan have broken up equipment in various salons, as Cherry Lee calls them, and word has traveled among the owners of these places that Cherry Lee is trouble, which means that she must go farther and farther afield to find work. Jewett seems to remember that she is currently rinsing, washing, and setting the locks of ladies in Chatsworth or some other remote corner of the San Fernando Valley. "I'd go to another state," he says, "a faraway state. And I wouldn't leave a forwarding address."

Cherry Lee grunts. "You know what's the matter with me? I'd worry about him. I love him. Isn't that crazy?"

This part of the conversation is also a repeat. Jewett says, "Think about it seriously. I have to hang up now. You keep calm. Don't have a fight. It's not worth it. Bill won't be home till late."

"He won't call anyway," Cherry Lee says gloomily. "He's sick and tired and fed up with us. I guess I can't blame him, but it sure as hell makes me feel bad, sometimes. He was my firstborn. You always love them the most."

"He loves you," Jewett lies. "It's just all the things Dolan has done over the years. He can't take it anymore. It's not you—it's Dolan." In fact, it is the whole tribe, including the dog. "All right, I'll ring off now. You let me know about Gramp and Gran."

"All right. Thank you. I'm sorry to bother you but I don't know where else to turn." The mouthpiece goes away from her mouth, but he hears her snarl, "Old fairy!" before the line goes dead. He raises his eyebrows at the receiver in his hand, then puts it down. His glass is empty. He pushes up out of the chair and goes to the beautiful bar and fixes another drink for himself. He laughs and shakes his head. Phone calls from Cherry Lee have ended this way before. Why is he surprised?

Sipping scotch, returning to the wing chair, putting up his feet, watching John Hurt in a ghastly kitchen slip the ax out from under his coat and hang it on the wall over the black stove, Jewett frowns, trying to remember for sure whether she doesn't save this ending exclusively for the times when she has asked a favor and he has granted it. It would be orderly of her, and that isn't characteristic. Still, she hates his guts, and it must pain her to have to beg aid from him and pain her worse still for him to grant it.

No. That's wrong. That's attributing to her feelings he would have. Her sneer at the end gives the lie to that. She feels deep down that he owes her every dime, dollar, hundred dollars he has ever given. If she is ashamed at all, it is because she imagines she is accepting money in exchange for the body and soul of her firstborn. Jewett pictures her in the harsh fluorescent glare of that vinyl-floored, glass-sliding-doored family room behind the kitchen, where wax crayon scrawls are the only decoration on the white plaster walls, where wood-grain plastic peels from a television set never silent but never truly audible above the yelling of the kids, the raving of the adults, the barking of the dog.

He pictures her, lath-thin, shiny-faced, in a faded pink shorty housecoat with cigarette ash dribbled down it, knobby legs bare, feet in dirty woolly pink slippers, hair in big pink plastic rollers, cigarette hanging from a corner of her mouth. He pictures the contemptuous and vengeful twist of that mouth as she puts a finger on the phone to break the connection so that her final words will stay with him to gall him, she hopes, forever. She is as childish in this as her youngest who jabbered dirty words into the phone tonight before she came on. She knows it, too. Jewett isn't going to let himself be shocked or hurt. He will give her what she asked.

He gets up and switches off the television set. He goes around the room, turning off all the lamps but one. The door is locked and not bolted. He picks up his drink and takes it to the bedroom, where he strips. He showers. Maybe what makes her spiteful is that she can't understand. She is bright but ignorant. It must drive her crazy that Jewett won't show her any anger, the way Bill does, or pretends to. Jewett washes shampoo out of his hair. No, it's not ignorance. It's lack of imagination. She can't see that Jewett and she are in the same fix. As she can't make herself leave Dolan, Jewett can't make himself leave Bill. And if you take on one Haycock, you take on all the Haycocks. He towels himself, blow-dries his hair, brushes his teeth. No one comes into anyone else's life unhampered and alone. It's no good wishing they did. They never do. It's a truth he learned very young from Joey Pfeffer.

He piles up pillows, gets into bed, switches on the clock radio that plays something by Brahms for horn, piano, and strings. He reads smoking, finishing his drink. He would like to be awake when Bill comes in, so as to apologize for standing him up. But he is too tired. His mind won't take in what he is reading. He closes the book, and lies staring blankly at the walls, which Bill has hung with posters from films in which Jewett played feature parts in the late 1940s and early 1950s, the foolish years when he believed he had a future. It took Bill time and trouble to find these tawdry artifacts in secondhand stores. He did it secretly. In secret, he gave them handsome mountings, handsome frames. He waited until Jewett was away on location, filming something for television, and hung them in the living room to surprise him when he returned.

Surprised Jewett did not feel. He felt appalled. He winced in embarrassment. And he wasn't able to hide how he felt. Bill was badly hurt. He couldn't seen why Jewett wasn't proud of the posters, didn't glow at the notion of friends and strangers coming in for drinks and being impressed by these trophies of Jewett's triumphs. God knew, Bill was proud of them. Bill was impressed. Jewett couldn't make him understand, but he did finally get him to agree, sulkily, to hang the wretched things in here in the bedroom where they might, with luck, escape notice. Jewett scarcely notices them himself anymore—they are too familiar now to give him pain, except for the crudity of their artwork.

He jettisons the extra pillows, switches off the lamp, settles on his side, and shuts his eyes. But it isn't sleep that comes. Unnecessary memories—those are what come. He lets them come, hoping they will transmute into nonsense and then from nonsense into dreams. It is a trick he plays on himself that sometimes works.

Elevator doors hissed softly behind him. Open. Shut. He sat leafing over a magazine on a deep leather couch in Morry Block's spacious, dark-paneled waiting room with its cool, hanging fern baskets. A handsome brown pottery mug of coffee steamed on the low teak table in front of him—to make him feel welcome because he was working regularly that year, 1970, bringing in as much as a thousand dollars a week from small television roles, earning Morry a steady ten percent, nothing to overexcite him, but enough to merit for Jewett a prompt mug of coffee when he walked in and a glowing smile from the receptionist, who also troubled to remember his name.

This wasn't only in thanks. It was also in anticipation. Jewett was getting better roles all the time. The improvement was measurable only in increments of seconds on camera, but Morry was aware. He watched and waited for the day when a break would come—a feature role, maybe a running part in a

series, week after week, at possibly two, three thousand dollars
a segment. Morry's optimism reached Jewett and made him like
coming here. He was forty-seven years old and knew better than
to let himself get excited over bright promises in this business.
The casting people could get bored with him tomorrow and
find another lean, handsome, gray-haired actor to put on
judges' robes or sit in a pinstripe suit at a corporate boardroom
table or a college chancellor's desk. Yet sometimes, like this
morning, he shrugged off cold reality and like a kid warmed to
the notion that he was in for a run of good luck.

The agency of which Morry was a part occupied the entire
twelfth floor of this white tower at the top of south-sloping La
Cienega Boulevard. Anyone leaving those elevators behind
Jewett had only one place to go, the reception desk that was in
Jewett's line of sight among lush philodendrons, where a telephone switchboard buzzed discreetly and the young blond
woman's voice was softly musical and cheery. For a look at
whoever had got off the elevator, Jewett needed only to wait. It
would be no surprise here if the newcomer were a celebrity,
film star, rock musician, television detective. But Jewett didn't
care about celebrities. He simply, unfailingly, looked up when
a stranger entered a room.

It wasn't that people fascinated him. It was deeper than that.
It was deeper than obsession. It was a reflex. It had taken his
mother years to break him of staring. She never really had. He
had mastered tricks to make her think he wasn't staring, but he
was. He had taught himself to see between blinks of an eye what
he knew others couldn't register in an hour or a lifetime. Why?
To memorize mannerisms, gestures, ways of walking, talking,
looking, listening, standing, sitting, eating, drinking, taking off
a jacket—so as to make himself a better actor? That was the easy
explanation. It satisfied people when they noticed what he was
doing. It didn't satisfy him. No, it was some longing, some
hunger that he didn't understand that sometimes saddened
him, sometimes made him angry with himself, sometimes wore
him out with its futility, but that he could no more rid himself of
than he could stop himself breathing.

He looked up now to see a small, trim, brown-skinned young man, hardly more than a boy, cross the deep, tawny waiting-room carpet. Head just a little too large for the rest of him, like a jockey's, good shoulders, narrow pelvis, a dark suit off the rack at J. C. Penney in Fresno. He carried a little bunch of flowers, orange and blue. His walk was a bantam strut. His eyes shone, and his wide mouth grinned as at some private joke. Past the farthest grouping of couches and chairs, he set the bouquet in his teeth and turned a cartwheel. The young woman at the reception desk stood up in surprise and Jewett laughed. The young fellow bowed, handed her the flowers, tucked his necktie back into his jacket, and said in a country-boy twang, "William Haycock, miss. To see Mr. Morry Block, please?"

Jewett sighs and turns over in bed. The bouquet and the cartwheel were meant to bedazzle the young woman, to make her remember William Haycock, miss, forever. Which she may or may not have done. It didn't help. Morry was mistaken about Bill. He had looked as shiny and full of promise as a new toy on that little-theater stage in Fresno. It turned out that his voice was light, he was short, his teeth needed work, and he couldn't act. These flaws weren't fatal, but he also photographed badly. To a camera, every time he turned his head he looked like someone else. So he wasn't often back in Morry's waiting room.

Jewett shivers. The night has turned cold. He switches on the lamp, gets up and narrows the window gap, finds a sweater in a drawer, pulls the sweater on, crawls back into bed, and switches off the lamp. He huddles down under the bedclothes and shuts his eyes. And he is sitting beside Bill in Bill's wreck of a car, rattling along a broad, sleek street garish with neon signs, on the way to a motel outside San Diego, where Jewett is sleeping during a run of *Macbeth* at the Globe in Balboa Park, part of a summer Shakespeare festival. The theater was a recon-struction of Shakespeare's playhouse in London, a tall wooden cylinder. Lately a crazy boy burned it down. Jewett gives a rueful laugh into the blankets.

At the time, he felt like burning it down himself. He was no good as Macbeth. He thought the week would never end. The local critics bitched about the beauty of his voice and how he relied too much on his voice and its beauty. The second night, he rasped and growled, and the director asked him if he'd lost his mind. The Los Angeles reviews came a day later. They sneered that Jewett moved like a dancer. He tried moving like a bear, shuffling, like a lame football player, hobbling. Backstage, Lady Macbeth offered to buy him a truss. She'd been struggling not to laugh with her hands full of bloody daggers. He was no good as Macbeth, and he never would be.

He was bleakly grateful to Bill for coming. Not that Bill could tell him how to do the part. No one could do that. But he didn't want to be alone with the knowledge in that damned motel room all night long. He was weary of the jibes he threw over and over again at himself, at his purblind vanity that had made him believe he could handle the role. It wasn't the fault of the director who had flattered him, the other cast members who had marveled at the skills and graces he showed in the rehearsals. It was his own fault for believing them. He was disgusted with himself and he needed Bill to hold him through the night as if it didn't matter that he was a fool.

Bill parked the car on noisy gravel at the far end of the long, shake-roofed, sand-color buildings that housed the motel units, in whose ground-cedar plantings spotlights crouched. He reached into the rear seat for the canvas airline bag he'd brought, while Jewett climbed wearily out of the car and slammed the loose door that wouldn't latch unless it was slammed. Bill got out on his side and looked at Jewett across the roof of the car, which was pitted with rust—sea air is hard on paint jobs. Bill had seen the performance and congratulated him on it. Little else had been said by Bill during the drive. Nothing had been said by Jewett, slumped grouchily in the seat, staring out the window, lost in self-contempt and self-pity.

Now Bill said, "You know why I could never be an actor?" He slammed the door on his side of the car. "Because I never loved it. You love it. You know what I love? Making wood shine."

Jewett said, "But you can do that. I can't act."

"Oh, Christ!" Bill snorted, jerked his head, started off along the gravel, the small bag with its chipping white airline logo very blue in the glare of the lights. "What is the matter with you? The fucking reviews?" He looked back and came to a stop. "Are you coming or not?"

Jewett sighed, pushed hands into pockets, trudged after him, head down. "The reviews are right," he said.

"The reviews are wrong." Bill shifted the bag to his other hand and gripped Jewett's arm. "Macbeth was a weakling. That line about 'vaulting ambition which o'erleaps itself'? That's not him. That's his wife. Don't you know that? Macbeth was a weakling. He let his wife push him around. He hated it. He was just doing what she wanted so the bitch would leave him alone."

Jewett glanced at him, took out keys, unlocked the door of the motel unit, reached inside and turned on the lights. "And that's how I'm playing him?"

"Aren't you?" Bill walked in and set the bag on the bed and ran its zipper open. "Shit, the only time Macbeth is brave is when he knows he's going to be killed. He knows. He doesn't believe that shit about 'no man born of woman'—he doesn't believe that any more than he believed the witches. *She* believed the witches."

"He believed Banquo's ghost." Jewett took the bottle of scotch that Bill had pulled from the bag, and went into the bathroom for plastic glasses. "He believed the vision of the bloody child, the bloody dagger." Jewett came out of the bathroom. "Do we want to go for ice?"

But Bill had already opened the bed and was stripping off his clothes. It was summer, warm. Now tugging up the blankets of his own bed against the February chill, Jewett sees Bill's trim, brown-skinned body and smiles as he smiled at that moment. Bill was surprising the hell out of him. With his mind. His body never surprised Jewett now. It simply pleased him as nothing else did in this world. Bill got into bed and sat there naked without pulling up the sheet and held a hand out for his plastic glass of whiskey and water. "To hell with ice," he said. He drank some of the whiskey and patted the bed with a small brown callused hand. "Come on."

Jewett undressed. Orange makeup had smeared his shirt collar and the shirt smelled of sweat. "I need a shower," he said. When he came out, Bill lay on his side, pouring more whiskey into his own glass. Cigarette smoke hung in the air of the clean, impersonal room. He said, "He believed Banquo's ghost because she'd driven him nuts by then, making him do things he wasn't strong enough to do, evil enough to do. It's an old story." He set the bottle on the nightstand. "People let other people push them around, wreck their lives. It happens, doesn't it? They always say it's for your own good."

Jewett sat on the bed, back to Bill, picked up his glass, drank from it, and lit a cigarette. "You're quite a Shakespeare scholar. You surprise me."

"Shit," Bill said, "I didn't figure that stuff out. That was my high-school English teacher." The bed moved under Jewett. Bill's mouth was on the back of Jewett's neck. Bill's arms came around him, Bill's body pressed against Jewett's back. "I wouldn't even have remembered it, except I read those stupid reviews and then I saw you tonight doing it the way it was supposed to be done." He took the cigarette from Jewett's fingers and laid it in the ashtray stamped with the name of the motel chain. He took Jewett's glass away from him and set it beside the ashtray. He switched off the lamp.

Jewett turned his head and kissed Bill's smoky mouth. "Your high-school English teacher was wrong," he said, "but you still make me feel a lot better."

Bill pulled Jewett down onto the sheets, whispering a laugh. "You ain't seen nothing yet," he said....

Jewett wakes in the February cold and dark. He blinks at the red digits of the clock radio. One-twenty. Where the hell is Bill? Bill is standing in the bedroom doorway, silhouetted by lamplight from the far living room.

"Hello," Jewett says. "I'm sorry I was late. I've never seen the freeways so bad. A lot of accidents." He switches on the lamp and winces in the brightness. "What's your excuse?"

Bill comes in, unknotting his tie. He sits on the side of the bed. He gives off a strong alcohol smell. "The man in the seat next to mine struck up a friendship." He laughs a quick, ironic laugh and begins unbuttoning his shirt. "A stray-hand-on-the-thigh kind of friendship."

Jewett feels outraged and threatened. "That never went over very well with you before," he says.

"It didn't go over well with me this time." Bill strips off the shirt and drops it. He bends to take off his shoes. He emits a little grunt as he does this, as if he were fat or old, neither of which he is. There isn't an ounce of extra flesh on him, and he will be thirty-two in November. Maybe he is unwittingly imitating old Jewett. Bill stands to get out of his trousers, fold them, hang them over a ladderback chair that is one of his best pieces of work. He says, "He tried to buy me a drink at intermission. When I went to the men's room instead, he followed me in there. Ugh. I zipped up and left, but he was back in his seat, wasn't he, when intermission was over? I sat in your seat as soon as the lights went down, and he didn't quite have the nerve to move after me." Bill strips socks, T-shirt, shorts, puts out the light, and with a moan of exhaustion puts himself under the covers.

"So he isn't the reason you're late." Jewett says. "You're going to be cold without pajamas. It's cold. Or won't all that antifreeze you've been drinking let you feel that?"

"Come on." Bill paws at him groggily. "Keep me warm."

Jewett lies against Bill's back.

"Put your arm around me," Bill says. He sounds almost asleep. He draws a deep, slow breath and lets it go. He says, "He had one more trick up his sleeve." Bill takes Jewett's hand and places it over his genitals and makes a contented sound. "He does publicity. He knew everybody in the cast. Naturally, I wanted to meet Oscar Sereno, didn't I?" Sereno is a prodigiously fat actor worth watching even in his tacky mad-scientist roles on television. "He said he'd introduce me to Oscar Sereno. It's been a long time since you did a stage show. I miss those cast parties. I was pissed off at you, so I went."

"What about the boy—Bo Kerrigan? Is that his name?"

Bill is silent for a moment. Then he gives a little shrug. "He's all right. There's dozens of him on TV. Sereno kept smooching with him. It was in the Music Center bar, you know? I mean, everybody was staring. It's not that dark. Christ, I thought Sereno was going to start doing it to him right there. The kid was really embarrassed. I don't think he's even gay."

"So you didn't learn the secret of great acting from Sereno?" Jewett says. "You didn't ask him the key to playing *Macbeth*? A fat man played it for Shakespeare's company. Burbage."

"I asked him for his autograph. He groped me while he was signing my program. Naw, he didn't say anything about acting. I don't think he thinks about it. I think he only thinks about one thing."

"You stayed a long time," Jewett says.

"The booze was free and there were a lot of laughs."

"Did you know your father was here?" Jewett says.

Bill stiffens. "What? You mean when you got here?"

"In the guest room with a woman," Jewett says.

Bill pulls away from him, half falls out of bed. "Excuse me. I have to throw up." He staggers away through the darkness. Jewett waits for him to come back, and falls asleep waiting. He wakes up with Bill talking to him, sitting up in bed, wearing a white turtleneck jersey. Bill says, "He came just when I was getting ready to leave. He won some money and he wanted to brag about it. He bought some awful clothes."

"I agree," Jewett says.

"I ran him out when I left. But when we're downstairs, he says he forgot his hat. I gave him the key to go get his hat. He comes back with the hat and introduces me to this huge lady in the fancy fake car. And I take off. He must have left the door unlocked."

"They were humping in the guest bedroom," Jewett says. "When are you going to stop letting him manipulate you? Do you know where he got that money? From Gramp and Gran. It was their Social Security money. Your mother called and told me."

Bill flops down in the bed and pulls the covers over his head. "I don't want to hear about it."

"Sorry," Jewett says.

Bill crowds against him. "I just want you to hold me," he says, and finds Jewett's hand again, and puts it where he put it before. He says bitterly, "And the reason she called was to ask you for money so Gramp and Gran won't starve to death, right?"

"And to say she's going to kill Dolan for this."

"Yeah, well, I wish she'd shut up about it and just do it for once," Bill says. "Then they'd both be off my hands and all I'd have to worry about would be Larry and Tillie and Newton and Jo Ellen, and—" His diction slurs and he can't finish the roll call of his younger brothers and sisters. Jewett thinks he is asleep. He is not. He says clearly, all of a sudden, "You didn't open that notice from Calcoast, did you? You know what it says? We have to clear out."

"What?" Jewett says. "Clear out of where?"

"Here. These aren't going to be apartments anymore. They're going to be condominiums. We get first bid, though, on this place, seeing we've been here ten years. A hundred and fifty thousand dollars. Have you got a hundred and fifty thousand dollars? Or did you give it all to Gramp and Gran?"

"What did they give you to smoke at that party?" Jewett says. But now Bill is asleep. Deeply. He rarely snores, even when he sleeps on his back. He is on his side, now, but he has begun to snore.

March

THE DRIVE takes an hour, up snowy old logging roads through towering ponderosa pines in the San Jacinto mountains. The drive starts in darkness, from a little ski town where Jewett, ten other actors, and a crew of twenty-odd sleep in shingle-sided motels, eat supper at a shingle-sided diner with COORS in red neon in the window, and buy cigarettes, liquor, and digestive tablets at a shingle-sided general store. Boxy little buses jounce and creak up the twisting roads through the cold dark, laboring, small pistons noisy. The actors are packed in tight. They smell of soap, deodorants, perfumes, and cold remedies. The lukewarm air that the rattly heater blows smells of exhaust fumes. Jewett is always a little sick before the drive ends.

It ends at sunrise among main-street banks, shops, a church, side-street houses, backyard sheds and barns that are mere fronts and hollow shells, constructed in Hollywood, carted up here on flatbed trucks, and set up by studio carpenters to make real for the cameras a scriptwriters's terrorized mountain town, isolated by a scriptwriter's paper blizzard, where a scriptwriter's paper townsfolk are being systematically and bloodily slaughtered among the silent pines by a paper teen-age boy with hurt feelings and a paper chain saw. It isn't the carbon monoxide fumes alone that sicken Jewett, coming here every morning. The picture sickens him.

The crew doesn't appear to care. They shift their heavy lights, cranes, trucks, lay their thick black taped-together cables, shift their reflectors, stoically tend their noisy generator on its big wheels. It's another job. Their pay is the same whether the picture is decent or not. Assistant directors, dialogue and script people, camera operators, lighting men, sound recorders, wardrobe women bitch about the cold and about technical problems, but not about the quality of the product. They are pleased to be working. The makeup people are enjoying themselves. The relentless mayhem in all its grisly detail makes it their sort of picture. If what they do is art, this is a chance for them to practice their art.

The actors are either young and hopeful of getting a better picture next time, or old, or sick, or drunk, or resignedly second-rate, and happy to have any kind of work at all. The good ones—saddest of all—grimace, shrug, and study their lines. The biggest role belongs to the teen-age girl friend of the crazed boy killer. She made a sensation in a similar picture, but with a bigger budget, last year. Now she appears to Jewett to be on some sort of drug. Her actions have the clockwork jerkiness of Elsa Lanchester in The Bride of Frankenstein. She is supposed to look frantic, but she is in fact frantic. Not always, but too often, when she makes mistakes, she cries. Not always, but too often, when others make mistakes, she screams at them.

Cast and crew have commented on it. Quietly, among themselves. Not to the director. He wouldn't want to hear. A bearded, big-bellied, loud-laughing man in a cowboy hat, he arrives up here on the mountain from Palm Springs far below every morning at sunup, and drives back down in his World War II jeep when daylight begins to fade. With his lady for the day, slim, suntanned, and with his gangly buddy the writer. Not the writer of this picture. A rich writer. The director is

living in the rich writer's big house in Palm Springs—
swimming pool, tennis courts, a French chef. That is where he
is getting his fun out of this picture.

Hulking around up here, in his sheepskin jacket and cowboy
boots and dark glasses, he is getting his job done. He goes about
it like an elephant setting up a circus tent. He doesn't want to
know what the hell he is involved in. He certainly doesn't want
any trouble. Everyone understands this and respects it, or simply wants to get home and out of the cold as soon as possible. So
no one gives the director any trouble—except the girl. And
somehow she has become Jewett's responsibility. The director
hasn't time, the picture hasn't time. When the director tries to
deal with her, he keeps his voice low, but he swells up, gets red
in the face, veins stand out in his thick neck. Everyone on the
set holds his breath, expecting an explosion.

Jewett stepped in the first time, hung the girl's arctic fox coat
across her shoulders, put an arm around her slim waist, and
walked her away into the trees. He sat her down with him on a
log, kept the consoling arm around her, laid her head on his
chest, stroked her back, crooned to her, dried her eyes,
smoothed her hair, told her something funny, and in five
minutes had her smiling damply—and shooting could resume.
He has repeated this routine until he has lost count. Either the
director sends for him or, if Jewett is on hand, he doesn't wait,
he moves in. Yet it hasn't brought him close to the girl. She
never speaks to him or even smiles at him except at those
moments. This doesn't worry him. What worries him is that she
speaks to, smiles at, no one. She seems awesomely alone.

Now he comes out of the steamy warmth and boiled-coffee
smell of the almost deserted little eatery into falling snow. To
jam into the place with the hungry first wave of actors and crew
isn't worth the jostling and the short tempers of the sweaty, fat
owner who cooks, the fat, sulky wife who snarls the orders, the
fat, pimply daughter who slogs back and forth carrying the
plates. The food is certainly not worth rushing for. Tonight's
was meatloaf, mashed potatoes, peas and carrots from the

freezer, leaden apple pie. Yesterday it was mushy roast chicken. Tomorrow it will be frozen fish fried in gummy batter—tempura, on the handwritten menu. Jewett has made suggestions for improvements. "Sounds great," the fat man said, "and if you ever need a job cooking come see me." Meantime the food remains unfit to eat, but it beats the so-called meals that come tilting onto the set at noon in a ribbed-aluminum catering truck. The young eat it. The older actors and crew skip lunch. The director brings up food in handsome wicker hampers from the kitchen of the writer's French chef, and he and the writer and the lady for the day disappear into a trailer to eat it. No one knows what it is, but the rumors never omit peacock tongues. Jewett pines for his own kitchen. He puts himself to sleep nights reciting recipes.

The sad girl's big mobile home parked back among the trees, windows already dark, is a cheerful enough looking vehicle but for some reason it reminds him of a giant coffin. He is walking, shoulders hunched inside a down parka, hands pushed deep into pockets, beside Rita Lopez, also in fox fur, though hers is far from new. It is even a little mangy. Rita has been an actor even longer than Jewett has, in parts monotonous and repetitive in their way as his. She started as the brassy-voiced girl friend of the ingenue, crude, oversexed, but warmhearted. Then the funny-sad floozy with the heart of gold. Then, when movies grew brave enough to call a whore a whore, Rita was a whore, with a heart, by then, of mush. When the years marked her face and she got too heavy in the bust and hips, she became the cowtown madame. And finally she was the fleabag landlady in police shows. In this film, she noses into the doings of her roomers and is killed for what she learns. She and Jewett are both wearing boots, but hers are soft leather, show tufts of fluffy lining at their tops, and zip up the sides. The snow creaks under their boots. Snowflakes settle on Rita's long, false eyelashes.

Jewett stops. "Doesn't that child have a mother?"

"Kimberly?" Rita walks on. "What does she need with a mother? She's got you." Rita stops, turns, comes back to him.

"Oliver, she's not a child. She's twenty-five, been married and divorced. There aren't any children in this business. You know that." She takes his arm. "Come on. We'll freeze to death out here."

"She ought to have someone with her." Jewett leaves the road, walks down among the thick gray tree trunks, raps on the door of the mobile home. The door clatters to his knock. "Kimberly?" he calls. "Are you all right?" No answer comes. He raises his cold hand to knock again, but he doesn't knock again. "Kimberly?" He stands, irresolute, feeling foolish, overprotective, interfering. He stuffs his hand into its pocket and trudges back up to the road, where Rita stands watching him with a mocking smile that twists a corner of her mouth.

Behind her looms the Antlers, a tavern that was probably once a stable for the horses that used to drag the big wagons and sledges when this was logging country in the 1890s. The place is a slumping frame hulk, freshly painted red, with a neon sign over its door. Crossed skis are nailed to the door. From inside the place, through the old boards, leaks the twang of country-and-western music. From young throats come whoops and hollers, cowboy style. Dancing boots stamp and stutter on drum-hollow planks. Jewett asks Rita to wait a minute, crosses the perfect whiteness of the road, works the heavy iron latch of the door, and peers inside. A whirl of purple and orange satin shirts, a glitter of silver belt buckles, a smell of beer, the cutting edge of amplified guitars. A girl's slim body snaps like a whip aboard a mechanical rodeo bull that bucks and rocks below the flick and glitter of a turning ball of mirrors. She is not Kimberly. Kimberly is not in the Antlers. He didn't think she would be. He shuts the door, making sure the latch catches because a wind has risen, driving the snow. Leaning into it, head down, he returns to Rita, shivering in the road.

"Why isn't she in there having fun?" he says.

"Because she's the star." Rita takes his arm and starts him toward the motel. "These days, one picture, and you're a star, right? A superstar. She can't socialize with them. What are you, some kind of Communist? Maybe on the last night. Even these cheap bastards will throw a party on the last night, won't they? Stale crackers, moldy cheese, and two lousy jugs of Red Mountain?"

"Will she even be here by the last night?" Jewett looks over his shoulder for another glimpse of the mobile home, but the night and the snowfall obscure it. "That is one unhappy girl, Rita. She's doping herself with something, and she's falling apart."

"I hope you're wrong," Rita says. "They'd have to reshoot all her footage. If I liked this kind of weather, I'd have signed on with Napoleon in 1812."

"She shouldn't be alone," Jewett says.

"That's the best way to get your sleep." Rita is regarding the Antlers. "She makes more sense than they do." She gives her head a shake. "Every night till midnight. If I tried it, I'd drop dead on the set in the morning."

"They're young," Jewett says. "You remember young?"

Rita snorts. "Who wants to remember?" She turns a key in the door of her motel unit, stamps snow off her boots, pushes the door open, and steps inside, where weak-watted lamps go on. She says, "Living through it wasn't enough?"

"Living through it was a narrow escape." Jewett follows her into the unit and shuts the door on the snow and the cold. He watches her shed the coat and drop it on the bed. Her hat is fox also but with a sheen to it that says it is much newer than the coat. She tosses the hat onto the bed, shakes out her dyed red hair, rubs her hands, blows on them, and goes to fetch plastic glasses from the bathroom. She digs a fresh pint of Old Overholt from a suitcase of soft, fake cowhide. Rye is a man's drink, and Rita, for all her false lashes, lavish lipstick, long enameled nails, for all her curves, is and always has been manly.

She sets bottle and glasses on a maple coffee table between two maple armchairs that have thin cushions tied to overvarnished, spooled backs and hard seats. The cushions are covered in a folksy patchwork quilt pattern that has been used in the bedspread and the pleated curtains too. An oval braided rug is underfoot. The walls are knotty pine. The lamps imitate frontier coal-oil lamps, with frilled shades. The aim was coziness. Why doesn't the place seem cozy? Jewett drops his parka on the bed and brushes snow out of his hair.

He says, "You can control it, can you—remembering?" He sits down opposite her, digs a cigarette out of the pack in the pocket of his red wool shirt, lights it with a throwaway lighter. "How?"

"Don't keep scrapbooks," she says. "Don't keep pictures. Don't watch your reruns. Don't listen to old songs." A deck of cards buzzes and flutters in her hands. "I really despise actors who keep scrapbooks. 'I did this in 'forty-eight, I did this in 'sixty-two.' Pathetic!" She deals. The cards whisper across the scratched varnish of the tabletop. She thumps the deck facedown in the middle of the table. "But what you really want to avoid is bumping into old friends."

"Too right." Jewett gathers his cards together and arranges them in his hand. Too many face cards. "When I climbed onto that bus and saw you sitting there, I wanted to turn and run. Trouble is, I need the money."

"Would anybody work on this piece of garbage that didn't need the money? Would I work with you?"

She doesn't mean it any more than he does. They are happy to be working together, pleased to be sitting again in the same room at night, a room with a bed in it—though the bed of course is no more than a reminder—and playing cards again after—dear God, how long has it been?—twenty years. Either of them could, at any time, have picked up the phone and talked to the other. They could have met for lunch or drinks or the theater. Why not? On the other hand, why? No—it took a casting accident to bring them together. That's how the picture business goes. And after these weeks of shooting, first here on location, then at the studio for interiors, they will part with promises to keep in touch, but they won't keep in touch. They have long since learned to get along without each other. It will take another accident to join them. And if he leaves the business, it will take a miracle.

They lay down cards and pick up cards for a time in silence. Snow whispers against the window. Now and then, a gust of wind rattles the window, which is loose in its frame. The wind sings hoarsely in the tall pines. Jewett wonders whether they will be able to shoot tomorrow. Will those false building fronts stand against the wind? Won't it take a long time to clear the snow from the road up to the set? Will the storm stop by morning? He is disgusted with the storm. This is March. Down on the desert, the wild flowers are out, carpeting the ground. When the writer of the script hears about the storm will he think of himself as a prophet? Or as a god, even—creator of blizzards? He knows a few writers. Most of them think that way when they get the chance.

Rita chain-smokes, leaving red lipstick on the butts that pile up in a stingy glass ashtray. She pours tots from the flat bottle into the plastic glasses. They sip the whiskey. Rita says, "That's why you worry about Kimberly." She twists out her cigarette. It has no filter. It's the short, old-fashioned kind. In a moment, another hangs tough from a corner of her mouth, smoke trickling up into an eye always half shut against the smoke. "You don't like the weather, either. You don't like the picture. You want it over with as soon as possible."

"If the industry wants to be squalid, let it. I don't want to be squalid."

"And that's why you take such care of her," Rita says.

She knows him better than this. She is ragging him.

"I want to get out. I want to earn an honest living for a change." He picks up an eight and discards a ten. "There's a little bakery for sale in my home town. I'd like to buy it. I'm a good baker."

"I remember," she says. "It was one of your ways of getting back at me when I threw chairs at you and ran out and slammed the door and said I was never coming back. When I came back, the place would be full of the smell of baking bread. Beautiful."

She lays her cards on the table with a flourish. "Gin!" Jewett blinks at the neat progression of low cards, sighs, bends, and reaches to gather in all the cards. She says, "But that's not the same as getting up every morning at two and baking for a whole town. Actors go to bed at two in the morning." She doesn't mean in the picture business. He knows what she means. She is talking about the stage. "How long have you been an actor, Oliver?" She knows, but he gives her an answer anyway.

"I got the idea at age six." He shuffles the cards. "Six-year-olds make a lot of mistakes." He sets the deck in front of her, she cuts it and hands it back to him. He begins to deal. "It's taken me a half century to see that."

"Please, Oliver, not midlife crisis." She picks up her cards. "You're a failure, right?" She fans the cards in her fingers and the red nail enamel glints in the lamplight as she shifts and tucks the cards. "You've wasted your life?"

"Not quite all of it," he says, "and I'm going to start doing something I'm fit for while I've still got a few years left." He arranges his own cards. "When I saw that sign in Pfeffer's window, I knew what it was." He lays down his hand to pour whiskey from the bottle, into her glass, into his. "Something real, satisfying. Something I'm good at."

"If you weren't good at acting"—she picks up a card and gets rid of another—"you'd have been a baker for the past forty years, whether you wanted to be a baker or not. If you're not good in the acting business, you don't last. You've lasted, dear."

"I had something a little better in mind."

"You mean you wanted to be Laurence Olivier?"

"I wanted not to be second-rate." Jewett picks up a deuce and lays down a jack. "You don't know what that means, because you're good. I don't care how they miscast you and waste you—you're good, and you have the satisfaction of knowing that, of knowing that everyone with intelligence in the business and out of it knows it too."

"Oh, la, sir," she says, and lights a new cigarette from the stub of an old one. "I have a funny face and a funny voice, dear. It's the luck of the draw. They pay me. It's a boring way to earn a living, but it beats working." She draws a card and gets rid of another.

He says, "When you're second-rate and too dumb to realize it, that's one thing. Too dumb, too egotistical, too easily flattered. But when you finally see it, when you finally face the awful truth, you're ashamed to show your face. And an actor who's ashamed to show his face is in deep trouble." He lucks out with another deuce and slaps down a ten. "My sister always said I was a numbskull, but fifty years of it must be a record."

"You learn your lines, dear, hit your marks, and look the other actor in the eye. As old Spence said, that's all there is to acting." She sips some of the whiskey from her plastic glass. The smoke is a blue halo around that orange hair. "All you need is a break. Don't be impatient. You get better-looking every year. My God, if it could happen to Charles Bronson, why not to you? It's never too late, Oliver. Wait for it, love."

"I'll wait." He picks up still another deuce, and, by Christ, discards an eight. "Till I've saved enough to buy that bakery. That's how long I'll wait."

"How is your sister?" she says.

He stares at her. He has forgotten that they ever met, Susan and Rita, but they did. Susan arrived without warning, bad foot clunking up the long, rickety outside staircase of a paint-flaking hulk of a house at the beach, on a sunny Sunday morning. The summer of what—1954? It had to be. Rita and he were still new to each other. The famous battles hadn't yet begun. They'd been making lazily delighted love on that bed in the tower room with the curved glass windows. The moment comes back to him now with a sharpness and sweetness so vivid he half stands up, the legs of the chair catching in the braiding of the rug and almost toppling him backward.

"Something the matter?" Rita says.

"Bathroom," Jewett says, for an excuse. He goes to the bathroom door and with the knob in his hand turns to tell Rita,

"She's dying. Leukemia. The doctors don't sentence you anymore—but she thinks she's got a year."

"Oh, God," Rita says glumly.

He goes into the bathroom, uses the toilet, washes his hands, splashes his face, uses the towel. Memory has ambushed him, as it so often does. They meant to pack food and spend the day on the beach. But neither was willing to let the other out of bed. Time stopped. There were moments of high solemnity but there was much laughter and, in the end, because those curved windowpanes acted like lenses, sweat that made their skins squeak against each other. In a sharp smell of sweat he flapped into a blue cotton happy coat. He went barefoot to answer the door. The noise of her climbing should have identified Susan to him, but she was too far from his thoughts. And there she stood, short, pudgy, crooked, in a dazzle of sunlight off a yellow shiplap wall. He was so surprised, he didn't even wonder how she had found him.

"Are you all right?" she asked through the screen.

"Fine." He heard amazement in his voice. "Is anything the matter?" He seemed unable to move from his place on the gritty kitchen linoleum. The only way into Rita's apartment was through the kitchen. "Mother all right?"

"Worried," she said. "Wondering what became of you. I wouldn't have arrived on your doorstep like this, but you don't seem to have a phone."

"They cost money," he said. "Which I haven't got."

"Oliver," she said crossly, "it's been three years."

She meant since their father's funeral. 1951. November. Rain. At the dark house on Deodar Street, their mother had worn a stiff, white face, had moved stiffly, spoken stiffly, controlling her temper. She had lost it after the ceremony at the church, when they were in the undertaker's limousine, following the glossy blackness of the hearse to the cemetery, had lost it in a bitter storm of tears and reproaches, which Susan had quieted. But under the gloomy old cemetery trees that shed cold drops upon them while the coffin went down into the grave, Susan had taken her turn at him—muttering furiously, eyes on her prayer book. Why had he even come to the funeral? In ten long years why had he never spoken to his father, never even tried? What kind of hypocrisy was this?

"He was in the wrong," Jewett murmured. The coffin had slipped a little. Its dull pewter-colored bulk splashed quietly in the rain that had pooled at the bottom of the grave. "He drove me out. He never called me back." He heard the words about returning to dust, and bent to pick up a handful of wet earth and drop it down on the coffin lid. He turned back to her. She was staring at him with flared nostrils, stony eyes. Rubbing the mud from his fingers, he told her, "I wanted to please him. Nothing else mattered to me so much. When I disgusted him instead, it seemed like the end. Did he say he wished I'd come back? Did he ever say that?"

"He didn't have to," she said sharply. "Not to me. Really, Oliver—don't you ever think about anyone but yourself? Can't you imagine anyone else's feelings?"

The minister, at the head of the grave, under a black umbrella held by a grouchy-looking altar boy, closed his book and dropped it into a pocket of his cassock. The boy clumsily hung a mackintosh over the old man's frail shoulders. Touching his cornered black cap, the minister came to shake hands with the widow and orphans, and to wheeze ritual words of comfort, then made off at a brisk totter down the grassy slope among the tilting old headstones, the spongy earth squishing under his shoes. Susan put away her prayer book and took her mother's arm.

Jewett said quickly, "I came because I'm sorry. I should have tried to patch it up. But don't you see—it wasn't something I'd done that made him angry. It was something I was. Not something I could help, not something I could change. So what was the use in trying?"

Susan looked at him with pity and scorn, turned with her mother, and followed the clergyman and altar boy down toward the curving lane, where the black cars waited. Jewett watched their retreat for a moment, Susan tilting as she always did, his mother having a wobbly time because the spike heels of her new black patent-leather pumps kept sinking into the soft earth. He stepped again to the edge of the grave and looked down at the coffin with its dark splash of symbolic earth. "I wanted to please you," he said. "The times I was able to please you were the proudest times I ever knew. I was all right then. Those were the only times I was all right. You want to remember that? I'd like it if you'd remember that." He was crying. Workmen trudged toward him from a stone shed. Wearing dull black slickers, carrying shovels, they were coming to fill in the grave. They must be used to seeing people cry over coffins. And who cared what they thought? Still, he turned his face up to the rain, so they wouldn't see his tears.

"I know how long it's been," he said to Susan from the unkempt kitchen on the second floor of the sagging old house at the beach. "Somehow, I had the impression that it didn't matter. That I didn't matter."

"What do you mean, you don't have any money?" She glanced up at the sun that was climbing toward noon. Its brightness made her wince. "Do you think I could come in?"

"What?" He was startled and abashed and hurried to unhook the door whose black screens bulged in their warped frame. "Come in, come in." He pushed the door wide. "Excuse the mess. We're not much on housekeeping."

She looked him up and down. The happy coat was short. She made him feel naked. The length and straightness of his legs made him ashamed. She said, "You're not much on clothing, either." She limped indoors and he let the screen flap shut. "Who is 'we'? Not your fat friend Fogel—the one who brought you home for the funeral in that pretentious car. He certainly made himself scarce."

"He doesn't like funerals," Jewett said.

"He doesn't like you, either," Susan said. "Not anymore. He was very curt with me when I phoned yesterday to ask about you. He said he didn't know where you were and, what's more, he didn't care. Wasn't he your agent?"

"Past tense—you've got it," Jewett said. "Excuse me—just let me see if the coast is clear." He peered into the tousled bedroom. The bathroom door beyond was open, a big rainbow beach towel hanging crooked over it. A shower splashed. Rita sang under her breath. If she sang aloud, neighbors would come flocking with requests. He closed the bedroom door, went back, and led Susan through the hall to the living room, where a bay window faced the ocean across a street of patched asphalt and a beach teeming with summer youngsters. Sea light was harsh in the room. He cleared a dumpy tan daybed of paperback books and old copies of *Daily Variety* and *Hollywood Reporter*. "Sit down," he said. "It's hot. Can I get you something cold to drink?"

"I'm all right." she said, and sat. She peered up at him through her distorting lenses, blinking. "What's happened to you? We keep looking at the movie ads in the papers. Your name isn't there anymore. When we saw it, we always went, and you know how I hate to go out."

"I appreciate it," he said.

"What went wrong? It's that Fogel, isn't it? I don't trust people who wear dark glasses in the rain."

Jewett smiled wanly. "I'll remember that." He made to sit down and remembered that he couldn't sit down in the happy coat and not reveal what Rita called the tropic zone. He said, "Let me put on something," and turned, and Rita stood wrapped in the rainbow beach towel in the doorway, drying her hair. She wore it short in those days and its natural dark brown color, almost black. She looked surprised when she saw Susan. Jewett said, "My sister, Susan. This is Rita Lopez."

Susan gaped. First at Rita. Then at him. She moistened her lips with her tongue, and her voice came out faint. "Are you— are you married?"

"I am," Rita said brightly. "He isn't."

Susan's face flushed. Her clumpy little fists dug into the padding of the daybed and she struggled to get to her feet, crying at Jewett, "What about what you are? What you told me at Daddy's funeral? That you couldn't help it, you couldn't change. What

about that?" She did manage to stand up, almost falling forward from the effort. "You *could* help it. You *could* change."

"I didn't know that then," Jewett said. He looked for Rita, but
she was retreating down the hall. "I don't know it now. Things
happen we don't expect. Did you expect it? Be honest, now.
You're surprised as hell."

Susan was staring after Rita. "What does she mean—she's
married?"

"She means her husband walked out on her when the studios
blacklisted her, and she couldn't get parts anymore and support
him in the manner to which he'd grown accustomed."

Susan's face lost color. "She's a Communist?"

"Her father was a Communist," Jewett said. "In Mexico. In
the period when they wanted democracy and everybody was
fighting everybody else about it. 1917. He was dead before Rita
was born. She's not a Communist."

"But it's because of her that you're not working," Susan said.
"Oh, Oliver, why? You were doing so well."

"Will you let me change my clothes, please?" he said. "It's
not that simple. Will you wait?" She didn't have words, but she
nodded, and plumped down on the daybed again. Jewett
bumped into Rita, who was coming out of the bedroom in jeans
and a red-check gingham blouse. She put a quick kiss on his
mouth, then wrinkled her nose.

"Whoo!" she gasped. "You stink."

"I can't think how it happened," he said.

She went off to the kitchen. He shed the happy coat and got
under the shower to wash off the stink of sweat. He couldn't
find clean pants and ended up kicking into the crumpled,
grubby white sailor pants he found on the floor beside the bed.
He couldn't find a shirt, either, but it was too hot for a shirt
anyway.

In the living room, a brown quart bottle of Acme beer sweated
on the battered coffee table. Rita sat on the other end of the
daybed with a glass of beer. A glass of beer untouched stood in
front of Susan. She stared at it. In high school a boy had invited

her out. She thought it was because he cared for her. He got her drunk on beer and brought his friends to laugh at her when it made her sick. She had not touched beer or anything else alcoholic since. Not that Jewett knew of. Smoke hung in the hot air. Rita chain-smoked even then. She was saying:

"I was acting in a play in a little theater off Sunset, and scouts come around to those, scouts from the studios, looking for new actors. Not me. I'm not new and I'm blacklisted anyway. But new kids. And Ziggy Fogel came with Oliver. They were sleeping together, you know." Rita was a model of discretion. "Ziggy had rescued him from some janitor's closet in New York in 1948 and brought him back out here and got him into pictures."

"During the war," Jewett said, "I'd had some pretty fair parts on Broadway. I thought it was because I could act." He bent over the table to fill a water-spotted glass with beer from the chilly bottle. "It wasn't." He sat on the dusty floor and crossed his legs. "It was because all the good young actors were in the service."

"Oh, Oliver," Susan said.

"It's true. How true it was, I learned when they came back from Europe and the Pacific and suddenly nobody wanted me anymore. Cockroaches were my only friends. We lived together on a share-and-share-alike basis. Until Ziggy saw me in some butchered Shakespeare outdoors in the summer for the poor unwashed, you know, and decided the movies needed one more pretty face."

"Oh, Oliver," Susan said again. "Stop." She looked to Rita for help. "He's very good. Isn't he very good?"

"I make it a rule never to go to movies," Rita said, and grinned at him over her beer glass.

"When I left him for Rita"—Jewett got to his knees and took a cigarette from Rita's pack on the table and lit it from the flame of Rita's Zippo, and sat cross-legged again—"it made him spiteful. He warned me I'd never work in this town again."

"But you're not a Communist," Susan cried. "That's so unfair!"

"It would be unfair," Rita said, leaning forward to twist out her cigarette and light another, "if he was a Communist. What the hell's that got to do with a person's right to earn a living?"

Susan looked desperate. "But what will you do?"

"He makes a mean taco," Rita said. "Worst comes to worst, I'll hock my ass for ten pounds of hamburger, and we'll peddle tacos to the hungry on the beach."

"We're working," Jewett said hastily. "Don't worry. Life is full of ironies. All the other Communists, who really are Communists, adore Rita. A bunch of them have got a little-theater group. She's in all the plays. They pay Equity. And because she's in the plays, I'm in the plays. They think I'm a Communist too. Some of them are very great actors." He looked at Rita. "Get Susan some tickets, all right?" Rita set down her glass, hopped off the couch, went away. "They even praise my work. They know better. But politics makes liars like nothing else. All the same, I'm glad. I'm learning a lot."

"But you're getting in deeper," Susan wailed.

"How's the painting going?" Jewett asked.

"The gallery closed," she said wanly. "I took my pictures around, up and down La Cienega. God how I hate it—the way strangers stare at me. They wouldn't take them. It was charity on Zimmerman's part. Poor man. I went to see him in the hospital. His face is all twisted. He drools, Oliver. I couldn't understand a word he said."

"You'll be all right," Jewett said. "When things can't get worse, they get better. New York taught me that. What about the advertising agency? At the funeral, didn't you tell me they kept phoning, trying to get you to come back?"

"I don't want to do that. I did it for so long. I'm taking pottery classes. But it's not going to work. I just end up looking like a mud pie, and everything comes out crooked. Like me." She gave a grim little laugh. "What we are—that's what we make." Her shoulders sagged. "Oh, I suppose I'll go back to the agency. What else is there?"

Now, in the smoke-stuffy motel unit, the snow blowing outside, whiskey warm in the veins, Rita clucks over her cards.

"Poor woman. She had rotten breaks from the start, didn't she? Crippled? Now this."

"She's rich and famous," Jewett says. "It took her a while to learn what she was supposed to do. Not half as long as it's taken me." He picks up the last deuce, lays down his hand for her to admire, and says, "Gin."

Rita grunts and, cigarette smoldering short in a corner of her painted mouth, one eye squinting, gathers up the cards and reaches for the cardboard box they fit into. Jewett drinks off his whiskey. He says:

"She even found a man to marry her, finally. She loved him. Very much. Unluckily, he was blind."

Rita cocks a painted eyebrow. "What is this, some kind of sick joke?"

"No, it's a fact. And Lambert's trouble was that he wouldn't admit it. And it killed him. He stepped in front of a car one night. And I've been watching her, and I'd say she gave up on life right then. It just took death seven years to get around to her. Love was all she ever really wanted."

"We all want what we can't have." Rita slips the pack into the box. "What we've got, that's no good to us. That's why I kept throwing plates at you." She sighs. "Listen, love, I'm pooped. Go off to bed, Oliver, okay?"

He stands stiffly. "I like remembering the house at the beach." His watch tells him he has been back there in 1954 a long time tonight. "Don't you?"

"It was hell," she says, "but we had some fun." She tucks the rye bottle back into the suitcase, picks up the fur coat and hat, and hangs them in a stingy closet. "I got a lot of target practice." She laughs.

"Your aim wasn't too bad by the end." He picks up his parka from the bed and works himself into it. "You damn near killed me."

It was a clear day like that other day, but eight years later. And this time, kids were witnesses, little kids, Connie's snotty-nosed, grubby-handed little redneck kids, watching big-eyed from open windows, hanging arms and legs over the stair rails, grinning gap-toothed at Rita flinging Jewett's clothes down that long rickety outside staircase at him, then pitching the drawers the clothes had lain in, then rushing back inside the apartment, dragging out the cheap little chest and heaving that after him. Accurately. It broke his left arm. Or the fall did.

And this time, she wasn't sorry, tearful, apologetic. She didn't go all frantic with love and sympathy, the way she used to when she cut him with flying glasses or scalded him with pots of hot coffee. This time she spat down on him, ran back inside, slammed the door. She didn't even phone for an ambulance. One of the strangers in bathing trunks who had clustered in the street, attracted by Rita's loud curses in Spanish and English, and gaping up in amazement at the poor naked bastard trying to get back up the stairs—one of them phoned for an ambulance. And asked Jewett for his dime back as the attendants were sliding Jewett into the truck.

"You want to forgive me now?" She struggles to pull off a wildly striped turtleneck sweater, orange, scarlet, magenta, green, over her head. "I didn't know what I was doing, all right? What could I do, what could we do?" She drops the sweater on her chair. Her bra looks strong as canvas, holding up the massive breasts. Her flesh is an old woman's, mottled. He turns his eyes away. She says, "Connie was the problem, Connie and her kids."

"No," he says bleakly, "it was me. I didn't want us to be finished, couldn't accept it, couldn't bear the thought." He zips up the parka. "And you didn't have the heart to tell me I was a fifth wheel. You were kind as long as you could be. No wonder you kept losing control."

"Kind? Me? Shit. I couldn't have looked after them without you." She goes into the bathroom. Water splashes in the hand basin. He hears her make spluttering noises. She is washing off her makeup. She calls, voice echoing off the hard, shiny surfaces of the bathroom, "I lied to myself that I could. But it went to pieces right away. Twenty-four hours a day with nobody but Connie? Forget it."

"Good night," he calls, pulls up the hood of the parka, opens the door. The cold is breathtaking. He drags the door to after him, hunches his shoulders, puts his head down, and makes for his cabin. Connie used to grin when Rita threw things at Jewett. Rita would have needed a target, it was her nature. With Jewett gone, Connie would have become the target. God knew, she was big enough—beautifully proportioned, but tall and large-boned, a Michelangelo sybil bred in an Arkansas sharecropper's shack. She wouldn't have liked being Rita's target—not after Otto, her 360-pound meat-cutter husband who had beaten her up at every full moon for eleven years before she fled to Rita. Does Rita really believe it was her boredom with Connie that put an end to the two women living together? Maybe. Time can do funny things to truth. More likely, Rita said that tonight to make Jewett feel better—as if it mattered now. His scars only hurt when it rained.

The key to his unit is warm because he has been clutching it in his pocket. The lock is cold. The motel room, identical to Rita's, is warm and smells vaguely of perfumed room-deodorant spray. It is tidy. The maid has built a neat stack on the dresser out of the script he left in the bed, the floppy blue crossword puzzle book, the paperback novels. His big, two-speaker portable cassette player stands on the bedside table under the lamp. He presses a button and it begins to play a Brahms quintet. He sheds the parka and looks at his own bottle of whiskey. Scotch will taste wrong after the rye, but he pours himself a nightcap anyway. He tried to telephone Bill before supper and didn't get an answer. It's pretty late now. He'd better let it go. He removes his boots, stacks pillows, lies on the bed propped up by the pillows, lights a cigarette, and slowly works on the scotch.

What did he say to her that morning to make her so mad? They were in bed together. She had tiptoed in with mugs of coffee and had slipped between the sheets naked beside him before he was awake. This didn't happen often—not after Connie and the kids moved in. Rita slept with Connie. The kids slept all over the place, kitchen, bathtub, couch, floor. There were four of them—they only seemed like a dozen. And it was an event when Rita sneaked in to be with Jewett. He glowed about it.

They made drowsy love, marveling in whispers at each other, as if their bodies held nothing but surprises, as if they hadn't been together this way two thousand times before. And then, with the coffee mug at his mouth, he said something. And she began yelling at him and hitting him, first with her fists, then with the straight chair she'd propped under the doorknob. And that was why he was naked out there on the bright morning stairs, arms over his head to keep the missiles from crowning him, feet tangled in his flung clothes.

He gives his head a baffled shake, gets off the bed, goes into the bathroom for aspirin, washes it down, switches off the bathroom light, goes back to the bed. He was trying to get back up the stairs. No point in that. He could have put on what she'd flung at him, covered his nakedness right where he stood. Why was he trying to get back up the stairs? To make it right with Rita, grab hold of her and keep hold of her till she stopped raging? She was much smaller than he. He was stronger. He had done it before. But it wasn't that—not this time. This was their last battle, the end of the war—and he knew it.

He stands scowling beside the bed, taps ash from his cigarette into the little ashtray, tastes the scotch, and remembers Darlene. The smudged faces of all the kids he sees with a sharpness no amount of time will ever dim. God, they are grown-ups now, even Bubby—sneak, bully, four years old. But Bubby doesn't figure in this. It's Darlene, the oldest, twelve. He gives his head a shake and stubs out the cigarette. Can this be true? Was it Darlene for whose sake he was trying to get back up those stairs?

He remembers her—all elbows, knees, thin white face, straw hair straggling over it, big eyes filled with pain and longing. He sees her standing in a dirty rag of a dress, on Ocean Front Walk, hands clasped behind her, staring up at the blind man who played there, a scruffy little dog asleep at his feet, a tin cup attached to a wheezy accordion mended with soiled adhesive tape. The scrawny child was spellbound, everything else forgotten—including the smaller kids whom she was supposed to mind, to keep from drowning, stealing, falling under the merry-go-round, making themselves sick on greasy french fries. He sees her at a summertime park, where a band played on a portable stage, sees her stick-thin arms and legs moving in an awkward dreamy dance on the grass in the shadows of the trees. He sees her face, washed for the occasion, wet with tears on the night he took her to a symphony concert at Hollywood Bowl.

Could he have saved her for the kind of life she ought to have had? How? He sits on the bed and pulls the boots back on. He shrugs into the parka and yanks the hood up. He makes sure he has his key, then pulls open the door and goes out again into the snow. The wind is at his back now, pushing him along the white street. Music still twangs from the Antlers. Its sign is a pinkish blur through the falling snow. He crosses the invisible road and moves into the trees, wading in drifts, just able to make out a yellow glow of small windows in Kimberly's mobile home. He raps the door again. Does he hear her voice? "Kimberly?" he calls. "Are you all right?"

The door jerks open. She stands there in jeans and a sweater, the light behind her making her hair shine like shredded silk. "Will you please leave me alone?" she says. "Will you please just leave me the hell alone?" And she slams the door.

In the morning, the storm has stopped. A yellow machine with a high glass cab, driven by a youth in a green earflap cap and mackinaw, chugs up the logging road ahead of the vans that carry actors and crew. The machine scoops up the snow from the road and blows the snow away into the trees. It is a pleasant sight, if monotonous. Jewett watches it, seated cramped beside Rita, paperback book in his lap, a finger stuck in it to keep his place. Kimberly's Alfa-Romeo is buried in snow, so she rides in the van this morning. She doesn't make it more crowded. She is too thin for that. Jewett does his best not to look at her.

April

JEWETT HELPS Susan up the cracked cement stairway under the dark deodars to the house. It is slow going. She has lost weight, but she depends on him for half her strength, and her bad leg gets in the way. She feels sick and weak, and he feels old, and they stop to rest every few steps. It is always worst on the sixth and final day of each month's series of treatments, which this is. Both of them have become attuned to the fine shadings of wretchedness, which darken with each day's treatment.

He has learned to take empty back streets home from the distant University Medical Center, because it is always necessary to stop at least once so she can open the car door and miserably vomit into the gutter. It isn't nice. It is unsanitary and antisocial, but she stubbornly refuses to use the plastic container with lid he has stowed in the car. (It is her car she insists they take, with tiny stuffed toy replicas of Lambert's dogs dangling from strings off the rearview mirror.) She is repelled by the idea that Jewett will empty and wash the container. When he brings up the idea, she threatens to hire a nurse. And that puts an end to it.

The day is sunny but cool, and the retaining wall against which they lean, side by side, catching their breaths, is cold. The rusty moss is thick on this portion of wall. The pine needles are thick and slippery underfoot, making the ascent harder than it might be. Yet he hasn't swept them away because they form a cushion, and he is afraid that sometime he may lose his grip on her and she will fall. It is important that she not cut herself. If she starts to bleed, it will be hard to stop, maybe impossible. The chemicals that drip into her veins during these dreary five-hour sessions will in time, if they haven't already, end her blood's ability to coagulate. Then there is the danger of infection. Week by week she is losing her ability to fight infection.

The danger is worst in the days following treatment, when a common cold could turn swiftly to pneumonia, and this chilly spring he has made her bundle up. She wears an old stocking cap that started life a cheerful blue but has faded with the years to a sickly lavender. Moths have been at it, and through the holes her pale scalp shows. All her fine, white, old-woman's hair has fallen out. She won't let him buy her a new cap. Over her protests, so that she can make a neat appearance at the medical center, he has hauled her heaps of soiled clothing to the dry cleaner's and to the laundromat: he rather enjoyed sitting in the blank white room on a chair of flimsy molded orange plastic, warmed by winter sunshine through plate glass, reading while the washers sloshed and shuddered. But her clothes are all old, faded, threadbare, and she refuses to let him take her to buy new ones.

"A waste of money," she says. "I'm dying, remember?"

Now they commence climbing again, he with an arm tight around her, lifting, she making low, miserable sounds under her breath. These switch him back in time fifty years. After the polio, she had to go for therapy to the hospital three days a week, to try to regain the use of her leg. He pleaded to be allowed to go along in the Model A when their father drove her in the early mornings, having carried her in his arms down these long steps—though she could manage them, slowly, wearing her brace. Jewett sees his father's straight back, lean shoulders lifted against Susan's weight, disappearing down the steps, the dark tree branches shutting him from sight. Jewett ran to his mother, who was dressing for school, and hopped around her, tears in his eyes, begging to go to the hospital with Susan.

"Idle curiosity," his mother said, "is an unattractive thing in a civilized person. I'd suggest you do your best to suppress it." She bent to give her bobbed hair a hurried brush in the dressing-table mirror. "Starting now."

"But it's not idle curiosity," he said. "I want to help her."

"Casuistry"—his mother put on a little tight-fitting brown felt hat—"is even less attractive." She brushed past him to lift down from a rattly hanger in the closet the light jacket that matched her skirt and hat. Her blouse was pale yellow silk, with a floppy bow at the throat. Alice Jewett had no use for what eight-year-old Oliver already understood to be a rule of life— that teachers had to look dowdy. She always looked pretty, even in those pinchpenny Depression days when they'd had to sell his father's Dodge to help pay Susan's medical bills, so Alice didn't get to drive her trim Model A anymore. And no one could pay lawyers, so his father had to knock on doors in the evenings, trying to sell cheap life-insurance policies. " 'Casuistry' means," she told Jewett, "making up pious excuses to cover impious motives."

From the built-in oak drop-leaf desk in the living room she gathered student papers she'd sat up late last night correcting and stuffed the papers into her neat briefcase. She frowned at her pretty little gold wristwatch. "Magdalena's late again." She kissed the top of Jewett's head and ran for the front door. "If she comes before you leave for school, tell her I won't need her Friday. Tuesday, next week." She was out the door and her high heels were rattling across the hollow porch boards when she called back, "And her money is in the cookie jar." Then she was off, slim and brisk as a girl, down the long steps to wait for her ride.

"My motives are not impious," Jewett called after her before he shut the door. He touched his hair where she had kissed him, and put his fingers to his nose to smell the trace of her perfume those quick kisses always left. But he did it without thinking, from habit. He was scowling, angry with her. It wasn't idle curiosity. She didn't know, his father didn't know. They were too busy and too worried. Susan's brave smiles could conceal from them how she felt. Jewett knew. He was with her more than they were, and he had time to pay attention.

Susan's therapy went on and on, and she was tired of it and full of anger and despair because her leg was hardly getting better at all. She cried. He knew. He had caught her at it, and the sound of it was bitter. He never told her. She was trying hard to appear strong and hopeful. It would be cruel for him to tell her he knew she cried. But he did know—nothing could change that. And he wanted to help her. He felt sure that if they let him go with her to the hospital, he could help her. His father and his mother didn't understand how alone Susan felt, having to get better all by herself. He understood, and it was mean to let her go on alone when he could help.

He went to the kitchen, dragged a chair across the blue linoleum, climbed on the chair, opened the cupboard, and took down the cookie jar, heavy pale brown pottery with California poppies painted on it, egg-yolk color. He set it on the shelf and lifted the lid. Inside, his hand found a little wax-paper packet. He unfolded it. There were six wilted one-dollar bills. He must be wrong. He climbed down off the chair, separated the bills, and laid them out on the counter. He was not wrong. None of them was a five or a ten. Magdalena was gray-haired, heavy in the hips and breasts, and her ankles swelled out over the tops of her worn, misshapen shoes as she waddled about. Every Tuesday and Friday she came early and worked all day, vacuuming, sweeping, mopping, washing dishes, making the window-panes shine, leaving a cedar-oil gloss on the furniture. On Tuesdays, she also ran the washing machine and hung the clean clothes out on the line, and brought the dry clothes indoors and folded them and put them away, smelling of starch and sunshine. On Fridays she stayed and cooked dinner. And three dollars a day was what they paid her. He wrapped the bills in the wax-paper packet and dropped it back into the cookie jar. He put the lid on the cookie jar, climbed on the chair again, slid the cookie jar back into the cupboard, and shut the door.

He had meant to take coins so as to ride a bus to the hospital. He had never ridden a bus alone, but he knew where the hospital was, and knew how to ask directions from a bus driver. He couldn't take Magdalena's money. Not even if he could persuade himself he was only borrowing. *Casuistry*, his mother said. You weren't borrowing if you knew you'd never be able to pay the money back. He set the chair in its place at the kitchen table and left by the back door so he wouldn't meet Magdalena toiling up the stairway from the street, puffing and panting. She would scold him for starting late to school. He fought his way through the thick brush and untrimmed trees in back of the house to the street above. He wished he had a bicycle on which to roll swiftly down the hill. He didn't have a bicycle. He walked to the hospital.

It seemed a long way. He was afraid he would arrive too late, that Susan's session would be ended, that their father would have come back in the Model A from his law office to pick her up and fetch her home again. He kept reading clocks through store windows. Then he saw the hospital looming up white and tall on its hilltop, windows catching and flashing back the sunlight, and it no longer seemed far. His legs were tired, but he made them go faster, climbing the strange streets of shacks and broken fences. It was a Mexican district. Maybe Magdalena's house was somewhere here. A dog came running at him, and he stopped dead still, afraid. But the dog only sniffed at his shoes and trouser legs. It didn't try to bite him. It went on.

The hospital was big and confusing to him. But he told a round-faced woman in starchy white about his sister and her leg. He rode the elevator and followed children in wheelchairs, old men with twisted faces, hobbling on crutches, to the physical-therapy room. It was like the gymnasium of the high school where his mother taught. Except no one here was playing basketball, as had been the case at the high-school gym when his father took him there. Everyone here was crippled. Most of them wore pajamas and bathrobes and bedroom slippers. They were all being helped to stand and walk by nurses or by young men in white jackets and white trousers. From somewhere, Jewett heard the echoing cries and splashes that meant there was a swimming pool. He was short, and found it hard to see between the many cripples. No wonder Susan was discouraged. All these cripples. He dodged this way and that, looking for Susan. He saw her, far away across the room.

She stood between long parallel bars of yellow wood. She had pushed up the sleeves of her sweater, and stringy muscles showed in her thin forearms. Her knuckles were white from gripping the bars so hard. Her face was tight. A red-haired, plump young man was leaning his freckled face to hers, nodding, urging her to try. Her leg would never get strong if she didn't put weight on it. Did she want to wear that heavy brace forever? Susan wasn't looking at him. She was looking down at her bad leg, which swung foolishly, and appeared to Jewett frail, not up to any weight.

She was making those low, miserable sounds under her breath. They broke Jewett's heart. He lunged toward her. She didn't see him. She tried to take a step on the bad leg. It gave under her, she lurched, and the bar caught her in the armpit. It jarred her and she winced. The young man's big, freckled hands came out to keep her from falling. He smiled, and she smiled back at him, heaving herself upright again. The smile was so brave and false that Oliver felt a surge of pity and cried her name. She turned. "Oh, Oliver, no!" She looked stricken. She let go the bars and dropped in a heap on the gray buttoned canvas mat beneath. Jewett ran to her, fell to his knees, and threw his arms around her. She was sobbing. He said, "I came to help you." But he knew, too late, that he hadn't helped. He had only made her more miserable....

When he unlocks the front door, she stops making the sounds. He helps her through the house, past the silent loom, down the hall to the back bedroom, which he has made clean and tidy and brightened with fresh wallpaper. He lets her down gently onto the bed that he keeps always fresh now with clean sheets, pillow slips, blankets. He unzips and gets her out of her awful old mackinaw jacket, and helps her lie back against the pillows. He removes her scuffed little shoes, sets them by the bed. She shuts her eyes. "Television?" he asks. The set is old, black and white, but she stares at it these days, not up to the effort of reading. She shakes her head. He stands gazing down at her. She looks as if she might die, right now, this afternoon. But he knows there is no cause for alarm. If not by this evening, then by tomorrow, she will be working, some of her color will return, and for three weeks, until the next set of treatments, she'll be a fair replica of her old self, able to joke, maybe even able to hope.

She begins to snore softly, and he slips off her old blue knit cap and stands inspecting it, poking a finger through the biggest of the moth holes. He recalls when it was bought, and why. The winter of 1932–33. For skiing. Because she finally did regain the use of that leg—such use as it would ever be to her. The brace hung for a while in her closet, then was taken to the garage to hang off a nail, the metal rusting, the pads graying, curling away from the metal, the straps stiffening and cracking.

She changed when she could do without the brace. The change was temporary, but he didn't know that. Instead of lying in bed all day, reading, drawing, painting, she wanted to walk. Not alone, no. Jewett must walk with her. Later, she tried to run, and did run in a crazy, lurching way, and pestered Jewett to race her along the tilted street at sundown, when no cars passed, when neighbors were busy indoors. She wouldn't play in the gym at school for fear of being ridiculed. But early on Saturday and Sunday mornings, she made Jewett play basketball with her on the quiet street, a barrel hoop nailed up over the garage doors. The hoop is gone now, but the nails that held it are still there. He hated basketball, he was no good at it, he wanted to be alone with his little cardboard stages, his little cardboard actors, but he played with her, played with her to help her leg grow strong—while his father slept, his father who loved basketball.

Then she saw a short subject about skiing. In those days, all four of them went, one night each week, to the movies at the Fiesta down on Main Street. Two features, a newsreel, a cartoon, and sometimes a short like the skiing one. The flower face of Freddie Bartholomew flickers in Jewett's mind's eye now, in dense black and white, weeping. Joan Crawford, big eyes outlined in black, a black spit curl at her ear, comes sneering through a bead curtain. Ugly old Marie Dressler howls at Wallace Beery in lashing rain aboard a storm-tossed tugboat. And tiny skiers squat as they whisk down a long chute, then fly above pine trees in long, heart-stopping trajectories, before they come to earth. She wanted to do that—fly.

Instead, she broke her leg. She learned to ski first, crookedly but loving it, and with a great sense of triumph. She whizzed down slopes around Big Pine. Jewett liked the look of the snow but not the cold of it. He shivered and however much his father sighed, never kept his skis on for long, though he skied with natural grace and almost never fell. He preferred to sit in the Model A with the heater humming, the heater bought specially for these weekend treks up to the snow, and read. If there'd been a radio, he'd have listened to the radio, running down the car's battery. But it was the time before car radios.

Then Susan found a little ledge to jump off. It wasn't three feet high. But her leg wasn't strong enough for even such a jump, and the bones snapped. She had sneaked off alone to try this jump, sure her father wouldn't let her if he learned about it. So she lay alone in pain in the snow for a while before they found her. The bone mended poorly, and three operations were needed to make the best of it. And after that, she returned to her old habits—never getting out of bed again unless she absolutely had to.

Jewett drops the cap on the bedside chair and leaves the bedroom, softly shutting the door. In the kitchen, he washes the breakfast dishes—they got a late start this morning. It is hard for him to hurry her to the torture he knows lies ahead, so they often get late starts. He has something she likes in mind for supper, and he cuts up a chicken and some big, floppy fresh mushrooms. She won't eat more than a few small bites, so he wants the bites to please her.

Also, this is the last meal he will cook for her for a week. He will make enough to freeze a couple of packets that she can easily reheat if she will—though usually she won't. Packets from last week lie close-stacked in the grudging old freezer compartment, gathering snow—from last week, from the weeks before. He coaxes her, mildly scolds her, tries to exact promises, but he is losing the struggle to keep her weight up. Five nights on the living-room couch is his limit. To move in, he'd have to dislodge those twine-bound heaps of weaving from his old room. Where to? The garage is full of them already. And short of moving in, being here, every day and night, he can't keep her eating. It's hopeless—one week out of four is already too many for Bill. Susan is not Bill's sister. Bill has no use for his own sisters.

"Dying?" Bill says. "We're all dying, for Christ sake." He stands naked in the steamy bathroom, peering into the shaving mirror. He pushes at his thick, dark hair, pushes it back from his smooth, clear forehead. "I'm sure as hell dying. Look at that." He faces Jewett, thrusts his head close. "My stupid hair is coming out by the handfuls." He taps the back of his head, lowers his head. "Look there. A bald spot big as a dollar." There is no bald spot, but Bill gives Jewett no time to say so, which is probably just as well. Bill faces the mirror again, lifting his upper lip with two fingers. This plays hell with his diction, but Jewett gets the gist of it. "My fucking gums are receding." He lets his lip go. He talks into the mirror. "You know what happens next? Your teeth start to fall out." With flattened hands, he drags down on his cheeks so the red inside his lower eyelids shows. "Look at me. Will you look at me for once? I've got as many wrinkles as a fifty-dollar suit."

"Stop pulling at your face." Jewett regrets sounding like a mother, and puts his arms around Bill from the back, hugs him, kisses the nape of his smooth, brown neck where the neatly trimmed hair is still damp from the shower. "Anyway, fifty-dollar suits are the ones that never wrinkle, never stain, look as awful after years of wear as they did in the store. Nothing can harm them." He caresses Bill's chest and flat belly. "They're nonbiodegradable."

"Yeah, well, I'm biodegradable," Bill says, "and I'm biodegrading fast. No wonder you don't want to come home anymore." He picks up a red comb and works on his hair. "I'm getting old and ugly."

"You don't know what old is, you don't know what ugly is, and you don't know what dying is." Jewett lets him go, turns away. "Come on. I'll fix you a beautiful breakfast. You'll feel more cheerful then." He walks along the hall.

Bill shouts after him, "I know you're never here."

A film of dust lies over all the shiny surfaces in the kitchen. Not the bedroom, not the bathroom. They're immaculate. So probably is the rest of the place—he was too tired to notice last night. But the kitchen is neglected. Why is it the people he loves can't feed themselves? He can guess how Bill has survived—on afternoon cheese and wine at the gussied-up canyon houses of interior decorators, on brunches of quiche and Irish coffee on Malibu sun decks among keepers of Beverly Hills boutiques. Bill excites these types with his easy masculinity. What do they excite him with—how easily he excites them?

Jewett, briskly sponging counter tops, stove top, breakfast bar, the red cushions of the barstools, can't think of another reason why Bill flocks with these chichi queens, in their skinny-ass designer jeans, shirts open to the navel, sunlamp tans, and loops of thin gold chains at their withered throats. Bill doesn't feel superior to them—of that Jewett is certain. There is always something wistful and lost about Bill in their shrieking company—like a little brown sparrow among flamingos. Yet he keeps going back. It saddens Jewett, but seemingly it doesn't sadden Bill, so Jewett does his best not to question or comment anymore. Bill works for decorators. That's probably explanation enough—along with the fact that he adores parties.

The supermarket date-stamp on the package of sweet Italian sausages puts it a little past. He cracks the clear plastic butchers' wrap and sniffs. They will be all right if he washes the grease off. He rinses the sausages carefully under warm water and lays them in a skillet over a low flame and puts a lid on the pan. The tomatoes have gone a bit soft and one or two of them have developed black spots. He washes the red, smooth skins, cuts away the spots, and chops the tomatoes fine. He observes the eggs carefully as he cracks them into a red bowl. They appear as fresh as supermarket eggs ever do these days. He cuts butter into a pan and starts it melting. He beats the eggs. And he hears Bill come into the kitchen, smells his cologne and his cigarette smoke.

"The treatments are brutal. She can't drive herself," Jewett says, and fits the coffee maker together and puts coffee into it. "It's only one week out of the month."

"And every Saturday," Bill says. "And it was three weeks in March. That fucking chain-saw movie."

"That wasn't supposed to take so long," Jewett says. He goes to the breakfast bar, where Bill has placed himself, shakes a cigarette from Bill's pack, and lights it with Bill's lighter. "They fired Kimberly Wells. There was nothing to do but shoot everything over again with the new girl. I explained that."

"You missed every meeting of the renters' association. You missed the meeting with the city council. Building snowmen with Rita Lopez. I'll bet when she stuck the carrot on, it wasn't for a nose."

"You're confusing her with the roles she played in those old movies." Jewett pours boiling water into the coffee maker. He peeps under the lid at the sausages, which sputter. He finds a fork and tenderly rolls the sausages over. They have begun to brown, and they smell fine and fresh. "She's as indifferent to sex as a Camp Fire Girl. You can't be jealous of old Rita."

"She wasn't indifferent to sex when you lived with her. I know you. You wouldn't live with anybody who was indifferent to sex. Not for eight years."

"She liked fighting better," Jewett says. "Anyway, that was twenty years ago." Again, the thought makes him a little dizzy. "Bill, we played gin rummy—like down at the senior citizens' center? No two golden-agers could have been more chaste. We'd never even have met except that both of us needed the money from that disgusting picture."

"You had laughs," Bill says sulkily.

"We needed all we could get, believe me." Jewett lifts down from their brass hooks red mugs marked with big white initials, O and B. These were Bill's notion some Christmases ago, like the monogrammed red bath towels. Jewett has yet to see the point. He is careful always to give Bill the O mug, always himself to use a B towel. He hoped this might draw an explanation from Bill. It never has. It made him mad at first, and grumpy later, but never rational. Jewett keeps at it to test his father's repeated assertion that the key to success is never giving up. Jewett lives in hope—and curiosity. He fills the mugs now, stirs sugar and cream into the O mug and sets it in front of Bill. "It's true, I missed the renters' meetings." Jewett stubs out his cigarette in the ashtray. "But I earned the rent, all right?"

"You don't want to face facts," Bill says. "Rent won't help if they convert this place to condominiums. We'll have to buy. And you'd have to do fifteen chain-saw movies to earn that kind of money."

"That is certainly a fact I don't want to face." Jewett returns to the stove to cook the eggs with tomato mixed up in them, to scoop the eggs onto plates, to lay the sausages on the plates beside the eggs. "What about the injunction?" Jewett sets the plates on the breakfast bar. He has forgotten forks and napkins. He fetches these, the napkins red, of course. He sits on the red-cushioned stool beside Bill. "Didn't you say the renters were going for an injunction?"

Bill unfolds the napkins and lays it in his lap. He is wearing worn old corduroys stiff with spilled varnish and dotted with paint, but the napkin is ceremonial. He says, "If the city council won't act. We're giving them another week, and then we go into court." He stabs at a sausage with his fork, and hot grease squirts his faded red sweatshirt. The sweatshirt, sleeves torn off to show the hard muscles of his brown arms, is part of his work outfit, like the corduroys, and has often been used as a paint rag. All the same, he says "Shit!" and wipes at the grease spots with his napkin. "If we get the wrong judge, you and I will be out on our ass in the street." He forks a chunk of sausage into his mouth and chews. "This is no movie, buddy. This is reality."

Bill is at his least winning when he calls Jewett buddy. Jewett wonders what Bill thinks his days with Susan are. He doesn't ask. The other man's reality is rarely so real as one's own. Isn't that what's behind acting—the attempt to make strangers share another stranger's reality? Behind writing too, painting, music, dance. Bill isn't without sensitivity. He sometimes walks changed out of a theater. He rarely reads, but Jewett has known books to change him. Eating quietly, Jewett decides that Bill is simply absorbed for the first time in his young life in a political cause, fighting alongside a crowd of like-minded people. This can be a heady experience, obsessive, apt to blind a man to anything else. At the risk of being called buddy again, Jewett asks tentatively:

"Would it be so bad—getting kicked out of here? It's only an apartment. We can find another."

Bill chokes, hurriedly drinks coffee, gulps, wipes his mouth with the napkin, stares at Jewett over the napkin as if he can't believe what he has heard. "Are you serious?"

"You mean it's a matter of principle?" Jewett asks.

"Wrong. Don't you know what this place is to me? 'Only an apartment'?" He lays down the napkin. He appears stunned and injured. "Is that what it is to you?"

Jewett is nonplussed. "Isn't it? What makes it so special? Your beautiful pieces. But we can take those with us wherever we go."

"Ah, Christ." Bill looks ready to cry. Turning away, wagging his head in mournful disgust, he gets off the stool and crosses the kitchen, carrying the red mugs. He rinses them at the sink and fills them again with coffee. Jewett gets the O mug this time. Bill doesn't sit down beside him again. He stands, holding his B mug, studying Jewett, who does his best to keep his face blank. "You really don't know, do you? You had a home—you've still got a home, your sister is still in it. You were born there, grew up there with parents who looked after you and fed you and sent you to the same school all your life. You had a home."

Jewett nods. "Yes. All right. And?"

"This is the first home I ever had. The only home. Did you ever stop to think of that? This is the first place I ever lived more than six months running in my whole life. This is the first place I ever lived with anybody I wanted to live with, anybody I loved, anybody who loved me." Tears fill his eyes. He picks up the cigarette pack, shakes a cigarette from it, lights the cigarette. "This is the first place I was ever happy in my life." His mouth begins to tremble. His voice wobbles. To keep from crying, he shouts at Jewett. "Now do you understand, you cold bastard? It's not just another goddamn apartment. This is my home, Oliver. This is my *home!*" And he can't help it—he starts to cry.

Jewett gets off the stool and takes him in his arms, holds him tight, they sway together. Jewett strokes Bill's back. "Don't cry," he says. "Don't cry. I didn't know. I'm not a cold bastard, Billy. I understand, now. Don't cry anymore. I understand."

Bill clumsily kisses his mouth. "I'm sorry I said that." He hiccups, reaches for his stool and sits down, wipes his face on the red napkin. "I didn't mean to shout at you. But I don't want to go back to drifting around. I had that, Oliver." He hunches miserably over the coffee mug, smoking, sniffling a little, wipes his nose on the napkin. "Trailers—shut up with half a dozen babies. You ever smell one of those dinky old trailers with half a dozen little kids in diapers when you have to keep it shut up in the rain? You ever eat cold cereal a week running for every meal? Eat out of whatever cans your old lady could rip off at the supermarket when nobody was looking—okra? You want to try okra cold out of the can sometime. You don't know what you've been missing. You ever try fitting in at a school where none of the kids ever saw you before, and your tennis shoes are rotting off your feet? He'd take me and one of my sisters and stop the car in front of some house and we'd go to the door and say we were lost, and could we please use the bathroom, and he'd keep the old lady talking while we found her house money and picked up any little items we could hide in our pockets and hock later. Summers, he'd canvass new towns in a pickup truck with asphalt cans in the back, long-handle brushes, ladders, selling roofing jobs, getting down payments and never going back. He had twenty dodges. We were lucky he was only in jail half the time. Dolan Haycock. Father of the year. Shit!"

"Forget it," Jewett says. He has of course heard this litany before. But not lately. He is disturbed that it still haunts Bill. "It's over. You're all right, now."

"Was all right." Bill gloomily crushes out his cigarette, gloomily swallows coffee. "Everything's going sour, all of a sudden. We're losing this place. Your sister's dying. You're never home."

"It can't be helped. It won't be forever."

Bill grunts skeptically. "And I'm losing my looks."

"You are not losing your looks," Jewett says. "Bill, you are not yet thirty-two years old. You are a very young man. This is ridiculous. I'm here every minute I can be."

"You get along fine without me," Bill mumbles.

"I breathe in and out," Jewett says. "I'm sorry you feel neglected. Just put up with it for a while, all right? And stop imagining things. You're beautiful. I love you."

Bill sighs and sits straight. "I have to go to work." He slides off the stool. "How is she? Don't think I don't care. But losing this place is all I can think about. We had happy times here. Every room. I don't want to leave them behind. We'd never be the same anyplace else."

"That's crazy." Jewett laughs so as not to sound exasperated. "We'll be the same no matter where we go. And maybe we won't have to go at all. You're fighting back. Why won't you win?"

"Because money talks," Bill says. "Especially to politicians. And we haven't got that kind of money." He picks up the cigarette pack and lighter and stuffs them into a pocket of the corduroys. "If we did, we wouldn't be renters, would we?" He brushes Jewett's mouth with an absentminded kiss, and walks out.

"She's all right," Jewett says to the empty kitchen. "She's as well as can be expected."

They sit on the long, windowed porch at the Skipper's, under drooping strings of signal pennons whose crimsons, blues, greens have faded to an almost uniform gray. The bentwood chairs at the small square tables are rickety. The tablecloths are mended. Jewett and Bill lazily drink coffee and brandy and smoke cigars. They never smoke cigars anywhere else. While they ate crabmeat salad, sand dabs fried in butter with toasted sesame seeds, washing the food down with a crisp Chablis, they watched the sun set, a bulging red fireball. The sun has drowned in the ocean now. Far out, long streaks of cloud are flame color, slowly turning smoky. Overhead, the sky has a green luster that will soon fade.

Jewett leans his forehead against the windowpane. Below, at the foot of the ragged bluff on which the old wooden restaurant perches, little beach-running birds skitter on long legs among the jutting rocks and in the foam-edged tide. Spotlights shine down on them from the restaurant, but they don't seem to care. There are no gulls, no cormorants, no noisy sea lions now. Maybe the birds enjoy the extra feeding time the spotlights give

them, even if it cuts in on their sleep. He doesn't know where
they sleep. He wonders. He turns to tell Bill to look at the birds,
and a hand appears between his face and Bill's. A hearty voice
says:

"Oliver Jewett, how about that!"

Jewett looks up, frowning. No one has ever asked him for an
autograph in a restaurant. No one ever will—not by his reckoning. Why should they? So who is this bald man, sagging jowls,
pouches under his eyes, drip-dry suit of baby blue, blue shirt of
oxford cloth a little too tight where his belly bulges? Red light
glancing off the sea gives his face a false rosiness, but there is
nothing false about his smile. It looks delighted. Jewett rises
awkwardly, unsure, and takes the proffered hand, but he must
look as blank as he feels, because the man says:

"You don't recognize me, do you? Fred Heinz."

"Good God!" Jewett laughs and gives him a clumsy hug and a
couple of slaps on the back. "Where in hell did you come
from?"

"Illinois. I manage a television station there. Been in L.A. for
a network convention. Fly home tonight, damn it." He turns
and calls, "Joanie?" And a stocky, gray-haired suburban ma-
tron in a beige double-knit suit punished by an aircraft seat
comes to shake Jewett's hand and smile with neat false teeth.
"My wife, Joan?" Heinz sounds almost as if he were asking
Jewett to confirm this identification. "Oliver Jewett."

Her handclasp is damp. "Fred's always thrilled when you
turn up on TV. He always makes it a point to watch."

"And then she has to hear all about New York," Heinz says,
"for the five hundredth time."

His expression is innocent, his tone all self-effacing good
humor, but Jewett knows he is lying. Joanie may hear about the
long flights of stairs up to that crack-windowed room where the
heat seldom climbed to the radiators, where cockroaches
poured in a black rush down the drains when you switched on
the bathroom light, about the greasy hot plate behind the tin
shutter doors, about the sardines and crackers and the cutoff

credit at every deli within a mile, about their waiting tables for one free meal a day, about the super seizing Heinz's typewriter for the unpaid rent. She may hear about Jewett's failed auditions in clothes borrowed from other actors, about how he lined his shoes with cardboard after walking the soles through from producer to producer, about how the little-theater group in the abandoned church put on Heinz's play and never paid him as they'd promised. But she hasn't heard, and never will, how the two boys, twenty-one, twenty-two, kept each other warm under thin blankets in winter, and consoled each other for their daily failures and dashed hopes—and how they laughed, holding each other tight, in bed.

Jewett is stunned by the recollections that rush into his mind. It's been thirty-five years. He's scarcely ever thought of these things. Yet now, it's suddenly as if they'd happened yesterday. Except to look at Heinz—puffy, gray, gone to pot. What became of the skinny kid with the beautiful grin and the thick sandy hair he kept pawing out of this eyes while he crouched over that ugly typewriter, rattling away with four fingers, ribbon growing frayed and pale, yellow pages spouting out of the machine? Jewett searches the slack face before him now for traces of that wild obsessive ambition. He doesn't find any.

Joan Heinz appears to be talking. Jewett blinks and gives his head a shake so as to make himself hear her. "But it must have been absolutely gruesome." She laughs. The sound of it is artificial. "I can't understand how anyone can be nostalgic about it."

"We were so young," Jewett says, "we thought we were having an adventure."

"Sure," Heinz says. "The bad bits didn't matter. We were going to be famous. All geniuses have to starve first."

"Strengthens the character," Jewett says. Plainly starve is only a word to Heinz now. He hasn't gone hungry in a long time, by the look of him. Jewett wonders how he likes being manager of a television station in Illinois. Is it any worse than acting in chain-saw murder movies? He doesn't ask. Instead he looks at Bill, who stands up. "Bill Haycock, Joan Heinz, Fred

Heinz." Jewett watches the man's face as Bill shakes his hand. Something sad and regretful happens to Heinz's jollity. The way he looks Bill up and down suggests to Jewett that he has, after all, gone hungry for a long time.

"Are you an actor too?" Joan Heinz asks Bill.

Bill shakes his head and says to Heinz, "How does somebody get to manage a TV station?"

"He goes in as a newswriter and has luck," Heinz says.

"You musn't think we watch a lot of television," Joan Heinz tells Jewett. "But Fred notices when you're going to be on and makes an occasion of it. It's so empty, so addictive, such a waste of time. And really, there's plenty of guilt, just taking your living from it."

Heinz gets red in the face. "The money's nice. Don't tell them the money isn't nice."

"No more playwriting?" Jewett says.

"The money's nice, of course, but—" Joan begins.

"I might get back to it when I retire," Heinz says. "I'm creative all day. After eight hours, I'm out of gas. I hear some people can write after dinner—not me."

"He has to sleep off the double martinis," Joan says. She is not speaking to anyone in particular. She is frowning into the shadowy main dining room. She grabs Heinz's arm. "Look. Those people are trying to take our table." She raises a hand, calls out to the waiter, and hurries off.

Heinz looks grim. Not about her going, but about her picture of how he lives. He doesn't try to erase it. In self-disgust, he fills it out. "So I can wake up in time for double scotches to clobber me for the night—well, at least till three in the morning, Scott Fitzgerald's dark night of the soul." He makes a face. "What went wrong? You're still acting. How come I'm not writing?"

"Because you've got good sense," Jewett says.

"To hell with that. You made it. Maybe I was good too. Maybe I gave up too soon. Now I'll never know."

"Forget it. I didn't make it, Fred. I was not good, and I never will be good. And believe me, there's no satisfaction in learning that. If I can find a way out of the acting business, I'm going to take it. You were the smart one. The money is good. Stop drinking. Take a walk before dinner, take a walk before bedtime. Stop regretting."

Heinz sighs and shakes his head. "Doesn't anybody end up satisfied in this life?"

"Nobody who wants very much," Jewett says.

"Are you coming or not?" Joan is back, agitated. "People are lined up, waiting for tables. It's embarrassing sitting there alone with them staring at me."

"Right. Coming." Heinz works up a smile. "Listen, this was great." He pumps Jewett's hand, pumps Bill's hand. "Nice to meet you, Haycock." With Joan tugging at his sleeve, he fumbles a business card from his wallet and gives it to Jewett. "Let's not lose touch, now," he says. "You must fly to New York sometimes, in your business. If you get a layover at O'Hare, give me a ring." Joan drags him away. He shouts over his shoulder, "I'll drive into town and we'll have a drink."

"I'll do that," Jewett says, and sits down again.

Bill is already seated. He tilts his head. "You were lovers. How does it feel, seeing him again after all this time? The nineteen forties, wasn't it?"

"December 1947. He got pneumonia. His father came from Rockford and dragged him home." Jewett pushes the card into a pocket and tries his coffee.

"That was a year before I was born," Bill says. "How does it feel? I can't imagine how it would feel."

The coffee is tepid. Jewett looks for the waiter. "He weighed about a hundred thirty. Lots of hair. When there was money from home—his home, not mine—I went to the barber. I was the one who had to look neat for auditions. Haircuts didn't help." Jewett catches the eye of the waiter, a stoop-shouldered, middle-aged son of the fearsome Portuguese lady. Jewett holds up his coffee cup and brandy glass. The waiter nods. "When Fred was gone, my hair grew long. I couldn't keep the room. I slept a lot with friends and, when I'd used them all up, with men and boys I'd never seen before and would never see again, just to have a place to sleep in out of the cold. Sometimes I got breakfast, sometimes not."

The waiter comes with the coffee urn and two more little slim glasses of brandy. He fills the cups and takes away the empty brandy glasses. Jewett goes on:

"When I got breakfast, I was set for the day, which I mostly spent in the public library with the bums and bag ladies—the other bums and bag ladies. When I got filthy enough, ragged enough, hungry enough, I put my pride in my pocket and shlepped around to a little theater I knew. I swept the place out, scrubbed the toilets, painted flats, rigged spotlights, anything, and they let me sleep there and gave me pocket money. Then an actor got sick or drunk or something and I got a part. It turned my luck around. I was seen and hired for the summer Shakespeare plays. Because of my hair—what else? Men cut their hair short in those days. The city of New York could save the price of a wig. Wigs weren't a dimestore item in the forties."

"It wasn't the hair," Bill says wearily. "Why do you always put yourself down?" He stirs sugar and cream into his coffee. "You still haven't answered my question. How did it make you feel—seeing him again?"

Jewett shrugs. "Sad, what else?" He smiles to himself. "I had a nickname for him—the Ivory Mischief. It's a quote from someplace, I don't know where. That's what he was like, white and smooth to the touch, like ivory." Jewett shakes his head. "Lean and good to hold. Now he's a bag of lard, isn't he? And about as mischievous as a sea slug. Sad, Bill, that's all. Time is not kind."

"Are you different too?" Bill says.

Jewett gives a small, bleak laugh. "I thought I was wonderful, beautiful, talented, and that the world would one day be sorry for how it was treating me." His cigar has gone out in the ashtray. He knocks burnt wrapper and ashes off it with his table knife and relights it. "Fred kept me from dying of self-pity by making me laugh. He had a lovely zany streak. One night when we were asleep, a rat tried to eat our feet. Big rat, big as a cat. Fred called him the grandfather of all rats, and when he finally trapped him in the bathroom and bashed his head in—it had to be Fred, I can't kill anything—Fred said that if we didn't give grandfather a decent burial, all his five hundred thousand children and grandchildren would come after us. I'd told him about my toy theaters at home, and he made me sew a suit for the rat and make a little top hat out of cardboard, and fix up a coffin from a shoe box. Then we took the Staten Island ferry and tossed him off the back while Fred recited 'Sunset and evening star, And one clear call for me....' It was touching."

"Jesus," Bill says, but vaguely, his mind on something else. He frowns. "You never told me you wanted to quit acting. Why him? Just to make him feel better about how he's thrown his life away?"

Jewett knows he should say yes to this and let it go. Bill is anxious about losing the apartment, anxious about losing his looks. This was supposed to be a happy evening. But Jewett's own anxiety is up. Heinz looks so old. Life is slipping away. So Jewett goes ahead and says:

"He hasn't. I have. I haven't talked to you about it because it'll only upset you, you'll only argue. And arguing won't change the facts. Do you remember *Hobson's Choice*? The scene where the strong-minded daughter who wants to marry John Mills goes to break off his engagement to the slum girl with the fat mother? And while the women shriek at each other indoors, Mills stands outside in the street, and the camera is on his face. He doesn't blink, doesn't move a muscle. But something happens to that man inside, something terrible and beautiful, and he makes you feel it. Now that is acting. Bill, I could no more do that than I could climb down to those rocks right now, strip off my clothes, and swim to Hawaii." Bill tries to interrupt. Jewett won't let him. "I can't go on pretending to be an actor. It makes me feel like a liar and an ass. I've got to find a way out. I've got to find some self-respect. It's already very late."

"Are you drunk, or what?" Bill says.

Jewett says eagerly, "You remember my telling you about the bakery at home—my first real job, Joey Pfeffer, the war? The bakery's for sale. I'd love to buy it. I'd make a good baker. You know I'd make a good baker."

"Will you talk sense?" Bill says.

"It's honest, useful work," Jewett says. "Like you do. With your hands. Making something people need."

"Bakers get fat." Bill tosses back his brandy. "From people ordering wedding cakes and then not getting married." He grinds out his cigar, backs up his chair. "Come on. Sleep it off. You'll feel sane tomorrow." He gets to his feet.

"I mean it," Jewett says. But Bill has gone to pay the check. On their way out, they pass through one of the bars where, high up in shadowy drifts of cigarette smoke, hangs a color television set. It is election year. A wrinkled presidential candidate with a crooked grin and dyed hair is talking. He can't be heard above the noise of the drinkers. Bill says, "There's your old buddy." Jewett worked in two films with the candidate thirty years ago. Bill says, "If he wins, maybe he'll get you a job in Washington."

"You forget how wholesome he is," Jewett says. "I am not wholesome." Out on the sea cliff where the car is parked, he says, "We can live above the bakery."

"Please shut up about the bakery," Bill says.

ay

A HUSH used to lie over the town. Even here, between the brown brick storefronts of Main Street, sound was subdued. The brooding old trees grew here too. But while they quieted the noise of cars, and around the schoolyards damped the cries of children, and around the churches muffled the Sunday hymn singing, it was not to the trees that the hush was due. It was to the sanatorium.

Back before the First World War, a doctor had come here from Iowa to die. Instead, he had got better—or at least no worse. Concluding that the elevation, easy temperatures, and dry air had cured him, he built a set of deep-eaved, shake-sided cottages on high ground, where people with tuberculosis could come and get well. He may have been right, because soon a town had spread out around the sanatorium. But almost everyone in the town was sick, and not disposed to excitement, and so the atmosphere, without anyone's particularly meaning it to, became like that of a hospital. And that explained the hush.

The hush became a habit, and hung on long after tuberculosis ceased to be the reason for the town's existence, and even well after the sanatorium went out of business and became retirement cottages for rich old people. The town continued to keep its voice down, walk around on tiptoe, and never honk an automobile horn. The common unspoken agreement to keep quiet had the effect of slowing everyone down. Speed, recklessness, tearing around could lead to forgetting not to yell. Acting silly could provoke laughter, another sort of noise. This meant that even the very young soon learned to behave soberly, though they rarely learned to enjoy it.

Jewett is amused now by the noise. Not only do horns honk. Tremendous trucks rumble through the town. Trucks were banned in the old days. Motorbikes carrying shiny-helmeted students from the new state college sputter past in the tree shade. Children large and small flock along the sidewalks where storefronts now gleam with happy plastic. The youngsters laugh, shout, jump, push each other, tilt back their heads to gulp soft drinks from gaudy cans. They stuff down tacos, hamburgers, french fries, pizza. Eating on the street? This is not the old Perdidos. Everyone moves briskly, even little old ladies with fat, asthmatic dogs.

The theater has lost its glowering old marquee. Its front is tiled in zigzag serape stripes, with FIESTA in jaunty neon script above a row of glossy plate-glass doors. Just past the theater is the drugstore, where he is lucky enough to find a parking space. He feeds a sturdy new parking meter a dime, and leaves a prescription for Susan at a pharmacist's white Formica counter at the rear of a long aisle of rakes, hoes, trowels, coiled green garden hose, pots, pans, toaster ovens, stuffed plush animals, hanging tricycles. Filling the prescription will take a little time. Jewett goes out to wander along the busy sidewalk.

Here is the Gray Shop, where he used to browse among the new books. He rarely had the money to buy one, but Mr. Gray always had a smile for him. And here he could open any book. At the public library, soldierly, square-jawed Miss Walton kept a sharp eye on him. If she thought he was too young to read something, she would march over, take it from his hand, close it with a snap, and set it back on the shelf. She bumped against him once, in her haste to keep his mind unsullied. Her corsets were like armor plate. He remembers one of the books forbidden him, *Young Joseph*, by Thomas Mann—the scene where the boy sheds his coat of many colors and dances naked in the moonlight. It made Jewett's heart beat fast in the summer hush of the library. Miss Walton must have known things about him he didn't know himself. He had hunted, dry-mouthed, for that scene again, but he'd never found it. She hadn't given him time.

Jewett looks in at the door of the Gray Shop. The place is blindingly shiny. In the old days there was wood paneling, the shelves were of wood, the tables too. The new book jackets provided the only brightness. It was comfortable, homey. Carpets lay soft underfoot. Today not a wooden surface shows. The floor is gleaming vinyl tile. A college-age girl with hair like a water spaniel's, wearing a red-and-yellow-striped tank top and tight jeans, is lifting books from a carton at a counter and checking off titles on a clipboard. She is nothing like Mr. Gray, in his Shetland sweaters, tweed jackets, gray flannels, soft calfskin shoes. Startled and chagrined, Jewett realizes at this late date that Mr. Gray must have been homosexual.

He smiles ruefully to himself. Why had he never suspected Gray? Just because, unlike young pastor Ungar, unlike poor, tormented Le Clerc, Gray had kept his slender, well-tended hands to himself? They'd often talked. What had they talked about? Jewett can only remember one moment. Gray had gently corrected the boy's mispronunciation of Michelangelo's name. Jewett sees his quietly amused smile, hears him speak the syllables, *mee-kail-ahn-jel-lo*. At this moment, he likes Gray very much. What if—? He stops himself. He had been no more ready for Gray than he'd been for the other men. He walks into the cooled air of the shop and asks the girl:

"What's become of Mr. Gray?"

She wears big round glasses with amber lenses smoky at the top. She blinks behind the lenses. "Mr. Gray?"

"It's the name of the shop," he says.

"Oh," she says and shakes her head and smiles. "There is no Mr. Gray."

"There used to be," he says.

"I suppose so." She lifts another stack of books from the carton. "I haven't been here too long." She pushes up the glasses, which have slipped down her nose, and jots a check on the clipboard list. She corrects herself. "Very long."

Jewett looks for someone older, but no one else is in the shiny aisles, and he decides he doesn't need to ask his question anyway. He knows what has become of Mr. Gray. Either he is shrunken, wrinkled, brittle-boned in some nursing home at eighty-five, fretful at how the type blurs when he tries to read—or he is in his grave. If the bookshop hadn't changed so much, this would be harder to accept, and Jewett would be tempted to go looking for him. Now he walks out into the bright spring sunlight and the rollicking children and the noise and smell and windshield sparkle of traffic, and goes looking for himself.

Down the block, across the street, Pfeffer's bakery waits for him. This fact stops him in his tracks for a minute. His heart begins to beat quickly. Why is this? What does he feel, exactly? Excited and at the same time frightened. Excited by the prospect of getting the bakery and a whole new start in life. Frightened at leaving the known for the unknown. He feels something else as well, something that surprises him—guilt. It is a fifty-seven-year-old failure who has been yearning for the bakery, who knows, or thinks he knows, that the bakery will redeem him, gain him pardon and forgiveness for his misspent life.

But what about the fragile little Jewett of six, with the big, dreaming, liquid eyes, dressed in whispering silks, rouged and powdered and grave, dancing in an empty house, the ghost of a girl-child never to be born? What about twelve-year-old Jewett, frowning at his desk, tongue in the corner of his mouth, toiling with ruler, cardboard, colored papers to duplicate the sets of new plays he'd read about in Burns Mantle? What about the gangling, show-off Jewett of sixteen, all unfamiliar hands, feet, elbows, in the glamorous glare of spotlights on the dusty stage of the high-school auditorium? The Jewett of twenty on Broadway, so scared and elated he vomited before every entrance? The dazzling juvenile Jewett of the thick Technicolor makeup, face looming huge and inhumanly beautiful in the popcorn-smelly dark?

Jewett, an old man laboring for breath in a glaring, hot, three A.M. kitchen, flour stuck to the sweat of his face—what kind of end to all those dreams was this? Somewhere lost in time, in a shabby Upper West Side rooming house, a naked, hungry boy turns on his face in a grubby bed that rattles when he turns, and weeps. On the sunny, midmorning sidewalk of a little foothill town three thousand miles away, the gray-haired man who was that boy long ago finds his eyes wet, the cheerful street, the carefree colors of the clothing of the passersby, the sun flashes of the cars all smeared together. He wipes his eyes.

"Sir, are you all right?" A boy and girl have climbed off a little yellow motorbike at the curb. The boy is without a shirt, skin smooth, honey-color. The girl wears little yellow shorts. They lift off their safety helmets. Each has hair so blond as to be almost white. Their blue eyes regard him worriedly. "Sir? Can we help you?"

He blinks, gives his head a shake, swallows to get his voice back. "Thank you—no, I'm all right. I'm fine." He could seize their arms, as the Ancient Mariner seized the arm of the Wedding Guest, and make them listen to a long, strange tale of a painted man upon a painted stage. He says instead, "Got something in my eye. It's gone now." He smiles. "Kind of you," he says, "I appreciate—" But they have already begun to walk away.

'You do too know him," the girl tells the boy in a loud, indignant whisper. "On 'The Rockford Files' last week. When they shot him, he fell in the swimming pool. He was the rich art collector who ran the drug-smuggling ring."

Not Oedipus, thinks Jewett. Not Hamlet. Not Richard II. *For God's sake, let us sit upon the ground,/And tell sad stories of the death of kings.* Kings—not actors. You can't wring much pathos from the sad stories of actors, certainly not the sort who are shot weekly and for whom stuntmen fall to their fictive deaths, screaming, arms flailing, into swimming pools, or down curving marble staircases, or off expensive terraces into the sea, in endless reruns of "Barnaby Jones," "The FBI," "The Streets of San Francisco." For God's sake, how many suave, effete art-collecting villains has he been? How many more can he stand to be? He takes a deep breath, straightens his shoulders, walks to the corner, and crosses with the green light.

What does he miss from the window of the bakery? The NRA poster, red, white, blue, a steely eagle clutching a jagged lightning bolt? The curling, fading war bonds poster? He couldn't have seen it here, but he had seen, in the windows of shops like this in New York, the gold star that stood for a boy's death, little pacifist Joey crouched in the raw tail-gun turret of a B-17, shot down in a lash of machine-gun bullets and the howl and helpless roll of wounded metal over Italy. Not that. No—what he misses in the bakery window are the flags, a little fan of fading U.S. flags like those his father fastened to the radiator cap of the Model A every Fourth of July. The Pfeffers didn't wait for the Fourth of July. The little flags were always there among the glistening white and chocolate cakes, the trays of frosted cookies, the gingerbread children.

Jewett didn't understand what the flags meant until too late. The recollection makes him feel a little sick and he shakes it off. He is pleased that the flags have vanished. That must have happened in the 1960s, when youngsters began to patch the worn-out seats of their jeans with flags. Flags would never mean again what they meant to Hermann and Ursula Pfeffer, and to Jewett's father and mother, when the bright little scraps of color had fluttered from the radiator cap on the drive to the picnic grounds at Brookside Park in the 1930s. What did they mean then, he wonders—the country going under, no one understanding why, hungry, jobless, hoping against hope? What the hell is he thinking about? He shrugs and steps into the bakery.

"Hi, Mr. Jewett," young Joe Pfeffer calls.

Young Joe Pfeffer is, of course, not young at all. He is, by Jewett's reckoning, thirty-seven. His father begot him at age nineteen, and was dead before the boy was born. Frances Lusk was the boy's mother, and it is Frances Lusk's smile that beams at Jewett across the sleek white cash register now. Young Joe doesn't favor his father, who was short, snub-nosed, blue-eyed, fair-haired. Young Joe is tall, dark, his nose is long and straight, and there is a dimple in his chin. Frances Lusk was renowned in high school for the dimple in her chin. And her radiant smile. Jewett doesn't know what has become of Frances Lusk.

Young Joe hands across a white counter three white bags lettered Pfeffer's in red. A young woman in a blue jogging outfit and striped blue and white jogging shoes pushes the crackling bags into a wire carrier basket on to the back of a pram where a pale baby dozes. She wheels baby and bakery goods out the door. She can't jog fast, not in the foot traffic, not with the pram, but she does jog, almost in place, breasts jiggling inside the loose blue jacket, baby's head jiggling slightly, though it gives no sign of waking up. Young Joe watches the girl and the baby out of sight.

"Still interested in becoming a baker, Mr. Jewett?"

"I'd like to talk seriously about it," Jewett says. "Have you got a few minutes? I'll buy you a cup of coffee."

Young Joe glances around the cheerful white and yellow room. A tall, gray-haired woman in a checkered coat bends peering through counter glass at an array of petits-fours. She is the only customer at the moment. A swing door flaps, and a teen-age boy in a white cap and white wraparound apron comes through from the kitchen, carrying a tray of crullers. He is short, fair-haired, snub-nosed, blue-eyed. Young Joe slides open a rear door in a glass display case and the boy sets the tray inside. As the crullers are glazed with sugar, the boy's face is glazed with sweat. Young Joe tells him:

"This is Mr. Jewett. He knew your grandfather."

The boy wipes a hand on his apron and holds it out across the countertop for Jewett to shake. He says he is glad to meet Jewett, but he doesn't smile, which underscores his likeness to the dead Joey, a solemn boy. The new solemn boy says, "Were you in World War II with him?"

"High school," Jewett says. He hears himself remark on how like his grandfather the boy looks, and ask if the boy's name is Joe Pfeffer III. He registers the boy's name, Peter-Paul, hears young Joe tell Peter-Paul to wait on the customers while he has a cup of coffee with Mr. Jewett. Jewett is aware of sitting on a yellow bentwood chair at one of three little round yellow tables at the front corner of the bakery, drinking coffee from a paper cup set in a yellow plastic holder, and of eating one of the fresh crullers from a paper plate. Young Joe himself eats a cruller, and Jewett is aware of thinking that he can't do that often—not and stay so thin. Jewett somehow manages to ask questions about the business, supplies, quantities, costs, overhead, profits, waste, work hours, shop hours. But he speaks and listens as if in a dream. None of this is real. The boy's question has toppled him backward in a long fall. Only the past is real.

Joey drove the bakery truck along a straight, narrow road edged by tall eucalyptus trees rooted in their own noon shadows. Beyond their ragged trunks stretched flat, empty farmland. Far off, a scatter of white shacks slept under trees. Away on the left, the mountains dozed under rough brown blankets in the cool winter sunshine. Rolling high and stiff-jointed on its wood-spoke wheels, rattling empty on a Sunday, but still smelling of fresh-baked bread, of chocolate and cinnamon, the truck was old. But Joey had outfitted it with a radio from Pep Boys auto supply store. Fat, bald, testy old Hermann, in the thick German accent he never shed, objected. But Joey was the one who drove the truck, and when he said he'd spend his own money, his father grudgingly agreed. So now symphony music poured from the radio that hung black under the dented dashboard in a snarl of wires, like a fly in a spider's web.

Jewett was listening to the music, but he was also staring at Joey, because he looked different today from the Joey whom Jewett ordinarily saw. He was dressed up in a suit and tie. So was Jewett, but Jewett was vain of his appearance and, like his mother, always took care to dress well. Joey was indifferent about clothes—except when he took out Frances Lusk. Old jeans, cords, flannel shirts, shapeless all of them, sometimes torn, not always even clean—these satisfied Joey. He had no idea that he was beautiful. Jewett knew better than to tell him. Joey would look at him with scorn. But this noon, Jewett was aching to tell him.

"Got your eyes full?" Joey said.

Jewett looked away. "It went off all right, didn't it?" He meant the Bible passages they had read aloud under the high, gray, pointed arches of a big cement church in Cordova, as part of a Christmas cantata with choir in wine-color robes. Here, in the clear morning brightness of the bakery, sipping his coffee, talking to Joey's middle-aged son, hearing in the background the voice of Joey's almost grown grandson, the soft electronic beeps of the cash register, Jewett can't recollect why, of all the young actors in the area, he and Joey were chosen for this chore. He can recall that they lied to the minister, so as to be able to leave the church as soon as their part was over, so as to be able to hear the New York Philharmonic broadcast in the truck. This had been Joey's idea. Joey couldn't get enough of good music. It was scarce on the air in those days.

"You did fine," Joey said. "You always do fine."

"Nothing the matter with how you did," Jewett said.

"You'd say that if I got every word wrong."

It was one of those insights of Joey's that always startled Jewett. It often seemed to him that Joey hardly knew he existed—apart, that is, from when they were naked together. And even at those times, Joey could seem remote, detached, thinking of something else, probably something beyond Jewett's scope. Jewett's scope was narrow. On the radio, it was plays he listened to, how the actors read their lines. At the record store, he watched for albums like *Macbeth* with Maurice Evans and Judith Anderson. The grooves of his set were by now so worn their gritty noise almost drowned the actors' voices. He read the newspapers and his father's *Time* magazines, but only for the reviews of plays and movies. No longer did he browse idly at the Gray Shop—he walked in knowing what he wanted, plays, books on acting, makeup, how to do foreign accents. These were crowding the children's stories, poetry, art books, novels off the shelves in his room. He hated having to attend to schoolwork, to making his bed, cleaning his room, getting up his laundry, sweeping the pine needles down the long front stairs, washing the car, trimming back the ground ivy and the shrubs—anything not connected with greasepaint, footlights, laughter, and applause.

Except Joey. And if Joey too hadn't liked acting, in the dark, echoing gym, the fusty, gray radio room at St. Barnabas Church—what then? Because the boys were not much alike. Music aside, when Joey listened to the radio it was for the clipped reports from overseas by H. V. Kaltenborn, the grim singsong of Edward R. Murrow speaking from bombed and blazing London. Joey read the papers and magazines to follow with alarm Hitler's progress across Europe with his tanks and snarling planes and steel-helmeted, goose-stepping troops in long overcoats. Jewett had seen these things in the streaky gray newsreels at the Fiesta and had been disturbed by them, but he couldn't understand why they were always on Joey's mind. Europe was eight thousand miles away.

Over the rattling of the truck, the soaring of strings, the shout of trumpets, Joey said, "You don't have to say those things. I'm not as good as you, and it's okay. Why apologize for how good you are?"

"I didn't mean that," Jewett said. "You and your damn psychology classes." He laughed impatiently. "Why is it all right for you to praise me and wrong for me to—"

"Hold it. Listen." Joey lifted both hands off the knobby steering wheel and for a second held them high, like a trapped badman in a Western. Only Joey's was a reflex of surprise. His mouth was open and his eyes were wide. He grabbed the wheel again before the truck could slope off into the eucalyptus trees, but he steered badly. He bent forward, face twisted in concentration, to listen to the announcer. Jewett wondered what had happened to the music. The announcer said, "—news department. We now return you to the regular Sunday broadcast of the New York Philharminic Orchestra." The music took up again in the middle of a phrase.

Jewett laughed. "Did you hear that? He said 'Philharminic'!"

Joey switched the radio off. He stared at Jewett. He was pale and he seemed angry. "That doesn't mean anything. Who cares about that? For Christ sake, didn't you hear what he *said*?"

"He said 'Philharminic'," Jewett said.

"He said Japanese planes have bombed Pearl Harbor."

Jewett blinked. "What's Pearl Harbor? I never heard of Pearl Harbor."

Joey threw his head back and howled. The truck strayed again, this time into the left lane. Just in time, Joey jerked the wheel. A car shot past, horn blaring. "It's in Hawaii, for God's sake," Joey said. "It's a U.S. Navy base. Boats, Oliver. You know? What you play with in the bathtub?"

Jewett grinned. "Not what I play with in the bathtub."

Joey looked disgusted. "This isn't funny, Oliver. You act like a moron. Don't you know what this means? We'll be in the war now. America will be in the goddamn war."

He wasn't just pale now, he was a bad, greenish color. He pulled the truck onto the shoulder of the road, where dry leaves and seedpods from the big trees crackled under the tires. The truck's motor stalled. Joey climbed, half falling, down from the truck, ran a few steps, and began throwing up. Jewett sat stunned. He couldn't take it in. It seemed like such a beautiful day. Numbly, he climbed down from the cab and went to Joey. He didn't know what to do. He touched Joey's heaving shoulders. Joey shook his head fiercely and threw up some more. Then he staggered away from Jewett, wiping at his mouth with the back of his hand. He leaned against the thick, peeling trunk of a tree, face in his arms. Jewett watched. He couldn't make out what Joey was doing. Then he heard. Joey was crying. Jewett went to him and very tentatively stroked his back.

"Don't cry, Joey," he said. "Don't cry."

Joey turned to him, face smeared with tears, strings of mucus from his nose, vomit yellow on his chin. "I'm not going, Oliver, God damn it, I'm not going."

"We signed up," Jewett said. "Remember? Last summer." He took a neatly folded white handkerchief from his hip pocket, opened it, and wiped Joey's face. Joey stank of vomit, but Jewett didn't care. Here was a chance to show tenderness to Joey—something Joey hated for him to show. And this time Joey wasn't rejecting it. Jewett's heart swelled. But he was still bewildered by Joey's words and he said, "They made us sign up. They'll make us go, too."

"Not me," Joey said stubbornly. "I'm not going to kill any-body. I don't care how evil they are. They never did anything to me." He took the handkerchief away from Jewett. He fumbled with it, trying to find a clean spot. He dabbed at his necktie. "Look what I did to my new suit." He wiped at the jacket. Holding on to Jewett for balance, he wiped his splashed shoes. He held the handkerchief out. "Thanks."

Jewett gave a small laugh. "What am I supposed to do with that?" He made a face. "Throw it away."

Joey shrugged and dropped the handkerchief. He started back to the truck, walking like an old man, feet dragging, shoul-ders slumped. He kept silent while he started the engine and rolled the truck back onto the long, straight strip of asphalt, heading for home again. Jewett broke the silence.

"What will you do? Go to jail like Gandhi?"

To Jewett, Gandhi was a comical-looking skinny little old man in big glasses and a huge baby's diaper. But to Joey he was a god. Joey had a photo of Gandhi torn from *Life* magazine tacked to the wall of his bedroom above the bakery. In the photo, Gandhi sat in the dirt, at some sun-scorched place in India, cranking by hand the wheel of a funny little sewing machine. Joey often quoted Gandhi to Jewett, but all Jewett remembered about him was that he said the only good machine was the sewing machine, that he often went to jail and starved himself until they let him out again, that he once sat down in

front of a locomotive. And, of course, that he was against vio-
lence. Jewett said:

"I may be a moron like you say, but I remember why we went
and registered last summer. If you don't do what they tell you,
they get to put you in jail. It's the law. Unless you're a conscien-
tious objector. Are you?"

"You have to be religious. I don't believe in God."

"Then you'll have to run away. Where will you go?"

"Nowhere. I'll tell them I'm queer."

Now it was Jewett's turn to stare. "You can't!"

"Why not? It's the truth, isn't it?" Joey's laugh was harsh and
unhappy. "And the army won't take queers."

"But—everybody'd find out. Your parents—"

Joey shook his head. "That's against the law. They can't tell
your parents anything. Nobody will know. Nobody but you."
He frowned. "What's the matter with you? Why are you arguing? Do you want me to go kill people?"

"I'll have to go," Jewett said bleakly.

"You could tell them the same thing." At a Sunday-vacant
intersection Joey half stopped the truck, then swung it onto a
road that curved up into the foothills. "Stay here with me." He
looked straight into Jewett's eyes. "I don't want you to go."

It was the first speech of its kind Joey had ever made to Jewett,
and it moved him. His eyes became wet, and he turned his face
away. Why did it take the fear of death to make Joey admit he
cared about him? Why did it have to happen now, when it was
too late?

"I couldn't do it," Jewett said.

He stands now with Young Joe in the bakery kitchen. It seems
smaller than he remembers from that happy summer of 1941,
smaller yet less crowded and far brighter. What remain the
same are the fierce heat and the good smells. When he labored
here with Joey, the long tables where the loaves were shaped
and the batters poured were sheeted in zinc. The oven doors
were dark, inset with small, thick double panes of glass
browned at their edges from the interior heat. Jewett thinks he

remembers brick. The scaffolding of the cooling racks had been chipped white enamel, the racks themselves wood.

Now all is stainless steel. Banks of varicolored push buttons beside the ovens control temperatures and baking times. Crisp numerals of red light wink. Small electronic alarms beep. Young Joe has no need to carry in his head, as had grumpy Hermann, awareness of what went into which oven when. Nor need he keep recipes in his head. Computers measure flour, shortening, yeast, sugar, milk, vanilla, baking powder, at the touch of a button. If he were capable of feeling, Jewett would feel disappointment. He has dreamed of working with his hands, hasn't he? But he can't feel much about this moment. The feelings of forty years ago are too strong in him.

Perdidos went war crazy. There were blackouts. Fat businessmen in tin helmets limped the neighborhoods at night, pestering householders who forgot to draw the shades. The Japs might be here at any minute. Sirens howled, and in the high-school hallways kids bumped into each other trying to act as if there were an air raid. Rumor said an anti-aircraft battery on a rooftop in downtown Los Angeles had caught Japanese planes flying over in the beam of its spotlight, had fired at them and missed. A Japanese submarine was supposed to have been sighted in the Catalina channel. Everyone hung out flags. The cheerful brown crinkly-faced Japanese people who sold fruits and vegetables at the market were shipped off overnight to some barbed-wire camp. So were the five quiet kids with Japanese names at the high school. On the screen at the Fiesta three times a night Kate Smith sang "God Bless America."

Deodar Street echoed with the racket of housewives and little kids flattening tin cans on sidewalks with hammers. The steel was needed for tanks and ships. Victory gardens were planted in steep backyards and washed away by the winter rains. Food, clothing, gasoline, tires—everything was going to be scarce. Jewett's father was appointed to the rationing board. Boys in new uniforms that didn't fit, boys Jewett scarcely knew, shook his hand and smiled and said good-bye. The stocky, red-faced

army officer who ran the ROTC at the high school sat down at
his desk one morning and put a bullet through his head. No one
knew why. At the hamburger shack across from the high
school, the jukebox played "The White Cliffs of Dover" and
"Der Führer's Face." Jimmy Stewart joined the air force. Clark
Gable. Jewett's father tacked a map of the Pacific to the dining-
room wall and jumped up from supper during newscasts to find
islands no one had ever heard of before.

In February, Jewett's notice came. The weather was cold and
rainy. His mother looked for a minute as if she might cry, but
she didn't. It wouldn't have been patriotic. Susan said, *You'll
get to dress up—you always liked that.* His father drove him
before dawn to Cordova, where he waited on a gray corner,
hunched and miserable, till the big red streetcar heaved to a
halt with scraping brakes, its trolly showering sparks, when he
climbed the slippery iron steps, dropped his dime rattling into
the glass-sided fare box, and packed himself in with the damp-
smelling crowd clinging to overhead straps and seat rails, to
sway with the heavy rocking of the car, telling himself wretch-
edly over and over that he couldn't do it. If Joey's notice had
come first, if Joey had already done it, that might have given
Jewett courage.

But he was afraid. And ashamed. His cheeks burned with
shame. There was nothing to be ashamed of. It was no lie—he
was queer. And he didn't want to kill anyone. Just because
maniac politicians overseas had turned loose murder on the
world, did that make it right for him to turn murderer?
Wouldn't that be a real reason to be ashamed? But these were
Joey's arguments, and this morning they seemed weak. Telling
the truth was fine, but what about your reason for telling the
truth? Most of the boys in his class had gone, simply gone
without question, and the rest would soon be going. Every day,
all over the world, hundreds of people were being slaughtered.
They didn't want to be involved, either, did they? But could he
save them? How? The streetcar rumbled between green hills.
Jewett closed his eyes. He couldn't think straight. He wanted to

lie warm in his bed and cling naked to naked Joey, and that was all. He didn't want to die, he didn't want Joey to die. These things didn't seem much to ask. Yet no one else was asking them. He had to be wrong. He couldn't do it.

The induction center, above the carbarns, was an immense barren room with dirty windows and a dirty wooden floor and a scattering of battered folding chairs. Rooms smaller but no less barren opened off the main room, and in these Jewett glimpsed weary-looking, unshaven men in soiled white coats, seated at long, dirty tables, as if they had sat there endless days and nights. The main room was crowded with lost and frightened men being herded in straggly bewildered lines this way and that by men in stiff-looking woollen army uniforms. Each naked man held over his crotch the paper sheaf he had been handed on reaching this place. There was no heat in the room. The bodies heated it. A couple of minutes passed that Jewett didn't understand when he and those he had arrived with sat on the broken chairs and were given a short, foul-mouthed lecture by a pudgy officer standing beside a dusty flag. Jewett could hardly hear. His heart was pounding so, it deafened him. Then he too was naked and shuffling along in a stupefied line. The smell of unwashed bodies was strong.

With the rest, Jewett tried to piss into a small bottle and pissed as well on his bare feet and on the urine-soaked floor. He stood at a table and squeezed his penis for a doctor so bored he looked and sounded ready to fall asleep. Jewett and the rest of the line next had to bend, grip their buttocks, and spread them for the regard of a doctor whose disenchantment understandably went the penis inspector's one better. Jewett began to look for someone in uniform he could speak to. He thought he had already had enough of the army. It was urgent now to speak. He tried to speak to the young doctor who pressed a cold stethoscope to his chest and was frowning hard into Jewett's eyes. A nurse with acne scars had wrapped a black cuff around Jewett's arm and pumped it tight and now was staring at her gauges and at Jewett's face and back at her gauges again. She too frowned.

"What the hell have you been taking?" the doctor said.

"Taking?" Jewett said. "What do you mean?"

"Drugs. People take all kinds of junk to try to screw up their medicals." The doctor scribbled on Jewett's papers. "Your heart's going a mile a minute. Your blood pressure would kill you right here on the spot if you were fifty."

"I'm not fifty," Jewett said. "I'm nervous." The nurse took off the cuff. Jewett rubbed his arm. The way the doctor peered into his eyes bothered him. He looked at the floor. He mumbled faintly, "Can you please tell me how—" But the doctor had pushed his papers back into his hands, gripped his shoulder, and moved him roughly on. The doctor had five hundred more hearts to listen to.

Jewett stumbled out into the big room again, following, as he had done for an hour, a bald man with big surgical scars slicing around a body the color of candle wax. A woman army officer was pointing Jewett's line the way to go now. She was short, with thick legs and a bulldog jaw, but her rough, jokey voice and the wry twinkle in her eyes made Jewett think she was the person to ask. *Don't ask them*, Joey said sharply, *tell them*. Jewett wondered bitterly how Joey came to know so much. But he told the woman, "I have to see the psychiatrist."

Five stiff chairs stood in the psychiatrist's waiting room, which was a wooden box about six by nine. On two of the chairs others already waited, staring straight ahead at nothing. One was a dwarfish black boy whose head kept jerking to the side and backward, out of his control. The other was a baby-fat boy with Down's syndrome. With stubby fingers he played absentmindedly with his penis under the cover of his sheaf of papers. Jewett felt ashamed of his handsome body and its perfect health. He didn't belong here. These boys were sick and sad. Why had they even been forced to come here and go through this? It was cruel and absurd. The army called every sort of cripple, even the blind and deaf—he'd seen them all this morning. Did he belong with them? Was he a cripple too? He started to get off his chair and leave the room. But Joey said,

Stay here with me. Joey looked into his eyes and said, *I don't want you to go.*

The psychiatrist leaned back in a creaky, golden oak swivel chair and waved in a delicate hand a little red rubber hammer. He was a small, fragile-looking man, with a bush of fiery red hair. At his back, rain made runnels in the dirt of a window without blinds or curtains. The psychiatrist asked if Jewett ever went out with girls. His speech was sibilant, ladylike. Jewett made his own speech like that. He never went out with girls. He adored classical music, movies, art, ballet, the theater. What was he going to be? An actor. Why did he think he wouldn't work out in the army? Well, all those naked male bodies around him all the time—think of the temptation! The naked bodies here today had only stirred his pity and disgust. But he didn't tell the psychiatrist that. Instead, he mentioned Michelangelo's David. He was acting a part now, and for the first time since he'd wakened this miserable morning in the cold rainy dark to come here, he was at ease. He was even having a good time. He forgot to wonder if it was wrong. All he thought about was how well he was doing with the role.

At a desk in a cramped office, crowded with men waiting, and with file cabinets and clerks at noisy typewriters, a bored officer stamped his papers with a red symbol that had blurry letters or numbers inside it. Jewett couldn't make them out. "What does that mean?" he said.

"It means"—the officer was already holding out his hand for the next man's papers—"you can get your clothes and go home, kid. The army doesn't need you."

Jewett stood stunned. He must explain to the man. It was all lies. He hadn't meant it. He was all right. He wasn't queer. He would go. He wanted desperately to go with the others. He didn't want his clothes, he wanted a uniform. He didn't want that mark on his papers. He opened his mouth. It was dry. He gulped. "Listen—" he croaked.

"Go on, pansy face," the officer said. "Get out of here."

Jewett stands with Young Joe in dappled tree shade on the

sidewalk in front of the bakery. "A hundred fifty thousand dollars," Young Joe says. "That's all new equipment in the kitchen, less than a year old. If I'd known Grandma was going to die right away, I wouldn't have put it in. Now the price scares everybody. But it's not out of line, not when you consider the goodwill, the location."

"I guess not," Jewett says. "How much do you want down?"

"Oh, I'll have to have the cash. The ranch I want up north, they want cash, so I'll have to have cash."

Jewett smiles a little, shakes his head sadly. "I don't have that kind of cash, Joe. I couldn't even raise it. Not unless my luck changes."

Young Joe sighs. "You worked here with my dad. I'd like you to have it." He stares off across the busy street. "But I really have to have the cash."

"Do this for me," Jewett says. "Don't sell to anyone else before you let me know, all right? I mean, an actor's life is chancy. I might get a break, who knows?" He doesn't believe this, but he isn't willing to let the dream of the bakery go. At this sad, sunlit moment, it seems to him that's all he has, that dream. "Promise me," he says.

"Sure, okay, Mr. Jewett." Young Joe shakes his hand. Jewett thinks Young Joe doesn't take him seriously, but he doesn't know how to change that. Young Joe says, "Thanks for coming," and walks back into the shop, which is crowded with lunchtime shoppers now. A girl younger than Peter-Paul is tending the cash register. She looks like Frances Lusk.

Jewett has the prescription in a small white paper bag, and fresh-baked rolls from Pfeffer's in a big white bag. He unlocks the car, relieved that though his time on the parking meter has run out there is no police ticket under the windshield wiper. He tosses the bags on the car seat, bends to get into the car, and feels the heat. Sun has been beating down on the roof. He straightens and sheds his jacket, tosses it into the rear seat, gets into the car, and quickly starts the engine so the air-conditioner will work. He waits for cold air to jet from the openings in the dash and cranes to see himself in the rearview mirror. *Pansy-face?* No more. If ever. The man had seemed accessible until he spoke those words. Then Jewett was glad to leave. He looks into the side mirror to see the traffic. When there is a break, he pulls away from the curb and heads for Deodar Street. He checks his watch. He will be late getting Susan her lunch. He is annoyed with himself about that. Like his father, he believes meals should be on time.

His father climbed long flights of dusty wooden stairs to reach him. Anger and the effort of the climb made him short of breath. The Playloft was what it sounded like—a vast room on the top floor of a business building at the shabby end of Mountain Street in Cordova where plays were put on by young actors fed up with being rejected by the famous Cordova Stage. They had painted the loft black—walls, floor, ceiling, even the skylights. The double doors at the top of the stairs had glass panels, and these too had been painted black. It was a thriller they were rehearsing, about a handsome young man—Jewett in his first big role outside school—who marries rich lonely widows and murders them for their money. So the lighting was dim, sinister. Which meant that when Jewett's father yanked open the doors at the top of the stairs, the light that struck in from the hallway was glaring, and the man standing with his back to it was only a silhouette. Yet Jewett knew who he was.

"It's my father," he said, and left the murky spotlights, the carved sofa, the older woman on the sofa with her cup of make-believe tea, and stepped out into the long rectangle of light. "What's the matter?" he said.

"I don't want to discuss it here," his father panted. "Come with me. Get your coat. It's raining. You won't be coming back here." He looked beyond Jewett, though he can't have seen much in the gloom. "I'm taking Oliver with me. It's a family matter, I'm sorry." His manners never failed him. Jewett found his coat in a heap of other coats and went out onto the landing. His father carefully closed the doors. "Come on," he said.

"What's it about?" Jewett flapped into his coat.

"Shabby place for a theater." Jewett's father went on down the stairs. "You always talk about the bright lights." He squinted up at the flyspecked forty-watt bulb in the ceiling at the landing. His voice echoed hollowly in the bleak stairwell. "Grim atmosphere to want to spend your life in."

"Is it Susan?" Jewett asked. It was so often Susan.

"It's you," his father said. "Are you coming?"

Jewett felt wary. His father had never before said a word against his ambitions. Andrew Jewett was a commonsense man, but if his son wanted to be an actor, if his daughter wanted to be an artist, he left that up to them. Not coldly, either. He listened amiably to their hopes and dreams, took pride in their small triumphs, sympathized with their setbacks. Not so much lately. His war work kept him away from home. He took it seriously. Added to his law practice, it left him little time even for sleep. He waited for Jewett at the foot of the first flight of stairs.

"Do you know who Harold Cochran is?"

He was a warden at St. Barnabas, a neat, slender man with a pencil-line mustache and rimless glasses. He owned a Ford agency and read the lesson Sunday morning in a high, pinched voice. Jewett nodded. "Of course."

"He's on the draft board," Andrew Jewett said, and started down the next flight of stairs. Jewett felt cold in the pit of his stomach. Andrew Jewett said, "Did you know that? Perhaps you should have known that."

Jewett said, "I don't understand." He stopped on the landing and watched his father reach the bottom of the flight, turn back, look up at him. Jewett said, "What are you talking about?"

"He telephoned me tonight," Andrew Jewett said. "Asked me to come to the draft-board office. I went. He showed me your papers from the induction center."

"No." Jewett held on to the sticky wooden railing of the stairs. "He didn't have the right to do that. That's against the law."

Andrew Jewett's smile was thin. "What are you going to do

about it? Ask me to take him into court, spread the story all over the newspapers? I don't think so." He turned away. "He felt an obligation to me as a friend." He was out of sight now, going down still another flight of stairs. Numbly Jewett followed. "And as a father himself." The sound of footsteps ceased. He was waiting. Jewett went down to the third floor. He looked down at his father. Andrew Jewett said, "And to you, since you obviously didn't understand what you were doing."

"It's none of his business," Jewett said.

"He'd like to keep you out of prison," his father said. "Lying to the army to avoid the draft is a serious crime."

Jewett didn't want to say this but he couldn't think of anything else to say. "I didn't lie. I told the truth."

"That you are"—Andrew Jewett's handsome, haggard face lost color, a nerve twitched below his left eye, he fumbled for words—"not sexually normal? That's ridiculous. You know what such men are like—that pathetic little Le Clerc, years ago. Oliver, I've dealt with homosexuals—lawyers often have to. Believe me, you are nothing like that. How could you do this to your mother and me? And poor Susan, as if she didn't have enough to contend with. Who put this idea into your head?"

This was dangerous ground, and Jewett wasn't going to set foot on it. "It's not an idea," he said wearily. "It's how I am, it's how I always was. I should have told you first, but I was afraid of how you'd take it. And I was right, wasn't I? Look how you're acting now. You hate me."

"What I hate is the lie you told and your reason for telling it. What you should have told me was that you were afraid. I would have understood that. Every man is afraid sometimes. I wouldn't have blamed you. We could have talked it out, and you wouldn't have done this disgusting thing." He looked past Jewett up the stairwell. "It was someone up there who gave you the idea, wasn't it? Some degenerate like Le Clerc—the theater is full of them. Well, you're not coming back here." His eyes were hard, his tone was hard. The nerve kept twitching. "Understand me? Never again." He turned sharply and started down the remaining stairs. "Play-acting is over for you. You are going to face reality." He reached the landing and dropped out of sight again, but his voice rose up the stairwell. "Do you suppose anyone likes it? Do you suppose anyone wants this terrible war?"

It was late. There was little traffic on Mountain Street. The signal lights went from red to green to yellow like people talking to themselves. Rain sifted down. In the gutters, the runoff gurgled. Jewett trudged along the puddled sidewalk after his father, coat collar turned up, hands pushed into pockets. He wondered why his father had parked so far down the block. Not that it mattered. Nothing seemed to matter now. He supposed his father had been going fast when he passed the address. He was more angry than he had shown. That was how he was—controlled. You learned that in courtrooms. Now his father held open the car door for Jewett to get inside, then slammed the door. When they were under way, he said:

"Harold Cochran has agreed to get the draft board together for a hearing on this stupidity of yours tomorrow morning at seven o'clock. These are busy people with responsibilities. It will be a sacrifice for them. So you will be up and washed and ready to leave the house with me at six-thirty. We'll straighten out this sordid mess, and give you back your self-respect. Is that perfectly clear?"

Jewett turns his car onto Deodar Street and is surprised. In front of the garage, where he ordinarily parks, stands a moving van. Its rear doors hang open. So do the garage doors. Inside the truck stands a hefty black man. When a brown youth comes staggering out of the garage, bearing a clumsy, twine-bound bundle in torn brown paper, the black man squats to take it from the boy. It is one of Susan's wall hangings. As Jewett rolls closer, he sees that the van already holds quite a heap of the hangings. He finds a place to park up the street, takes the paper sacks and his jacket from the car, and walks back down to the van. The smell of camphor is heavy in the air. He has to sidle past the high boxy white cab of the van in order to reach the

cement steps. They need sweeping. After he finishes the house-
work today, he will sweep them. Now he climbs them, shoes
sometimes slipping on the carpet of brown pine needles.

At three o'clock in the morning he stood beside his rucksack
in the alley where the bakery truck slept next to the brick back
wall of the bakery. His face was turned up to the gentle rain. He
was gazing at Joey's window. The alley was paved but there
was always a scattering of gravel. He stooped and picked up a
wet handful. If he could hit Joey's window with it, maybe Joey
would wake up and put his head out, and Jewett could signal to
him to come down. But he was afraid of hitting the wrong
window. Or breaking Joey's, which would waken everybody.
He stood in his raincoat and a canvas hat his father wore for
fishing, and couldn't decide what to do. Then a light went on
upstairs. And soon afterward, Joey's light went on. Jewett had
forgotten how early they started. He went away.

There was no place to go. He ended up in the Greyhound
depot, where the blue linoleum was strewn with cigarette butts
that a black man in coveralls was pushing around with a dry
mop, and where winos slept on chairs with cracked blue cushions and shiny curved-metal tube arms. Jewett slid his rucksack
into a pay locker, put the key in his pocket, and sat on one of the
chairs. He gazed blankly at the cigarette and candy-bar
machines, at the wavery reflections of the overhead fluorescent
tubes in the smeared glass of these machines, until he fell
asleep. When he woke, stiff, bleary, his watch told him he still
had time if he hurried. He jogged all the way and reached the
end of the alley just as Joey drove out in the truck. He flagged
him down.

"What are you doing here?" Joey said. "You're all wet. Get in.
What's the matter?"

Jewett told him what the matter was. "They don't keep it
secret, Joey. That's a lie. You mustn't do it."

"I got you into it," Joey said. "What kind of shit would I be if I
didn't do it?"

"It's no use now," Jewett said. "We can't be together. I have to leave here. When the bank opens, I'll get my savings out and get on the bus and go."

"We can be together," Joey said. "Just tell me where you're going. When I've done it, I'll come to you."

Jewett lit up inside. "Will you? Great. I'm going to New York. I'll write you my address."

"Who do you know in New York?"

"Nobody, but if you're going to be an actor, that's where you have to be."

Halfway up the steps he meets a man coming down, a rotund man in a rich dark blue velvet suit, a saffron man, smooth-shaven, with crinkly black hair. He flashes Jewett a smile of beautiful white teeth. Jewett does not like his yellow silk shirt and pink Sulka necktie. The collar of the shirt is loose, the knot in the tie very large. The man stops and extends a dimpled hand. "You," he says, "must be Susan's brother. Armie Akmazian, her dealer, I'm proud to say." His voice is lyrical. Jewett shakes his hand, which is damp. "Susan's been expecting you. She thought we might lunch together. But"—he glances at a wristwatch made of a large gold coin—"I've got a meeting at the County Museum. Too bad." His onyx eyes look Jewett up and down in a frank caress. "I'd have enjoyed a chance to chat. I'm sure we have much in common."

"Maybe some other time," Jewett says. "What's happening?" He tilts his head to indicate the van. "It looks as if you're taking everything. I thought you were keeping it off the market."

"Letting pieces go at intervals, yes," Akmazian says. "But I think it's time for a complete retrospective exhibit, don't you? Won't it be good for Susan's morale? We're doing a beautiful catalog. That's already under way."

"Good," Jewett says. "Did you surprise her with this?"

"Oh, no. We've been talking of it since December. When she began—began not feeling well." He looks grave. "What a shame. What a loss."

"Not yet," Jewett says. "She's not lost yet. There can be remissions, you know." He hears himself with amazement.

This is what he wants but he knows better than to count on it. Akmazian's unctuousness makes Jewett want to cross him. "Her hair is coming back."

"Yes." No matter what Jewett wants to think of Akmazian, the butter-colored man seems honestly, selflessly pleased. "That's made her happy. She hasn't an ounce of vanity, but it makes her happy that her hair is coming back." He flashes the gold-coin watch again. "I must run." He squeezes Jewett's hand a last time, and goes down the steps, light on his feet. Near the bottom, he pauses and turns back, half obscured by branches of deodar heavy with new green needles. He calls, "The men won't need to bother you. They're all done in the house, and they'll lock the garage when they leave."

"Thank you," Jewett calls, and climbs to the house. Indoors, there is a new sense of emptiness. The sound of the old clock echoes louder than before. The door to his parents' bedroom stands open. He peers inside. It was crammed with bundled hangings. Now the furniture looks stark, abandoned, among sprawls of yellowed newspaper. He opens the door to his own room. His bed, stripped to its mattress, is visible again, his dresser, its mirror opaque with dust, his chair and bare worktable. He is startled by the poster on the wall—for the film of *The Petrified Forest*: Bette Davis, bob-haired, forlorn; unshaven Humphrey Bogart clutching his machine gun; Leslie Howard golden-haired and death-haunted in ill-fitting, rumpled tweeds. Jewett had forgotten the poster, forgotten how he loved that picture, worshiped Leslie Howard. He saw the film again every time it came back to the Fiesta. The last time, he dragged Joey to it. It made Joey gloomy. He saw more in it than Jewett could see.

When Jewett found his room in Manhattan, he wrote to Joey at the bakery. No answer came. The silence dragged out, a week, a month, another month. Jewett changed some of his dwindling supply of money into quarters and tried to telephone, but it was wartime, and long-distance lines were overburdened. He gave up on the third try. Joey would come as soon as he could. He didn't. A letter did. In hot August. From some air force base in Texas.

I'll be going overseas soon. I don't know when I'll have time to write again. I'm going to be a gunner. I'm sorry, but I couldn't do what you did, I couldn't do it to my parents. You know how patriotic they are. Remember the flags in the bakery window? It's because of their German name and their German accents. They hate Hitler for making Germans look bad. They want everybody to know they love America. It would kill them if I hadn't joined the service.

No mention of Gandhi. Mention of Frances Lusk.

We got married on my first leave. Oliver, you and I—that was kid stuff. It couldn't last. Grown men don't live that way, not real men. There was more, but Jewett didn't read it. He tore up the letter and flushed the scraps down the toilet. First he was sad and stood in the bathroom and cried. Then he was lonely. He went to a window and looked out. In all those buildings, on all those streets, no one knew or cared about him. Now, no one knew or cared about him anywhere. It frightened him. He closed and locked the windows, pulled the cracked shades. He locked the door and bolted it. He crept under the bed where no one could find him, and curled up on his side, clutching his knees and shutting his eyes tight. He could still hear, and the roar of the alien city alone frightened him. He went to the bathroom and came back to the bed with a towel. He bound the towel around his head to cover his ears, and crept under the bed again. He meant to lie there until he died. He laughs bleakly at his young self, and shuts the door to his room.

He touches Susan's door with light knuckles. She speaks and he steps inside. She lies on her bed looking pale. He says, "Tired you out, didn't it? I should have been here—I'm sorry. You didn't tell me anything about it."

"Armie often has grand ideas," she says, "and forgets them the next day."

"I'm pleased as hell," Jewett says.

"It will be nice"—she turns her head away, with its soft fuzz of new white hair, and gazes at the old black-and-white television set, where fuzzy figures move without sound—"if I live to see it."

"Come on, now," Jewett says. "You're feeling better and you know it. You had Akmazian expecting lunch, right?"

She turns back and smiles guiltily. "He loves good food. He'd have been more rewarding to cook for than I am."

"He looks as if missing a meal now and then wouldn't finish him," Jewett says. He holds up the little white bag. "I got your prescription."

"Thank you. What about the bakery?"

Jewett tells her. "I'll keep hoping. Evidently there isn't a long line of would-be buyers. What happened to Frances Lusk? I was leery about asking Young Joe. Why don't I see her at the bakery?"

Susan looks puzzled for a moment, then remembers. "Ah, of course, you were in New York. You couldn't know. When the telegram came that Joey had been killed, she packed up and left. She'd been living with his parents above the bakery. She never came back. No one knew where she went, not her parents, no one. Not to this day. The old Pfeffers raised Young Joe. It was quite a scandal at the time. But Mother wasn't surprised. She said Frances had a reputation in school—she was fast. Isn't it funny how slang dates? Mother said all the boys laughed at Joey behind his back. He was so proud of her being his girl. She was pretty, wasn't she? But, of course, she wasn't his girl at all. She was anybody's girl. Did you know that? You and Joey were good friends, weren't you?"

"Not good enough," Jewett says.

June

HE IS hiking with Richie Cowan up a canyon back of Perdidos. They have climbed higher, farther than ever before. A thin gray rain falls, and when they sit down in the shelter of big pines to eat, they watch mist form into rags of white cloud below them down the canyon, swirling among the sharp tops of pines, sharp outcrops of rock. They are hungry, and the sandwiches Richie's mother has packed for them are thick with sliced beef, and ketchup has soaked into the bread. They devour the sandwiches. Coffee comes steaming out of a thermos into metal cups with folding handles. Jewett doesn't open the handles, and he burns his fingers on the metal. There are candy bars. Scrupulously, they stuff paper bag, candy wrappers, ketchup-stained napkins back into their rucksacks. The cold and the coffee make them have to piss. They do this against a pine trunk. The urine runs down steaming in the chill, foaming around their shoes. Jewett reaches over and touches Richie's cock. Richie smiles and takes hold of Jewett's cock. I'm dead, he says. He lies facedown on the dying grass of the football field behind the high school. Spindly tall boys, in football garb too big for them, stand panting and dumb around him.

The coach kneels over him. Wisps of his thinning red hair move in the November sunset breeze that crosses the field from bleachers empty because this is only practice. The coach rolls Richie over and lays his head on Richie's chest to listen for a heartbeat. Richie lies too still for that. Jewett says to the gaping boy next to him, *This is only practice.* He sits with Richie on the back row of bentwood chairs in a big plank-walled room of the music building. The windows are open. Blue sky can be seen through the lacy leafage of a jacaranda tree. Mrs. Castle in her old black dress and loops of jet beads lifts and lowers fat arms. The voices of the boys rise to the plank ceiling in harmony: *Summer, you old Indian summer.* Richie Cowan's hand is on the back of Jewett's neck. The fingers caress and gently knead. Jewett does not know what to make of this. His body knows. He gets an erection. He hopes Mrs. Castle will not ask him to stand, as she sometimes does, and sing his part alone. The coach kneels up straight. *For Christ sake,* he says, *don't just stand there. Call a doctor.* The football boys grunt and mumble and begin to run away toward the school buildings, whose windows reflect the setting sun. Jewett looks at the sky. Three crows fly black above a row of dark old trees that edges the football field beyond the bleachers. The coach shakes Jewett by the shoulders. *Who are you?* he says. *Wake up!*

Jewett wakes up. Bill, dressed only in his work pants, the old corduroys, bends over Jewett where he lies in bed, and shakes his shoulders. "Wake up," he says. "What the hell does this mean?" He rattles in Jewett's face a square white card and a square white envelope. Jewett shuts his eyes, groans, and rolls over, dragging the blankets up to cover his head.

He mumbles, "What are you doing up so early?"

"It's trash day. I forgot it last night. I heard the truck down the street, and I ran around dumping the wastebaskets into the bags, and I found this." He sits on the edge of the bed and pulls the blankets off Jewett's head. "Did you mean to throw it out? Do you even know what it is? It's an invitation to a reception for the dude who is probably going to be the next President."

Jewett makes a sound, rolls to the far side of the bed, gropes for pillows on the floor. Clumsily he stacks them against the headboard and pushes himself upright and leans against them. He rubs a hand down his face.

"It's got a personal, handwritten note on it to you," Bill says. "He calls you Oliver."

Jewett shrugs and reaches for cigarettes on the nightstand. "Oliver, Shirley—it's meaningless, Bill."

"It's not!" Bill cries. " 'Looking forward to seeing you again after all these years. Ron,' he signs it. 'Ron,' God damn it. He still remembers you."

"Don't be naïve." Jewett lights two cigarettes and hands one to Bill, who looks unhappy. "I don't hear any trash truck."

"It's been and gone. I ran the bags down just in time—just barely. They took it all."

"Not all," Jewett says. "Not that thing."

"What's the matter with you? It will be a great party. All kinds of big shots will be there. Television will cover it. Everybody will get their picture taken."

Jewett takes the ashtray from the nightstand and sets it on the bed. "You wouldn't want to make some coffee, would you?"

Bill stands. "You don't get around enough. That's one of the reasons you don't get more work. Being seen at a party like that could do you a lot of good."

Oliver snorts. "Where is it? The Century Plaza, right? Bill, there'll be a thousand people there."

"Not with personal, handwritten notes on their invitations, there won't." Bill waves a frantic arm at the posters on the wall. "Oliver, he remembers you. He's your friend, for Christ sake."

"He had somebody make a list of every two-bit actor he ever worked with. They got the addresses from the Screen Actors Guild. He was president of the guild once. He doesn't want to see me. He wants me to vote for him, that's all." Jewett reaches. "Give me that thing."

Bill steps back, clutching the invitation against his chest. "Oliver, do you know it's been years since we went to a decent party? It was when you did that dinner-theater *My Fair Lady* in Orange County. I loved those cast parties. Don't you want to have any fun anymore?"

"Let me show you." With a lecherous laugh, Jewett lunges for him. The ashtray bumps the floor.

Bill steps back. "Not that." Grumpily, he crouches for the ashtray. Cigarette butts from last night strew the carpet. He gathers them up, puts them in the ashtray, sets the ashtray where it belongs, under the lamp. He brushes hands together, stands, rubs the ashes into the carpet with his naked foot. "Why don't you do those dinner theaters anymore? They ask you."

Jewett makes a face. "People weren't born to eat and pay attention at the same time. Besides, the work is too hard. All I get out of it is tired." He sits back against the piled pillows again, smooths the blankets. "If we can't have sex, could we have that coffee, please?"

"Oliver." Bill looks grim. "I want to. Go. To. This. Party. If what I want makes any difference to you anymore, you'll call that number and say you're coming."

"I'm sure Good Ol' Ron will pick up the phone himself," Jewett says. With a flounce, Bill leaves for the kitchen. He can't manage effeminate mannerisms, and Jewett wishes he would stop trying. He throws back the covers, swings his feet to the floor, stubs out his cigarette, and heads for the bathroom. When he comes out of the shower, Bill is standing in the bathroom door with the O mug in his hand. Reaching for the red towel marked B, Jewett says, "You've had a taste of politics lately." He dries his hair and the towel muffles his words. "You know how it feels. The landlords' association probably gives nice parties." He dries his shoulders, his chest, where the hair is grizzled. "If they asked you, would you go?"

"Come on," Bill scoffs. "You're not political."

Jewett arcs the towel over his head and begins drying his back. "You don't have to be political not to want to be killed. The dumb son of a bitch thinks he's in another movie, the guns are props, the bullets are blanks, the bombs are stock footage. He believes in Good Guys and Bad Guys. He'll get us into a war." Jewett lowers the lid on the toilet and puts his left foot up on the lid to dry the foot and leg, then puts up his right foot to do the same. "I don't want to encourage him."

"It's just a party, for God's sake." Bill sets the mug on the surround of the washbasin. "You think everybody who goes will vote for him? Shit. They'll go for the booze, the laughs, the music, to be in on what's happening."

"That's up to them." Jewett switches on the blow dryer. Its whine prevents his hearing Bill's answer, if Bill makes one. When his hair is dry, he shuts off the machine, combs his hair, and edges past Bill to get his robe off the hook on the bathroom door. "Anyway, Saturdays I spend with Susan." He puts on the robe and cinches the sash tight. "You know that."

"You could make it Friday for once," Bill says. Jewett picks up the coffee mug and leaves the bathroom. Bill comes hurrying after him. "Susan, always Susan. Will you please think about me for once?"

"I think about you all the time." Jewett takes four eggs from the refrigerator, butter, plastic-wrapped bacon slices. "That never changes."

"You said yourself," Bill argues, "there'll be a thousand people there. Nobody's going to blame you for his politics. In a crowd like that, who'll even notice you?"

"I'll notice." Jewett finds Bill's coffee-filled mug on the counter and sets it on the breakfast bar. "Bill, I can't go to that party. You go if you want to. Take the invitation and tell them you're me. The men on the door won't know the difference."

"Alone? Shit, that's how I am all the time now. You're never with me anyplace. I don't want to go alone. I want to go with you. You're the celebrity."

Jewett is separating the cold greasy strips of bacon, which come apart grudgingly, trying to make lace of themselves. Over his shoulder, he tosses Bill a smile. "And you're beautiful when you're angry."

Bill shouts exasperation and flings his coffee mug. It misses Jewett's head by a yard, bounces off a cupboard door, splashing sweet white coffee around, and ends up undamaged in a corner.

Bill has vanished. From the bedroom he yells in a tight voice, "Don't cook for me." He comes back to the kitchen doorway, tucking in the tails of an old cotton plaid workshirt, yellow, green, brown. "I don't want any breakfast. You don't want to be with me? Okay, then I don't want to be with you either." His voice shakes now, and tears brighten his eyes. "I don't want to look at you, I don't want to listen to you." He forgets to flounce this time. He stamps off. From the living room, he shouts, "I'm going to work." And the front door slams.

"It's your day off," Jewett tells the emptiness. He untangles a blue sponge mop from a crowded little broom closet that smells dustily of soap powder. "The shop is closed." He mops up the spilled coffee, rinses out the sponge in the sink, and puts the mop away. He is disgusted with himself for not having torn up that invitation and burned it. The fact is, he hardly noticed the damned thing. He frowns and shakes his head. He didn't so much throw it away as let it slip from his fingers. He often feels that way now, careless, indifferent. His list of things that are simply too much bother grows. Part of the cause is his sadness over what is happening to Susan and his helplessness to stop it. But it began before that—when he discovered that he was growing old, and that all the years added up to nothing.

He sets two of the four eggs back in the refrigerator and cooks for himself, which he doesn't like, which makes him feel useless. He wasn't meant to live by himself, for himself. But no, he doesn't want to have any fun anymore—not fun in Bill's terms. And here, in the sunny morning kitchen, this truth chills him. Bill has begun to mean the things he says during his tantrums. And keeping Bill happy is becoming a chore. It seems incredible, but for quite a time now, he has had to pretend to Bill. Last summer, Jewett was reluctant to drive to Oregon for the Shakespeare Festival. The coastline on the way was beautiful, the ocean beautiful. But the plays seemed flat, stale, threadbare. Last winter's ballets, operas, symphony concerts he felt as if he'd seen and heard once too often. He didn't tell Bill. But Bill hadn't needed telling, had he? *Don't you want to have any fun anymore?*

Carrying his plate and a mug of hot coffee to the breakfast bar, he smiles at his stupidity. The extremes to which he's gone lately to keep Bill amused because of guilt for the time he must spend with Susan have been absurd and useless. *You're never with me anyplace.* He mounts his stool and eats cheerlessly. Except for the weeks when Susan has her chemotherapy, he has taken Bill, on his days off—today was to have been the Queen Mary tour—to Sea World, Knott's Berry Farm, Disneyland. But the dolphins, leaping sleek from their jewel-blue tanks, the mechanical hippos yawning at the African riverboat, the fake cowboy shoot-outs were no answer to Bill's need. On the Universal Studios tour, he kept cornering strangers in Western hats, dark glasses, Hawaiian shirts, telling them excitedly that Jewett once played in pictures there. The strangers, from Missouri and Japan, from Idaho and Holland, reacted with wary smiles, as if Bill were retarded or harmlessly crazy. Jewett winced and afterward scolded Bill. A mistake. For that was the one day out of all those boring days when Bill had his idea of fun.

With a wry shake of the head, Jewett snuffs his cigarette in the little red kitchen ashtray, gets off the stool, carries plate, fork, mug to the sink, washes them, dries them, puts them away. He can't take on a dinner-theater show now, nor even an ordinary stage play—not with Susan needing him so much of the time. Small television bits would be welcome, manageable. But these wouldn't involve parties. And parties are what Bill needs. If all he gets out of them is the pathetic little thrill that comes when others realize he is with Jewett, that he is Jewett's closest friend, then so be it. Jewett cleans up the frying pans and hangs them, with their shiny copper bottoms showing, on their hooks above the stove. From a trigger bottle of Windex, he sprays stove top, counter tops, cupboard and refrigerator doors, and wipes these clean with paper towels. He knew from the start, didn't he, that actors have a special shine for Bill? If he loves Jewett for any better reason, he has never said so. Jewett doubts it and doubts that it matters. He throws away the soggy paper towels and sets the foamy Windex back on its dark, low shelf.

He makes the bed, grateful that Bill isn't as awful as he used to be. When they first started living together, he dragged home strangers from the shops where he worked, from hamburger and taco stands where he ate lunch, from supermarket checkout lines, to prove to them that, yes, honest to God, he really did live with Oliver Jewett, the actor. *Didn't I say that was him in that Longines commercial?* Jewett felt like something in a zoo. He tried to stop it, but he only slowed it down a little. And it peaked when he made three successive appearances on "All in the Family" as an elegant and expensive auntie frigid with hauteur. Bill turned every afternoon into a reception awash in gin and vermouth. The apartment swarmed with lissome youths of every age, voices shrill as peacocks. Bill was happy. Jewett was unhappy. He took to leaving every day at four-thirty and not returning until dark.

"You do it to make me look silly," Bill said.

"Better you than me," Jewett said.

But it wasn't better. It was selfish. It hurt Bill, and he had no right or reason to hurt Bill. Bill has given him much happiness and very little pain. No pain at all, really. Discomfort, now and then, annoyance—no more. And loyalty, stalwart and foolish. Where Bill's beautiful brown bare foot scuffed the ashes, the beige carpet is smudged. Jewett fetches the vacuum cleaner, unwinds the red cord from its shiny cleats, squats to plug in the cord, runs the red machine over the smudge half a dozen times. Frowning. *You're the celebrity.* He isn't, but he's never been able to get this through Bill's head. The best hope for Bill would be for him to finish with Jewett before films, television, commercials finish with Jewett, before the only part left for him on some hole-and-corner Hollywood side-street stage is the dying grandfather in the wheelchair in *Night of the Iguana.* It's the best hope, but a faint one.

Jewett prays it will remain faint. He knows he is going to lose Susan. If he also loses Bill, what the hell will he have left? The bakery? *I have to have cash.* The bakery is a fantasy. He will stop in there one of these Saturdays, and Young Joe will tell him it has been sold. No, all he has for sure is Bill. For sure? With his old man's idea of fun? Spending half a day in the kitchen, whipping up elaborate meals. Eating them alone with Bill. By candlelight, God forgive us. A good wine. Mozart quiet on the stereo in the shadows. A dessert all liquor, fluffy egg white, thick cream, in a tall glass. Apples and crumbly yellow cheese. Coffee with brandy. Idling afterward in deep chairs by lamplight, chatting aimlessly about yesterday and tomorrow, or maybe reading aloud—Bill loves the sound of Jewett's voice. Or watching an old black-and-white movie rich with chiaroscuro lighting on TV. And early to bed. It will be decades before Bill can or ought to settle for this. And has Jewett got decades? Lately he wonders if he's even got years.

The smudge is gone. He runs the vacuum lightly around the rest of the room, and catches sight of himself in the mirror over the General Grant chest of drawers. He stops to stare, the vacuum tugging feebly at his hand, whining like a pettish child till he taps the off button with his toe. What he sees is startling and perplexing. He doesn't look old. He looks younger than his years and, in spite of how he feels, the line of his mouth suggests he is about to say something genial. His eyes seem amused. Where is the image he has been carrying around in his mind—of a doddering, toothless gaffer, all dry skin and brittle bones, shuffling feebly after a pretty boy half his age, and uttering pitiful, piping cries? Something out of Congreve, Wycherley, Otway. Or worse, if there is worse. The mirror says he has been playing a role inside his head. Why? *Handsomer than ever, aren't you?* Susan says. *Tall and straight and trim. Beautiful Oliver.* Rita Lopez says, *You get better-looking every year.* They are right. So why does he feel like Pantaloon? What the hell is wrong with him? Is he losing his mind?

He unplugs the vacuum, lashes its cord to its cleats once more, and wheels it back to the coat closet in the living room. He wants another cup of coffee and, in the kitchen, lights the gas under the glass coffee maker. He returns to the bedroom and dresses. Old jeans. A sweatshirt. Sandals. The day is already warm and if it is like yesterday will be very hot by noon. He peers into the clothes hamper in the bathroom—wicker, spray-painted red by Bill. There aren't enough dirty T-shirts, shorts, socks to warrant a walk to the laundromat. He will think of supper and walk instead to the supermarket. Tonight it had better be what Bill likes best, hadn't it—veal spiedini? It sure as hell had. Because Jewett is not going to that party.

The phone rings. He runs to the kitchen, turns off the burner under the coffee, snatches the red receiver down off the wall. He always runs for telephones, like every actor he has ever known, always snatches at them. The big break is always about to announce itself from the other end of the line, right? The role that will make him a star forever, and millions of dollars? He knows better. But his heart still races at the ring of a telephone. It races now. It is an idiot. He pants hello into the receiver.

"Mr. Jewett? Oliver? I hope you remember me. It's Mavis McWhirter." He remembers her, big and bulky, in handsome and expensive clothes, a little drunk and more than a little humiliated when Oliver surprised her here with Dolan that dark, far-off winter evening. On the telephone, her voice is as plummy, her diction as elegant as Margaret Dumont's. "We haven't had that lunch you promised."

"I haven't forgotten," Jewett lies. "My sister is ill. She lives out of town. I'm tied up with her much of the time. Please don't feel neglected."

"I won't, if we can have that lunch today," she says. "It's terribly important. I'm afraid I'm desperate for advice and counsel."

"What play are you doing?"

"It's not about acting. It's personal. I'm embarrassed to have to bother you, but you're really the only one who can help."

"Don't tell me—let me guess," Jewett says. "It's Dolan, isn't it? What's he done to you?"

"I'd rather not discuss it on the phone."

Jewett checks his watch. "Let's not wait for lunch. Come here, why don't you? If you're starving, I'll fix something light."

"I'm too upset to eat," she says, "but I'll be there. In twenty minutes." To Jewett she looks like a lady who can always eat, and he makes preparations. Including bloody Marys. And he turns out to be right. She is in blue denim today, a blue and white polkadot blouse, a little red scarf knotted under her chins, red lipstick, red nails, little red bows on her blue shoes. She polishes off the tall red drink in a hurry. About the delicately poached eggs, crisp bacon, cheese sauce on English muffins she exclaims, "This is heavenly. You ought to open a restaurant." She won't talk about Dolan until she has finished the last bite, lost most of her lipstick on the tip of a cigarette smoked with her coffee, and carefully renewed the lipstick. "I wish I were wrong, of course, but I doubt that I am. A housebreaker wouldn't have been so picky. Only one ring is missing, a large, square emerald." She drops lipstick and mirror back into her big shoulder bag. "Anyway, we're burglar-proof at Sandoval Estates. All kinds of security devices, guards, television scanners."

"You don't need me," Jewett says, "you need the police." He takes her plate to the sink, lifts the red phone down again, and holds it out to her. "Here. Call them. He deserves it."

"But what if I'm wrong?" Appalled at his suggestion, she shakes her head, gets quickly off the stool so she can back out of reach of the phone cord. "Suppose I lost it somewhere and didn't realize it. Perhaps he didn't take it. Think how hurt he'd be. I could never face myself."

"Try asking him, why don't you?" Jewett hangs up the phone, begins washing the pans under hot water. "He's a rotten liar. You'd know from the way he smiled whether he took it or not."

"Oh, I couldn't. That's why I rang you. I couldn't accuse him myself. I thought you—well, you know him. You seemed to handle him with such—authority that time. I have no right to ask, I know, but if you—"

"You give him money, don't you?" Jewett says. "Be honest with me. He asks you for money all the time, doesn't he? Come on—you won't shock me."

"That's why this is so incomprehensible," she cries.

Jewett dries a pan. "How much do you give him?"

She shrugs her massive shoulders. "A hundred here, a hundred there. And, of course, I pay for the dinners and drinks. And the motels." She eyes the empty glass with its mottling of tomato juice and crushed wedge of lemon on the breakfast bar. "I wonder if I could have another drink, please?"

"If I do the driving." Jewett looks at her with raised eyebrows as he hangs up the pan. She nods anxiously, hiking her bulk on the stool again, rummaging in her bag for cigarettes. He collects the glass, rinses it, and puts together another drink for her. "I take it a large, square emerald is worth more than a hundred here, a hundred there, and who's counting?" He sets the drink, clinking with ice cubes, in front of her, and she begins on it greedily.

"Many thousands," she says. "Where are we going?"

"To find Dolan and get the pawn ticket from him. If he still has it. You don't want to prosecute him. You just want your ring back, right?"

"He didn't mean any harm." After clicking her jeweled lighter half a dozen times, it springs a flame, and she lights a cigarette. "He wouldn't have taken it if he didn't think I could afford the loss."

"Don't count on it," Jewett says. "Just pray he's still got the ticket. When did this happen?"

"I discovered it was missing this morning—but then, I don't always wear it. I couldn't believe my eyes. I searched high and low. You should have seen me crawling on hands and knees all over that shag carpet. No use. That's when I called you." She twitches a thin, crooked, sad little smile. "It's a good thing Dolan is so ignorant, He took the biggest one, not the most valuable."

Jewett dries and hangs up the second pan. "He'll be back for that. He'll get it by hit or miss sooner or later. Unless you shake him. He's bad medicine, Mavis."

"He's a lot of fun." Wistfully, she wipes tomato juice off her chin with a red napkin. "We have so many laughs together. And he's very good in bed."

"Dear God," Jewett says. "Come on. Let's go get that pawn ticket. Have you got your checkbook?"

She has her checkbook. He gets his car out of the garage under the apartment building and makes her take the Excalibur off the street and put it on the slot he has left. They drive out the San Diego freeway to the Valley, where the heat hammers down through a brown overcast. When he finds the street he panics for a minute as to whether it is the right one anymore. The Haycocks change residences often. He hasn't heard from them since bailing out Gran and Gramp, and that was months ago. It's one of those Valley streets that harks back to the thirties—no sidewalks, scabby, tilting picket fences, rusty chain-link fences, the street itself bordered by gnarled, shag-headed pepper trees, fruit trees in shiny leaf in the yards, orange, lemon, walnut, the houses boxy, meager, the older ones clapboard, the newer ones—forty, fifty years old by now—cracked stucco, sun-faded yellows, greens, pinks. Grass in the yards sometimes, a sprinkler system hissing here and there, ivy in the yards, now and then a parched flower bed, sometimes nothing in the yards but packed earth, a ragged dog now and then, now and then pecking chickens, waddling ducks, or only auto bodies propped on chunks of gray eucalyptus trunk, their disassembled guts strewn around them in dry weeds. Here and there house trailers and vacation vehicles with drawn curtains wait, soaking up heat. The Haycock place is not, surprisingly, one of the tackiest. Jewett parks. Youngsters in dirty jeans, boots, cowboy hats sway on horseback up the middle of the bleached blacktop, in and out of tree shade. Big hoofs clop. There is the creak of leather. After they have passed, Jewett gets out of the car into the stunning heat. Mavis McWhirter fumbles sunglasses from her bag and gets out too, but not eagerly. She slams the car door, then stands and stares. It is possible that she thinks this is a bad dream.

"Watch out for that plumbago," Jewett tells her. "The twigs

can tear your clothes." The plumbago has overgrown the fence and given time will pull the fence down. Among dense, fuzzy, gray-green leafage, it shows flowers the faded blue of the eyes of grandmothers. It has lately been trimmed back around the chain-link gate. Unexpectedly, the latch on the gate works. Jewett pushes the gate open and holds it for Mavis McWhirter, but she hangs back.

"What if his wife is here?" she says faintly.

Jewett shakes his head. "She's the one who works."

"Why don't I wait in the car?" Mavis turns away, bends to reach the door handle.

"Because I want you to see Dolan's face."

She looks up and down the street. "His car isn't here." She takes a few steps along the street edge, which is thick with the dry, curled leaves of pepper trees. These crunch under her handsome shoes. She peers past the house. "I don't see a garage."

"Someone will be here," Jewett says. "The Haycocks are a cast of thousands. Do me the kindness? You really ought to know more about him than that he's a lot of laughs and good in bed." He starts up the cracked squares of cement sunk in grass grown too tall that make a path to the front stoop. Beside the flat veneered door that is scaling its varnish is a bell push. He tries it but doesn't hear a buzz inside. He hears music. "And a thief," he adds, sensing her behind him at the foot of the short steps, reluctant, anxious. He uses knuckles on the door. The music is loud. The dog, who barks at everything, doesn't bark. No one answers the door. Jewett turns the knob, opens the door, and looks inside.

The furniture has been pushed back against the walls. If there is supposed to be a rug, it has vanished. The floor is vinyl tile printed to represent parquet squares. On a television stand of corroded metal tubing a color television set whose wood-grain covering is curling off and whose brightwork has been scraped shows a startlingly beautiful color picture. Jewett knows what the film is. *Nijinski*. It is not being broadcast today. If it were, he would be at home watching it, and to hell with the Queen Mary tour, and to hell with Mavis McWhirter and her ring. Then he sees on the rack under the television set what he recognizes from advertisements to be a videotape recorder. All of this he takes in at a glance.

It is not the center of interest. The center of interest is a sixteen-year-old boy in nothing but a slippery coat of sweat, dancing with the dancer on the screen. He is as brown-skinned as Bill. His profile is Bill's, his mouth is Bill's but without the sulk, with the idiot sweetness and good humor of Bill's ten years ago. His hair is shoulder-length, his brown eyes with their fringes of long, dense lashes, are as empty and unregarding as those you'd find in a box on a taxidermist's shelf. He is a little taller than Bill, which doesn't make him tall, and he moves with a grace Bill couldn't begin to manage. With the door open, the music is almost deafening.

"Ho!" Jewett shouts. "Larry? May we come in?"

The boy throws a panicked glance over his shoulder and runs from the room. The television blares on. The beautiful young man on the screen moves to the music. Jewett goes to the machine, squats, puzzles over it for a minute, punches a stop button. Blessed silence fills the room, and the screen above the recorder goes gray and blank. A film of dust is on the screen, with one handswipe across it.

"Just a minute, Mr. Jewett," Larry calls from somewhere remote that echoes. "Be right there." Water splashes. Jewett stands up. Mavis McWhirter is still outside at the foot of the steps. She has lit a cigarette to give her hands something to do. Larry comes back into the room. He has put on jeans and a clean T-shirt. A towel hangs around his neck. His hair drips. He gives an embarrassed smile with teeth better than Bill's—no gaps, straight, very white. "I'm sorry I didn't hear you." He snatches up Jockey shorts from the floor and jams them under a chair cushion.

"I should have phoned first," Jewett says, "but I hoped to surprise your father. He's not here?"

"Nobody's here. It's like paradise. It's the first chance I've had to use the Betamax. I've got a job at Colonel Sanders, but I phoned in sick."

"So it's new, then?" Jewett says. "Excuse me." He motions to Mavis McWhirter, and she comes doubtfully up the steps. "Mavis McWhirter—Larry Haycock." They shake hands, the boy bashfully, but his smile is better than hers. Hers is forced. Jewett touches the recorder with his sandal. "Where did it come from?"

"Dolan bought it, a couple days ago. Gave us kids cash to buy the movies we wanted. Only Newton bought a spider bike instead. Dolan said he won the money on a Dodger game."

"Did you believe him?"

"Shit," Larry scoffs, and says to Mavis, "'scuse me."

"Where is he?" Jewett asks.

"At Magic Mountain. He took everybody—except me and the dog. Mom's at work. Where did he get the money? Is it about the money—is that why you're here?"

"Mrs. McWhirter is missing a ring," Jewett says.

"Are you a friend of Dolan's?" Larry sounds amazed.

Sweat trickles from under Mavis's tasteful wig. It makes runnels in her thick makeup. "He probably picked it up"—she trudges to the door to flick ashes from her cigarette—"and absentmindedly put it in his pocket." She turns back with an unconvincing smile. "I'm always dropping things."

"Yeah, and he's always picking things up." Larry eyes the videotape player. "It must be some ring."

Jewett says, "Shall I go through his pockets, or will you?"

Larry looks puzzled for a second, then his frown clears. "For the pawn ticket, right?"

"He may have thought"—Mavis McWhirter tries, maybe for the boy's sake, maybe for the sake of her own illusions, to beatify Dolan—"it would be wiser to put it in a safe until he could return it to me."

Larry's look pities her. "I'll be back," he says, and leaves the room, rubbing his hair with the towel.

Now it is Mavis's turn to gaze at the machine. "You see?" She turns to Jewett with tears in her eyes. "He is kind and thought-ful and generous. After all, he might have spent it on himself and never told his family."

"Don't worry—he spent most of it on himself," Jewett says. "The gifts were only to raise his stock around the house. As you can tell, it needs raising. They all know what he is. When are you going to find out?"

"This is all guesswork," she says, crossly, and goes to toss her cigarette from the doorway into the yard. "The truth is, I drink too much, and I black out. There's no telling what I might have done with that ring."

A faint cheer sounds from the back of the house, also the excited barking of the dog.

Jewett says, "If I know Dolan, he made the smallest possible down payment on that video deck, and in ninety days the dealer will be back here to haul it away."

Mavis says, "I wish I'd never come."

And Larry runs into the room, holding the pawn ticket high in triumph, the dog yelping at his heels. It is a big, floppy dog, with long taffy-color hair. It jumps happily up on Jewett, stag-gering him a little, and, when Larry puts the ticket into Mavis's hand, the dog jumps up on her.

"Get down," she says snappily, "get down." Larry drags the dog, its paws firmly planted but skidding on the vinyl tile, to the hall and closes the door on it. It barks beyond the door. It claws the door. Mavis peers through her sunglasses at the tick-et. Jewett looks over her shoulder. The date is only four days past. She turns her head, meets Jewett's eyes briefly, looks away. "Schoenfeld's," she says, and drops the ticket into her bag. "I suppose that's the next stop? It's on Woodman." Over her shoulder, as she goes out the door and down the steps, she calls back in a cheery stage voice, "Thank you, Larry, dear. Bye-bye. Nice to have met you."

"Yeah," Larry says, "bye-bye."

Jewett says to him, "Don't tell Dolan about this, all right? Let her tell him."

"Will she?" Larry looks after her doubtfully as she retreats down the grass-grown cement squares. He says to Jewett, "Don't worry. He'll never miss it. You should see the pocket I got it out of—shredded Clorets wrappers, empty cigarette packs, used-up matchbooks, old bar checks, old betting slips. What would he want it for, anyway? The ring? Shit, all he wanted was some fast bucks."

"Right." Jewett smiles. "Go on with your movie."

The boy blushes, but before Jewett reaches the gate, the music of "Afternoon of a Fawn" blares out the open front door. The gate latch clacks behind him. When they are inside the car, waiting for the air conditioning to suck out the heat, Mavis, panting, wiping her streaming face with tissues, says plaintively:

"Can we find a drink, please?"

They found a drink—in Mavis's case two drinks—in a stone-fronted tavern all cushiony leather, dark woodwork, shadows, icy air. They found the ring in a spacious, shiny shop where on shelves and in display cases hocked electric guitars and wedding-present silver plate glittered like new. This graveyard of lost hopes radiated promise. Where were the grubby cellar light, the dusty clutter, the glum, unshaven fat men in cages of his New York days? To get the ring back cost Mavis a thousand dollars, but she has the ring now. For how long? He doesn't like to think.

In the fern-effulgent foyer of the apartment building in Mar Vista—how long has it been since anyone saw the sea from here, if anyone ever did?—he checks his watch. Ten past two in the afternoon. The mailbox holds an envelope addressed to Bill from the office of a city councilman. Jewett's hands shake as he tears it open. He wants it to contain good news for Bill's sake, but he dreads the kind of news it almost has to be if Bill's reports on the renter-versus-owner meetings in front of the council have been accurate. He reads. He smiles. There will be a three-month moratorium on conversion of apartments to condominiums. New hearings will begin in October. He tucks letter back into envelope, folds envelope, pushes it into a hip pocket, and turns for the heavy glass doors again. Maybe some of Bill's gratitude will be given the bearer of good tidings. Maybe Bill will forget the damned party. Jewett won't telephone the shop. He will take the letter there. He hopes Bill will hug him.

West L.A. is not so hot as the Valley, but it is hot, though awnings and leafy curbside trees give these blocks of Robertson Boulevard a cool look. The slim women in the boots and blowsy, crumpled clothes that are 1980s apogee of fashion, strolling the sidewalks in the shadows of the awnings and the trees, look cool. The modest lettering in neat gold leaf on the shop windows, the sleek glass of the windows, the handsome old furniture, oriental rugs, long swags of lavish fabric beyond the window glass look cool, the glossily mounted chunks of broken Greek sculpture, cracked medieval wood carvings, time-darkened paintings—all look cool. That anyone sweated, fashioning these things, is as unthinkable as that those able to buy them ever sweat. Corniches, Mercedes-Benzes, Alfa-Romeos line the curbs. There is no place to park.

Jewett wheels his Toyota up a side street and into an alley where bougainvillea flowers red on cement-block walls, and where treetops can be glimpsed above the walls. Bill's junky car stands close against a wall near a high gate of redwood planks. He is well paid by the shops that vie for his services but he is as attached to his car as to the apartment. He likes excitement but not change. A new yellow sports car is parked behind Bill's car. Jewett drives on and finds space down the alley beside a lavender-painted latticework that hides a trash module. He walks back to the redwood gate, starts to lift the wooden latch but does not have to because at his touch the gate swings inward—not far, a few inches. He pushes it open and is in a yard paved in terra-cotta tiles, with plantings in redwood boxes, and plants in clay pots hanging by macrame strings from overhead redwood beams. It wasn't like this when he was last here. Can he have come to the wrong shop? Is this a nursery? But no. Bill is here.

Jewett sees him through the drooping leafage and bristly red flowers of a bottlebrush tree. He stops in his tracks. Bill sits in a redwood armchair. The wood is rough. This is outdoor furniture. Its cushions are covered in a floral print, greens, blues. Bill's knees, in the work-stained corduroys, are spread. Between them, facing Bill, kneels a young man in a yellow tank top and yellow cotton drawstring pants. His very blond head is at Bill's crotch. He lifts and lowers his head slowly. The traffic noise from the boulevard out front is loud, but Jewett would almost swear he can hear the young man humming to himself. Bill is smiling down at him. His hands rest lightly on the young man's head. He has not seen Jewett.

Jewett touches his own hip pocket, where the letter is folded. He takes the letter out of the pocket, looks at it blindly, puts it back. He is not going to deliver the letter. What is he going to do? He feels as if he has been struck hard in the chest. He would like to sit down. In fact, he would like to lie down. Like Richie Cowan on the dry-grass football field. Facedown, motionless, unable to see, or hear, or think, or feel. Not forever—*this is only practice*—but for some time. One thing is certain: Bill is not going to hug him. He turns his head slowly, as if turning it quickly might make a noise. He looks at the open gateway, at the rust-red tiles littered with small bottlebrush leaves and tufts of bottlebrush flowers. He gauges the height of the hanging pot of trailing vine above him and to his left. He backs out carefully, and carefully pulls the gate almost shut after him. *Practice?* For what? The sun hot on his back, he returns to his car.

He pushes a shiny wire cart along the aisles of a supermarket. He is not seeing the colorful cartons and cans. He sees the long dark patch of sweat down the back of the blond boy's tank top, right at the center, along the spine. He shakes the vision away. He cannot find a plastic-wrapped package where the veal slices are thin enough, and rings for the butcher to cut them specially. In the deli section he finds prosciutto in a neat transparent envelope. Has he any dried rosemary leaves at home? He takes a bottle from the spice rack. In the produce department he bags

Spanish onions and brittle-skinned garlic. He remembers Romano cheese, and wheels back to the deli section for it. Circles around again to the produce section for parsley and mushrooms. Sunlight, broken by the ragged shadows of the hanging plants, gleams on the blond boy's naked shoulders. In bed, in the cold winter dark, Jewett asks, *Bo Kerrigan—is that his name?* Bill shrugs. *He's all right. There's dozens of him on TV.* Jewett finds wild rice and seasoned breadcrumbs. Bill blesses the boy with his hands, and smiles. *I don't think he's even gay.* Jewett drops a carton of cigarettes into the shopping cart. In the liquor department, surrounded by bottles that glow like stained-glass windows in some hedonist cathedral, he chooses a pricey California pinot blanc, and heads for the check-out stands. A heavy-bellied, stoop-shouldered old man waits ahead of Jewett in the line, denims baggy at the knees, holes worn by his toes in the stained blue canvas uppers of his shoes. His cart holds a stack of frozen TV dinners, a six-pack of cheap beer, the new *TV Guide.* Bill says, *You get along fine without me.* Jewett shuts his eyes.

He wishes grimly that Bill's favorite dish took longer to prepare. At home in the kitchen, he cuts the thin veal slices into little squares, salts the squares, peppers them, chops prosciutto, parsley, and a clove of garlic, grates the cheese, stuffs and rolls up the squares of veal, ties the rolls neatly with string. He half fills a shallow bowl with bread crumbs and coats the rolls. He lays them on a plate, slips the plate into a plastic bag, sets it in the refrigerator. And it still lacks six minutes of being four o'clock, and Bill won't be home until a quarter past five. That's when he always comes home. For dinner. Always.

Jewett takes down a pan, melts butter in it, chops the mushrooms, sautés them. He dumps the wild rice into a colander and washes it. After bringing water to a boil, he sets the colander over it, stirs in the browned mushroom bits, puts a lid on it, and leaves it to cook long and slow. He cleans up knives, plates, bowls, the chopping block, the counter. With lemon juice he rubs the garlic smell off his fingers, washes his hands, dries his hands. From deep in the beautiful old sideboard-bar in the living room he fetches out the expensive gin kept for special occasions and in the kitchen puts together martinis, turning the ice gently with a glass rod and removing the ice cubes before they can lose their edges. He sets the closed pitcher in the coldest spot in the refrigerator and with a very sharp knife cuts twists of lemon peel. These go into the refrigerator too, in a plastic bag. He crouches to check the broiler to be sure it is clean. It is clean. He reads his watch again. Four twenty-five.

He has been working hard, with frowning concentration, and he is sweaty. The Valley was hot—how long ago it seems to him now, dimmer than a dream—the yard back of the shop was hot, the alleyway. He will shower. He strips in the bedroom and notices that the glass over the posters is dull. Naked he goes back to the kitchen for Windex and paper towels and carefully cleans the glass. Bill will be pleased. He returns the bottle and the towels to the kitchen. He is fussing like a bride over her first dinner party. He is fussing like a fool. He is making believe that something is going to happen that is not going to happen. He is making believe that something that has happened has not. He is a frightened man who doesn't know what to do.

Under the shower he tells himself he will take Bill to a film. Bill is movie crazy. For a long time Jewett went with him to all the new films. But also for a long time, Jewett has refused. No one who knows how to make films is making them now. Amateurs are making them. The lighting is flat, the sound inaudible or too loud to bear. Editing is a lost art. Scripts take up and drop situations with the indifference Jewett gave that invitation. None of which seems to matter, because audiences pay little or no attention. They talk and never stop talking, and almost never talk about the film. If they react to what is on the screen at all, it is to laugh raucously at the most tender moments, or at moments when murder and mayhem are at their bloodiest. At such times, Jewett's mind reels. He can't believe he is awake. But Bill doesn't want to hear about his outrage and despair—and Jewett never goes to films with him anymore.

Except tonight. Tonight he will suggest they go. It will make Bill happy. Like the dinner. Jesus, he has forgotten dessert! He lunges out of the shower.

There are apples. There are sugar and flour, cinnamon and nutmeg. He nicks his thumb peeling the apples. His hands shake. He coats the apple slices with sugar, cinnamon, nutmeg, butters a pan, dumps the slices in the butter, cuts more butter onto them, stirs them around, clatters the pan into the oven. He sweats again in the heat leaking from the oven as he mixes the batter. It is five o'clock. He waits ten minutes and tests the apple slices with a fork. Tender enough. He pours on the batter, sprinkles it with more cinnamon and sugar, closes the oven. Well timed. There will be dessert, after all. Twenty-five minutes later, there is dessert. He uses oven mittens to take it out of the oven and set it on the back of the stove.

There is no one to eat the dessert. Nor the spiedini. Nor to drink the icy martinis, nor to savor the pinot blanc. The wild rice is perfect. It stands and steams in a bowl on the stove top and stops steaming after a while. Jewett gets a fork and, standing in the kitchen where the light is fading, eats a little of the rice, but he soon stops. He is not hungry. He begins to feel tired. All that stupid racing around to prepare food he knew, he knew in the sour place where he keeps his common sense, Bill wouldn't come to eat. *You don't want to be with me? Okay, then I don't want to be with you either.* Jewett pours a martini for himself and takes it into the living room, where he sits and sips it and smokes and watches the daylight redden and die. He sits in the dark. He goes to the kitchen without turning on the lights and squints in the glare from the white inside of the refrigerator when he takes out the martini pitcher again. He tries the rice again. It is not appetizing cold. He takes the second martini back to his living-room chair. He sits there with his feet up, no light but the faint glow at the window from streetlamps below, no sound but of the occasional car on the street, none of them Bill's car, whose sound he knows. He falls asleep, waiting for the sound of Bill's car.

Something wakens him later. The martini is warm. He goes to bed. And what wakens him after that is Bill. Not turning on a light. Just climbing naked into the bed beside him, smooth, warm, familiar. But not the same, not quite the same, never the same again. Jewett says, "Your ineffable father stole a ring from that big old woman he was here with last winter."

"The one with the jazzy car?"

"We got it back," Jewett says. "It wasn't hard."

"You mean you got it back." Bill turns toward him, draws him close, puts a kiss on his mouth. It tastes of barbecue sauce. "You know, you're a very nice man," he says. "You make me mad as hell sometimes, but you're a very nice man. I don't want anybody but you. I thought I did. I thought we were through, this morning. I was wrong. I don't want us to be through."

"It's up to you," Jewett says. "You got a letter from your councilman. The owners lost. Temporarily. I drove to the shop to bring you the letter. This afternoon, about two-thirty. I used the back gate." He feels Bill stiffen. "Next time you want to try out another man, will you phone and say you won't be home for dinner?"

"It was the first time," Bill says.

"I know that. You were smiling. Did it prove to you you're not getting old and ugly?"

"There won't be a next time," Bill says.

July

JEWETT JUMPED out of a taxi into warm summer rain. "You don't have to come in." He shut the curbside door. "There's nothing much to carry. I'll be right back."

"I'm coming."

Plump little Ziggy Fogel climbed out the streetside door and told the driver to wait. Ziggy acted as if the rain didn't exist, though he wore a beautifully tailored lounge suit. His small feet in handmade shoes stepped delicately across the black rainwater pushing trash along the gutter, but he ignored the waterfall down the steps into the black-railed areaway where Jewett pushed a key into the theater door. Maybe Ziggy could afford to throw the shoes away if the rain damaged them—and the suit too. His suite at the Plaza Hotel must be costing him more than Jewett had earned in his whole short life.

Jewett had slept the night with Ziggy in that suite. This morning, over a room-service breakfast involving a lot of stiff, snow-white linen and a silver ice bucket that held French champagne, Ziggy had asked Jewett to move in with him and, when his business in New York was finished, to fly with him to the Coast and continue to live with him there. He would find parts in pictures. He hadn't promised to make him a star. Maybe he feared Jewett wouldn't believe him if he exaggerated. Jewett didn't believe him anyway.

Years of going hungry, not just for food but for the chance to act, had turned him skeptical. He had nearly given up hope that anything good could happen to him. And this morning he had focused on only one thing Ziggy said: that he would fly Jewett home. There might never be a part in a picture, but at least he'd be back in California.

If Ziggy wanted to feed him for a while, as he had fed him this morning, and last evening after the Scenes from Shakespeare in the park, Jewett could take as much of that as time allowed. And Ziggy was tender and worshipful in bed. He thought this tall, slender, broad-shouldered, narrow-hipped California boy was almost as beautiful as the boy thought himself to be. Jewett had been waiting a cold, lonely time to hear it from someone else. Since Fred Heinz, the half-friends, the strangers he'd had sex with didn't pay compliments. Some of them, mostly actors, wanted compliments, even asked for them straight out. *Tell me I'm pretty. Everbody says I have beautiful eyes. Do you think I have beautiful eyes? Look, see how big it is. Did you ever see one so big?* Ziggy paid compliments. Maybe they were sincere, maybe not, but they made Jewett feel better than he had felt for a long, long time.

So here he was, back at the only place that had made reluctant room for him, to pick up his belongings. And with the door open into the cellar smell, the dark emptiness of the little, low-ceilinged theater, he was seized with shame. He switched on pallid houselights that showed disordered rows of folding chairs on a cement floor strewn with heel-marked mimeo-graphed programs, crumpled Kleenex, crushed cigarette butts, and he hurried off, dodging the chairs, jumping up onto the low stage and loping long-legged across it, pushing through musty-smelling curtains into blackness, finding his way from habit. He didn't want Ziggy to see how he had been living.

He pulled the string on the hanging light in the janitor's

closet, where, on a canvas fold-down cot, lay the sleeping bag he'd begged secondhand from a kid too old and horny to be a Boy Scout anymore. Jewett bent to pick it up, and dropped it. It was greasy, stained, it smelled. The rags that were his shirts, sweaters, underwear, socks, he gathered up, soiled and clean alike, and stuffed into his rucksack. His extra shoes, the pair whose uppers, at least, he thought of as good, he saw now, with changed vision, were scratched, scuffed, dull. He kicked them into a corner where something let out a sharp squeak and rustled away. The suits he had bought in the early days when he got Broadway parts he'd long ago sold for eating money. His one jacket, corduroy with leather elbow patches, left here by a playgoer who had not cared enough about it to come back for it, Jewett was already wearing. Down from a shelf of stacked toilet paper, disinfectant bottles, soap powder, scrub brushes, he pulled his scrapbook of clippings and the fake-leather folder of photos he'd had taken when he first reached New York. He tucked these under his arm and bent for the rucksack. When he turned, there was Ziggy, watching him.

"This is where they made you sleep?"

"This is where they let me sleep. It beat the park, alley doorways, the mission." It had never been that bad, but he wanted Ziggy's pity, not his scorn.

Tears filled Ziggy's eyes. "I'm so sorry."

Jewett handed Ziggy the scrapbook and folder, and reached up and yanked the light string again. He touched Ziggy in the dark. "Let's go," he said. But when they were out in front of the stage once more, he halted. "I ought to sweep out. It's my job. Every morning."

"Not anymore." Ziggy took his arm and thrust him out the door, where sun was shining down into the areaway, turning the raindrops to glittering glass beads. Ziggy reached to pull the door shut.

"Wait," Jewett said. "I have to leave the key." He stepped inside again, laid the key on the little shelf of the ticket booth. He took a last look at the place, switched off the lights, stepped out, and closed the door behind him. "Hell, I should have left a note."

Ziggy's look pitied him. "Of thanks?"

"They kept me alive."

"And you swept out every morning," Ziggy said.

In the taxi, Ziggy rolled down the window, picked up Jewett's rucksack, and heaved it out. It hit a trash barrel but didn't drop inside. It knocked the barrel over, and the barrel strewed its contents onto the wet paving. Jewett was shocked. He turned to look out the rear window. Lying in the street, the rucksack looked forlorn to him, like a dog abandoned that had thought all along it was loved.

"Those were all my clothes," he said.

"We are going now," Ziggy said, "to buy you new clothes. God knows, you need them."

The night before they were to leave New York, Ziggy hosted a party at his suite, and Jewett was happy to have new clothes, because everybody who came was well dressed. Many were actors but he didn't know their names: he hadn't been able to afford theater tickets for a long time. Some of them played charades. They called it "The Game," and they went at it noisily, crawling on the floor, stamping up and down, howling, jumping on the furniture. Jewett recognized Paulette Goddard and Burgess Meredith and Charles Laughton—they had been in pictures.

The names of producers he shook hands with were familiar. Most of them had, at one time and another, refused to see him when he limped into their offices. Most of the directors had fobbed him off with unkept promises at auditions. Producers and directors who had once hired him, back before the war ended, acted glad to see him, shook his hand hard, slapped his back.

"Where the hell have you been?" they said. "Look, I've got a great part for you, let me send you a script."

He didn't tell them he had been right where he always was— around. He didn't say they never returned his calls and were always out when he went to see them. They knew it. He just said, "I'm going to Hollywood."

A tiny lady with flame-red hair cornered him, demanding to know where he had been keeping himself hidden, and why. She called him glorious. He didn't tell her about the janitor's closet. She wanted credit for discovering him. He said that belonged to Ziggy, and she forced herself through the pack of nibblers, drinkers, laughers, to argue with Ziggy, and Jewett didn't see her again. He was excited, and kept pouring down champagne, until he suddenly felt dizzy and sick to his stomach. He reached for the knob of the bathroom door, just as it opened, and he collided with a slim, brown man, who threw his arms around Jewett and kissed him. It happened very fast. The brown man laughed softly, said something in Spanish, and squeezed Jewett's genitals with a warm hand. Jewett pushed him aside, stumbled into the bathroom, slammed the door, and threw up before he could reach the toilet. He kept conscious long enough to clean up the mess, and to stagger into his bedroom, shedding his clothes.

The night was hot, and the clothes seemed to be smothering him. They used a lot of material in suits in those days: it was like wearing curtains. He wanted the feel of cool sheets on his skin. He lurched toward the bed, but it was occupied. Light fell into the room from the hall, and Jewett still remembers their startled faces, though he doesn't know to this day whether they were a man and a woman, two men, or two women. The voice that spoke was high-pitched. *Didn't you ever hear of knocking?* He veered toward the chaise longue and fell on it. *It's my room,* he mumbled, and sleep pulled him under like a shark. He had a headache and diarrhea all the way to Los Angeles. It gave him a permanent hatred of aircraft washrooms.

With Ziggy, parties were a way of life. He lived up twisting trails lined by lacy eucalyptus trees high in the Hollywood hills, in a six-bedroom, three-level California Spanish house, all sun-dazzled white walls and red tile roofs without, cool white walls and hand-hewn black beams, black ironwork chan-

deliers, black ornamental ironwork door fittings and stair railings within. In a central patio of lush plantings and cool shade,
water played in a mossy fountain. The sound all night made
sleeping easy. To reach the house from the road above, you
drove down past tennis courts. From the ground-floor terrace
you looked down on a big, blue swimming pool. At night, the
lights of Los Angeles stretched off to the sea.

It was like living on a movie set, and it was as alive with
people as a movie set, strangers with famous faces, most of
them, or simply famous names, writers, directors, producers.
Ziggy scrupulously introduced Jewett to them all, but they
scarcely noticed, most of them. Those who did notice ended up
trying to get him into bed, men and women alike. At first he was
happily startled at their attention and their flattery—they
praised his looks, his nice manners, his lovely deep voice, his
way with words. And he let them take him to lunch, until he
realized that by so doing he was letting them think he would
have sex with them. This he wasn't going to do, because he was
loyal to Ziggy.

Ziggy didn't always make it easy. He gave a lot more attention to his endless flow of guests than he gave to Jewett. He
spent such time as he could snatch from brunches, lunches,
cocktail parties, dinner parties, after-theater parties on the telephone, setting up deals, renegotiating contracts, turning down
scripts, scuttling directors his stars didn't like, making travel
arrangements for clients. It was corny, but he actually lay in
flowered swim trunks on an inflated raft in the middle of the
swimming pool and dictated letters to a secretary at an
umbrella table on the deck. Sometimes the phone would ring in
the middle of the night and Ziggy would leave his place beside
Jewett. A car would arrive. Jewett could see the lights sweep the
bedroom ceiling. And Ziggy would spend hours downstairs
with some weeping client, drunk or drugged or sick or simply
sad. Holding hands, murmuring kind words.

He had an office he went to, mornings. And he kept traveling.
Sometimes he invited Jewett, sometimes he forgot even to mention that he was leaving. It was up to Jewett, missing him, to

learn from some secretary where he'd gone. Or even from the cook, a waddling old Mexican woman who reminded him of Magdalena long ago at home. Ziggy neglected him, but Ziggy had rescued him, clothed him, fed him, and when he could find the time, gave him great tenderness. So Jewett kept his distance from the beautiful ones who wanted to bed him. He listened to records or the radio, sat by himself in the dark of Ziggy's projection room watching old films, or swam in the pool, or lay beside the pool, reading, soaking up sun. Ziggy let friends—and he had a thousand friends—use his pool and tennis courts whenever they liked. If someone came by alone in whites with a racquet, Jewett played tennis. If no one came, he got Ziggy's little MG with the big red wire wheels out of the garage and drove to the beach to watch the shorebirds while he ate lobster. Or he drove just to be driving, the coast road, hills, canyons.

These lonesome, aimless weeks seemed endless. Shame began to overtake him in the nights when Ziggy was away and the big empty house slept silent in the dark and silent hills. He was a rich man's kept boy, good for nothing but to look at and play with. He hadn't asked Ziggy what he was doing about finding Jewett those parts in pictures he had promised. It wasn't in his upbringing to ask more of anyone who was already giving so openhandedly. Ziggy didn't owe him anything. It would soon be November. The nights were growing cold. One night the cold wakened him. He got out of bed to find another blanket—and instead he got dressed.

It was time to leave, past time. He slipped his watch on his wrist, thrust his wallet into a hip pocket, pocketed change, cigarettes, lighter, lifted down his car coat from a hanger in the big closet packed with his clothes, and suddenly couldn't move. The car coat wasn't his, the hanging clothes, the clothes he stood up in. They were Ziggy's. Ziggy had paid for them. And the watch, the lighter, the cigarettes. The wallet was Ziggy's, and the money in the wallet. When Ziggy couldn't find time to say anything else to him, he always managed to ask if he was all right for money. He was always all right for money. What was there to spend it on? But Ziggy didn't hear his answer. He handed him money anyway. When there got to be more than the wallet would hold, Jewett tucked it into dresser drawers. He carried a hundred dollars. There must be five hundred hidden. He hung the car coat up again. To walk out of here any way but naked would make him a thief. He went back to bed.

Ziggy's driver was a former boxer named Mick Clockerty, a hulk with a flattened nose, crumpled ears, scar-tissue brows. In black riding breeches, puttees, a white shirt with the cuffs turned back, he hosed and sponged down Ziggy's maroon Packard brougham. Broughams were scare in Hollywood by 1948, and for that reason this one got a lot of attention, which was why Ziggy kept it. Jewett leaned in a side door and watched the water slide off the gleaming car onto the drive. When Mick had reeled up the green hose and wheeled its green cart out of sight, Jewett stepped out and shut the door. Mick didn't look up. He began wiping waterdrops off the wax with a chamois.

Jewett said, "I can pick him up."

Mick regarded him with tiny, hostile eyes. "It's my job. You trying to lose me my job?"

Jewett shrugged. "I just thought you might have work you'd rather do."

Mick went back to wiping with the patch of soft, yellow leather. "Get lost," he said.

Jewett was already lost. "I'll ride with you, then."

Mick grunted, and with lumpy fists wrung out the chamois. He flapped it in the sun to get the wrinkles out of it. "I can't stop you." The seat in the open part of the car was maroon leather. Mick leaned in to wipe imaginary dust off it with the deep chamois. He wiped the maroon instrument panel. He bent to pick up the sponge. "I'm leaving right away." He disappeared through a small door into the garage. When he returned, he was wearing his high-collared jacket with the two rows of buttons, his billed cap. He pulled on gloves. Jewett was sitting in the front. Nick scowled. "What do you think?" he said. "I want your company?" He jerked his head. "Get out. You ride in the back."

Jewett got out. It was a fine, sunny day. He wanted to ride in the open. He slammed the door. "You know," he said, "Ziggy is a homosexual too."

"He isn't a whore." Mick got behind the wheel, closed his door, and started the engine. Jewett got into the back.

Under the high, carved rafters of Union Station, Mick wouldn't let him help carry Ziggy's bags. They were too many for one man, but Mick carried them anyway, all of them, through the shafts of sunlight from the high, clear windows, a long, long way down the beautiful tiles to the doors, outside which olive trees grew in a forecourt. Ziggy pattered along, chattering brightly. Jewett's arms felt useless. They flopped from his shoulders, heavy, absurd. They felt yards long. His whole body seemed heavy, absurd, useless. Except his cock, of course. That was of some use—at least to Ziggy. Gloomily Jewett watched Mick load the luggage into the trunk, his battered face sweating. In the car again, heading west through traffic between glum, gray buildings, he drew a deep breath and said to Ziggy:

"When do I get a part in a picture?"

Ziggy looked at him astonished. "Do you want a part in a picture?"

Jewett felt himself flush. "Isn't that why you brought me out here?"

"I brought you out here to make two people happy—you and me. I've been very happy. Haven't you?"

"Yes, sure, but—" It was a disturbing question. He frowned at his sandals, gave his head a sad little shake, and said softly, "No, I haven't been happy."

"I thought," Ziggy said, "you'd enjoy the contrast from the way you were living in New York."

"I do, I do." Jewett tried to smile. "It's just that—I'm sorry, Ziggy. I feel ashamed. I ought to be earning my living. I feel like, I don't know, like a parasite or something."

Ziggy twinkled at him. "Aren't orchids parasites? It doesn't mar their beauty. Not in my eyes."

"Mick called me a whore."

"Ah, dear Mick. He's very religious, you know."

Jewett knew. He had looked into Mick's rooms above the garages. He had no business there—he was idle and curious. A shrine with a painted plaster figure of the Virgin stood, blue and gold, against one bare sitting-room wall. The bedroom was a plain white cell, crucifix over a narrow iron cot, rosary strung over a lampshade.

Ziggy said, "He'd like to be a priest, but the church won't let him because he was married and divorced and there were children, so he can't claim the marriage was never consummated. The church thinks highly of immaculate conceptions, but not for everyone." He patted Jewett's knee. "Forget what Mick said. He's a fanatical ascetic."

"He picked a funny man to work for," Jewett said.

"Many years ago, before I learned discretion," Ziggy said, "I got involved in a sordid little encounter with some very rough trade in a dark alley. I think they would have ended up killing me. Mick came to my rescue. He's worked for me ever since. I hope he always will. He cares about me—he even cares about my immortal soul."

"I thought Jews didn't believe in immortality."

Ziggy said sharply, "I don't know what they believe."

It was a lie. With Jewish clients, two famous comedians, in particular, Jewett had heard and watched Ziggy revel in Jewish inside jokes and Yiddish expressions. He knew all about what they believed. Ziggy was a Jew. But he didn't like people who were not Jews to use the word to him. Jewett was sorry he had done it now, but he was going to finish what he'd started.

"I'm not a whore," he said, "and I'm not an orchid. I'm an actor, Ziggy—remember? I want to work."

Ziggy studied Jewett's face, put a light kiss on his mouth, and sat back with a sigh. "All right," he said, as if bidding good-bye to someone in a coffin, "if that's what you want, that's what you shall have."

"All right," Ziggy says now, thirty-two years later, "if that's what you want, that's what you shall have." But he says it with sweetness, and he is a changed Ziggy, parchment and bone, seventy-seven years old, bald, his handsome false teeth too big for his mouth. Only two things show him to be the Ziggy of old—his clothes are conspicuously expensive, and his eyes are bright, clear, eager as ever. To read the contract pages lying on the desk in front of him, he does not wear glasses. He makes a mark on the contract with a slim gold ball-point pen. A gold cuff-link clicks on the desk top. He lifts amiable eyebrows at Jewett's agent, fat Morry Block. "Anything else?"

Morry has loosened his necktie and unbuttoned the collar beneath his rubbery chins. He has pushed dark glasses up on his thick, crinkly hair. He looks at Jewett. Jewett can't think of anything else. He is dazed. Ziggy's office is as bare and white as Mick Clockerty's rooms, except for a group of framed *santos*, crude Mexican holy pictures on tin, on the wall above Ziggy's head. Stranger still, a frowsty, middle-aged priest sits quietly in a corner, reading. This priest shepherded old Mick to a peaceful, joyous end, according to Ziggy. Mick didn't suffer. He had God and Jesus and the Blessed Virgin comforting him, making it easy to bear the pain. He didn't die alone. Ziggy foresaw a lonely death for himself and it sobered him. He became a Catholic. In case he should die suddenly, he keeps the priest with him all the time. Jewett wonders if he asks the priest every day how he is for money. Probably. This is all strange enough, but it is not what has left Jewett stunned and wordless.

What has done this is a telephone call that came this morning after Bill left for work. It was the call Jewett had long given up believing would ever come. At first he had flat-out doubted it. He had never known Morry to play practical jokes, but that Ziggy Fogel, of all television producers, had rung up wanting Oliver Jewett, of all actors, for a principal role in "Timberlands," the most successful dramatic series now on the tube, was impossible to take as anything but a joke.

"Morry," Jewett said, "he hates my guts. We haven't spoken in a hundred years."

It was a February morning in 1954, sky silver-gray with coming rain over hills velvety with new spring grass, when Jewett had walked out of the elegant Spanish house for the last time to go live in love and squalor at the beach with Rita Lopez, never expecting to hear from Ziggy again. When he did, the call was brief. It came to the little theater where Rita was working, and where Jewett was waiting for her. When was Jewett coming back to Ziggy? He wasn't. In that case, Jewett would never work in pictures again. The connection broke. The line hummed. Jewett stood dumb in the theater office, with its beaverboard walls and fly-specked glossy eight-by-tens of actors' faces, until someone took the receiver from his paralyzed hand and hung it back on its hook.

Morry said, "Judd Norton, the old guy who played the father, dropped dead on the set from a heart attack. Monday. The writers are going to replace him with a younger brother who comes out from Wall Street to take over Timberlands—elegant, educated, classy, your shtik, Oliver. You're a natural for it. It will make for great script material. That son of a bitch, T.J., the oldest son—he expected to run the empire, right? Now it will be this uncle—you—instead. The old man shafted T. J. from the grave, right? Look at the danger you'll be in, look how smart you'll have to be to frustrate T.J. at every turn. It could build up to the biggest role in the series."

"Morry, you ought to stop snorting that stuff. It plays hell with the sinuses."

"Would I kid you about a thing like this?"

"Did he mention money?" When producers mention money, it sometimes means they are serious. "How much, Morry?"

"Seven thousand a week," Morry said.

Jewett's knees gave. He leaned against the kitchen counter and struggled not to believe any of this.

"That's not bad, is it? I told you it was gonna happen sooner or later, didn't I? Hey, are you all right?"

"I don't trust Ziggy Fogel." Ziggy's telephoned threat had come only days after their big, dramatic face-off, when Ziggy wept and wailed, begged and pleaded, and finally tried to commit suicide, and maybe would have, except that he fainted at the sight of his own blood, a trickle from a razor-scratched wrist. His ravings that night meant nothing but that Ziggy Fogel hated to lose. He wasn't in love with Jewett anymore, if he ever had been. Jewett was an elegant, dependable fixture in his life, that was all. But he meant what he said on the phone. And his threat would have come true if television hadn't very soon changed the picture business, put an end to the studio system, and drained people like Ziggy of a lot of their old clout. For the time being. Now Ziggy was powerful again. "He may have thought up a new way to punish me for walking out on him. He's had a lot of years to brood, Morry. He's old. Maybe he wants to really stick it to me before he leaves for Forest Lawn."

"You talk like a writer," Morry said. "Do you know where Blackbird Productions is?" He didn't wait for an answer. He gave the address. "I'll meet you there. If you don't like anything about it, we don't have to sign, do we? Let's hear him out. What harm can it do? You with me? I made the appointment for eleven. Jesus, Oliver, you're hard to please. You been a long time hungry. You deserve this break."

They have signed the contract. The priest and a trim little black secretary with her hair in cornrows and tiny, red-beaded braids have signed as witnesses. The secretary has gone. The priest sits and reads again. Across the glossy desk, Ziggy holds Jewett's hand in a frail, old man's grip. He looks tenderly into Jewett's eyes, and his smile, with the big false teeth, is saintly. "I did you a great wrong, Oliver. I hope this will make it up to you."

Jewett can't think of an answer. He nods. "I'll save the money. I plan to buy a little bakery. In my hometown. What do you think?"

"If that's what you want," Ziggy says.

Noon sunlight falls steeply in at the wide office window. It shines on the dirty gray hair of the quiet priest, and makes it glow as if with a halo.

August

"YOU SAID yourself the price scares everybody." Jewett leans urgently across the little yellow table, morning sunshine warm on his back through the bakery window. The smell of fresh-baked bread is strong in the air. The taste of streusel and raspberry jam from the pastry he has just eaten mingles in his mouth with the taste of coffee from the paper cup in its yellow plastic holder. "I don't honestly think you're going to get the cash, Joe. It's a lot of money at one time."

Young Joe Pfeffer frowns past Jewett, mouth tight, fingers pulling solemnly at his long nose. He laughed and cheered when Jewett walked in with the news about "Timberlands." He was pleased as hell, pleased and proud, and pumped Jewett's hand till Jewett had to shake loose. Joe yelped the good news to the girl who looks like Frances Lusk, and she ran in a flurry to the kitchen to tell Peter-Paul, who came out with flour in his hair to give Jewett grave congratulations. The Pfeffers are fans of "Timberlands," never miss it. This morning, Jewett has become awesome as a god. And Joe is plainly finding it hard to say no. He sighs, gives his head a troubled shake. "That ranch I want to buy up north. They want cash."

"We don't always get what we want." Jewett smiles. "Talk to them. See if they won't accept partial payment." He has no real knowledge of business, but he has often played bankers, businessmen, brokers. He falls back on the simpleminded psychology of television scripts. From his inside jacket pocket he takes a crisp oblong of paper and unfolds it in the middle of the table for Joe to look at. It is a cashier's check for ten thousand dollars, made out to Joseph Pfeffer, Jr. Jewett is a little staggered at his profligacy, but the paychecks come from the network as promised, week after fat week, and the money piles up in the bank like faery gold. He gives the check a little nudge toward Young Joe, who watches it as if hypnotized. "This is earnest money," Jewett says. "If I default, it's yours—all right?—free and clear, no questions asked. If we close the sale, it goes toward the purchase price."

Joe drags his gaze away from the check. He blinks at Jewett, shifts uneasily on the flimsy yellow chair. "And you want—" He is hoarse, scarcely audible. He clears his throat. "And you want to pay me one-fourth down, and the rest in monthly installments based on the shop's income—is that it?"

"With a floor under them," Jewett says. "We'll work that out with the savings and loan people." He pushes back his chair and stands. He gives his smile all the assurance he can muster, and holds out his hand. "Done?"

Young Joe digs worriedly in his ear with a little finger, staring at the check again, which he still won't touch. "Jesus," he says to himself. He looks up from under a wrinkled brow at Jewett. "I don't know."

"Has anyone else made you an offer?"

"Well, no—not really. I mean, they inquire, but no, nobody's made me an offer." He grins sheepishly and picks up the check. "They sure as hell none of them put any money on the table." He gets to his feet.

"Think the ranch people will agree up north?"

Young Joe's sallow complexion darkens in a blush. "Ah, hell," he says, "that was just talk. I wanted cash. I figured if I said that about the ranch, it would be easier to get the cash. They'll take it in sections, sure. I just didn't want it to drag on for years, is all. I wanted to have it over with."

"That For Sale sign's been in your window at least since January," Jewett says.

"Yeah." Thoughtful, running his gaze over the check again, Young Joe sighs. Then he looks up a final time, grins, says, "What the hell," and shakes Jewett's hand. "Done. When do you want to draw up the papers?"

Jewett unties the stretch of bristly cord that has held down the trunk lid. He tosses the tangle into the trunk and bends to wrestle out a bulky carton. It is at least as heavy as he feared. He ought to have paid the kid who loaded it to come with him. He sets the carton on the retaining wall at the foot of the steps and turns his gaze up to where the straight horizontals of the house show through the dark deodar branches. It's a long haul. He goes back to slam the trunk shut, grapples with the carton, and starts to climb. The dour old trees cast shade but there is nothing cool about it. After a dozen steps, he feels sweat begin to trickle down his ribs. His arms tire, his legs tire, he stops often to catch his breath. He wonders if he is going to make it, but somehow he makes it. Setting the carton on the porch, however, is more like dropping it. The sound is loud and hollow. He has to sit down and he sits down on the wooden steps. And hears the house door open behind him.

"Oliver? What in the world?"

His mouth and throat are dry. He can't answer. He can only pant. He hears her crooked footfalls, thump-*thump*, thump-*thump*, nearing. He hears her draw a breath in happy surprise.

"A television set? A color television set! Oh, Oliver, how wonderful. You shouldn't have." She plants a kiss on the top of his head the way their mother used to do. "How marvelous!" And like her young self, quick and impulsive when pleased, she plumps down beside him on the steps and gives him a clumsy hug. "How good you are. How good you are to me."

"Can't have you watching 'Timberlands' in dingy black and

white," he says. "Not now." He smiles into her homely face, the crooked teeth, the eyes distorted by the thick glasses. She glows. The remission has come, the devouring horror in her bloodstream has quit. She feels fine these days, the weakness banished, the nosebleeds, the great bruises fading. If she knows, as he knows from talking to the doctors, that it isn't likely to last, not at her age, she gives no indication. He pushes to his feet, not ready to put out more effort yet, but not wanting her to have to wait. "Come on. Let's set it up and plug it in."

She holds open the screen door and he plods past, moaning inside at the ache in his muscles that the weight of the damned thing reawakens. She hobbles happily after him through the living room, dining room, where the loom holds a now almost completed panel that blocks off much of the daylight, the dark colors of the lumpy yarns soaking it up. He staggers down the hall to her room, and lets the carton slip out of his aching hands onto the bed, which, to his pleased astonishment, is smoothly made. Not that he minds making her bed. But this is the first time she has made it since she took sick. It is a sign of how good she feels. A begonia with buttery yellow blossoms sits in a foil-wrapped pot tied with a blue ribbon on top of the old television set. She removes it, places it on the dresser. It is good to see her old quickness back.

He digs under the flaps of the carton with his fingers and begins to pry them up. "The lady from the Humane Society again?"

"Well, at least it's not another chrysanthemum." Susan laughs. Jewett seems always to be carrying to the back porch chrysanthemums whose leaves have drooped and whose blossoms have dried to brown, brittle pom-poms. Mrs. Fairchild keeps bringing them when Jewett is not here, and Susan hasn't had the strength or presence of mind enough to look after them. Jewett routinely trims back the dead growth and waters them, and the hardiest come back to life in long, leggy stems that put out puny buds and pathetic, scrawny little flowers and flop like vines. "She's so kind to keep coming to see me. After all, it was Lambert who was the dog lover."

Jewett lays the flaps back. Swathed in thick clear plastic, the television set is lodged inside the carton by means of molded Styrofoam fittings. These leave no space where Jewett can slip his hands down inside to pry the thing out. He tips the carton onto its side, and kneels to tug at the packing, which comes to pieces in his fingers. He sighs, rises, turns the carton upside down, and shakes it by its flaps. Grudgingly, still clamped in its stiff white brackets, the set squeaks out onto the bed. He pries the brackets off, peels up the sticky transparent tape, unwraps the plastic swaddling. The set gleams with newness and gives off a strong warehouse smell.

Susan has unplugged the old set and folded down its bent, corroded antenna. Jewett picks it up and carries it across the hall, through the kitchen, out to the back porch to join the sad chrysanthemums. When he returns, Susan has undone the skein of power wire on the new set. She carries it after him to the corner, where he rests the new set in the old set's place. She squats and plugs it in, and for the next twenty minutes, confused by the badly translated Japanese of the instruction book, they fuss over getting the flesh tones to look like flesh tones, the reds, yellows, blues of the detergent cartons and cereal boxes of the commercials to match those on the supermarket shelves.

Susan is enchanted. She sits on the edge of the bed and stares through those thick, distorting lenses of hers as if she'd never seen color before, anywhere. Her shoulders are hunched up in glee, her hands are clasped between the knees of her threadbare jeans, and her smile is as bedazzled as a Christmas child's. What she watches involves beautiful wholesome youngsters, scrubbed and combed, dressed in clothes obviously never before worn, playing at suburban impishness in a supposed home that is a dream of middle-class avarice. It doesn't matter. All she cares about for now is the color. Jewett looks at his watch and clears his throat. She doesn't hear. She is enraptured. He steps to the set and snaps it off. She jerks with surprise.

"Have to get moving," he says. "The preshowing is at three,

and you wanted to get in and out before people arrive, no? Also we have to buy you clothes."

She makes a face, groans, gets off the bed.

"You promised," he says.

She hobbles to the new television set and strokes it. She smiles at him. "Even if I hadn't," she says, "I'd have to do it now, wouldn't I?" The smile goes. She opens a dresser drawer, takes a small brown folder out of it. "You can't afford gifts like that. You let me write you a check."

"You're forgetting, I'm a big star now. Us big stars give away television sets all the time." He goes to her, takes the checkbook, drops it back into the drawer, closes the drawer. "Come on—talk to me while I fix lunch."

She catches his arm. "No. You're always drudging for me in that kitchen. Today, we eat lunch out." She is feeling better for sure, isn't she? She is feeling wonderful. She is beside herself with how good she feels. She hates to eat in public. "Furthermore," she says, "I will pick up the check."

He cocks a skeptical eyebrow. "And you won't try to get out of shopping?"

"Cross my heart"—she makes the solemn childhood gesture—"and hope to die."

That her clothes are worn, raveled, faded, shabby isn't alone what makes them pathetic. They are too big; they hang on her. The disease has turned her from a pudgy little woman to a fragile child. An old child, spooked no more by imaginary fears but by real fears, so that the horrors department stores have forever given her she passes off now, as she limps beside him between towering refrigerators, gleaming stoves, washer-dryer pairs, toward the boys' department, passes off with a wry laugh. "God, how I hate the smell of these places. It makes me want to turn and run."

" 'Courage, mon amie,' " Jewett quotes from a book they loved together as children, The Cloister and the Hearth, " 'le diable est mort.' "

"I certainly hope so," she says, and peers up at him pleadingly. "Shoes, too?"

"Look at those. Absolutely, shoes. What's wrong? Your socks have holes in them?"

She drops into a chair in the shoe section. "You threw all of those out," she says grumpily.

It is the boys' department because this is where she can find clothes to fit. And the boys' size that fits her now is smaller than ever. Still, when she has put on the dark blue corduroy suit with the brass buttons, the light blue wool shirt, the very small blue suede shoes, she looks better, trim instead of starved and sick. Her eyes, so magnified by the glasses, seem bright as a boy's. She looks almost pleased at her appearance in the tall mirrors, almost lets show a streak of vanity like her mother's, like her brother's. He wanders off, so she won't see him grinning. When she is paying for the clothes and isn't looking, he finds a dark blue corduroy cap for her and pays for it at another counter. He will probably have to force it on her. Caps on women are stylish right now, and she wouldn't want to look stylish. But she surprises him. She is delighted, and keeps peering into the side mirror of the car, setting the cap at a more and more rakish angle, as they breeze along the sunshiny freeway toward Los Angeles and lunch.

Armie Akmazian wears seersucker today, in deference to the heat. The rolled collar of his forest-green shirt, the broad knot of his apple-green tie are soaked with sweat, discolored by it. His smooth blue jowls gleam with sweat, and he mops his face and the back of his fat neck with a large, apple-green handkerchief that has no dry inch left. It isn't the weather alone that has him in a sweat. His plans are running late. The catalogs have not been delivered. And around him, a scant hour before the exhibit is to be previewed by journalists from near and far, youths on stepladders still paint the high walls and partitions of the gallery's front room with sheepskin rollers. The smell of paint is strong.

"I can't apologize enough." He holds Susan's elbow so that she won't stumble and fall on the paint-spotted gray tarpaulins that lie rumpled underfoot. "I thought there was ample time, ample. But you can't count on people anymore. They give you their word, and then where are they? What's time to them?"

But under high, flat, shadowless fluorescent light, the farther rooms of the gallery show that he exaggerates. He is only working off excitement and anxiety. The farther rooms are perfect. Against the flawless whiteness of their walls, Susan's great, dark, rugged fabrics brood in silence, like eternal truths, ancient, ineluctable. Jewett has only seen one hung before—the one in the Tate. Their size alone is daunting, and in such numbers, their emotional power stuns him. He thought he knew her, was closer to her than anyone on earth. He has never known her, not till this moment. These vast, knotty rectangles, with their mysterious overlaps, like strata from the boiling and tormented crust of earth on its first day, show him as they will soon show a world of strangers, a mortal story, tragic, courageous, sometimes breaking out in savage laughter—those unsettling, snaggly braids of brilliant crimson that he never understood till now.

He is struck dumb. Thank God, Akmazian keeps talking, talking. Jewett looks at Susan, who has fashioned these tremendous slabs of anguish, and has to look away and fight back tears. He bends and pretends to examine the cards behind small plates of beveled Plexiglas, cards that identify the works. Akmazian has been busy. The hangings come not just from "Collection of the Artist," which means from the dark, cobwebby garage, the bedrooms of the dead and lost on Deodar Street, but from Denmark, Finland, Paris, Berlin, London, Rome, from Japan, even from Australia. Can people really hang these things in rooms in which they live their daily lives? What kind of people can they be—impervious to pain?

He turns to ask Akmazian a question, but Akmazian has fled. He can be heard whooping and clapping his hands, hastening the painters on their way. Jewett resumes studying the little cards. He can't look at the hangings—not here, alone with her. They reproach him. Yes, he's doing the best he can for her. Now, when his best is pathetically too little and too late. What about those seven years after Lambert's death? He tells himself it's no good regretting. It can't be helped. But he does regret—bitterly. And she has woven her loneliness into her work and he can't face it. She is watching him. She stands in the middle of the farthest room, where a long table glitters with bottles and glasses beneath the largest, somberest, most neolithic of the hangings.

"Well, what do you think?" she calls.

He summons a smile. "It's overwhelming," he says.

She comes titling toward him. "We'd better go. I don't want to be trapped here. I don't want them taking my picture."

"They'll do it eventually," he says. "Why not get it over today? That way, they won't come swarming around the house, invading your privacy." She has reached him. He takes her arm, skin and bone through the thick fabric of jacket and shirt. "I'm serious. You look nice today. Susan, these things you've made are marvelous. People are going to want to know about the woman who made them. You can't hide—not any longer. It's your moment in the sun. Why not relax and enjoy it?"

"You'd enjoy it, wouldn't you?" She teeters along beside him through the wide, white rooms hung with her misery and greatness. "It's the breath of life to you, having your picture taken, being the center of attention." She gives him a teasing, sidelong smile. "I don't suppose I can bribe you into putting on a dress and wig and pretending to be me."

"God would strike me dead," he says, and means it.

"Oh, hell," she says. "Here they come."

He is, of course, having his own moment in the sun. His picture is often taken. He is often the center of attention. Within hours of his signing the contract with Ziggy, the network publicity machinery began to hum. He is, if not relaxed, resigned. He is certainly not enjoying it. Bill is enjoying it. Feverishly. He comes home each night from the shop, smelling of sweat and shellac, bright-eyed, grinning with eagerness to learn who has interviewed Jewett on the set between takes or at lunchtime, photographed him, put his image on videotape, his voice on audiotape, for what telecast, what radio report, who has taken notes for what magazine, what newspaper. Jewett, busy fixing dinner, his cues and lines for tomorrow's shooting repeating themselves from a flat, black cassette recorder propped against the red can opener, script lying open on a counter where he can peer at it from time to time—Jewett has humored Bill, told him all he asked to know. But he has lately tired of the game.

"Bill, who cares?" he says. "It's meaningless."

"What are you talking about?" Bill is always, at this time, on his way to the shower, and always does his undressing in the kitchen while Jewett reports or avoids reporting. Now he stands with his shirt dangling from a grubby hand. "It means everything. The whole country wants to read about you. Sixty million people watch that show every week. They don't give a fuck about the presidential campaign. They don't give a fuck about Iran. 'Timberlands' is all they care about. What do you mean, it's meaningless?"

Jewett stops the cassette machine. "Bill, it could have been twenty other actors. It's got nothing to do with me. What have I done to deserve it? It was an accident. Blind, crazy luck. Ziggy Fogel is angling for sainthood."

"He owed you!" Bill cries.

"If you say so." Jewett lifts the lid off a double boiler and with a wooden spoon gently stirs hollandaise sauce. "It still had nothing to do with acting ability. On that tacky show, nobody needs acting ability."

"Okay, so what are you mad at yourself for?"

"I'm not mad at myself." Wearily, Jewett raps the handle of the spoon on the edge of the double boiler, lays the spoon on a square of aluminum foil on the stove top, and replaces the lid over the sauce. "But I'm not fooling myself either. The network is blowing me up like a balloon. Bill, those sixty million morons won't be seeing me on 'Timberlands' for a month yet. What the hell kind of celebrity does that make me?"

"You paid your dues." Bill kicks out of ragged shorts, torn-off Levi's. He is wearing tiny red briefs. Jewett feels a flicker of lust. Bill's body never bores him. "It's time you collected big, after all those years of nobody paying any attention."

"The network is terrified they're going to lose viewers because of Judd Norton's death. They're using me to make them forget." Jewett snorts a laugh. "I wish them luck."

Bill regards him with disgust. He opens his mouth to continue the argument, but instead says, "I'm going to take my shower. Then we can have a drink. You'll feel better after you've had a drink." He carries his clothes off down the hall, calling back, "I don't know why you always want to spoil my fun."

Jewett knows. He wants to put Bill in the wrong because he, Jewett, is really in the wrong. He has said nothing to Bill about the bakery. This is contemptible. He is scared to death of how Bill will react. He hasn't the guts to face him with the truth. So he keeps up this badgering. What difference does Bill's childish excitement make, what harm does it do anyone? Maybe he's right. Maybe Jewett does deserve to be a star. Considering the number of them these days, all created in exactly the same way as Jewett is being created, out of ballyhoo, why should he mind? It's the system. It has nothing to do with him. And yet, and yet. Frowning, he leafs over the pages of the script. He can't dismiss his disappointment. This wasn't what he dreamed of as the pinnacle of his career. And he is back at square one again. It was all a mistake. His whole lifetime. We get what we deserve. He is right about the bakery. Somehow, he has got to make Bill see that. And his heart sinks at the prospect. He closes the script on the counter top and washes the asparagus under the cold tap at the sink.

Ten years ago, when Bill's abilities weren't yet celebrated, he sometimes went for weeks, even months, without work. Jewett didn't mind. He was earning enough to keep both of them fed, clothed, and out of the rain. He had to quit buying the best groceries, liquor, wine. They couldn't afford to see every show that came to town, every new film released. They couldn't afford restaurants, not often. But Bill had never known the best and didn't miss it. And so far as Jewett was concerned, Bill was the best and he needed nothing more.

But Bill fretted. He didn't like living off anyone. Dolan lived off others. And whatever Dolan was, Bill wanted to be the opposite. The instinct was good, Jewett admired it, but it made for some unhappy arguments. Bill would come home in despair after a day's job hunting in Jewett's car—he didn't have one of his own then. And he would try to move out, ashamed of not being able to pay his half of the rent and the food bill. He gave in to Jewett, who used every tool of logic and emotion he could muster, but he grew steadily more restless and disgusted with himself.

Jewett was sure that if things didn't change for Bill, he would leave. So one Saturday, Jewett got him into the car, and they prowled junk shops, searching for a piece Bill could restore on his own to show the decorators what he could do. Two or three hours of breathing dust and brushing cobwebs off his face with hands that smelled of mildew were enough for Jewett. But not for Bill. Each time they returned to the car, he snatched up the yellow phone book from the seat and doggedly leafed the pages over to find another place to look.

And toward sundown, on a street of grimy-windowed warehouses, in a shadowy back room, he found what he wanted. It lurked, as if ashamed, in a corner behind a stack of cheap 1920s dining-room chairs, a slumping collection of rolled-up bamboo blinds, and three rusty lawn mowers. A heap of moth-eaten Spanish shawls half covered it. Jewett couldn't really make it out, but Bill was excited, gleeful, eager. He began taking down the pile of chairs. "Wheel those damn mowers someplace, will you?"

Jewett tried. The wheels wouldn't turn. He carried first one, then another, then the third, and left them blocking a cross-aisle at their backs. Bill pushed the musty shawls into his arms. Jewett heaved them to the top of a mountain of grubby rugs. No shopkeeper came to protest. Jewett wondered if there was a shopkeeper. Bill wiped at the dirt on his discovery with a jacket sleeve. Lovingly, crooning. Jewett was appalled.

"You can't do anything with that."

"Cherrywood," Bill said. "Chippendale. Early nineteenth-century American. It's gorgeous." He was on his knees, gently trying to open the drawers. When he looked up at Jewett, his eyes shone. "It's a masterpiece."

"It's a wreck," Jewett said. He saw cracks, warping, he saw clamp marks, chisel gouges, paint-can rings. The finish was a crusted century of dirt. "Some yahoo used it for a workbench."

"It's all here." Bill got to his feet. "That's all that matters. Come on, help me move it."

"Bill, it's too far gone," Jewett said.

"You too?" Bill edged in beside a golden oak tabletop like the one on long-ago Deodar Street, and got a grip on the desk. He heaved, and the desk stuttered on the cement floor. "I thought you believed in me."

"It would take a miracle," Jewett said.

"Okay—I'll give you a miracle," Bill said. "But first we have to get it out of here."

They got it out of there. It cost Jewett twenty dollars. It cost Bill weeks of work, sometimes late into the night. He was obsessed, driven, but happy all the time. With tenderness and caution he dismantled the grubby old hulk. The warped panels had to be soaked and slowly flattened with gradually increased weights. The grime on all the surfaces, the cracked glue in joins and dovetails, slowly came away. No archaeologist could have worked more patiently than Bill, more reverently. The old varnish was stripped, the naked wood planed and sanded to remove the dents and gouges. The guest room was the wood-shop, and the whole apartment reeked of paint remover, hot glue, linseed oil. At moments, Jewett wished he hadn't thought of the project. He doubted that it would ever end. But the day arrived at last when the old desk stood on its grubby, rumpled underfoot of newspapers, glowing sleek and smooth and perfect as the day it was hauled off on a horse cart from Thomas Seymour's Boston cabinet shop in 1811—Bill had traced its provenance.

Photos taken before, during, and after were the proof he had needed. It got him the jobs he wanted. It humbled Jewett. He hadn't been at all sure that this twenty-two-year-old gypsy kid was much more than brag when it came to the craft he claimed. But he had given Jewett the promised miracle. He was offered startling money for the desk. He wouldn't part with it. It meant, it means, something special to him. And it stands in the guest room now, its elegantly bowed drawers heavy with old theater programs, scrapbooks of clippings, photographs and lobby cards, movie magazines—anything ever printed about Oliver Jewett, and not just from Bill's time with him but almost from the ancient start. Bill is a tireless plunderer of secondhand bookstores and thrift shops, where he will sit by the hour, cross-legged on the floor, thumbing tattered pages. He has mastered the intricacies of the microfilm systems in the periodicals rooms of libraries. With an education, he would have made a fine researcher. As it is, he is a magpie, a pack rat, not a collector but an accumulator. No matter how often a movie with Jewett, a series episode with Jewett shows up on television, no matter how obscure the channel, how inaccessible the hour, the *TV Guide* describing it goes into a drawer of the desk.

"The descriptions are always the same," Jewett says.

"The dates are different," Bill says.

Long ago, Jewett let Bill watch these reruns, even made believe he enjoyed them himself, when the truth was they depressed him for days afterward. Finally, he began arranging nights out keyed to those pernicious listings. Bill was upset.

"But it's your 'Starsky and Hutch' tonight."

"Bill, you've seen it. Half a dozen times."

"Four times," Bill said.

"That's enough. Bill, my performance doesn't improve."

"It doesn't have to improve. It's fine. That's why I want to watch it. I want to see the look on your face when you taste that heroin and it's powdered sugar."

Jewett put on his jacket. "I'm going to the Bogart festival at the Nu Art." He picked up his keys and made for the door. "You watch 'Starsky and Hutch' by yourself."

"I hate that. If I wanted to watch TV by myself, I'd live by myself. When you're not here, I just turn it off."

"Good. Now I know I'm going." Jewett pulled upon the door.

"Shit. Okay. Wait. I'm coming with you."

But the scene repeated itself for years. It still does, now and then. And Jewett fears worse is coming. For a long while now he has watched glumly as video recorders grow cheaper. One of these days, Bill will wake up to the realization that he can collect not just paper and print about Jewett's old movies and television segments, but the movies and segments themselves. This is why Jewett said nothing about the Betamax Larry danced to that hot afternoon in the bare Haycock living room in the Valley. He dreads the day when some family outrage too awful to ignore drags Bill out there. Unless the store has reclaimed it, or Dolan has hocked or sold it, Bill will see it, and understand that you don't have to be rich to own one. Then he will insist on viewing all those meaningless moving images of Jewett speaking all those meaningless and unmoving lines yet again, so as to preserve them in a drawer of the desk, from whose darkness and silence he can bring them whenever he likes, to look at, years after Jewett himself lies in a darkness and silence from which nothing and no one can bring him—not even Bill, who wants company when he watches TV.

Jewett lays the slim asparagus spears in half an inch of water in a pan, dots them with chips of butter, covers the pan, and sets it over a low fire. Bill, smelling of soap and steam, and dressed in a very tight white T-shirt and clean jeans whose blue has faded with years of wear and that fit him like a second skin, stands at the breakfast bar to pick up his martini. Jewett pours it for him into a frosted glass, rubs the rim of the glass with a curl of lemon peel, drops in the lemon peel, hands Bill the glass. He fixes a martini for himself, returns the pitcher to the refrigerator, sips at the martini, whose taste makes him very happy not to be shut up just yet in darkness and silence, peers under the lid at the hollandaise sauce to make sure it isn't curdling, then follows Bill into the living room.

He starts a Brahms piano sonata on the turntable, sits down with a sigh, puts his feet up, lights a cigarette. Bill stands at a delicate Sheraton sewing table by the door, where Jewett always lays the day's mail. Bill sorts indifferently through the white envelopes, and comes to his chair with the brown-wrapped *TV Guide*. Jewett never opens it. Bill sits down, tears off the wrapper, lets it fall to the rug, and parts the pages. He stiffens, frowns, blinks, says aloud, "What?" slaps the magazine closed again, and stares at the cover. He breaks into a smile. He laughs. He looks at Jewett. "You sneaky bastard. Look at that." He flaps the fat little magazine. "You're on the cover of *TV Guide*." He jumps out of the chair with a war whoop, and spins around the room, holding the magazine aloft like a prize scalp. He stops. His eyes shine. "You never told me. You knew, and you didn't say a word. Look at that." Breathless, he pushes the magazine into Jewett's hands. "Look. It's you."

"With Ellen van Sickle and Archie Wakeman," Jewett says. "Who are in the foreground. I am in the background. The man nobody knows."

"Read, why don't you?" Bill sits on the arm of Jewett's chair and runs a shaky finger under the caption. "See what it says? 'New boss of "Timberlands." Actor Oliver Jewett.' " Jewett grunts, and Bill snatches the magazine and turns pages, fast, almost tearing them in his hurry. "Here," he says. "See? Pictures of you, no one but you, color pictures. And all this write-up. Look, three pages. All about Oliver Jewett. Hey, these pictures were taken here. That's you in the kitchen."

" 'Old auntie whips up spinach soufflé,' " Jewett says.

"Will you stop that?" Bill slaps him on the head with the

magazine. "God damn it, this is wonderful. I'll bet people have been phoning up all day, haven't they?"

"One or two," Jewett says. There were nineteen, some with voices he hadn't heard in years, some with names he scarcely remembered. These hadn't wanted to know an actor who stood in line at the unemployment office. But everybody wants to know a star. He is going to have to change the telephone number and keep it out of the directory. "Your drink's getting warm."

Bill returns to his chair, tastes the martini, starts to read the article, looks up. "Don't you think you ought to give a party?"

Jewett smiles. "How about Sunday?"

St. Barnabas is smaller and dowdier than he remembers. The street has been widened and almost crowds the steps. In the narrow margin of lawn remaining, dandelions have gone to fluff, and big milkweeds die against the mossy foundations. Like most of the oldest buildings in town, the church is sided in thick shingles, weathered now, discolored. The gilt lettering of the black signboard is tarnished. The minister's name is strange to him. He pulls open the right-hand leaf of the pair of heavy doors and the smell of the cool air inside takes him back, a sweet, chaste, waxy smell he cannot name. Church, it says, church. It doesn't bring memories, only feelings, and he has no name for those either, but they tug at him. He holds the door so Bill can come into the vestibule, and he shuts the door. The light is dim. But the vestibule has not changed. There is a bell in the short wooden tower directly overhead. The bell rope is wrapped around a cleat in a center post. On a long oak table pamphlets are arranged in racks. These were black enameled metal as Jewett remembers them. They have been replaced by clear plastic. The pamphlets themselves are brighter in color. There used to be rather a bad color print of St. Barnabas on the wall facing the door above the table. It is gone. A crucifix hangs there now.

"Catholic?" Bill says.

"Episcopalian," Jewett says, and pushes the swing doors at the head of the center aisle, and knows at once what the smell is composed of—cut flowers and candles. Women in jeans, their hair covered by scarfs, are arranging flowers on the altar. The flowers they have not yet used stand in plastic buckets on the altar steps. The women are chatting, laughing. The sound is loud and echoes among the empty pews. They have heard the clack-clack of the doors through which Jewett and Bill have come, and they pause to look for a second or two. One calls:

"May we help you?"

"Just looking," Jewett says, "thanks." He is startled by the women's clothes. To his mother's set, pants would have been unthinkable in this place, for this task. They wore smocks, but under them they dressed up. "My mother was always a member of the Altar Guild," he tells Bill.

Bill runs a hand along a pew back and frowns. "You can't treat beautiful wood like this. Bet it hasn't been varnished in ten years. And the last time"—he bends for a closer look—"they didn't even sand it first."

Jewett moves down the aisle, under the high rafters, the pitched roof, between the stained-glass windows. Here and there, bits of colored glass are missing, have been replaced by cardboard dyed ugly by rain. He used to be vain about the windows. They were better than those of any other church in town. A famous artisan had been brought from Austria to make them. He knew the name once. He has forgotten it.

What he remembers now is how sad he was at Richie Cowan's funeral. The cheap little stucco Evangel Church, so new the ground around it was still raw dirt, had windows that looked not like glass at all but like panels of rusty tin. The congregation sat on folding chairs. There was no organ, only a jangly upright piano, and the hymns sounded like ragtime. The minister wore a wrinkled business suit. Jewett supposed it was what Richie was used to, but he deserved better. Jewett couldn't stop staring at those dismal windows and thinking how bleak the place was. In a life as short as Richie's, couldn't his church at least have been beautiful? He says to Bill, "I was an altar boy when I was thirteen, fourteen."

"What's that?" Bill scuffs worriedly at the aisle carpeting that is worn down to the backing. "Oh, yeah. You hand stuff to the priest, and kneel a lot."

"And light the candles," Jewett says, "and put the candles out at the end, with a brass candle snuffer on the end of a long pole. The first time, I was so nervous it took forever. Everybody was sitting out here coughing, waiting for me to finish so they could leave. I damn near knocked the candelabra over."

"You wore robes," Bill says, "and looked like an angel, right?"

"I thought so," Jewett says. "There were a lot of cottas on the racks, always freshly washed and ironed. I tried to get the one with the most lace. And I was never late. The first service was at seven in the morning, but even if it was raining, I was always on time. I had to come on my bike, and I got soaked, but I got here."

"There was an audience, wasn't there?" Bill grins. He drops the grin and tilts his head. "Why are we here?"

"I'm showing you my childhood," Jewett says. "Come on. There's more." He climbs the aisle in long strides, not wanting Bill to ask him why he is showing him his childhood. It is a stratagem, and he is a little ashamed of it. He means to exploit Bill's sentimental streak. Bill is in a good mood. The party on Sunday made him happy. Canny Jewett saw to that. He rounded up every celebrity he could, and particularly urged Archie Wakeman to bring his mother, who in the thirties and forties was a star of Broadway musicals—the kind of star beside whom today's performers look like twenty-watt light bulbs. So, to his interior-decorator friends, Bill was able to show off not only Jewett, but the fabled Mamie Wakeman. For once, they gave up all thought of being queens themselves. They were ladies-in-waiting and loving it. Not a shriek was uttered. They fetched and carried. They sat at her feet, murmuring adoration, while she left lipstick stains on her champagne glass. It was the best party Bill had ever been to. That's what he said, and Jewett thought he meant it. He hoped it would hold Bill for a long time. He hopes it will hold him forever. He pushes open the door at the head of the aisle and turns. "When you bury me," he says, "make it from here, all right? And ask the padre to use the old prayer book, not the new one. The old one has beautiful language."

Bill shows shock, and Jewett hastens to smile. Bill's face clears. He steps past Jewett into the vestibule, saying in the voice of a tired comedian, "Why would I bury you? You're still breathing. Heh-heh."

"Heh-heh," Jewett says, and pushes out the big door into sunlight already beginning to feel hot. Under a shingled overhang, the parish-house door is locked.

"What's in there?" Bill stands at the foot of the steps, squinting up at him, sun in his eyes. "Oh—the radio station—that's right."

Jewett comes slowly down the steps. "Where Joey Pfeffer and I kept trying to sound like Orson Welles and Westbrook van Voorhees." He starts for the car.

"Westbrook van Who?"

" 'The March'," Jewett says in a stentorian voice, " 'of Time!' " They are passing a supermarket parking lot, where a stout woman in a muumuu, unloading sacks from a shopping cart into the back of a monster station wagon, looks up, startled, then smiles. But she has gray hair. Bill only looks blank. Jewett says with faint hope of being understood, "A famous radio announcer?"

With a sad shake of his head, Bill gets into the car. Jewett sighs, and drives off to try to find the grammar school and can't find it. He knows the streets, he is certain he knows the streets. He walked them hundreds of times on small-boy legs, rode them hundreds of times on his bicycle. He remembers with timeworn pride his sixth-grade stint as a crossing guard, wearing the cap and armband, holding the Stop sign, shepherding the little kids across, between the broad white lines of the pedestrian walk. Here. Right here. The filling station with the corner pepper tree still stands. But the school has vanished. In its place stretches a shopping mall.

"I can't show you where I first performed on stage," he says. "They've torn down the school. I was George Washington. Purple satin coat, ruffles at my chin, knee britches, buckles on my shoes. My mother made me a wig out of a silk stocking sewed with angel hair—you know, the curly white spun stuff they put on Christmas trees?" He glances at Bill. Bill plainly does not know. Bill's experience of Christmas trees is scant. "Fiber glass," Jewett says. "The itching nearly drove me crazy."

"How old were you?" Bill says.

"Six. It was a nice school." He remembers brown corridors that smelled of the oily red sawdust the janitor sprinkled on the thick linoleum before he began to push his wide, silent mop. There was never bright sun in the chalk-smelling classrooms. There was tree shade, and the green of trees to look at out the windows. He regards the dapple of leaf shadow on the roofs of cars aligned in the parking lot, the dapple of tree shade on the neat, new, flat-roofed shops. "I'm glad they kept the trees."

"The light's green," Bill says.

The high school is still there. Junipero Serra High School. He parks on the far side, where a chain-link fence under those big trees guards the playing field. A gate hangs open. A Little League team in yellow and green uniforms is playing another in red and white uniforms on a dusty corner diamond. Jewett leads Bill across the field, whose grass is a springy mat still green. He stops, frowns back at the bleachers, takes some lateral steps to get himself positioned.

"Here," he says. "Right here. This is where Richie Cowan died. Ran head-down into another boy and broke his neck. It was scrub football. Practice."

"You told me," Bill says.

"I wanted you to see," Jewett says. "It was supposed to be over at four. I'd been waiting for him. After he showered, I used to walk him home, and we'd jack off together. He didn't have a sister. Nobody home."

"You always say you hate remembering," Bill says.

"I dream about it," Jewett says, and turns away.

The music building is far from the rest, across wide lawns where old trees cast cool shade. The music building is wooden instead of pale brick like the others. Jewett steps up on the porch. Beside the door are posters about student musical events, an orchestra concert, an operetta, both past now. Summer term is over, fall term not yet begun. A band-recruitment announcement is tacked to the door. The door is locked. Jewett comes down the steps and leads Bill around to the side of the building, under feathery jacarandas. He peers through windows. The room is bare as ever, chairs scattered, music racks, a baby grand piano, and, signs of the times, loudspeakers, amplifiers, and what at a guess is an electronic keyboard in its case on thin metal legs. Bill has to crane to see in at the window.

"Don't tell me," he says. "This is where you and Richie Cowan sang in the glee club. This is where he got you thinking about sex."

"I wanted you to see it," Jewett says again.

At the top of the wide, shallow cement steps of the auditorium building, doors stand open. The air of the hallway, with its high, sunny, steel-frame windows, smells of paint. Somewhere out of sight, spray guns hiss. A stepladder leans outside an open classroom door, paint cans gathered around its feet. Jewett pushes open an auditorium door. The paint smell is strong here, too. The houselights are on, and steel-pipe scaffolding laid with planks rises along both high side walls. The big, somber figures of monks in brown robes and Indians in brown skins have been painted out—murals of events in the life of Father Serra. The walls are plain sand color now.

He walks down the sloping aisle and leans elbows on the dusty apron of the stage. "I had to wait two semesters," he says, "watching. They wouldn't let you act in your first year. I was dying to be up there with paint on my face and the lights shining on me. Dying. There was a senior play about some

Britishers holed up in a fort in India or something. The boys wore kilts, tam-o'-shanters, and tartans. I died of envy. Of course, everyone would have laughed when I opened my mouth. I had a high, sweet soprano voice. But I never thought of that. My public-speaking teacher loved my voice, and when I came back the next fall, and it had changed, she was so put out she wouldn't speak to me. As if it was my fault."

Bill laughs and shakes his head. He is being patient. Jewett doesn't want to try his patience, and takes him away from the school. They drive toward the foothills. In the foothills, he drives along side streets, some still with the old, low-roofed houses, some with the new apartment buildings.

"This was my newspaper route. The Cordova Courier. An hour and a half, two hours, every morning. It only paid a few dollars a week, but in those times a few dollars meant something. My father had clients, but not many of them could pay. Most of them were ranchers. We got free eggs and milk. One of them paid in limes and honey. Nineteen thirty-five—that was the summer. I've never liked limes or honey since."

"Are you trying to tell me you were poor?" Bill says.

"Not you, Bill," Jewett says. "Not you." Bill is turning grim and Jewett tries to make him smile. "Delivering those damned papers, I used to scare myself, when it was dark and nobody was awake but me. I'd imagine werewolves and walking mummies and the Frankenstein monster hiding in the shadows, waiting to jump out and grab me. There weren't as many streetlights then, and there were more trees. Sometimes I'd get so terrified I couldn't move. I'd stand at a corner, right in the middle of the intersection under the light, till I heard the rattle of bottles in a milk truck and I was sure somebody'd hear me if Dracula swooped down on me and I yelled for help."

Bill does not smile. "You're talking a lot," he says. "What are you so nervous about?"

"I want you to like it here," Jewett says. "I want it to mean to you what it means to me. Just give me a few more minutes, all right?"

Bill regards him poker-faced, without comment, and Jewett

drives back down out of the hills to Main Street. His plan isn't working. It might, if he really cared all that much for the place, did cherish the memories. He doesn't. And Bill senses that. Bill knows him. But Jewett can't think of anything to do but go straight on. He has put this day off too many times, put off telling the truth, and he is growing sick about it. Main Street is not busy, and they cruise it slowly in the car. He tells Bill about the Gray Shop, the public library, the Fiesta.

"Once my mother won a set of dishes on keno night. I can't think how. We avoided keno night. She wouldn't have said anything. But Susan was holding the tickets and she shouted. She was thrilled. My mother was only embarrassed. Other people needed the luck more than she did—she had a job, she was a teacher, and everyone knew it. She wouldn't have kept them anyway—they were terrible dishes, cheap junk. She gave them to the rummage sale at church."

He points out a store where kitchen appliances gleam white in the show window. "That was Roosevelt election headquarters in 1932. My father was the local campaign chairman. I passed out handbills. It didn't make me popular. They were mostly Republicans here then, retired people, not rich but comfortable. One woman told me my father ought to be put in jail, making his little boy distribute Communist propaganda."

Bill smiles, but only with his mouth. His eyes are distrustful. Jewett parks in front of Pfeffer's bakery. Bill doesn't ask why. He regards the shiny front of the bakery, the breads and cakes in the window, the cheerful sign. His jaw moves. He is working his tongue in a back tooth, but Jewett is afraid it isn't a toothache that makes him frown. Jewett's heart thuds and the sweat he breaks into isn't from the growing heat of the sun as it climbs toward noon. He is anxious, and his hand trembles as he switches off the ignition. He opens the door and hardly recognizes his voice, saying to Bill, "Come on."

Bill looks at his watch. "Your sister will be wondering where we are. I know. This is where you and Joey Pfeffer worked together those summers before the war. I don't have to see it."

Jewett gets out of the car. "You'd better see it." He shuts the door, steps into a pool of tree shadow on the sidewalk, and cranks a coin into the parking meter. Resignedly, Bill climbs out of the car and slouches to join him, hands in pockets. Jewett takes his arm and turns him to face the bakery. He draws a deep breath, smiles, and says, "I'm buying it, Bill. I have the money now, and I'm buying it. I told you I would if I could. The title's being cleared, the papers are being drawn up. I've put down earnest money. Next month we'll close the deal."

Bill stares at him, mouth open. "You can't," he says. "What about the apartment? I thought when you got money, you'd buy the apartment. I told you—" He lets the argument go. Anger takes over from surprise. He knocks Jewett's hand away. He stares at the bakery. "Are you crazy? You've hit the top." He peers into Jewett's face, bewildered, outraged. "You're going to quit acting now? Now? You're going to quit acting and be a goddamn baker, for Christ sake?"

"Just as soon as I can," Jewett says. "Don't look so heartbroken. You'll get used to it."

September

JEWETT LIFTS from the coffee table the latest chrysanthemum plant and carries it to the kitchen. He lays a rubber stopper over the drain and lets cold water trickle into the sink while he removes the blue foil wrapping from the plastic pot. He turns off the tap and sets the pot in the shallow water so the roots can drink. The leaves show signs of drooping, and it is too soon: Mrs. Fairchild came and went only days ago. Jewett crumples the foil, drops it into the waste basket under the sink, shuts the under-the-sink door, and starts for the living room again.

Susan calls out, "Sure you don't want my help?"

He stops, backtracks, looks in at her door. She lies on the bed, neat in a new blue gingham shirt and new blue jeans, and watches the television set, where a bearded man and a man without a beard sit leaning toward each other from deep chairs, conversing in slow, earnest tones about a book one of them has written. Jewett says, "You get time off for good behavior." All morning, she shopped with him, hardly grumbling at all. "Seriously—you get all the rest you can. That flight tomorrow will be very tiring. They pack you in like sardines."

"I'm smaller than you," she says.

"You'll have Akmazian beside you," Jewett says, "and people like Akmazian overflow into any available space. Airline seats were not designed for hippos."

"I'll be fine," she says. "I'm looking forward to it." She nods at the television screen. "Can you see me sitting in one of those chairs? My feet won't touch the floor."

Jewett blinks at the set. "Is he interviewing you?"

"I'm watching to see how much he helps his guests. I'll be tongue-tied, I know I will." They both watch and listen for a moment. Then she says, "Can you see anything from so high up?"

"Unless there are clouds," he says. "That's the part I like—being able to see the country below. It changes your perspective. Man doesn't amount to much. He's hardly made a mark on the planet. It really reaches you at night. A tiny cluster of lights in a vast, black emptiness—that's man. It's a lonesome sight."

"Maybe we'll fly back at night," she says. "You make it sound romantic."

"It's sobering," he says, and returns to the living room, the packages from the stores heaped on the couch, the new brown simulated-leather luggage waiting. He removes the price tags and little keys from the luggage, lays the first grip open on the coffee table, begins ripping open the bags and taking out the new clothes. He sorts and arranges these in a kind of order he hopes will prove sensible, laying outer clothing, trousers, jackets, sweaters, in the bottom, tucking shoes into corners, adding shirts, laying underwear and socks on them, and pajamas and robe last of all. With minor variations, he repeats the routine with the second grip. It can rain in New York in September, though he remembers it as often steamily hot, and he does not pack her new macintosh or the canvas hat, but lays these across the grips where he has set them next to the front door.

The clothes she will wear on the plane are those she is wearing now, with the addition of a light windbreaker jacket and a sweater in case of cold—he remembers a flight from London when something went wrong with the heating on the DC-10:

the air is polar at thirty thousand feet. She has had her hair cut. Comb, toothbrush, and the like are in a little leather kit she will carry on board. He has brought her a fat paperback novel to read. He does not have to worry about the plane tickets— Akmazian is in charge of those. All Jewett has to worry about is getting her to the airport on time. It's enough. She is like a small boy when it comes to waking up. Bed has always been her safe haven. She still hates to leave it. He will probably sleep badly, worrying about getting her started on time. It's a long drive to the airport from here.

But sleeping badly won't be a novelty. He wakes often these nights in the dark bedroom of the apartment at Mar Vista, and reaches out for Bill, who is not there. He knows Bill has left him. But when his conscious mind is asleep, some deeper part of him does not know, will not accept the change. Habits of ten years' duration are hard to break. Here in the living room on Deodar Street, the old clock ticking slowly behind him, the television voices murmuring from down the hall, he shrugs and tries to smile. Maybe he'll sleep better here. It won't be on the cramped couch this time, as it always was during those weeks when he drove Susan every morning to the medical center for treatment. It will be in his boyhood bed, where he never slept a night other than alone.

Until Akmazian's truckers hauled them away, those great, newspaper-wrapped bundles of Susan's weaving stuffed his room. Afterward, there was no need for him to sleep over, since Susan's chemotherapy was stopped. So not until this morning did he think to examine the bed. The mattress smelled of mildew. He dragged it out into the sunlight of the steep, weedy backyard, and left it there to air in the sun. When they got back from the shops, he turned it over. He had better check it now. He goes out through kitchen and back porch. The shadow of an acacia falls across it. He drags it into the sun again. He glances skyward, and judges there will be another hour of sun warm enough to help.

Susan has fallen asleep. He switches off the television set, goes back to the living room. For that hour, seated in a big leather armchair that was his father's and, handsomely reupholstered in red with brass nailheads, became Lambert's, and now is no one's, he studies his script. In this one, Jewett's sixth episode, his wicked nephew T.J. is dealing at a rough, backwoods café with a pair of transient loggers, shifty-eyed, unshaven young men, beer cans in their hands, a rifle racked inside the cab of their pickup truck. T.J. offers them five thousand dollars to kill his uncle and make it look like an accident. The bald, fat café owner overhears and rattles coins into the wall telephone to try to reach Jewett at the spacious Timberlands offices high in a new glass tower in the city, to warn him, but...With a groan of disgust, Jewett tosses the script away. He fetches broom and dustcloth, spray cleaner, carpet sweeper from the back porch, and cleans his old room. He drags the mattress back indoors, finds sheets and blankets, and makes the bed.

He enjoys the chance to cook supper for two again. Too often these days he skips supper, stands in the kitchen alone with his martini and tries to work himself up to cooking, and then forgets it. It's too much trouble. He has tried eating out, but that is desolating. He is losing weight. Scales are not needed to tell him—the way his clothes hang tells him, the changed notch in his belt. So now he pitches happily into sharpening an old butcher knife and cutting thin slices from a thick steak. He rinses and cuts up mushrooms. For Stroganoff. Susan likes it. And it is rich in calories. He is pleased to have a new argument to persuade her to eat tonight—that airline meals are meager. She does her best. He does his best too, but it doesn't amount to much. Seated across from her at the kitchen table, he has already begun to miss her. They see each other only once a week, now that her illness has let up, but they talk on the telephone most evenings, and knowing she is here, still here, comforts him. He isn't quite alone in the world. The weeks while she and her art are being celebrated in New York are going to seem long. It's a good thing he is working.

He sleeps so deeply, so wearily that it is she who wakes him. For a moment, time is out of joint. Leslie Howard watches him sorrowfully from the far wall. Jewett is sixteen again. That Susan's hair is white and her face webbed by age and illness doesn't register. She is his sister. He is at home. Something is wrong. This he takes in, and sits up sharply. "What's the matter?" he says, and then understands that it is 1980, that he is fifty-eight years old, and that she has a plane to catch. "What time is it?" He throws back the covers and swings his feet to the floor. His heart thumps. He rubs sleep from his eyes with thumb and finger.

"It's only a little after six," she says, "but you said we have to start early." She is all dressed, and smells of cleanliness and cologne. "Did you sleep? I couldn't sleep. And I didn't dare take a pill for fear of not waking up on time."

"You can sleep on the plane." He reaches for his robe at the foot of the bed. "Can you put the kettle on for coffee?" He pushes groggily into the sleeves of the robe, feels about on the floor for his slippers, and pushes his feet into them. Tying the robe, he heads for the bathroom. "I won't be long."

He lets her out of the car in front of the terminal with her little kit, her mac and rain hat and paperback book. He sets her bags at the curb. The airport parking lots are jammed. He will have to leave the car a long way off, and he doesn't want her to have to hobble that distance. "Wait for me on that bench there," he calls, and because the car behind him honks impatiently, leaves her looking a little bewildered among the crowds of those who will soon fly and those who have just flown, and the porters, black and Latino, and the mounds of luggage, and the carts piled high with luggage.

When he reaches the terminal again, Akmazian is with her. A gray coat with an astrakhan collar hangs over his arm. He wears a gray homburg, dark pinstripe suit, white shirt, knitted tie, and the clothes alter his personality. He is brief in his speech and so reserved and businesslike, Jewett hardly knows him. When they have found seats in the waiting room, where children run squealing among the rows of chairs on the thick carpet, where very young adults with backpacks and soft drinks camp out along the walls, where large parties of Japanese huddle together eating noodles from paper cups with plastic spoons, and huge Germans make loud demands at reservation counters—Susan goes off to the women's room. And Akmazian says to Jewett in a choked voice, "Susan mustn't know, but I'm terrified of flying. Absolutely terrified." While he says this, he is peering around, stretching his fat neck. "Ah, there's the bar. I've got to have a drink."

"It's eight in the morning," Jewett says.

Akmazian pats Jewett's hand and heaves his bulk out of the narrow chair. "Don't fret. We'll have champagne. I'll go ahead and order. You join me when Susan comes back. Champagne is just the thing for breakfast." And he sets off, parting the shoal of anxious travelers like a whale making its way through fry.

Jewett stands, worrying about Susan. He glimpses her far off, peering around through her thick lenses, looking lost and scared. He goes to rescue her. "You have caused Akmazian to prosper," he says, steering her back to their chairs. He takes up her kit and book, coat and hat. "He's afraid of flying, needs a drink, and decides on champagne. He wants us to join him in the bar. It's sweet when an agent is willing to share his wealth with you—and it's your money."

"Those things would still be gathering dust in the garage, in your room, Mama's room, if it weren't for him." Susan teeters along beside Jewett, letting him guide her by the arm. Even so, because she is so short, she is bumped into. People in air terminals seem always to be focused on objects in the distance and never what's in front of them. "Armie isn't the only one who's rich. Why couldn't it have happened twenty years ago?"

"I'm glad it's happened now," Jewett says. They are among the glass cases of the gift shop. He stops. "There's the bar, straight ahead." He points the near-empty room out to her, with its dark woodwork. "You join him. I'll be along in a minute."

It takes more than a minute. Akmazian has chosen a table far from the glass wall where one can watch the great sleek planes waiting or taxiing along distant, sun-white runways or lifting off. The table is in a shadowy corner. Plainly he doesn't want reminders of flying. His back is to the window. And he has been putting away champagne at a good clip. There is little more left in the bottle than will fill Jewett's glass, once he has settled and laid Susan's things on the empty chair. He lifts his glass to both of them and smiles. "Here's to great success in New York." Akmazian murmurs cheers, cheerlessly, and tosses down all that is in his glass. Susan takes what Jewett guesses to be her first sip. She eyes him curiously.

"What were you doing?"

He pokes a hand into his jacket pocket and brings out a silver medal by its chain. He works the catch and leans across and hangs the medal around her neck and fastens the catch. She takes it in her fingers, peering down at it, purblind, more than a little cross-eyed.

"A St. Christopher," Jewett says. "I want you to get there and come back to me safe and well."

She looks at him, still clutching the medal in her fingers. Color blooms in her old cheeks. It is hard to tell because of the glasses, but he thinks there are tears in her eyes. She works up a smile and a taunt. "I seem to remember you sneering at me for popish mumbo jumbo once upon a time."

"Nothing popish about St. Christopher," Jewett says. "Not anymore. The Catholics have dumped him."

Akmazian has gone off to the bar and come back with another bottle of champagne that smokes at its open mouth. He fills Jewett's glass, tops off Susan's, fills his own, sits down. He reaches across for a look at Susan's medal, lets it go, sits back, and regards Jewett coldly. "What about me? Expendable, am I?"

"You're her real St. Christopher," Jewett says. "I'm relying on you to look after her for me and deliver her home unharmed."

Akmazian grunts, sulkily gulps champagne, and will not look at Jewett and Susan. He averts his face. He keeps the wounded look, the silence of the offended child for a few beats.

Then he brightens, waves an airy hand, and with a blithe, dismissive smile says, "Never mind—I can always summon a magic carpet, can't I? If not, what's the point in being Armenian? And he sloshes more champagne into his glass.

This is Susan's second Saturday away and it is too lonely for him. He wishes "Timberlands" would do some location shooting. That way, he could work Saturdays too. But location shooting is past for this season. He ought to be thankful that the daily grind of child's play among the hot sets, those islands of blinding light in the vast and lofty gloom of the sound stages, often these days runs from seven in the morning until eleven at night. He is. The accumulated exhaustion from a week of such hours has made him sleep this morning away. But there is still too much empty time ahead. Without Susan. Without Bill. He is sitting up in bed, drinking coffee, smoking, pawing around in the newspaper, not taking in what he reads. The radio may be playing old show tunes. He doesn't hear. The so-called entertainment section of the paper slips from his fingers. He stares at the wall. For a while, he sees nothing. Then, slowly, the posters come into focus.

He throws back the bedclothes. Newspaper pages drift to the floor. He pulls on briefs and jeans and lifts the posters down. Flimsy in their own right, the glass and the frames Bill gave them lend them weight. One by one, panting and grunting a little, he carries them to the living room, carpet soft and cool under his bare feet. He leans the posters, brown paper backs outward, against the wall, as near the door as furniture allows. Back in the bedroom, pushing his feet into deck shoes, he notes that the wall is bleached in big rectangles where the posters hung. Has it been that long since the room was painted? He'll paint it tomorrow. That will take care of Sunday.

He lugs the posters out on to the gallery. The day is not bright. Clouds make a low gray ceiling. Off to the south they look almost black. Below in the patio the big floppy leaves of the landscaping seem fiercely green. No one uses the swimming pool. The damp air is chilly on his bare skin. He gets into a heavy pullover the color of the sheep that wore it first, then one by one carries the posters down to the street. He fetches the Toyota from its gloomy slot under the building, parks it at the red-painted curb in front of the apartment building, and lays the posters facedown in the trunk. They stick out, but not far enough to warrant flagging them. He hopes. He ties the lid down on them with the frayed twine still in the trunk from the day he hauled Susan's television set to her. He gives the sky another glance. Will it rain? Does it matter?

He can find only two cardboard cartons and those not big. He takes them to the guest room and opens the drawers of the beautiful old desk and from them shifts the magazines, scrap-books, envelopes of photos into the cartons. He stacks the cartons and carries them down to the car, empties them on the rear seat, carries the empty cartons up again for another load. And a third. There still remain some faded, dog-eared color lobby cards, held in packets by rotting rubber bands. When he has shrugged into a lightweight Windbreaker and checked that he has wallet, keys, cigarettes, lighter, he tucks the lobby cards under his arm, and leaves the apartment, rattling the door after him to be sure it is locked. Halfway along the gallery, he hesitates. He has not shaved. The hell with it.

The sky has darkened. On the cinderblock wall, the leaves of the bougainvillea shiver in a chill, brisk wind. A smell of rain is in the air. Jewett parks. The plank gate hangs open, swinging a little with the wind, knocking the wall. The wind swings the potted creepers strung from the patio beams and tosses the branches of the bottlebrush tree. He crosses the red tiles and takes two steps down to the back door of the shop. He pushes inside, where Bill, by the light of fluorescent tubes in a white enamel reflector, stands at a battered workbench running an electric sander that snarls along a mahogany tabletop. The air is foggy with the dust of old varnish. Jewett coughs. Bill switches off the sander and looks at him. He says:

"This is all I can do today. The air's too wet for anything else." Blinking, he waves a hand in front of his face to chase the dust. "What brings you here?"

"You should wear a surgical mask," Jewett says. "You'll get cancer, breathing that stuff."

"I'm used to it." Bill lights a cigarette. Around them, outside the dazzle of the workbench lights, dark heaps of old furniture loom up. The smell is of moldy plush and horsehair stuffing. There is scant room to move about. When Bill needs space to work in, he pushes the wreckage around, or piles it higher. "It doesn't bother me." He picks up his cigarette pack from the workbench and holds it out. "Smoke?"

Jewett shakes his head. "What brings me is that when somebody tells you good-bye and takes his clothes and razor and toothbrush but leaves something important behind, it's supposed to mean he isn't too sure of the move he's made, and he wants an excuse to come back."

"I took everything," Bill says. "How's the bakery?"

"In escrow, which means they have my money and I have patience. You left the posters. You left the desk full of magazines and clippings. It's been six weeks. I decided this morning that the psychology books are wrong. You're not coming back for them. So I brought them. If you give me your keys, I'll put them in your car."

"Don't put them in my car." Bill drops his cigarette to a cracked cement floor thick with shavings and sawdust. And cigarette butts. He steps on this one, which he has hardly smoked at all, twists his shoe on it, as if it had done something to him. He turns back to the bench and runs his hand on the stretch of wood he has sanded. It is rose color. Jewett is jealous of the wood. Bill says, "I don't collect stuff about bakers."

"You can sell them," Jewett says. "They cost you a lot of money, some of them."

Bill turns and shouts, "I don't care." Tears shine in his eyes. "I don't want to see them. I don't want to remember, all right? Can you understand that? No, you can't understand that. You can't understand anything. You never understood anything about me in your life." He turns his back. "Get out of here and leave me alone."

Jewett says quietly, "I want you to come back."

"Yeah, well, I'm not coming back." Bill picks up the sander and switches it on. Jewett stands for a few minutes, watching him work in the rising haze of dust, which shines in the light. Bill wears one of those old plaid cotton shirts he won't throw away, worn thin by too many washings, faded, out at the elbows. He has folded back the cuffs. The way his square brown hands hinge at the strong wrists is beautiful to Jewett, heartbreaking, the curve of his strong, smooth neck bent above his work. He yearns, he dreams. Bill's voice jars him awake. "So you might as well go."

"I don't know what you mean about understanding," Jewett says. "I love you. That ought to count for something."

The sander rasps along the tabletop.

"The furniture," Jewett says. "That's yours."

Bill switches off the sander, lays it aside, crouches to unfasten big, dark C-clamps that have held the tabletop to the workbench. He shifts the tabletop around on the bench, crouches and fastens the clamps again. He straightens up, takes the sander once more, switches it on, and goes to work with it.

Jewett says, "You're with Bo Kerrigan, right?"

"I'm not with anybody," Bill says. "If you don't get close to people, they can't hurt you."

"Do you want the apartment? I'll move out. You said you loved that apartment."

"That was before," Bill says.

Jewett sighs. "Bill, what's the good of this? You're not happy, I'm not happy. It doesn't make sense. Why throw away ten years?"

"It was the ten years that didn't make sense," Bill says. "Look, I'm busy. This is a rush job."

"It certainly is," Jewett says, and leaves.

On the Coast Highway, the rain falls in cold, gray, windblown sheets. The beach is deserted, glassy. Surf the color of sand sloshes the beach with high, hurtling waves. There is little traffic on the road. Jewett drives fast. He ought to turn back, but pain and despair are stronger in him than common sense. He scowls. Why can't he get past human habitations? When he was a kid, there was no need to drive so far, but now there seems no end to the buildings. Miles of empty beach separated Santa Monica from Malibu then. Now he is in Malibu without realizing it. Rocks are scattered on the pavement, washed down from the cliffs by the rain. He presses on, wheels throwing fans of water where the road dips and does not drain. Here is Zuma, and houses and restaurants where there was nothing in the old days.

It is miles before he finds emptiness. He slows the car, looking in the side mirror, which streams with rain. Down the road behind him, nothing drives but the rain. A tanker truck comes toward him in the southbound lane. It passes with a roar, rocking the Toyota, showering it with spray from its big tires. Then he has the highway to himself, crosses it, stops the Toyota on a shoulder, and turns off the engine. Beyond a guard rail, a low band of white painted steel on stocky posts, the drop to the beach is sharp but not high. He will be able to get down it all right. When the time comes.

He lights a cigarette, and sits and waits for the rain to stop. It will stop before long. It rarely rains this early in the fall. It can't be a big storm. It is a freak. He finishes the cigarette, draws out the dashboard ashtray, stubs the cigarette out, closes the ashtray. Through the streaming window, he watches the big waves break, foaming, on the sand, hears the crash and roar of the waves, feels the earth shake beneath the car from the weight of the waves. The window glass clouds over from his breath. He falls asleep.

The sun wakes him, glaring into his face, hot on his face through the glass. The rain has stopped. Only rags of cloud remain in a sky so blue it makes him wince. The surf is still high, but out beyond it, the ocean is blue and sparkling. On rough rocks that extend out into the surf, cormorants sun themselves, holding out their wings. Stiff from sleeping sitting up, he climbs out of the car into a wind off the ocean that blows his hair into his face. He stretches, then pushes his seatback forward, leans into the car, and takes out the first load of old magazines.

Clutching them in his arms, he peers down the short cliff for a path and, after a walk of a few yards, finds one. He steps awkwardly over the guard rail and, cautious because the path is wet, picks his way down to the sand. At their inshore end, the rocks jut up high. Anything happening at their foot cannot be seen from the roadway. Ordinarily the rocks would not be black. They are black now from the rain. He bends his knees, sets the magazines down. The wind flaps the top ones. He weights them with a stone, and goes back for more.

When all the magazines, the manila envelopes of photos, the lobby cards and scrapbooks are piled at the foot of the rocks, he is out of breath. For no sensible reason, he has hurried. He rests, stands shivering in the wind, hair blowing, looking out to sea, hands deep in pockets, shoulders hunched. Then he draws a deep breath of salt air and trudges back along the sand, which is drying in white patches. He climbs the cutbank, undoes the twine holding down the trunk lid, and slides out the first of the posters onto the road shoulder.

Getting the poster down the path is awkward. He can't see well. A foot slips and he almost falls. His arms cramp. When he reaches the sand, he changes his grip and drags the heavy thing behind him. He lets it fall back against the rocks near the paper pile. He brings all of the posters this way, stands for a thoughtful moment studying them, squats, picks up a heavy rock from the wrack of brown, rubbery kelp on the sand, and smashes out the glass. He drops the rock.

Taking out his cigarette lighter, he squats again and tries to set fire to the heap of paper. The wind keeps the lighter from igniting. He gets to his knees, runs down the zipper of his windbreaker, holds one side of the windbreaker open, and flicks the lighter inside this frail shelter. It flames, but when he moves the flame toward the fluttering magazines, it blows out.

His nose runs from the cold. He wipes it on the back of his hand. He drops the lighter into a pocket, and shreds half of a magazine, a 1950 *Silver Screen*. This he rolls to form a torch, sets the shredded end afire, and pushes it into the heap of paper. The paper is mostly dry with age, so it catches quickly. He gropes around, finds a crooked stick of driftwood, and pokes at the stack. Flames leap up. Charred scraps whirl on the updraft of wind against the rocks. Smoke streams upward.

He gets off his knees, hauls a poster to the fire, shoves it behind the fire, against the rock face. It catches at once, his youthful image, the images of the other actors turning brown, turning black, curling, breaking away in the wind, flying upward on the wind. One by one, he drags the other posters to the burning. The heat is blistering. He steps back. The flames race up Bill's handsome frames, sparking green and blue from something in the varnish. Jewett feels like a vandal and wonders why. Bill was the only being on earth to whom this junk ever meant anything. Bill no longer wants it. Jewett never wanted it. It embarrassed him. He ought to be happy it is gone at last. So why isn't he happy?

He laughs bleakly and gives his head a shake. He must clear off. Fires on the beach are illegal. He just couldn't think of a better place. He gives the fire a last poke. It won't take much longer—not with the wind fanning it. He turns and jogs back along the beach to the path up the cutbank. He scrambles up the path, steps over the guard rail, shuts down the lid of the trunk. No one is on the road to see the smoke and ash. This disappoints him. Hell, it's a man's life that is burning here. He wants to be arrested. It would give him a chance to explain to someone what he is doing, what it means. "Dear God," he says in disgust, gets into the car, slams the door. He turns the key to start the engine, releases the parking brake, swings the car in a fast U-turn on the half-wet pavement, and drives away.

Why does everything take so much time? He sits on top of an aluminum stepladder, aching shoulders slumped, and smokes a cigarette. A bucket of nasty brown water rests on wet newspapers at the foot of the ladder. Wet newspapers cover the carpet, the bed, the chest of drawers. He has moved out the mirror and the two bedside tables and their lamps. His tank top and dungarees are soaked. His hair is soaked and smells of dirty water. He looks disgustedly at his watch. Once this job would have taken him an hour, two at most. It has taken the whole morning. He was looking forward to painting. Now he is so tired, the prospect nauseates him.

Still, he clambers stiffly down the ladder to pick up the bucket, empty and rinse it, and hang it away in the broom closet. He eyes the sponge in its brown puddle in the sink, squeezes it dry, and throws it away. He gathers up the newspapers, refolding them so they won't bulk too large, and pushes them into a corner of the small service room off the kitchen. Stripping his clothes, he eyes the damp walls and ceiling. They will dry in time. The day is hot, the windows stand open. He gets into and out of the shower. It has soaked some of the ache out of his arms, shoulders, neck.

He drives to the paint store on Robertson. When he returns, he stops at the red curb to unload the heavy cans, the clumsy sack of rollers, brushes, pans, and the folded plastic drop cloths he has bought. A thin young woman leans against the yellow flagstone wall that holds the landscaping in front of the apartment building. She has long, pale hair. Her skin is too white, as if it never saw the sun, and there is a big dark bruise on one cheekbone. She wears a loosely knitted sweater. Its V-neck shows a thin chest, the ribs defined. Her trousers are loose white cotton with a drawstring at the waist, elastic at the ankles. Fragile sandals are on feet like carved ivory. A small child sits on the wall, head resting against her shoulder, eyes shut. Jewett is no judge of the ages of children. He supposes this one is maybe a year old or possibly two. He has taken them in at a glance, and now crouches to load himself with the painting stuff from the sidewalk so as to carry it indoors and up to the apartment, after which he will hurry back down to put the car where it belongs before it collects a ticket. But when he stands upright, loaded with the paint cans, whose wire handles cut his fingers, and with the sack and drop cloths clutched under his arms, the young woman has lifted down the child and comes to him.

"Oliver?" She says.

Someone familiar looks out of her eyes, but he can't place her. It seems to him she belongs to the far past. "Excuse me," he begins, "but I have to—"

"It's Darlene," she says. "Connie's girl. Remember?"

"Good heavens," he says, and crouches to set down the painful cans and the rest of his burden. He takes her hands, and feels himself smile. He is excited and pleased. He says the first thing that jumps into his mind. "Are you a dancer?"

"A dancer?" She stares at him uncomprehendingly. Then she laughs. It is a bitter laugh. "No, I'm not a dancer. Did you think I was going to be a dancer?" The child starts to toddle away down the walk, and she takes four quick steps to catch its arm, swing it onto her hip, and bring it back. "What made you think that?"

"You loved music so. That was the way music used to take you when you were small. You danced."

She is frowning, not seeing him, seeing the past. "You took me to Hollywood Bowl once. That was why, wasn't it? You wanted me to be a dancer or something."

"I guess I did," he says. "Didn't you?"

"I do now," she says, and touches the bruise on her face. "I got married." She shakes her head and laughs to herself. "A dancer. Why didn't I think of it? Maybe—if you hadn't gone."

He laughs. "Do you remember that morning? When Rita threw the dresser at me down the stairs?"

"They put you in the hospital. I wanted to take you flowers, but they wouldn't let me. You were always nice to me. I'm glad you're getting famous."

He looks at the apartment building. He looks up and down the street. "Are you here to see me?"

"If you're not too busy," she says. There isn't much hope in the way she says it. She looks at the cans and the sack and the wrapped drop cloths. "You painting? Maybe I can help." The baby is asleep on her shoulder again, a thumb in its mouth. Its hair is the same color as its mother's but its cheeks are very red. She crouches and picks up a can. "I can take this, anyway."

"Thank you," he says. "You sure?" She doesn't look strong.

"I can manage fine." She gives him a smile. Her teeth are dingy and two are missing in the lower front. She would look in place standing on the sagging unpainted porch of that Arkansas sharecropper's shack from which her big-boned, beautiful mother so long ago escaped. Genes, he thinks, and leads the way, she following, burdened, stoical, resigned. He leaves her in the apartment, goes to park the car, and when he returns finds her sitting on a small Florentine chair near the door, her sweater pulled up, the baby nursing. A little color creeps into her face as he stands surprised, staring without meaning to. It's such a commonplace sight around the world, yet he has never seen it. It moves him. She says, "It saves money and it's healthy for him."

Jewett heads briskly for the kitchen. He has ceased to feel tired. He feels almost merry. "Like some lunch?"

"You don't have to feed me," she says.

"Have to feed myself anyway," he calls. "Have to stoke up to paint that bedroom."

"All right," she calls. "You're nice. That's how I remember you—a very nice, kind man."

Jewett smiles wryly to himself. If her father, the 360-pound meat cutter, is Darlene's standard for judging men, then Jewett has been only modestly complimented. He decides omelets will be quick and easy. When he opens the refrigerator, there, under a plastic dome, sits a coconut cake. Last Thursday morning he baked it—at three o'clock, worn out with trying to sleep. It was a favorite of Bill's. But Bill will not eat it. Jewett will eat some of it with this forlorn young woman. Maybe the baby will eat some. He hopes so. It is a big cake. Darlene comes and sits at the breakfast bar and watches him prepare the omelets. He takes her coffee in Bill's mug.

"Thank you," she says. "Could I have a cigarette? I quit while I was carrying Glenn. It deforms them, you know, babies, if the mother smokes. It makes her milk taste bad too. I'll just have one. Just one."

Jewett lays his pack and lighter on the counter. "I'm glad you came. I thought you'd forgotten me."

She gives him a quick glance. She looks down at her thin, nail-bitten fingers as they take a cigarette, at the narrow gas flame as she lights it. She lays the lighter down with a little click. Her voice is dismal. "Don't say you're glad." She touches the bruise on her cheekbone again. "You make me ashamed."

"Of what?" Frowning, he takes her chin and lifts her face so he can look at it. "What happened to you?"

Her laugh is quick, angry, and she jerks her head away from his grip. "I told you—I got married. It took me a long time. I was scared of men. You remember Daddy? Otto? How he used to beat up Connie all the time? How he used to pick us kids up and throw us against the walls?"

"I remember Otto." Jewett smells the butter overheating on the grill. He turns down the flame. "I tried to reason with him a couple of times." He dices tomatoes, shreds soft yellow cheese. "It didn't help."

"It helped when you took us in," Darlene says.

Jewett beats eggs together with a fork in a Japanese bowl. "Don't give me credit for that. That was Rita's doing." He pours the beaten eggs on the grill, lets them cook awhile, then sprinkles on the tomato bits, the shredded cheese. "She was the only one who wasn't scared of him."

Remembering that day can still make him shiver. He thought he was going to be killed. Otto came home from the packing plant on a payday, roaring drunk, which in Otto's case was never just a figure of speech. The back door slammed below. There were screams, thuds, crashes. Rita rang the police. Jewett ran down the stairs and beat on the door, yelling at Otto to stop.

There was a final scream from Connie, the door burst open, Otto knocked Jewett aside, lurched to his car and drove off, bellowing curses, threats, general abuse. Jewett picked himself up from a clutter of tricycles, sand pails, roller skates.

In the kitchen, chairs and table were overturned. The worn linoleum glittered with shattered plates and glasses. A big splash of spaghetti sauce ran down the wall behind the stove. Connie was sprawled like a broken and discarded doll in a corner, whining softly, hair, dress, apron drenched in blood. Rita came and crouched over her and sent Jewett to find the children. They huddled in the dark of a bedroom closet, cringing, wide-eyed, tear-stained. Rita ordered everybody out. It wasn't safe down here. Otto would come back. She helped big, moaning Connie up the long outside staircase, Jewett shepherding the children, who were dumb with shock and fright.

The police came, a pair of youngsters, blond and rosy-cheeked, looking as if the big revolvers in holsters on their hips could not be real. They listened without interest to what Connie told them, what Rita told them, what Jewett told them, then clumped down the stairs, one to use the patrol-car radio to describe Otto and his car and ask for an ambulance, the other to look over the scene of the crime. Rita washed Connie's scalp and bandaged it, but it was paining Connie to draw breath. The officers hung around in the alley by the patrol car until the ambulance came. After it drove away with Connie as cargo and Rita as supercargo, they told Jewett to call them if Otto reappeared. Then they too drove away.

Jewett fixed hot chocolate for the children. Their quiet disturbed him, the way they seemed to scrunch down on the kitchen chairs, shrinking into themselves, the fear in their eyes. Darlene, skinny, tangle-haired, kept shivering. Not steadily. In spasms. He found a blanket and wrapped it around her. He opened cans of chili and beans for them. Canned chili wasn't his idea of a meal, but to prepare anything himself would take too long. He heated the canned stuff over a high fire and ladled it into bowls and sat with them talking—about the beach, sea gulls, the amusement pier, a sea lion that had lately wandered up into the neighborhood, anything but what had just happened. They all ate except Darlene.

He pretended to her that he needed her help readying places for them to sleep. She trailed after him, mute, dully obedient. They took down blankets and sheets from shelves. She stooped with him to roll open the daybed so it would sleep two. They unfolded sheets together, blankets, tucked them in, remade the bed that Rita and Jewett slept in. Her hands and arms, her legs and feet moved, her back and shoulders bent, and the chores were done. The children were grubby. He filled the tub, and had Darlene help him lather the dirt off them, lift them out, towel them off. Beach nights are often cold. This was one of them. He found clean T-shirts of his for them to sleep in. He hoped they could sleep, hoped they wouldn't wake up screaming. They slept. Even Darlene. The house was quiet. He sat alone in the kitchen. On guard duty. He didn't think he was much of a guard. Otto outmatched him. Otto would tear his head off.

Footsteps sounded on the stairs. His heart jumped. He ran to the door and set the catch. He slammed down the window and worked the lock that was hard to turn, clotted with many coats of paint. The cracked roller shade came down all right but as soon as he let it go it rolled itself up again. The roller kept turning. The shade went slap, slap, slap. The sound of it was loud. He grabbed at the roller and it came loose and fell at his feet, the shade stretched from his hand to the floor like a sour yellow sail. He dropped it. The stair climber had reached the porch. "Oliver?" It was Rita. He almost fell down with relief. He worked the spring lock and jerked the door open and let her in. She looked him up and down. "Everything all right? You look terrible."

"Everything's all right," he said. "How's Connie?"

"He broke three of her ribs. She'll live. They want to keep her overnight, maybe tomorrow." Rita regarded the empty kitchen table. He had washed the cocoa mugs and chili bowls and put them away. Rita sat down on the chair where he had been sitting. "Whew! I'm pooped. Wouldn't you like a drink? I'd like a drink."

Jewett got down the bottle of cheap whiskey. He pried ice cubes loose from the old refrigerator. He ran tap water over the tray's bottom to loosen the cubes, then dropped the cubes in unmatched glasses—they didn't have matching glasses in those days, or matching anything else. He poured in whiskey and added water and brought the glasses to the table and sat down. "What about her head? All that blood."

"Just a cut, no fracture, no concussion. They stitched it up." She drank and rummaged cigarettes from her shoulder bag, which lay crumpled on the table. "How are the kids?"

He told her about the kids.

"Where are we supposed to sleep?" she said.

He reached for her cigarettes. "I didn't think of that," he said. And there was the noise of Otto's car, loose tappets, a muffler with holes in it. "Oh, Christ," Jewett said, and stood up.

Rita looked at her watch. "It's after midnight. How can he still be conscious?" She too stood up. She whispered. "Maybe he'll just go in down there and pass out." But her look into Jewett's face said she didn't believe it.

"Maybe." Jewett felt cold and looked at the roller shade in dirty ribbon-candy folds on the floor. He switched off the light. There was just the little red glow of Rita's cigarette. They stood listening. They heard him climb the short porch steps below, heard the door open and close. They waited. There wasn't long to wait. Otto let out a roar. The door slammed. Shoes crunched the gritty asphalt below. Feet struck the long staircase. They stuttered, stumbling, and the weight of them made the whole house shake. "Phone the police," Jewett said. "They said to phone them if he came back."

"Jewett!" Otto roared outside in the silent dark. "Where's my wife? Where's my kids? Jewett?"

Jewett heard the click of the telephone dial from the other room. It was a delicate sound. Otto's stumbling on the steps was loud. Had he fallen? Jewett went to the far corner of the blacked-out room, from which he could see the window. Otto had not fallen far. Otto had picked himself up. Now he loomed, broad and high in silhouette against the dim light of the alley below. Jewett's heart gave a lurch. Otto was waving a shotgun. He went out of the frame of the window. He pounded the door.

"Jewett? I want my wife. I want my kids." Jewett knew that this was the time to lie. He opened his mouth but no sound came out. Otto hammered the door with the barrel of the gun. "Come on. I know you're in there. I seen your light go off." He kicked the door. "I want my wife and kids. You got no right."

"You better leave," Jewett shouted. "The police are on their way." He felt Rita come up beside him. She squeezed his arm. Jewett shouted, "You'd be smart to get out of town. Connie's in the hospital. You almost killed her this time."

"If you'd stop fooling around with her," Otto said, and heaved his whole weight against the door, "I wouldn't have to hit her. She don't know nothing. She was all right till you moved in. A movie actor, for God sake! A movie actor." Something very loud crashed against the door this time. Jewett thought Otto had backed off a step or two and hit it with the flat of his boot. "Give me back my wife," he howled. "Give me back my kids."

"In the morning," Jewett said.

"I've got a gun," Otto shouted. "I'll kill you, pretty boy. I'll blow your ass all over Santa Monica."

Then he found the window. This is the part that can still make Jewett cold with fright. The gunstock smashed out the glass. Otto's thick arm came through, hand groping for the door knob, the spring lock. Jewett stood unable to move. Rita was the one who moved. She picked up a kitchen chair, took three fast steps across the room, and smashed the chair down on the groping arm. Something wet and black spurted at her from the window. Blood from an artery. Otto's arm had come down on broken glass stuck in the window frame and the cut was deep. He let out a bellow of rage and terror. His bulk no longer blocked the window. A clatter said the gun was slithering down the stairs. Thumps and creaks of straining wood said Otto was trying to go after it. He was bumping the railing, which was none too strong. His feet were slipping on the steps.

"Help!" he yelled at the empty night. "Help!"

In the dark kitchen, Rita faced Jewett, the broken remnant of the chair in her hand. "He won't be back," she said. "Fat son of a bitch."

Jewett went to peer out the window. "He could bleed to death."

"Let him." Rita dropped the broken chair and crossed the kitchen to switch on the light. "Who cares?"

Above Otto's whimpering and panicked yelps for help below, Jewett now heard the faint and far-off cry of a police siren. He unlocked and opened the door.

"What are you doing?"

"I better get that gun," Jewett said. "He might kill the cops." He stepped out and craned to see down the stairs. The gun lay on the landing. He ran down for it. Otto sat at the foot of the stairs, clutching his arm. Jewett could hear the dripping of his blood on the weedy blacktop.

"The spic bitch killed me," Otto said.

Jewett carried the gun back up the stairs.

Now, in the bright kitchen in Mar Vista, twenty and more years afterward, he says, "How is Connie?"

"Born again," Darlene says with a sad brief laugh. "She chased after this evangelist for the longest time. He wouldn't pay her any attention. She did crazy things, sneaking on his bus—he's got a bunch of people that travel with him, he has to have his own bus, like a rock group or a carnival or something. He got out restraining orders against her. He had her put in jail once in Texas, when he came back to his motel after a revival service or whatever they call it, and she was asleep in his bed. I was always getting these phone calls from hick towns to come and take my mother home." She puts out the cigarette in the red ashtray and gets off the stool. "I better look at Glenn."

When she comes back, Jewett has set her place at the breakfast bar with a red napkin and a fork, and when she is on the stool again, he brings her an omelet, golden brown and steaming. He likes food to make a pleasant picture and is happy when she tells him it looks nice. He fills her coffee mug and his and sits beside her on the other stool to eat his own omelet. She breaks off a forkful of omelet and laughs.

"And then you know what happened? He married her!"

Jewett laughs too. "Wonderful," he says.

They eat in silence for a few minutes. Then he is aware that she is looking at him. He turns to her. She seems grave. Small frown lines are between her eyebrows. "You say it was Rita's doing. But she had a reason. She was in love with Connie. I didn't know it then, but I figured it out later. There were clues. Plenty of them. Nobody hides much from kids."

"Not Rita," Jewett says, "not from anybody."

"But you didn't have a reason like that," Darlene says. "You just did it because you were kind."

Jewett gives her a smile and a shake of the head. "I did it because I was in love with Rita. Anything she wanted was all right with me. Even Connie, God help me, God help us all."

Darlene reaches for her coffee mug without taking her eyes from Jewett's face. She lifts the mug and sips the coffee and blinks thoughtfully at him. "And her four, dirty little snot-nose kids? What did you get out of it? She was sleeping with Connie."

Jewett attends to eating. "Where's your husband?"

"He didn't even want one dirty little snot-nose kid. You should have seen how he changed. I said I didn't ever want to get married because I was afraid it would be Otto, you know? And Daniel was so gentle, so sweet." She tilts her head at Jewett and cocks an eyebrow. "I guess I thought he was like you. I guess the man I was looking for, waiting for, was someone like you."

"But when the baby came he started beating you," Jewett says. "He turned out to be Otto after all."

"You've got it," she says grimly. "I kept going back to him

afterward because he was so sad and so sorry, but I guess he couldn't help himself. I had to go back, didn't I? Where else could I go? I tried Connie, but that husband of hers kept trying to get my clothes off. Some preacher! I couldn't tell Connie. I couldn't have stood it with them anyway, not for long. She doesn't talk anymore. She just quotes Bible verses."

"What did you do before you met Daniel?"

"Waitressing. But now I've got Glenn to take care of. I quit school too soon. I don't know how to do anything they pay you halfway decent for." She laughs bleakly. "I should have been a dancer."

"Right." Jewett pushes the pack at her. "Another cigarette?" He watches her take one, takes one himself, and lights both. He sips coffee. "Where have you been since you left Daniel?"

"A shelter for battered wives. But you can't stay there forever. There isn't enough room. New ones keep coming. Besides, I don't like how it makes me think. I get to thinking I was right all along—that every man is like Otto. Every man I see." She coughs on the cigarette smoke. Her eyes water. "Except you."

"You said you were ashamed. Of what?"

"Oh, hell." She averts her face, frowns across the kitchen, shrugs. "I read where you were going to be on 'Timberlands.' That meant you'd be rich. I came to ask you for money." She taps ash from the cigarette. "When you said you were glad I came, I felt ashamed. You fed me and clothed me and kept a roof over my head when I was small. So now how do I plan to thank you?"

"It's not something you owe anyone thanks for. You were a child. It was your right. You know that."

She makes a sound, breaks the cigarette in the ashtray, slides off the stool, and runs for the living room. Jewett blinks, lays down his fork. The baby gives a cranky cry. Jewett goes down the hallway. She has gathered up the baby again. It whimpers. She pulls open the door, throws Jewett a smile. "Don't worry about us. There's agencies—aid to dependent children, nurseries for working mothers, food stamps. We'll be all right."

"Let me help," Jewett says.

She shakes her head. "It wouldn't be fair." She loses the smile. "I couldn't do it—not to you. Why? Just so I didn't have to fill out forms and stand in line?" She comes back to him, tears on her face. She looks up at him earnestly, touches his chest. "Please be careful?" she says. "Everybody's going to try to take advantage of you, and you're too kind, too easy." She stands tiptoe and touches his mouth with a tear-salty little kiss. Then, baby jouncing on her hip, she runs down the room and out the door, slamming it after her.

"There's coconut cake," Jewett says to the silence.

October

THE WINDOW of the bakery shines cheerfully in the glum autumn dusk. The customers inside have the look of happy people because of the brightness of the lights and the yellow and white vinyl tile and the clean glass around them. Jewett parks in an empty space down the block, where the shops are only dimly lit inside though their signs glow through the foliage of the trees. It was not his plan to stop in at the bakery. He tries not to worry about the way time is dragging. Escrows take forever. Anyone knows that. This is an old building. Something about the title is obscured, lost, confused, confusing. It will be straightened out. Nothing is really wrong. But he can't help wondering if Young Joe has heard something that he, Jewett, has not heard. Young Joe has been away, up north, for weeks, dickering with the people who own the ranch he wants. But driving past just now, Jewett has seen him behind the counter. Since Jewett is in town anyway, it can't hurt to stop in and shake hands.

"Hey!" Young Joe hails him before he is even through the doorway. "Mr. Jewett." He stops a second from bagging sourdough rolls to give Jewett a wave of the arm. "It's the big night."

He takes money from a middle-aged woman in a pants suit, whose hair appears to have been electroplated, and who goggles up at Jewett, vaguely smiling. The cash register beeps and twitters. Young Joe gives her her change, and shakes Jewett's hand. "Can you stay and watch it with us?"

"I wish I could," Jewett says. Peter-Paul and the girl who looks like Frances Lusk are busy with customers but they throw him anxious smiles. He waves to them. "I'm afraid I promised my sister." The way their faces fall makes him want to invite them all up to Deodar Street. It wouldn't do. In the presence of strangers, Susan wouldn't enjoy the program. She would be worrying about her limp, her crooked teeth, her thick glasses. "She's alone, you know."

"Sure, sure." The woman with electroplated hair has not moved. Young Joe pushes the bag of rolls into her hands and tells her thank you. "Well, we want to do something to celebrate. How about we take you out to dinner first?" He looks at his watch. "There's time. Someplace fancy. How about the Chez Paree in Cordova? Champagne?"

"Come on, Mr. Jewett," Peter-Paul says with a grin. "Do it." He is, then, after all, not like his grandfather. Joey was never impish.

Jewett shakes his head. "I promised to cook for my sister. The car is full of groceries."

Joe boxes a lemon meringue pie for a pink-cheeked old man in a Dodgers baseball cap. "Bring your sister too."

"She'd never come. She's crippled and she's shy," Jewett says. "Look, I'm really sorry. If I'd known a little earlier, we could have planned something."

"I should have phoned you." Young Joe loops string around the box with Pfeffer's on it in red. He ties a bow and breaks the string. "Been a lot of bookkeeping to catch up on since I got back. You know, I don't think that damn computer saves any time. I lost track of the dates. Listen"—he gives the Dodgers cap man his change, hands him his pie box, and calls him Mr. Lasorda for a joke they both enjoy—"we'll think up some way to celebrate."

"Nothing new from the Savings and Loan?"

Young Joe sighs and shrugs. "All I can figure is we'll hear when we hear—right?" Customers crowd around. The yellow clock on the wall points its hands at 6:55. Young Joe is busy. He darts a glance at Jewett. "Hey, I'm sorry. Can you wait a few minutes?"

"I'd better get along," Jewett says. He looks at Peter-Paul and the Frances Lusk girl but they are too busy behind the counter to notice him for now. He calls, "Good night, all," and as he walks out into the cool night, they call after him, "Good night. Good luck." He is happy none of them knows the expression *break a leg*. It always reminds him of the skiing accident that put an end to Susan's hopes. He can't help seeing her lying crumpled on the sunset snow where they found her after looking for so long. She never called out. She was too ashamed. She didn't want to be found. She wanted night to come down and hide her so she could die there in the cold and dark.

She is bright and merry now, opening the big golden oak door, taking from him one of the sacks of groceries he has lugged up the long, shadowy stairs to the porch, where the light beside the door glows an old familiar welcome. "It doesn't seem right," she says, teetering ahead of him past the grandfather clock, past the sliding doors, the empty loom, to the kitchen, "for a glamorous celebrity to have to haul groceries on the biggest night of his life." She sets her sack on the counter next to the sink. "Elizabeth Fairchild? My brother, Oliver."

The woman sits at the deal table, where linger a teapot, teacups and saucers and spoons, and a plate with cookie crumbs. She is angular, wears a wash-faded sweatshirt and blue jeans, and when she rises to shake Jewett's hand, her grip is strong and her hand large. She wears her yellow-gray hair simply, parted on the side, fastened with barrettes. There are cat footprints on her sweatshirt. Her teeth are horsey but her smile is genuine. "I've been trying to leave. This is a special night for the two of you. Strangers don't belong."

"I wouldn't let her." Susan unpacks the grocery bags. "It's time you two met at last. You're the best friends I have."

"You bring the beautiful flowers," Jewett says. "I've enjoyed them. They've done Susan good."

"When you're feeling lousy," Elizabeth Fairchild says, "you want somebody to come with something cheerful." A war-surplus army fatigue jacket hangs over the back of her chair. She lifts it and flaps into it. "Now, Susan, I am going, for sure." Lanky strides take her to the kitchen door. The pockets of the jacket hang heavy and clink. Has she dog chains in there? "You enjoy this lovely man's company, now." She gives Jewett a grin and a broad wink. "Any woman ought to." Her face turns red.

"Oh, stay with us and eat," Susan says. "Look at all this food. He always brings too much." She is gazing at a heap of it she has made on the counter. Jewett agrees with her. "Besides." Susan looks at the gangly woman. "If you go back to your dogs and cats and horses, you'll forget to watch the program."

"No way. My husband is a 'Timberlands' junky. When he finds out I've met you tonight, he'll choke on his health food." Elizabeth Fairchild flees up the hallway. From the living room, she calls back, "Congratulations, Oliver. I'm so happy for you."

"Thank you," he calls, and hears the door close, feels the door close, feels the house tremble with its closing, and worries again about termites, dry rot, age. The house mustn't be allowed to fall down. The notion skips through his mind, as it often has lately, that he wants to come back here to live. He hates the loneliness of the Mar Vista place without Bill. He can rent out the apartment above the bakery. But he won't talk to Susan about moving in with her—not tonight. Maybe never. She might agree out of politeness, and then it might turn out to be a mistake, and he doesn't want to chance anything going wrong between them. He couldn't bear to bruise her again. "Martini?" he says.

Susan is washing the tea things under the hot tap, whose water steams. Life was lavish in New York. She arrived home with a little flesh on her bones, and with a little touch of daring as well. Martinis, she discovered in expensive Manhattan restaurants, whet the appetite. Jewett told her this long ago but to no effect. Now she gives him an eager nod. "Oh, yes—please. Nothing duller than tea." She rattles the clean cups and saucers into a cupboard. "I suggested a little glass of white wine. You'd have thought I'd invited her to leap straight into hell. I suppose she thinks that since animals don't drink liquor, it must be poison."

"I'm glad she didn't stay to dinner," Jewett says. "She's probably a vegetarian."

Susan laughs and claps her hands. "I never thought of that, but I'll bet you're right." She looks over the heaped meat and vegetables again, touching here and there. "What can I do to help with supper? String the beans?"

Turning from the refrigerator to set down the cold gin and vermouth bottles, he looks at her. It is so good to have her well that it wrenches his heart to remember that it can't last. He ducks his head quickly into the shelter of the open refrigerator door to keep her from seeing the tears in his eyes. "Good thinking," he says, and pries loose the ice-cube tray.

The "Timberlands" episode is worse than he expected—and he didn't expect much. He is used to the stale situations of the scripts, the ice-age dialogue, the mechanical direction, the acting that swings from mumbled indifference to eye-popping hysteria. But to sit and watch himself walk seriously through such fustian makes him flinch. It is childish to be sickened by what can't be helped. Since time began the theater has survived on junk. The actor who refuses anything but Sophocles, Shakespeare, Ibsen, Chekhov, Shaw, Beckett, Pinter starves.

Ellen van Sickle and Archie Wakeman and the other actors who people "Timberlands," and those who write, direct, produce it, feel the same contempt for it as he. But they lace their contempt with wry amusement. Jewett hasn't managed this. He has treated Uncle Julius as if it were a decent part. Aware as he has become of the shortfall of his talent, he can't betray it and the God who gave it to him. He has done his best, however out of keeping. To make himself feel better, he looks at Susan in the rainbow-shadowy room. She lies on the bed, propped on pillows, hands behind her head, unabashedly absorbed. She catches him watching her.

"Aren't you stiff and stodgy!" She laughs.

"Anyone that proper has to be a crook," Jewett says. "I suggest you keep a skeptical eye on Uncle Julius."

"Hush." Watching the screen, she frowns and holds up a stubby hand. "It's starting again." She hugs herself and gives the little nose-wrinkling grimace of shivery delight she used to give on those long rainy childhood afternoons when she lay here crippled and Jewett read to her from *Wuthering Heights* or Edgar Allen Poe, making his voice so spooky he sometimes scared himself. Looking back, it seems that as long as they were, those hours always ended too soon. On the stiff bedside chair, he wonders now whether this one will ever end. He lifts his wrist close to peer at his watch, and softly groans. Yet end it does, and he is on his feet quickly, to switch off the set.

"Marvelous!" Susan cries. "You were wonderful."

He laughs ruefully and shakes his head. "It's nice of you to say so. I was adequate. It's the story of my life. Never mind. I'll be a good baker."

"Nonsense. It was absolutely alive. I believed every word you said, every gesture, every expression." She frowns at him thoughtfully. "You were so different from yourself. How do you do that? So cold, so haughty?"

He waggles his brows. "Maybe that's the real me." She makes an indignant sound and throws a pillow at him. He catches it and throws it back. "How about a brandy to go to sleep on?"

"Would hot chocolate be too much trouble?"

He laughs. "My pleasure." It was the first thing he ever prepared in a kitchen, this kitchen. For her. When their mother made it, it was never sweet enough. He added extra sugar and always floated a marshmallow on top. "Hedonism," Alice Jewett said. She meant it too. But she never stopped him making it. She was relieved when anyone else would cook. She disliked cooking and never did it well. He says now, "I haven't got any marshmallows."

"Damn," she says. "Well"—she struggles off the bed to go switch on the news—"we'll just have to rough it."

From the kitchen, taking a box of sweet cocoa down from a shelf, fetching milk in its red and white carton from the refrigerator, measuring milk into a dented aluminum saucepan that has been here since he can remember, he hears faintly from her room the voice of the President, with its mournful down-home music, the voice of the jaunty actor who wants his job, the angry chanting of young men outside the chained gates of the American embassy in Tehran. He turns the circle of blue flame low under the pan of milk and spoons chocolate powder into mugs.

He pours a brandy for himself. He is queasy with worry. He was, alas, every bit as good as Susan claimed. He stirs the milk, frowning, remembering the disquieting review in this morning's *Times*. It called his work "startlingly sensitive and intelligent in a series so far notable only for its relentless vulgarity." It's a nice way of saying he doesn't belong on "Timberlands." He never thought he did. He tried to play as coarsely as the others. He didn't manage it, did he? And that could finish him on "Timberlands," and that could put the bakery and all it means out of his reach forever.

Steam begins to hover on the surface of the milk. The joke isn't lost on him—of never having been good enough to stand out until now, when the one thing needed is mediocrity or worse. But it doesn't make him laugh. Bubbles in the milk appear at the sides of the pan. He lifts the pan off the flame and turns off the burner. He begins to tilt the milk into one of the mugs, stirring, so the brown powder can absorb it. And he hears voices, real voices this time, not television voices. Footsteps thump on the porch. Frowning, he sets the pan back on the stove and goes into the hall.

"Someone's coming," Susan calls.

"I guess so." Jewett goes to see who it is.

It is, of course, Young Joe Pfeffer, Peter-Paul, and the girl who looks like Frances Lusk. The night has turned cold and they are in sweaters and fleece-lined jackets. Peter-Paul's cheeks are as red as a child's on a Christmas card. The sallow Joe and the girl have red noses.

"You were terrific," Young Joe says with a grin. He is carrying a big, flat box. The youngsters echo him. "Terrific," they say, and they too grin.

"We figured out how to celebrate," Young Joe says.

"We brought you a cake," the girl says.

Peter-Paul lifts a heavy green bottle that glints in the dim porch light. "And champagne," he says.

Jewett recovers from his surprise. "Come in," he says. He is worried about how Susan is going to react. As they troop past him into the living room, which can't have had a party in it for years, he calls out to Susan, "It's the Pfeffers. From the bakery? They're in a festive mood. Will you join the party?"

He takes the flat box that holds the cake from Joe Pfeffer's hands. With a foot he slides aside Elizabeth Fairchild's newest foil-wrapped potted plant, and sets the box on the coffee table. To his surprise, he hears the clunk-*clunk*, clunk-*clunk* of Susan's shoes down the hallway. She appears in the square arch where the sliding doors open to the dim dining room and the hulking framework of the loom. She wears a smile. The yellow lamplight catches in the thick lenses of her glasses, making her look a little like a jolly jack-o'-lantern.

"Hello!" she says to them all. This is a grace she must have picked up along with her newfound celebrity in New York. The way she manages it, every individual is bound to feel he has been singled out for a warm greeting. He admires the hell out of her. "It's so nice of you to come. Wasn't the program wonderful?"

"Wonderful," they all say, shedding jackets.

"There's a cake," Jewett says. "And champagne." He goes past her, giving her a light kiss on the cheek. "I'll get plates and forks and glasses."

"Let me open the champagne," Peter-Paul says.

"Do it out on the porch," Young Joe tells him. "So the cork doesn't hit somebody in the eye."

In the kitchen, collecting chipped and unmatched cake plates, and an even odder assortment of cheese-spread glasses (there used to be wineglasses: what has Susan done with them?), Jewett feels a cold draft come through the house from the front door. The champagne cork pops and everyone laughs in surprise. He collects forks and a knife to cut the cake with and, clutching all of it to his chest, heads back for the living room. Before he gets there, Susan gives a cry of delighted astonishment.

"Oh, Oliver, come see!"

He emerges from the dark dining room. She stands beside Peter-Paul, who hugs the champagne bottle as if someone might try to take it from him, and she is beaming at Jewett as if it were his seventh birthday. Eager, pleased. She points at the cake. "Look what these lovely people have done. Isn't it glorious?"

Having a time of it, hanging on to the china, glass, and silverware, he goes and looks. It is a flat cake, about a foot and a half long, and much decorated. Small pine branches and pinecones in icing frame it. The rugged Timberlands mansion stands against a background of snowy mountain peaks and towering pines. Above it, the lettering reads *To Our Favorite Timberlander.* And below, *Break a Leg!* He doesn't know what his expression is, but obviously it disappoints them.

The girl who looks like Frances Lusk says in a small, anxious voice, "It's what they say to actors on opening night, isn't it? 'Break a leg'?"

"Always." Jewett gives her his warmest smile. He gives it to all of them. "Thank you very much. It's beautiful." The plates and glasses slip and rattle. "Please, somebody take these things, before I drop them?"

Bill sits asleep in Jewett's chair, chin on his chest, feet up on the footstool, hand resting on the telephone. A magazine lies open in his lap. The television set flickers its colors in the near darkness of the long room. Its sound is turned low. Jewett stands in the open doorway with the cold night at his back and stares. For a moment he feels like crying with happiness. Then he laughs to himself, shakes his head, and closes the door.

Bill has written names and telephone numbers on the back of a yellow Western Union envelope. A glass with ice melt at its bottom sits on the envelope. Jewett picks up the glass and sniffs it. Scotch, of course. At the handsome sideboard he puts new ice and a new drink into the glass and brings it back to Bill. With the cold, wet bottom of the glass, he touches the back of the hand that rests on the telephone. Bill starts awake. He blinks up at Jewett in the soft lamplight.

"Well, hi," he says. He reads his watch. "You took your time." He yawns, stretches, gets out of the chair, grins, hugs Jewett, kisses him. "You were great. You know that, don't you? You made the rest of them look so klutzy. Did you see the piece in the *Times*? They thought so too." He stands back, gripping Jewett's upper arms, studying him, glowing. "How are you? Are you okay? You look tired."

"I don't feel tired," Jewett says. "Not now." He puts the glass into Bill's hand, bends, picks up the yellow envelope, reads the penciled names. "You've been playing answering service."

"They all called to congratulate you," Bill says. "Where have you been? At Susan's?"

Most of the names are familiar. One pleases him—Rita Lopez's. He smiles at that and thinks he will return the call tomorrow and knows he won't. He tears open the envelope. The telegram is from Ziggy Fogel. I KNEW I WAS RIGHT. YOU ARE THE CLASSIEST ACTOR IN THE BUSINESS. HERE'S TO A LONG, LONG RUN. GOD BLESS YOU. Jewett folds the message and fits it back in the envelope. "At Susan's," he says, and goes into the shadows again to pour himself brandy. "Did you read the piece about her in *Newsweek*? With all those beautiful reproductions of her work?"

"She must be a millionaire by now. When's she going to hire her own cook and dishwasher and chauffeur?" Bill sits in his own chair now, and reaches up under the shade to switch on the lamp on the table beside it. "When's she ever going to give you a break?"

Jewett returns with the snifter and sits in his chair. "I had a break while she was in New York. I didn't enjoy it. My life was pretty empty." He smiles and lifts his glass to Bill. "I'm glad you're back."

"Trying to live without you," Bill says, "was like trying to live without an arm and a leg." He lights a cigarette and tosses the pack to Jewett, who fumbles the catch. The pack bounces on the rug. Before Jewett can retrieve it, Bill is on his knees, picking it up, handing it to him. He stays on his knees, watching while Jewett lights a cigarette. In the gentle lamplight, he looks as he did when they first met. His gaze is worshipful. "I love you," he says.

Jewett should say, *You love Uncle Julius. You love my photo in the* Times. *You love the phone calls of congratulations from celebrities.* But he can't say these things. Instead, he smiles and roughly tousles Bill's hair. "Ah, Billy," he says. "You break my heart."

Tears brim in Bill's eyes. He takes Jewett's hand and kisses the palm. "You put some bad cracks in mine." He gives a quavery little sigh, lets go the hand, gets to his feet, falls back into the chair. "You're still going to buy that fucking bakery, aren't you? You know, they voted against the condominiums. We can keep this apartment. We can live here like we always did."

"If you want," Jewett says. "But it's a long way from the bakery. It will mean a lot of freeways every day. And there's a gas shortage. I thought we might buy you a shop over there. How does that grab you?"

Bill puts out his cigarette. He stretches and yawns. He grins. The meaning of the grin is unmistakable. "You know what I want to do?"

Looking into his eyes, Jewett gives a small, dry chuckle. He tosses off his brandy, puts out his own cigarette, switches off the lamp. He rises and turns off the television, holds out his hands to Bill, who takes them and gets to his feet. He closes Jewett in a hug and puts a long, hungry kiss on his mouth. They go down the dim hall to the dark bedroom.

In the morning, when Jewett brings him coffee and wakes

him, and he sits up to take the O mug, he smiles sleepily, brown, smooth, naked, beautiful. Then he frowns. "You painted this room. Where are the posters?"

Naked, Jewett gets back into bed and kisses his shoulder. "You didn't want them—remember?"

Bill is rigid. The mug is forgotten in his hand. He holds it tilted. Coffee runs up his forearm and drips off his elbow onto the sheets. "What did you do with them?"

"Watch it." Jewett takes the mug from his hand and sets it on the nightstand. He goes to the bathroom and hauls toilet paper off the roll. Bill is not there when Jewett gets back to the bed to soak up the spilled coffee. He knows where Bill is: from the guest room he hears the rattle and slam of empty drawers. An empty drawer hangs from Bill's hand when he appears in the bedroom door. He is a bad color, greenish. The elegant finish of the drawer glows in the fresh morning sunlight. Bill says, "There's nothing in the desk. What have you done?"

"None of that was me, Bill." Jewett lets the wad of coffee-soaked toilet paper drop into the ashtray, and he sits, suddenly old and weary, on the side of the bed. "This is me that you see here." Bill says nothing, only stares in misery. Jewett tells him gently, "I burned it, Billy, all of it. That day after I came to the shop. I took it to the beach and burned it."

Yeast and vanilla are the smells he brings home from the bakery, where since before dawn Peter-Paul has shown and explained to Jewett the moment-by-moment workings and work of the shiny, sweltering kitchen. Much of a television actor's day is spent waiting. Baking leaves no time for rest. His feet hurt, his back aches, he is arm-weary. The automation doesn't look after everything—nowhere near it.

A long white apron wrapped him, and he wore a starchy white cap, so maybe the yeast and vanilla smells aren't in his clothes and hair, maybe they are only in his nose and mouth. One thing he is sure about. Bill was wrong that night at the Skipper's. Jewett will not get fat eating unclaimed wedding cakes. He doubts that he will ever eat a cake again—certainly not one with vanilla in it. As for bread? He laughs to himself. He will be history's thinnest baker.

He swings the car down into the parking level under the Mar Vista apartment. It is gloomy but not late enough in the day yet for the lights, a line of feeble fluorescent tubes that bisects the low, roughly plastered ceiling. He wheels the car between painted lines so its square nose is under a small wall marker: JEWETT-HAYCOCK. He switches off the engine and sits staring dully at the names. Nothing would be served by changing the sign now. As soon as the bakery deal closes, he will leave here anyway.

He climbs out of the car, locks it, and trudges up the ramp into slanting daylight and a cold, steady wind from the sea that cannot be seen from Mar Vista. He follows the sidewalk to the shallow flagstone steps that rise to the lobby's glass doors. As he climbs, the big, cold, flappy leaves of the landscaping brush him. He wants a drink and a shower. He has scarcely eaten all day, but after helping prepare those mountains of loaves and rolls, croissants and crullers, cookies, cakes, pies for others to eat, he is not hungry.

Is "helping" the right word? He doubts it. Mostly he felt clumsy and in the way. Not that Peter-Paul once said so. He was driven and unsmiling but never rude. Jewett had expected Young Joe to teach him. It was unsettling—Peter-Paul's likeness to his grandfather. At moments, forty years dropped out of Jewett's memory, and Peter-Paul became Joey, and Jewett became young Oliver, sick with love and longing. He is glad it is over. He pushes a key into the lock of the glass door, and hears his name called. With a groan to himself, he turns.

Larry Haycock waves to him from across the street. "Mr. Jewett! Wait!" Larry has to wait for a string of home-going cars to pass before he can cut across the street. In a yellow tank top and jogging shorts, he looks beautiful but cold. His long hair flies in the wind. He takes the steps two at a time. He pants, combing the hair off his face with his fingers. "It's Mom." He points across the street, where Cherry Lee in sunglasses, slacks, high heels, and a short fake fur coat gets out of a rust-red 1960s Valiant. She bends back into the car, comes up with a silk flower-print scarf, and ties it over her hair. "She needs to talk to you," Larry says. He rubs his bare arms, brown and cleanly muscled. "Cold, isn't it?"

"It's always a little colder here than out where you live," Jewett says. "It's the sea wind." He looks at Larry sharply. "What's the matter? Has something happened to Bill?"

"No." Larry tilts his head, puzzled. "You'd know that. How would we know that?" The blank brown eyes blink.

The traffic has broken. Cherry Lee's high heels click-click-click across the street. Her well-muscled calves are not visible because of the slacks, but Jewett can picture them working. She moves quickly. She hustles up the steps. "Mr. Jewett, you got to help me." Her voice is as hoarse as ever. "That son of a bitch—he's really done it this time."

"Cherry Lee," Jewett says, "Bill and I are no longer together. I'm not a family connection anymore."

She actually staggers from shock. Larry has to grab her to keep her from falling backward down the steps. "Hey, Mom," he says. "Are you okay?"

"Do you mean"—Cherry Lee snatches off the sunglasses—"you kicked my Billy out, just when you got rich and famous? After he stuck with you and paid the bills all the time when you couldn't get anybody to give you a job acting?" Her eyes are small and sunken, but the lashes are false and long and black, and she bats them angrily. "And now you're not going to help his mother out when she's in the worst fix she was ever in in her life?"

The legend of Bill's sacrifices to keep Jewett fed and out of the rain springs from long ago when Bill still spoke to Cherry Lee and company. What Bill actually told his mother was that Jewett was not keeping him. Cherry Lee had been horrified by the notion of her pretty Billy as some fairy actor's kept boy. Bill assured Cherry Lee that he was working and paying half the rent and half the bills. Cherry Lee's interpretation of the facts

Jewett has heard before. It has not been made up for this occasion, though it suits this one better than the others.

"Come in," Jewett says wearily, and pushes open the heavy door and holds it so they can step inside out of the chilly wind. When they are up in the apartment, he says, "I didn't kick Bill out. He left. He was tired of me. I'm too old for him. Bound to happen." He doesn't mention the bakery. That would complicate matters beyond Cherry Lee's patience to sort them out. The apartment is pleasantly warm. He helps Cherry Lee off with her coat. "Would you like some coffee?"

She has never seen the apartment. Taking off the head scarf, she appraises it. "Coffee will be all right," she says, grouchily. "Larry, go make a pot of coffee."

"Maybe you'd rather have a drink." Jewett looks after Larry, who goes off seeking the kitchen. "I'm going to have a drink myself. It's been a long, hard day."

Cherry Lee slowly circles the room, running ruminative fingers with very long red nails on the glowing surfaces of Bill's handsome antiques. "I don't know what gets into that boy." She speaks almost to herself. "I sure as hell wouldn't leave a setup like this. It said in *Playboy* fairies live better than other people. It's because they only got theirself to look out for." She plumps down on the couch and pokes the scarf into a handbag. "No drink, thanks. Dolan does enough drinking for the whole Haycock family." She finds a cigarette in the handbag, lights it with a plastic throwaway lighter, drops the lighter back in the bag, and glares at Jewett through the smoke. "We waited for you out there more'n an hour. I read in *TV Guide* where actors go to work early. Figured you'd get home early too."

"There's a lot of overtime," Jewett says.

"TV studios use hairdressers," she says. "Could you wangle me a job in the studio? That would put an end to Dolan wrecking things for me all the time. They got guards at the studios. I read that someplace. Nobody gets in unless they got business there."

Jewett has an ear cocked for noises from the kitchen. Larry hasn't called for help. The rattles he has made sound like the right ones. Jewett goes to the bar and pours himself neat scotch. "I don't have any influence with the hairdressing department, I'm afraid." He comes back to his chair and sits down and puts his weary legs up. "What's Dolan done this time?"

"I got the qualifications," she says, "if that's what you're worried about. I been a beautician since I was sixteen years old. I got a list of references as long as your arm."

"I'll look into it for you," Jewett lies. "Now tell me what the problem is. This is a long way to come."

"Well, don't be in such a hurry," she says peevishly. "It's going to take some explaining first." She waits for him to speak. He doesn't speak. He is interested that she seems uncomfortable. That's the reason for the aggressiveness: she is embarrassed. She scowls past him and shouts, "Larry, are we going to have that coffee or not?"

"It's dripping." His voice comes from farther away than the kitchen. He is exploring the apartment. Jewett is surprised but not uneasy. Larry is not like Dolan. For one thing, Larry has a job. Larry is not going to steal anything. This leaves unanswered the question of why he is nosing around. But Jewett believes that if he asks the boy the boy will answer truthfully. His feet in soft-soled jogging shoes thump in the hall. "Mr. Jewett, is it all right if I use the bathroom?"

"Help yourself." Jewett smiles. He sips his drink, lights a cigarette, says to Cherry Lee, "I'm listening."

"Well"—she crosses and recrosses her legs, fiddles with trimming ash off her cigarette in the ashtray at the end of the couch. She has set the handbag against one thigh. As if it were the source of her discomfort, she moves it to the other thigh. "For a long time, I been saving up. To get a salon of my own."

Jewett blinks at her. He is remembering, and she must be aware that he is remembering, the numberless times when she has called, first Bill, then himself, for money to get her or Dolan or Gramp and Gran or a married daughter or son-in-law or a sick child out of trouble. He is remembering the numberless checks he has written. "A long time?"

"It wasn't easy," she says. "Not with all the kids. And keeping it secret, so Dolan wouldn't get his hands on it. Took me years." She looks everywhere but at Jewett. Her shoulders move impatiently. "Seven, maybe eight years."

"You certainly kept it a secret from me," Jewett says.

"Anyways," she hurries on, "I got a chance to buy into Monsieur Versailles, where I work, you know?" She pronounces it Monsoor Vursails. "Out in Thousand Oaks? I got a full partnership. You want to know why? Because they don't want to lose me. I get more ladies asking for appointments than any operator they ever had. They come from as far off as Laguna and Santa Barbara. They're always saying, 'Cherry Lee, why don't you work in a salon that's not so far away?' "

Jewett sighs. "What's Dolan done, Cherry Lee?"

"Well, there was papers to sign, wasn't there? And that means lawyers and the county and all that. And, of course, envelopes started coming in the mail. And I can't be home when the mail comes. I could trust Larry but he's got school and then he works. So, naturally, Dolan spotted the envelopes, and when Dolan wants to know what's inside of something—he don't care who it belongs to—he finds out. You know him. You know how he is."

"So he learned you'd bought half a beauty parlor," Jewett says. "I suppose he figured out a way to make something out of it for himself. How?"

A faint jingling comes from the hallway, accompanying the soft thud of Larry's feet. He has found a bentwood tray. On it stand the glass coffee maker, mugs, the red sugar bowl, a squat paper carton of cream. Spoons lie on the tray—it is the spoons that jingle. Larry sets the tray on the coffee table, sits down beside his mother, leans forward, and pours from the coffee maker into the mugs. The coffee steams. He starts to hand the B mug to his mother. She waves it away.

"Just let me light a cigarette first," she snaps. "I can reach that when I want it." She fidgets a cigarette and the plastic lighter out of the handbag again. The cigarette bobs in a corner of her painted mouth when she tells Jewett, "Number one—the place is insured. Everything in it is insured—fire, flood, theft, everything. He made sure to find that out."

"Dear God," Jewett says. "Don't tell me he set fire to it?"

She shakes her head. "He couldn't figure out how to make nothing for himself out of a fire." Cigarette smoke makes her squint one eye. The smoke lazes around her beehive hairdo. He can't remember its color the last time he saw it, but it is jet black now, with metallic blue highlights. It doesn't make her face look young. It makes it look like something you chop down trees with. "No, what he done was take my key and go in there at night and haul out the dryers and the chairs. Took bolts out of the floor to get the chairs loose." She lays the cigarette carelessly in the ashtray, picks up the red mug, and slurps coffee noisily.

Larry has stirred sugar into his coffee and made it very nearly white with cream. He says, "He doesn't mind work, as long as it isn't honest."

"He's your father," Cherry Lee says strictly. "So I don't want to hear that kind of talk from you."

"Sorry," Larry says and gives Jewett a wry smile.

"All new equipment," Cherry Lee tells Jewett. "Brand-new, just bought last month. Cost an arm and a leg. New sinks too. Guess the only reason he didn't take those was because he was afraid he'd get water on him."

Larry laughs and Jewett suppresses a smile. He is beginning to enjoy this. He drinks some of his scotch. "How do you know it was Dolan? No crime in Thousand Oaks?"

"Oh, we been broke into before." Cherry Lee picks up the cigarette, inhales deeply, puts it back in the ashtray. Smoke jets from her nose. "He knew that because I told him about it when it happened, fool that I was. I might have known he'd make something out of it for Dolan Haycock. You can't trust him with anything, not even information." She slurps coffee again, sighs, and says grimly, "I know it was him because he told me."

Jewett is startled and sits up straight. "You're not serious."

"He says it's insured, so it won't hurt the business any. He's got it hid someplace till he can file the serial numbers off and sell it." She makes a mocking face. "And he'll give me half the proceeds. Can you beat that?"

"Go to the police," Jewett says.

"And have them at Monsieur Versailles find out? Dolan Haycock is my lawful wedded husband. It was my key he used to get in there. They'll think I was in on it. Insurance fraud. I could go to jail. I could lose all that money I pinched and scraped for all them years."

"You should have left him." Jewett is trying not to laugh. "I've said so to you a dozen times."

"And I never listened, and I'm a damn fool." She pushes up off the couch and paces, smoking furiously. "If I just didn't love him so much." Ashes dribble on the carpet. "If he didn't know more ways than a snake to twist around me." She stops at the sideboard where the bottles and glasses wait. "Maybe I will have that drink after all. This is about the worst day of my life."

"I can drive," Larry says eagerly.

"Not till you get your license," Cherry Lee says. "All I need now is for you to get in trouble."

What she wants to drink is, of all things, a Tom Collins. Jewett retires with the gin bottle to the kitchen where there are lemons, oranges, powdered sugar, bottled cherries. She and Larry come trailing after him and stand watching him while he crushes ice cubes in the blender, ferrets out of a lower cupboard a cocktail shaker rarely used anymore, pulls off its dusty plastic baggie, and shakes gin, lemon juice, powdered sugar, and ice together. He slices an orange, drops ice cubes into a tall glass, pours the gin mixture over them, drops in an orange slice, a cherry, fills the glass with soda water, and hands it to her. She says, "You do that real professional. You could be a bartender."

"I have humbler amitions," he says, and holds out the halves of orange to Larry, who takes them and stands over the sink, chewing the juice out of them. Jewett leans back against a counter. "I still don't know what it is you think I can do, Cherry Lee."

"Find where he's hid the stuff."

Jewett stares. "How would I do that? I only know one of his haunts. They wouldn't let him stow stolen merchandise at the Skipper's."

"It's at the beach someplace," Cherry Lee says. "He told me that much. Far as he could get from home."

Jewett watches Larry splash his mouth and chin with water from the tap. The orange peels lie in the sink. Jewett wonders if Larry has told his mother about Mavis McWhirter. He hands Larry a red-striped dish towel, and leaves for the living room and his drink. Cherry Lee goes to the big window and stands looking out, jingling the ice in her glass. He sits in his chair and asks her: "What if by some freak I did find the things? What then?"

"Dolan's not the only one who can think up stunts. I'm not dumb. I just never had any education. I got pregnant too soon. You look at TV, every high-school girl in the country's pregnant, but it wasn't that way then. You had to drop out of school." She snorts, wags her head, and returns to the couch to plump down and rattle around in her handbag for another cigarette. "You move them. Put them someplace else. Then—"

Jewett swallows whiskey the wrong way and coughs.

"Then you get on the phone to the police in Thousand Oaks and tell them where they can find the dryers and chairs stole from the Monsieur Versailles beauty salon. And they'll come collect it, and turn it back, and that'll be that. Course, when you call them"—smoke streams from her nostrils again—"you don't give your name."

"He'd have to rub off Dolan's fingerprints." Larry comes in. Water has splashed the front of his tank top.

Cherry Lee tells him, "I thought of that. Don't always think you're so much smarter than your mother."

"I decline," Jewett says.

"You're not going to help me?" Cherry Lee yelps.

"I'm not going to protect Dolan," Jewett says.

"See?" Larry says. "I told you."

"Turn him in, Cherry Lee," Jewett says. "Tell the police what he told you. Tell your partner at the beauty parlor. Nobody's going to blame you. And maybe this time you'll get rid of him at last."

"I couldn't," she says, and starts to cry.

Sandoval Estates is new town houses built on flat steps of land bulldozed out of the Santa Monica mountains overlooking the Pacific. A high, strong-looking iron fence surrounds it. The grass and flower beds are new. And though most of the trees are tall, they too are new, brought in and planted full-grown in artful clumps—eucalyptus trees mostly, fragile-looking, lacy, the sea wind bending their slender pink limbs, turning up the silver undersides of their leaves. The houses are of raw cedar and glass. Jewett stops the Toyota where iron gates are closed between stone pillars. A large, plump youth in suntans with a gun on his hip gets off a director's chair, comes and stands beside the car. "Who did you want to see?" he says.

"Mavis McWhirter is expecting me," Jewett says.

"She didn't leave word," the guard says.

"Ring her, please," Jewett says, "and say I'm here. My name is Jewett, Oliver Jewett."

The guard bends his elephant knees, puts his hands on them, peers closely into the car. "You're the actor, aren't you? On TV. 'Timberlands.' " He snaps his fingers, laughs, gives a nod of satisfaction at having got it right. "Sure you are. I recognize you."

Jewett gazes steadily ahead through the windshield at the telephone beside the gates. "Could you call Mrs. McWhirter for me, please?"

"Oh, right away," the guard says happily. "Yes, sir." But before he lifts down the receiver, he turns and calls, "You're really putting that T.J. in his place, aren't you?"

"I'm giving it my best." Jewett grins.

Laughing, the guard punches buttons on the telephone. While he speaks into the receiver, he smiles relentlessly at Jewett. He hangs up and pushes a key into a slot below the

phone and the gates swing slowly open. The guard motions
Jewett through. "It's number twenty-one," he says, as the
Toyota's tires crunch the impeccable gravel of a curving drive.
"First on your left on the second level. You can park in the lane.
That'll be okay, Mr. Jewett."

Mavis McWhirter answers the door in a long flowing robe of
golden velour. The collar of the robe stands high. This and the
big gold medallion hanging heavy from a thick chain around
her neck give her the look of some ruler of an alien planet in an
episode of "Star Trek." Her wig is freshly washed and set—
there is more blue in it than before. "Oliver!" She spreads her
arms, the sleeves of the robe flowing. "What an unexpected
pleasure."

"Sorry to come on such short notice."

"Don't be silly. I'm thrilled. Come in, come in."

The place is good looking, the main room lofting high, with
beams, planks, clerestory windows. At the back is a loft with
steeply raked skylights. The furniture is Victorian—antiques or
good reproductions. Much carving and tufted plush. Didn't she
mention sometime a shag carpet? Not down here. Down here,
oriental carpets glow darkly underfoot. Akmazian would be
pleased. There are stretches of bare flooring, polished pegged
planks.

"A drink!" Mavis cries, as if she hadn't been thinking of it
since she got out of bed. "Sit down. Be comfortable. You like
my little pied-à-terre?"

"I do indeed." Jewett takes two steps up into an eating space.
He stands looking out a tall, narrow window at the sea spar-
kling blue in the sun. A trawler stands out near the horizon.
"Have you seen Dolan Haycock lately?"

She doesn't hear him. "Martini be all right?"

"Perfect, thank you," he shouts.

He steps into the kitchen. Nothing has been left out. Everything is in the right place. The burner deck is central, under a
big copper ventilation hood. A gas grill lies between the bur-
ners. Oven, rotisserie, and broiler are built into the walls. Doors

of black glass. Lots of cutting boards. Double sinks. Sunlight, a big, deep window full of flowers, and a view. He goes back through the eating space and down into the living room and Mavis comes with martinis in her large, jeweled hands. He has never seen such big martini glasses. He accepts his with a smile, a nod. "I envy you that kitchen."

"Isn't it glorious?" She sits down with a sigh and a billowing of velveteen yardage. Strong and expensive perfume gusts from her. "I don't deserve that kind of kitchen. You deserve it. You cook like an absolute angel. I really can't be bothered."

"It's no fun when you're alone." Jewett sits and tastes the martini. "Marvelous," he says. "Thank you."

She lifts her glass in a toast. "To your continued wonderful success." She sips her drink. She looks grave. "You know—you're much too good for that show. None of the other actors takes it seriously at all."

"It worries me. I should have been told. The director, somebody, should have told me." He shakes away his frown. "No use worrying. It's too late now."

"Oh, darling Oliver!" She reaches out to him. "I didn't mean to upset you. You're very good. That's all I meant to say."

"Thank you. Have you seen Dolan Haycock lately?"

She looks wary. She sounds wary. "Why?"

"I advised you to shed him," Jewett says.

She leans forward to lift the lid from a chased silver box. "Who says I haven't?" She takes a cigarette and slides the box toward him on the polished tabletop. "Cigarette?"

He takes one, sets the lid on the box, picks up a table lighter whose base is a cylinder of marble, and leans across to thumb flame from it so she can light her cigarette. He lights his own, sets the lighter down, settles back in his chair. "You didn't say no," he says. "When? Day before yesterday?"

Mavis braces herself with a long swallow from the enormous glass. "When I said 'why?' I meant, why do you ask?"

"Because he had a load of stolen beauty-shop equipment and he needed a place to hide it. He doesn't have a lot of friends—

something you can understand if you'll think about it objectively. He called and asked if you'd let him stow it in your garage—with the Excalibur. Didn't he?"

"It's distressed merchandise," she says. "He was able to buy it very cheaply. It will only be here a short while. Just long enough for him to find a buyer."

"That's what he told you? And you believed him?"

"It looks brand-new," she says defensively.

"It comes from a place in Thousand Oaks, called Monsieur Versailles. A business. In which his wife just bought a half-interest. He got it by using her key."

She plainly doesn't like what she hears, but she says nothing. She gulps the last of her martini and rises. All her radiance has vanished. She looks like the big, fat, disappointed old woman she is. She reaches listlessly for his glass. He gives her a little smile, a little shake of the head. "I'll stay with this awhile, thanks."

She goes off across the beautiful rugs, the beautiful flooring. Tonelessly she asks, "What shall we do?"

He follows. The bar is in an alcove behind the wooden staircase that climbs to the loft. Daylight pours down on glasses and bottles from a shaft to the roof. In a plain, squat pitcher of Swedish crystal, she mixes gin and vermouth and a carefully measured drop of olive brine, turning the ice with a glass rod. "What I should do," he says, "is tell the police where to find it."

"They won't like having the police here," she says. "I never let Dolan come here, anymore. We always meet at restaurants. We always go to motels. I was cross when he showed up with that rented truck. Of course, it looked much better than his own wreck of a car. But the driver raised some eyebrows among the neighbors. I mean"—she pours from the pitcher into her empty glass, where the olive bobs about—"Dolan is attractive in an earthy way, but not breedy, if you know what I mean. Not the country-club type." Her smile at Jewett is rueful.

"You couldn't tell them he was a deliveryman?"

She looks into Jewett's eyes. "I wouldn't do that."

"No, of course not." But he is surprised. He has misjudged Mavis McWhirter. He smiles to himself. She has, as the old song said, Klass. "You could send for him to take the stuff elsewhere. I hate for him to get away with this, but there's no reason you should be a victim."

"I make myself a victim, don't I? Because I'm lonely and old and sex-starved." She picks up her glass. "Shall we go and sit down?" He goes, she follows. She sits, drinking, smoking, brooding. Jewett moves about the room, carrying his drink. Eighteenth-century English theater prints are on the walls. There is a blown-up engraving of Garrick as Macbeth—just about life-size: Garrick was only five foot two. He ran to high heels, tall plumes in his hats, and popeyed scowls. When Jewett was in London with that awful musical, he went one cold rainy morning to see Garrick's burial place in Westminster Abbey. The slab over Garrick is small. Next to it, that of his large friend Samuel Johnson is large. For some reason, this brought tears to Jewett's eyes. He stands, sipping his drink, gazing out the window again. Little white boats bob breezily along offshore. Their sails have yellow and orange stripes. Above them, gulls wheel. Mavis says, "I'm not going to let him get away with it."

"Good." Jewett turns. "Where's the telephone?"

"No." She stands up, unsteady because of the gin, but resolute. "You're a celebrity. The reporters will notice your name. It will be on the newscasts. It will be in the Enquirer." She moves off, robe billowing, head held high. "They won't notice my name. And if they do, I deserve it. I'll do the telephoning, thank you."

"Dolan's sure it was you." Larry wears a bright green padded vest today, over a blue turtleneck sweater. His blue corduroys are rumpled from a laundromat dryer, and skimpy, as if he'd grown since they were new. "You're the only one who could connect him to Mavis McWhirter. And he says Mavis would never have turned him in on her own. He'd like to kill you."

Jewett smiles. "He says. Dolan talks a lot."

"He never heard about Mavis's ring from me. You said not to tell him, and I didn't." Larry plucks at the tab opener on an empty soft-drink can in front of him. He looks at that, and not at Jewett. He says softly, "I'll always do what you want," and lifts his head and gives Jewett a little frightened smile.

Jewett's heart bumps. They sit at a battered enamel table, one of three on sloping pink cement in front of a hamburger stand up the street from the studio. It is a busy street. Traffic surges past, home-going traffic on a workday. Pigeons peck around their feet, at scraps of lettuce, bits of french fries. The hamburgers here are broiled over charcoal, and Jewett judges them the best in town. Larry seems to differ. Half of his lies forgotten in its soiled wrapper in an oval red plastic basket. Jewett tries to ignore what the boy has just said. He wants to maintain the fiction that Larry has come to tell him of events at the Haycock household. He is mortified by an impulse to reach out and touch the boy's hair.

"Cherry Lee," he says, "should never have gone bail for him. She's making a new start in life. She ought to have left him in jail and filed for divorce."

The boy pokes at the wreckage of his hamburger. "Why is 'gourmet' always sour?" he asks.

"Is it?" Jewett laughs. "Maybe it is."

"I mean—McDonald's hamburgers—they're not expensive like these, but they're sweet, you know?"

"Right." Jewett loses his common sense. "Next time, we'll go to McDonald's." He doesn't mean for there to be a next time. This child alarms him. He crumples his napkin, stands, gathers together the baskets and the litter. "Come on. I'll drive you home." He goes to the trash receptacle and empties the baskets and stacks them with others on a shelf beside the serving window. When he looks at Larry, the boy has got up from his chair, but he seems distressed. He falls into step beside Jewett, who walks toward his car up the block at the curb.

"I didn't come to go home," he says. "I came to stay with you. In case Dolan comes and tries anything. He really is pissed off."

"I'll be all right." Jewett unlocks the car and opens the door for Larry. "I appreciate your worrying about me, but I can handle Dolan. I've done it before."

The boy says something but the traffic noise covers it. Jewett goes around and gets into the car behind the wheel. He closes his door. Larry drops into his seat and closes his door. "He's got a gun," he says.

Jewett turns the key and the engine starts. He watches in the side mirror for a break in traffic. It comes, and he hurries the Toyota away from the curb. Two blocks along, at a stoplight, he looks at Larry. "You wouldn't lie to me," he says.

"Why do you think I came all the way in from the Valley on the bus? Why do you think I came to the studio gate and called you out? He's got a gun. He showed it to Cherry Lee. I saw it."

The light is green. Jewett drives on. He is making for a freeway on-ramp northbound. "That doesn't mean he has the nerve to use it, Larry. He's a coward and a sneak. You know that. He might use rat poison. He'd never use a gun."

"You don't want me to stay over?"

"Your mother wouldn't like it." A wide green reflector sign predicts a freeway, and Jewett changes lanes. "She hated Bill's living with me. If she thought you spent the night at my place, she'd have a fit." Frowning, he glances at the boy, who looks dismally straight ahead. "You do understand about Bill and me? What we were to each other?"

"That's over," Larry says. "You said so last time. Where are you going?" Jewett is steering the Toyota up the on-ramp. Larry half reaches out as if to grab the wheel. "I don't want to go home. I want to stay with you. Don't you understand?"

Jewett willfully misunderstands. "To protect me from Dolan. I appreciate it." He makes his smile at the boy quick because he has to edge the car into the stream of cars rushing toward the Valley. "But it's not necessary. Dolan victimizes women, not men."

Larry doesn't answer. He slumps down a little in the bucket seat, hugging himself as if the padded vest weren't warm enough. Jewett glances at him. He looks ready to cry. Jewett switches on the heating system. Larry says, "I wouldn't lie to you. Dolan really did wave a gun around and say he was going to kill you. But I didn't believe it. I know him too. You're right about him. So I didn't lie to you. But"—he sits up straight, runs his hands through his hair, seems in an agony of embarrassment—"that wasn't why I came to you. Not really."

"Let's talk about something else," Jewett says.

"It wasn't why I wanted to stay over," Larry says. "Look—do I have to spell it out?" His hand is on Jewett's thigh, he is facing Jewett, twisted in the cramped seat. "I want to be what Billy was to you."

Jewett takes his eyes off the traffic ahead to look at Larry and give him the gentlest smile he can summon. "I'm old enough to be your grandfather." Up ahead, an eighteen-wheeler is having trouble climbing a long grade. All the cars in this lane slow. Jewett pushes the brake pedal. "I'm flattered. You're a beautiful boy and I like you but it would be wrong. I know that, if you don't."

Larry cries, "There's nothing wrong about it. It's just the way some people are. Nobody decent thinks it's wrong anymore. Bigots think that. Ignorant people."

"I agree." The truck has topped the grade, and the lane of cars begins slowly to move again. Jewett shifts the floor stick to drive. His hand brushes Larry's leg. He pulls the hand away quickly. "What would be wrong is that I'm an old man"—he inches the Toyota onward—"and you're a young boy, and we'd soon grow tired of each other. You don't know enough yet, and I know too much."

"I love what you know," Larry says. "I want to learn. About books and music and plays and ballet and all that."

Jewett switches off the blowing heat and rolls down his window. Traffic is moving normally again and the air that strikes his face, though it stinks of exhaust fumes, feels blessedly cool. "All those things can be found in books. In school. You don't need me for that."

"I need you for something else," Larry says.

"Find someone your own age," Jewett says.

"I have. It never means anything. Stiff cocks in a dark car. It doesn't matter whose. They don't care about you, you don't care about them. I hate that."

Jewett's heart beats heavily. He is short of breath. "Larry, please stop, all right? It's not fair. Even if nothing else made any difference—and it does, believe me it does—I'd be committing a serious crime."

Larry stares. He barks a scornful laugh. "Come on!"

"Not in your eyes," Jewett says, "and not in mine, but in the eyes of the law." He sounds like his father.

"Who the hell is going to know? You think I'd run and tell Cherry Lee?"

"I don't think you'd have to. She's far from stupid, Larry. If she found out you were spending time with me, she'd guess how and why. And there'd be trouble."

"Shit. Yeah. I suppose so." Larry grows thoughtful. "I'm the one who's stupid. I didn't think of all that. I was looking at your place. God, I'd love to live there with you. All those books and records." He chews his lower lip, frowning through the windshield. "I dream about it. I've dreamed about you ever since you caught me that day. I wasn't just dancing, you know."

"I had an idea what you were doing," Jewett says.

"I could go on living at home and going to school and Colonel Sanders and all that, but I could come see you sometimes, couldn't I?"

"I'm leaving here soon," Jewett says. "Moving back to my hometown. It's a long way from here."

Larry slumps down in the seat again. "Damn."

"Which off-ramp do I want?" Jewett asks.

Larry tells him bitterly which off-ramp he wants.

November

THE TRUNKS of the eucalyptus trees beside the narrow crooked trail that climbs to Ziggy Fogel's house have grown thick in the decades since Jewett was last here. Then, the house could be seen from below, its high white walls gleaming solitary in the sun. Now the trees are too tall, their dark, ragged foliage too dense. And the house is no longer lonely. Everywhere up these steep brushy hillsides, boxy structures perch on slim steel legs, staring blankly from wide glass faces at the city below. Sports cars, vans, costly, new, bunch beside clumps of mailboxes along the road. Irish setters, basset hounds, malamutes sleep in the shadows of the cars, on earth strewn with red and dun-color leaves. A cat scuttles across the road. There used to be quail up here, squirrels, opossums with naked pink snouts. At night coyotes yapped.

At first, steering down the driveway, he thinks things are the same at Ziggy's. The landscaping is trimmed and tidy. But weeds sprout through the paving of the tennis courts, where the green of the nets has faded where weather has rotted them. The swimming pool is empty of water. Leaves have piled up in its corners. He parks in the yard at the side of the house by the garage, where the daylight used to seem to him marvelously pure, distilled between the opposing white walls. Today's light is feebler than he remembers. But then, it is almost winter. The garage doors are closed. Is the maroon brougham inside? Or when Mick died, did Ziggy get rid of it? Did Ziggy, like everyone else in the industry, no matter how rich, now drive himself? Jewett can't picture it. Ah, no. He has forgotten the priest.

The priest opens the door to him, not the side door Jewett always regarded as his own private entrance when he lived here, but the front door with its wrought-iron hinges and latch, its studdings of crude black bolt heads. It is a wide and heavy door with a curved top. The priest gives him a solemn smile and a nod. His gray thatch still looks unwashed and uncombed. The nails of the hand he gives Jewett to shake are grimy. But his suit is not the threadbare, knee-baggy, moldy-looking thing he wore that day at Ziggy's office. His suit is spruce. To the patience of even the new and saintly Ziggy there are, then, limits. Ziggy never could stand scruffy clothes. But he evidently hasn't figured out how to tell his spiritual adviser to wash himself.

"He's expecting you." The priest whispers. He shuts the big door softly. The entrance hall is tiled and circular, a whispering gallery. *You, you,* whispers an echo. "Upstairs." *Ssss, sss.* The staircase is spiral, with wrought-iron railings. Jewett starts for it and the priest catches his arm in a soft grip. "Try not to show your shock." *Kk, kk.* "He's very ill, it's wasted him, and you know how vain he is of his appearance." *Sss, sss.* "He wanted to come to you. He insisted it was the only correct thing. But the poor soul is too weak. I'd have had to carry him to the car." *Car, car.* "Like a baby." *Be, be.*

Jewett is alarmed. "What's the matter with him?"

"Cancer of the pancreas. It's not painful." Is the priest taking credit for this? The power of prayer?

"Not painful," Jewett says. "Just fatal?" *Fatal.*

The priest's mouth forms a grim line. He nods.

Jewett does not want to go up the stairs. He is angry at Ziggy for summoning him here. Damn it, he sounded fine on the phone. True, he didn't talk long. It was important, he'd be grateful, that was all. Jewett assumed it was business and rang Morry's office to ask Morry to come with him. Morry is in Australia. Just as well. This is not business. This is good-bye, isn't it? He has been trying for months to prepare himself for Susan's dying and knows he hasn't managed it. And now this. Why? He and Ziggy have remained strangers. Not since that July meeting have they even spoken. Ziggy was never sentimental. Wait. Wrong. That day he was. Misty-eyed. Religion has done it to him. And the fear of death. Jewett wants to walk out of here now as he did in 1954. He can't. He follows the priest up the stairs.

Propped by pillows, with scripts and papers scattered around him on the counterpane, Ziggy looks like a mummy, shrunken, dried by centuries, yellow-brown parchment skin taut. His sunken eyes shine like those of an animal peering out of a trap. When he smiles at Jewett, his teeth look more false and ill fitting than ever. The hand that takes Jewett's is a claw. "Don't look so shocked. You should have seen me when I was sick." He laughs.

Jewett is speechless. He stares at the papers.

"You see?" Ziggy says. "I'm working again."

"I see." Jewett nods and forces a smile. The priest sets a Mexican painted chair with a woven grass seat next to the bed for Jewett. He sits on it. The legs are too short. The chair creaks. "That's great," he says hopelessly.

Ziggy taps a newspaper. "An actor in the White House! Isn't that the craziest thing you ever heard?"

Jokes are welcome in sickrooms. Jewett thinks of a joke. "Not the craziest. It could have been an agent."

Ziggy laughs again. It is a ghastly sight. He pounds the bed with curled claws. "Listen," he gasps through the laughter. "If he'd been my client, I could have got him real money, star money. He wouldn't have needed to moonlight." He laughs and laughs.

Jewett grins to be obliging. But he knows Ziggy. All this merriment is a cover-up. "You're busy and you don't feel well. I don't want to keep you. What did you want to see me about?"

" 'It might have been an agent!' " Ziggy laughs again. "That's a good one, it really is. Wonderful."

" 'He wouldn't have needed to moonlight,' " Jewett says. "That's not bad, either." He waits, distrustful.

"Moonlighting—being President? No, that's not bad." Ziggy makes believe his amusement is beyond control. He straightens his wasted face only to have mirth break it up again. Whatever he is postponing must be serious. Jewett doesn't laugh with him. And at last Ziggy sobers.

"I wanted to give you your script"—he frowns and scratches among the litter—"for the next episode."

"Why?" Jewett feels cold. "Toby Gold always gives out the scripts."

Ziggy finds the script and holds it out. "I wanted to see you before you read it." He watches Jewett, who accepts the red-covered thing as if it were a letter bomb. "It's the end of Uncle Julius. I'm sorry." Jewett stares at him. He can think of nothing to say. He flips over the pages of the script, but blindly. "The ratings are falling," Ziggy says. "The mail is bad. The viewers don't like him. Not the way they hate T.J. Not hiss the villain and enjoy yourself. Nobody believes in T.J. They believe in Uncle Julius. He's too real and that's no fun."

"Nobody warned me," Jewett says.

"They warned me. Schumacher, the writers. They came to me and said you weren't going over. I told them to wait. The viewers still missed old Judd. They'd get used to you. They'd get to love you. They'd want T-shirts with your face." Ziggy sighs, and his head falls back against the pillows, eyes closed. He looks dead. He says, in a frail, droning voice, "They didn't. The ratings don't lie. I couldn't buck dollars and cents." He opens his eyes for a moment and smiles a pleading smile. "Forgive me? I tried."

"Nothing to forgive." Jewett gets to his feet. "It never felt right to me. I just gave it my best shot. I'm grateful to you for the opportunity. It was generous."

But Ziggy doesn't hear. He is asleep and snoring.

"Don't worry about it," Young Joe says.

It is early afternoon, foggy, chill. He sits in a down parka with the hood up, on a freshly painted but old and tilted roundabout in a small park a block from the bakery. Long ago, Jewett and Joey flew kites here. Or sat on rickety benches and watched little kids play baseball with an adhesive-taped bat almost as big as themselves, and a fat gray ball with its cover flapping off. This bored Jewett, but it made Joey laugh—and Joey laughing was a rare and pleasing thing to see, so Jewett sat and didn't complain.

"You gave me a hefty down payment." Young Joe idly pushes with his shoe in the rut worn by children riding the roundabout and it slowly turns. He lifts his foot and rides, and when the motion slows, pushes again. "You took a risk. Why should you be the only one? Forget the floor under the monthly payments. The percentage will be enough. Shop's doing fine. No reason to worry."

"That's very generous," Jewett says.

The roundabout brings Joe full circle and he gets off it. "I'm sorry about your bad luck. Looks like in your business you never know." A gull glides down through the fog to perch at the top of the children's slide. Joe shakes his head. "We all thought you were sensational."

The weekend after Richie Cowan's funeral in that bare-bones church, Jewett hiked by himself. Far back in the mountains was a small lake, with four shacky tourist cabins and a rickety pier. It was among big pines on a side road and no one much went there. Andrew Jewett had taken him two or three times in the 1920s when he was small. To teach him to swim—"in real water, not chemicals"—to teach him to row, to teach him to fish. Fish were abundant in that little lake. Jewett learned, but it pained him to watch the fish gasp out their bleeding lives in the bottom of the boat. When later he led Richie to the lake, it wasn't to fish.

The cabins were all empty. The reedy old man with no teeth who looked after the place was friendly, but he minded his own business. The steel-pipe cot in the that stud-and-plank cabin was the first and only place where Jewett and Richie ever slept a night together. Free to smoke, they made themselves a little sick on cigarettes. In the bottom of the bottle of red wine they brought, they found leaves. They spent the day poking around the edges of the lake in one of the four leaky rowboats the old man rented out. The lake curved. At its far end, out of sight of the cabins, they stripped and swam together and wrestled in the shallows, and got erections, and reduced the swellings lying naked in mottled sunlight on the duff under the pines, where they were bitten by large, black ants. When they came back at dusk, the old man, pitying them the canned food they'd brought in their knapsacks, fed them fresh fish he fried on the woodstove in his shack. It tasted wonderful.

Jewett went back there because he was alarmed that he wasn't feeling anything. He hadn't cried for Richie. He went hours through his days at school without even thinking of Richie. This was wrong and inhuman and he believed something terrible was the matter with him. A tragic thing had happened. He had lost somebody he loved, lost him forever, and it seemed to be nothing but a cold fact. Being queer was bad enough. Having no feelings—that was too much to live with. In the nights awake, he tried to force himself to cry. His eyes remained dry. Desperate, he told his father. Not about the sex, about the worry.

"Richie was my best friend. What's wrong with me?"

"Maybe you only thought so," his father said. "Sometimes when we're young, we don't understand our feelings."

So he hiked alone back to the lake because that was where Richie and he had the best time they ever had together. It was late autumn again, and the cabins were empty again, and so he could sleep in the same iron cot as before, and smoke and drink

wine by the light of the same old kerosene lamp. And the next
day take out the same rowboat—or if it wasn't the same, it was
just as leaky. He rowed alone around the edges of the lake. He
found the reedy inlet with a thin glaze of ice on it this early
morning, where they had watched the muskrat, and the
muskrat, sitting up on a mound of dried reeds very still, had
watched them. Here Richie had let a hand drag in the water and
jerked it back in surprise when a fish kissed his fingers.

At last, here was the place where they swam. Shivering—it
hadn't been so cold before—Jewett stripped and lowered himself into the icy water. He swam around the boat, then waded
ashore and lay under the pines and miserably jacked off, eyes
closed, imagining Richie naked beside him, imagining it was
Richie's hand on his cock, not his own, Richie's cock in his
hand. He waded out again and climbed into the boat, nearly
swamping it. He hadn't thought to bring a towel. He got wet
into his clothes. As he rowed, he wished for the sun that had
shone on them that day. But the sky instead grew darker. He
sneezed. His nose began to run. He scarcely noticed. He was
waiting to feel grief, waiting for the tears to come. They didn't
come.

In the middle of the lake, he stopped rowing. He sat there
hunched, shivering, water dribbling cold down the back of his
neck from his hair. To this day he doesn't know how it happened. He supposes he fell asleep. But when he came to, the
oars were no longer in his grip. The oars had floated out of
reach. It was misting rain. A cold, mean wind was gusting
across the dark surface of the lake, making quick, slappy little
waves. The boat was drifting. At first he numbly sat and let it
drift. But the water in the bottom of the boat was over his shoe
tops. The lake was not big. But it was farther to shore than he
could swim in water so cold. He began to shout for help. It was a
long time before the old man heard.

He has remembered this because the phrase keeps coming to
mind—that he is adrift. He has worked almost every day since
August, often ten, twelve hours a day on the sound stages, small

worlds of their own that never turn, where God never separated the light from the darkness. There were lines to learn, often many lines. There was the drive each morning to the studio, the drive home at the end of each day's shooting. There were the flights to Oregon for location work in lumbering country. There were the Saturdays filled with cleaning, cooking, laundering for Susan. There were those absurd off-day excursions in the vain hope of keeping Bill amused. And now all of it has stopped. He still sees her, but Susan is looking after herself. Bill is wandering from party to party—people have rung up to say so. Jewett is out of a job. Morry is out of the country. The bakery is still in escrow. Jewett is adrift. And in danger.

He puts down the receiver. Inside his head, Mavis McWhirter says, *lonely and old and sex-starved*. He grimaces at himself and pushes up out of the chair where he has been staring at the local news on the television screen and drinking. He is drinking too much these days. He steps to the set in his stocking feet and switches it off. He frowns at the telephone, picks up his glass and finishes the scotch in it, sets it down, goes to find his shoes. The nights are always cold now. He puts on a corduroy car coat and a corduroy cap with earflaps. On the cold parking level, he pulls driving gloves from a pocket of the coat and works his hands into them. He drives south to Venice and east on Venice to the Mar Vista market. Before he swings the car into the parking lot, he sees Larry standing beside the pay telephones at a lighted corner of the building. He wears the bulky vest again, his hands are stuffed into his jeans pockets, an airline bag rests between his feet. Jewett halts the car in front of him, leans across, and opens the passenger door. Larry squints, then smiles, picks up the bag, tosses it into the backseat, drops into the front seat, slams the door. He radiates excitement.

"I figured out a way for us," he says.

Dodging abandoned shopping carts, Jewett drives slowly between rows of cars waiting for shoppers in the market. "What's in the bag?"

"Basketball uniform, socks, shoes, a jockstrap."

Waiting in the driveway for traffic to pass, Jewett raises eyebrows at him. "You want me to watch you play basketball?"

"Shit, I can't play basketball." He puts a hand in Jewett's lap and squeezes. "But I'll model the jockstrap for you, if you want."

Jewett gently but firmly takes the boy's hand and puts it in the boy's lap. "Easy does it," he says. Traffic clears. He turns onto Venice, eastward again, not in the direction of the apartment. "It's camouflage, right? Cherry Lee and Dolan and all the little Haycocks think you're playing basketball at school. You told them so."

"I hate lying," Larry says. "Dolan always lies. I don't want to be like Dolan."

"If you don't want to be, you won't be."

"It's not at school. They could check up on me there if they got suspicious. I don't know why they would. They've got Newton and the other kids to worry about. I never gave them any trouble. But just to make sure, it's a church team. They wouldn't go near a church. Oh, Dolan might, if he thought he could steal the collection. But Cherry Lee never would. Her old man was into religion. When she was thirteen and got knocked up, he made her and Dolan get married, and never let her come home again. Where are we going?"

"To McDonald's," Jewett says. "For those sweet hamburgers you like so much." He glances at the boy. The boy looks astonished. "And then, when you've had all you can eat, I'll drive you to the church. On time."

He climbs the long steps to the house on Deodar Street. The trees are darker in winter, the old needles darker, more brittle. The glossy ground ivy is strewn with brown needles, and the steps are cushiony with them. The sky is a clear, cold blue today. There is no sign of rain, but rain will come one day soon, so he must sweep the steps and dig the accumulated needles out of the narrow drains. He smiles to himself. Proust had it backward. It is the past that recaptures us. He frowns. The morning paper lies on the porch. He picks it up by its string, pushes the bell button, thumbs the latch. But the latch does not give. The door is locked.

He has a key left over from the months when Susan was so sick. He turns it in the lock, pushes the door, and walks into the dim front room, where all that breaks the silence is the immemorial ticktock of the big clock. "Susan?" he calls, but he is sure she isn't here. A house tells you when there is no one in it. At least, this house tells him. As a child, he always felt a queer little shiver of excitement, coming home, finding everyone gone. There was a sadness about it too. And, later, in his teens, a stir of secret sexuality. "Susan?" He closes the door, goes through the dining room, where the loom stands empty, and down the hall to her room.

The bed is unmade, blankets and quilt in a rumpled heap on the floor. The sheets are missing. And where are the pillows? Why would she start to change her bed and quit in the middle? Why would she leave the house so early? She is a dedicated sleeper-in. He steps across to the kitchen. It is not so clean as he was keeping it, but it is far from slovenly. Her illness changed her. When the remission came, she found joy in the ability to do chores she had scorned before as pointless drudgery. From its place on the cold stove he lifts the old drip coffee pot—blue enamel, white specks. Empty. No sign anywhere of a tea bag, a drinking mug, an empty cereal bowl. No bacon grease in a frying pan. Cupboards and refrigerator are well stocked. He always sees to that. No need for her to go to the market. "Susan?"

He glances into his room, his parents' room. No one. He goes out and down the long stairs to the garage. A corroded padlock fastens the sagging doors. He has a key. He rattles the lock apart, drags one leaf of the doors open, puts his head inside. Her car sits there. His frown deepens. He pushes the door shut and closes the padlock. He stands rubbing his forehead. She wouldn't walk anywhere. What the hell is going on? Can she be sick? He climbs the stairs again. He saw her only a few days ago. She likes him to be with her for the "Timberlands" shows. Had she been paler than normal for her lately? Maybe. Come to think of it, she had let him serve her supper in bed. He hurries through the now ominously silent house, pushes open the spring-twanging back screen door, looks over the steeply rising yard.

But through the untrimmed trees, overgrown shrubs, he can see she is not here. She wouldn't be. When they were children in summer, their mother had insisted Susan leave her bed to lie on a redwood chaise in the sun. Alice Jewett believed the sun had healing powers. Susan demanded the doctor tell her this was nonsense, but the best she could get from him was that it couldn't do any harm, and it might possibly do some good. To make it less disagreeable for Susan, Jewett sat with her, read to her, played chess with her, chinese checkers, rummy, worked jigsaw puzzles with her. She would never come out here voluntarily—not even today, fifty years later. Jewett lets the screen door fall closed.

He starts for Susan's room, where the telephone waits beside the bed, but he veers off. He needs to use the toilet. The bathtub is full of water. Submerged in the water are her sheets and pillowcases. They are stained with blood, and the water is pink with blood. For a minute he simply stands and stares, unable to take it in. Hideous things happen these days. Almost every night on the television news come reports of old women living alone stabbed, clubbed, shot to death. He runs to the dresser in her room and yanks open the drawer where she keeps her money, checks, papers. Nothing has been disturbed. There is almost two hundred dollars in cash. He shuts the drawer. He mocks his scared old face in the mirror. What sort of murderer would strip a bed and put the bloody sheets to soak? He turns for the phone.

The directory lies on the floor next to the spindly legs of the bedside stand. Open, soaked with blood. He reaches for the instrument and sees the notepad lying beside it. The top sheet is smeared with blood. But on it, in a shaky scrawl, is penciled a telephone number. Why hadn't she called him? Too far away, of course. Whom had she called? He lifts the receiver on which blood has dried, and pokes at the number buttons on the phone. The answer is a long time coming. *Hemorrhage*, he thinks, he knows. The damned leukemia is back. At last his ring is answered. With a single word. The voice is female, nasal, bored.

"Ambulance."

Above the San Fernando Valley the night sky in winter is vast, glossy-black, and cold. Jewett drives wide boulevards that shout light at that sky. He is looking for those high revolving red-and-white-striped buckets that mark Kentucky Fried Chicken outlets. Old Colonel Sanders smiles at him. Jewett wheels the Toyota into each parking lot in turn, gets out, locks the car, pushes into the glass and plastic shop with its clean, reflecting surfaces, and searches with his eyes among the look-alike, neat youngsters in their cheerful red and white outfits, behind display cases of pies and paper pints of coleslaw. He cranes to see beyond the service counters into the stainless-steel kitchens, where other youngsters move in and out of sight, boxing orders. He repeats his search three times.

At the third store, feeling conspicuous and ashamed, he stands in line. The lad taking customer orders, speaking them into a microphone for the kitchen help, ringing up totals on the cash register, taking money, making change, retrieving filled boxes, sliding these over to customers with a mechanical smile and a thank you is Larry. The queue is long. Jewett has time to change his mind. He ought to turn and leave. He is making a mistake. But he won't turn and leave, will he? Susan is dying. Life is desperately short. He is lonely and in need. Damn Bill, anyway. But no. If Larry hadn't offered himself, Jewett wouldn't be here. He could weather the loneliness, dismiss the need. He is old enough. Sex is no longer the demand it was. But Larry has offered himself. And Jewett is here.

When he reaches the counter, Larry is frowning at a tally on the cash register. He tears off the sales slip and turns with it to shout a question across the service counter into the kitchen. He listens for the answer, and when he has it, turns back with an armload of striped paper buckets, which he sets on the order counter. He tucks the slip into the topmost bucket, starts to turn back, sees Jewett, and begins a smile. He doesn't complete it. Puzzlement takes over. "What are you doing here?"

"What time do you get off?" Jewett says.

"Ten, but—" Larry raises his eyes to a clock with a red-and-white-striped face above the serving window, between the big posters that list prices. Jewett too looks at the clock. It is not quite nine. Larry fetches striped wax-paper cups from the service window and sets these with the buckets. Under frosty-looking plastic lids, crushed ice whispers. "But you said—"

"I'll be waiting," Jewett says.

Jewett waits. The parking lot is narrow, the number of slots scant, but he doesn't move. He watches because there is nothing else to watch, shoppers come and go, come empty-handed, leave with suppers. They aren't like the customers at the Colonel Sanders in Mar Vista: these are monotonously white and middle-class. He yawns. He checks his watch. He dozes. From the far end of the hall of the house on Deodar Street, on that long-lost day of rain, young Ungar in his priest's collar stares at sixteen-year-old Jewett naked, heading for the bathroom, where the water splashes steaming in the tub. He knows the look in the curate's eyes and it frightens him. He opens his own eyes. What the hell is he doing here? He turns the key in the ignition and for a moment runs the engine. But he doesn't release the parking brake, doesn't shift into reverse. He knows what he is doing. He doesn't like it, but he knows. He turns the engine off.

He must stay awake. He nods again. Le Clerc, in soft blue sweater, soft wide-wale corduroys, soft shoes, softly shuts the door to the dressing room. He is pale but he smiles. He sits on a bentwood chair and draws thin, mystified Oliver, eleven years old, between his thighs. Gently and with trembling hands he strips away Oliver's shirt. His hands travel young Oliver's skin, hands warm, moist, caressing. And Oliver takes alarm. He tries to get away. The man's thighs clamp him tight and he looks frightened too. His whispers turn to begging. But his panic panics Oliver. Oliver strikes out, slapping with his thin arms, thin hands, crying in his thin child's voice, *No, no, you mustn't. Let me go, Mr. Le Clerc. I don't want to. Let me go.*

Sharp tapping wakes him. A face is at the window of the car, a worried, middle-aged female face, framed in the white fake-fur lining of a parka. He blinks at her. "Are you all right?" she mouths through the glass. "My husband and I were afraid you might be ill." Husband stands behind her in a London Fog coat, a Tyrolean hat, clutching chicken boxes.

Jewett's neck is stiff. He kneads it with his right hand, cranks the window down with his left. He gives the couple a smile. "Just sleepy," he says. "But thanks for your concern."

"It is Uncle Julius," the man says. "Didn't I tell you it was Uncle Julius?"

"You really looked as if you might have had a heart attack or a stroke or something." The woman bends closer to the window, frowning to see in the poor light. "Are you Uncle Julius, really? You are. You are!" She is pleased. "Oh, listen." She turns and snatches a box from husband. She pushes it under Jewett's chin. "Could we have your autograph? Herb, have you got a pen?"

"At the ready," Herb says, and crowds her from the window to poke the pen at Jewett, who takes it, helplessly. "We're big fans of yours. What you're doing to T.J." He nods excitedly at the box. "Just anywhere there. We'll cut it out and frame it. Gee, this is nice isn't it?"

"Very nice." Jewett signs along a white stripe and they snatch the box and the pen and peer at his name. Their faces fall. "Oh, listen, Mr.—uh"—she squints at his scrawl again— "Jewett? Listen—could you just write 'Uncle Julius' too? So everybody will know?"

Herb pokes the box at him again, the pen. "We're not the sort of primitives that can't tell actors from the characters they play. You probably get a lot of those. But—well—if you don't mind."

"It's my pleasure." Jewett writes "Uncle Julius" after his own name, and, to forestall any additional requests, adds "of Timberlands." He is tempted to scratch out his own name, but he resists, and hands box and pen back once again.

"Oh, thank you," the woman gushes. They hurry off to their car in the dark at the rear of the lot. She calls back, "And we're so glad you're all right." She waves.

"Thank you," Jewett shouts, and rolls up the window.

The smell of Kentucky fried chicken lingers in the car. He reads his watch again. Eighteen minutes to go. He lights a cigarette and bleakly runs over again the scene with the parka woman and Herb while he smokes. He puts out the cigarette, laughs to himself, lets his head fall back against the high headrest, and lets his eyes drop shut again. A hand closes on his genitals, coaxing. Larry's? No—rain drips on the windshield. He is in Ungar's car, parked on a dark side street. It is Ungar's hand. *You've been waiting for this. You know it.* Jewett shakes his head and mumbles, "I'm waiting for Larry." Ungar says, *Don't pretend to me. You're the same as I am.* Young Jewett lies in despair: *I'm not the same as you. I'm not a queer.* And flings himself out of the car into the rain, on hands and knees on sodden grass. And Ungar jeers, *Then why are you waiting for Larry?* Jewett opens his eyes, sits up, revolves his head slowly to get the stiffness out of his neck. *The mind,* he remembers from some poem, *is an enchanting thing.*

"Hey." Larry jerks open the door on the passenger side and drops into the seat. "I never knew an hour could take so long." He regards Jewett. "Are you okay?"

"Fine. I napped. I signed an autograph."

"How can you be so laid back?" Larry takes Jewett's hand that reaches for the ignition key again, and puts the hand on his crotch. Inside the thin, worn corduroy, his cock is swollen stiff. "I'm like a bottle of soda that's been shaken up for an hour."

Jewett chuckles and gives the boy's cock a squeeze. Not like

Ungar. We're all friends here. He starts the car and lets the handbrake go. "Don't blow your top just yet, all right? You want to close your door?"

"Jesus." Larry laughs and slams the door. "I can't think straight." Jewett backs the car up, rolls it toward the glittering boulevard. Larry says, "Listen, I can't stay out late. It's too far all the way to your place. Half-hour to get there, half-hour to get back. Can we go someplace around here?" Jewett swings the car into the street. "A motel? I've got money. I'll pay."

"The hell you will," Jewett says.

The high, white hilltop hospital he ran to that childhood day to find Susan in the physical-therapy room with all the cripples looks no different outside. Inside, cheery wallpapers in the rooms, happy pastel enamels on the walls of corridors, nurse stations, and waiting rooms have replaced the old brown and white institutional look he remembers. There are frequent alcoves where growing plants relieve the bleakness. But nothing has been done about the hospital smell.

He knows he has no right to hate the place. But he hates it because Susan is here, and because she will never leave. They transferred her here for that reason from the Medical Center, where he so often drove her when the disease had her in its evil grip earlier in the year. They have given her transfusions. But all her blood platelets have disappeared. She will not make it. There is nothing they can do for her an ordinary hospital can't do. She might as well be near home. She wants that.

It is night. He has been reading to her. She lies very white and wasted against the pillows. Liquid in a bottle hangs above her bed, a long tube dripping health into her veins. Vainly. She dozes, wakes, dozes again, snoring sometimes, softly. Once, hardly awake, she whines about her sore throat, fretful, a child. She had the sore throat long before the night she called the ambulance—a sore throat, the old weakness, nosebleeds, the old tendency to bruise—and told him nothing. She wouldn't admit to herself what was happening. To tell him would have been to surrender the truth. Him, or anyone. He closes the book on his finger now, and waits for a sign from her that he should go on.

Nurses pass the open door with brisk steps and a whisper of starchy white uniforms. Young girls pass in peppermint-striped dresses. Orderlies, brown-skinned, black-skinned, wheel food carts, laundry carts. Trays of medications pass on wheels with delicate jinglings. From other rooms down the hall come soft television noises. Now and then a telephone gently burrs at the nurses' station. Electronic signals beep. Susan seems really asleep now. His watch tells him they will make him leave soon. He gets up from the minimal armchair and stretches away the stiffness of long sitting. He lays the book on the wood-grain plastic surface of the chest of drawers and starts to leave.

"Oliver?" Susan reaches out. He takes her hand, what is left of it, skin and bone. She smiles at him with dry, cracked lips. Her voice is weak. "I was so foolish all those years to be ashamed. I had a right to be here. As much right as anyone else."

"More." He bends, kisses her forehead. "You stick around. I'll see you tomorrow."

Dolan sits in Jewett's chair. From the door, Jewett stares in disbelief. Ten-gallon hat pushed back on his scruffy head, Dolan bends forward in the chair to study what lies on the coffee table. A long glass of whiskey is at his elbow. A cigarette smolders in a corner of his mouth. He squints at Jewett through the smoke, straightens his back, smiles. How much he looks like Bill! How much he looks like Larry! Gone to seed. Ashes from the cigarette dribble down his purple satin cowboy shirt.

"What the hell are you doing here?" Jewett holds the door open to the cold night. "Get out. How did you get in anyway?"

Dolan stretches out a leg so he can dig into his tight trousers. He holds up a key. "You had it made for Larry. I borrowed it."

Jewett closes the door. "Considering the trouble you got into the last time you borrowed a key, I'd have thought you'd learned your lesson."

Dolan scratches his ribs. "You'd have been smarter not to bring that up tonight. You ought to kept out of that. What did I ever do to you?"

"That would take too long." Jewett walks warily into the circle of lamplight, frowning at the objects on the table. "What are you doing with my bank statements?" His passbook lies there too. His check record. Everything.

"What is my sixteen-year-old kid doing with a key to your apartment?" Dolan's leathery face crinkles in a leer. "We both know the answer to that, don't we?"

Jewett sits in Bill's chair.

"There's nothing hard to figure out about an old pervert picking up a good-looking young boy from his nice wholesome little job three-four nights a week, is there? And taking him to motels?"

"Larry didn't tell you this," Jewett says.

Dolan gives his head a quick shake. "Newton told me." He takes a swallow of his drink. "Larry and me, we don't have too much in common. But Newton and me"—he laughs to himself—"we're like as two peas in a pod. He's only twelve, and he ain't supposed to be out at night. Cherry Lee's always giving him hell about it. She knows he's smart. She wants him to study. But he goes. And I guess he's all over the place on that little spider bike I got him. It's him seen you and Larry go into the Valley Oaks. Room eight. He didn't know what it was all about, of course. But he thought it was worth mentioning to me. Larry'd told him he was going someplace else—a school play or something."

"So Larry doesn't know," Jewett says.

"What for? It's not his fault, is it? You did it to Billy, and now you're doing it to Larry. You're the man. Larry's only a boy. They get pretty horny at that stage of life. But I don't have to tell you about that."

Jewett knows better than to speak. There is nothing to say.

Dolan is right. Larry is not to blame. That Bill was twenty-two when Jewett took him to bed, and had been to bed with other men before Jewett, is no answer. That Larry will find other men after Jewett is no answer. He goes to the bar and, in the shadows there, pours himself a drink as big as Dolan's. "What do you want?" he says.

"All this here. You're a pretty rich man. Looks like they been paying you seven thousand dollars a week. Hardly seems honest, does it?"

"Without Larry's testimony," Jewett says, returning to the light, "you can't prove anything against me. Entering a motel room is no crime."

"A few motel rooms. Not to mention this place, the nights he told us he played basketball with the Baptists." Dolan picks up an envelope from the table. "But you could say that don't count neither. What counts is what people do once they shut the door." He wags the envelope at Jewett, who is standing with his drink. "Go ahead, open it." Jewett won't touch it. "Well, all right. I'll open it. Lookee here." He lays photographs out on the table. Jewett glances at them and looks quickly away. They are black and white. The lighting is flat. They are pictures of Jewett and Larry, naked in a motel bed. He doesn't understand how they can be so ugly. Dolan scoops them up like a hand of cards and tucks them back into the envelope. "I guess that's proof enough." He grins at Jewett and pushes the envelope into a hip pocket. "Cost me a lot. I don't know how to take pictures, don't know how to sneak into a motel room when there's folks in there already. But I knew you was getting great big money, and there's private detectives know how to work all that. Do it every day. I figured it'd be worth a few hundred bucks."

"Not if I won't pay you." Jewett lights a cigarette with shaky hands and drinks from his glass. "If you have me arrested and tried, Larry will be hurt too. Or don't you care? You don't care, do you?"

Dolan shrugs. "Like I said—he's just a kid. Nobody's going to blame him. He'll get over it. You'll never get over it, Mr. Jewett.

It'll put you in jail." He stretches out a hand, picks up folded papers from the table, leans back and pretends to study them. Without looking up, he says, "A man like you don't know much about jails. But I can tell you, in there they don't like child molesters."

"I'm not a child molester," Jewett says.

Dolan looks at him with raised brows across the papers that are very white in the lamplight. He says, "I don't know how your face is going to look, time you get out. But it won't matter, will it? Because they aren't going to want you on TV again, anyway, are they?"

"Does Cherry Lee know about this?"

Dolan snorts. "If she ever finds out, she'll run screaming to the cops. You know that. Now, you just get this escrow money back from these here savings-and-loan folks." He tosses the papers on the table and picks up the passbook. "And you just withdraw all this. And put the whole wad in my hands, and nobody but you and me is ever going to know. What could be fairer than that?"

"But it's terribly embarrassing for us," Liz Pfeffer says. She stands washing dishes in the kitchen of the apartment over the bakery. Young Joe, looking pale and embarrassed, stripped of his long white apron and cap but with flour on his hands and forearms, is also in the kitchen, and so is Jewett. Peter-Paul and the girl who looks like Frances Lusk are at school. "We've made all sorts of promises," Liz Pfeffer says. Jewett has not known she existed until now. The youngsters had to have a mother, but somehow Jewett has assumed there must have been a divorce. He has never seen her in the shop. Young Joe has never mentioned her. Nor have the children. But now here she is, short, plump, snub-nosed, blond hair tied up in a bandana, her flannel shirt and jeans making her look all set for the ranch up north. "We've promised the kids, we've promised the Fergusons." She tosses soap-sudsy hands in the air. "I can't believe this. How can you do this to us?"

"Believe me, I'm sorry." Jewett holds out his hands. He is telling a lie. It isn't necessary. He doesn't have to explain. He can withdraw from the deal. It's his right. But the truth of why he is having to do this is so disgusting to him that something in him demands that he contrive an explanation. "I'm disappointed too. I want the bakery as much as you want the ranch. It was going to be a dream come true. And the chance isn't going to come again—not for me. You'll be all right. You're still young."

"Maybe it's not that bad," Young Joe says. "Maybe you'll land another series and get on your feet again."

"Sure." Liz yanks the plug from the sink. "And we'll still be here, you bet." Jerkily, she dries her hands. "God, how sick I am of this place! How I hate it!"

"Take it easy." Young Joe tries to put a comforting arm around her. She twitches away from him and stands looking glumly out the window at the brick wall of the building across the alley, where morning sunlight slants. "Liz, the man's got his own grief. His sister's dying. Her medical bills are wiping him out financially. He's lost his job. We've got a thriving business here, we've got our health, the kids, each other."

"You should have been a preacher, Joey—do you know that?" She snarls it at him, and slams out of the room.

"You understand," Jewett says to Young Joe, who looks after her dismally, "the earnest money is still yours—the ten thousand I handed you when we made the agreement."

"Thanks." Young Joe sighs, shakes his head, takes down a mackinaw—new: for the ranch?—from beside the door. He shrugs into it morosely. "Come on," he says. "Let's get over to the S and L and get it over with."

December

THE HOUSE on Deodar Street is silent. He has brought his receiver, turntable, tape deck. But he had not plugged them in nor strung them together with their patch cords. They stand on the floor in the living room, where he sits in the red leather chair, drinking. Their glass and metal glint in the soft lamplight among shadowy stacks of cartons that hold his books and records. He hasn't the heart to listen to music. He hasn't the heart to read. The old clock slowly ticks. The rain drums gently on the shingles overhead and taps against the windowpanes.

Susan is dead. Before he reached the hospital at noon—the car sunk on its wheels from the weight of his possessions, those that in the end he couldn't bear to part with—a massive hemorrhage flooded and drowned her brain. Not that his arriving late mattered. She'd been in a coma for days. *I had a right to be here. As much right as anyone else.* He laughs aloud now in the empty house, to keep from weeping. What a discovery to make, just when that right was about to be taken from her. Poor Susan. What a life.

He gets quickly to his feet. If he lets himself weep, it will be like his weeping as a child, a wild and bitter storm that will leave him wracked, bruised, drained for days. When these fits caught and shook him, he never knew where they came from, what it was he mourned so inconsolably. Maybe when we're very young we remember past lives and weep over what lies ahead for us in this one. Bad theology. He finishes his drink and goes to his room to take his clothes from cartons he has dumped on the bed. Some he smooths and hangs in the closet, where the smell of camphor still lingers from those pink, moth-repellent, hang-up pads he tried to peddle door to door during the Depression. Underwear, socks, sweaters he lays in empty drawers.

The top drawers smell faintly of lavender and are lined with yellowed shelf paper. The lower ones are lined with newspapers. He checks the date on one of these. 1957. The year Alice Jewett died. Aged sixty-two. Same as Susan. *We are simply not a long-lived family.* Why had Alice troubled to reline his dresser drawers? She'd seen him only once since the war—at Andrew Jewett's funeral, husband, father. Can she have expected Oliver to come home after that? He is surprised and moved. He'd thought there was room in her heart for only one man. He smiles wryly in the bleak light of the weak ceiling bulb. He also had thought he'd never come back here. Odd how the same ailment had killed both women. Not his father, though.

Jewett closes the last of the dresser drawers, jams cartons into each other, gathers them up, and carries them to the front porch. After he drops them, he stands in the dark, listening to the rain, the cold breath of the rain on his face. He never did unplug the drains. He can hear the rain cascading down the long steps. It was those steps that killed his father. Now that he is back here with no place else to go, will they kill him too? At the same age? He lights a cigarette and wonders at all the staircases in his life.

These forty cement steps deep in pine needles. The cabbage-smelling four flights to his room on Manhattan's dingy Upper West Side. The sunny yellow outside stairs to Rita's. The walled-in narrow flight to the wide white room filled with sea light in Venice where he lived out the 1960s alone among the strange, stray youngsters of that nightmare time. Even in comfortable Mar Vista—stairs. Why had he always to climb so far to find a place to lay his head? What does it signify? *Signifying nothing*, says Macbeth in Jewett's stage voice in Jewett's memory. He flicks the cigarette into the rain and dark, and goes back indoors.

He carries his glass to the kitchen and pours another drink. He sits at the kitchen table with it. He is tired. It's been a long day. Owens and Ewing, the undertakers, have a new building since he saw them last, at the time of his mother's funeral. The architecture makes no sense here, white pillars, red brick, wide lawn green even in December when the mountains rising behind it are brown. He spoke with aging plump men in suits and ties who answered in whispers and smelled of mouthwash. One remembered Susan well, from Andrew Jewett's funeral, Alice Jewett's funeral, Lambert's funeral. Jewett, against this man's sorrowing better judgment, chose a wooden coffin. Susan would want that.

In the dowdy, brown-shingled rectory, under dark magnolias behind St. Barnabas Church, Jewett found the priest, a gawky youth in raveled sweater, worn corduroys, grubby high-top suede shoes. He surprised Jewett by knowing not Susan herself but her work. The room was untidy. He dragged out of a stack of magazines on the floor the *Newsweek* issue whose art section featured her. "Maybe it's provincial of me," he said, "but I was proud we had such a world-famous achiever in town." He wagged his head in sorrow over the magazine. "If I'd known she was a member of this parish, I'd have gone to see her." He looked at Jewett with apology. "I'd certainly have gone to see her if I'd known she was ill."

"She was a very private person," Jewett said. "Will you use the old prayer book, please?"

"It's the only one we use," the youth said with a rueful smile. "That's why this parish is on its beam-ends. We're being punished for not keeping in line. It's stupid. No one likes the new book." He looked up from the pictures of Susan's work in the magazine. "Is that rain? Hell." He jumped up. "The church roof's a sieve. I have to go set out buckets to catch the leaks."

Trudging through the heavy drip of rain off the big leathery leaves of the magnolias, collar turned up, hands jammed into pockets, Jewett wondered about Ungar. What became of him? If it hadn't been for young Oliver, he might have grown gray as rector in this parish. It might be he reading Susan's burial service. *The first man who ever paid any attention to me in my life.* Getting into the car, Jewett wondered if there wasn't someplace he could call that would have a list of Episcopal clergymen. He shook his head and turned the ignition key. Ridiculous. Ungar wouldn't remember Susan. Was he even a priest today? Was he even alive? There have been wars. There was Ungar's war with himself. He let the parking brake go and drove down the drizzly street. Suppose Ungar had married Susan? Then she would have had a really dismal time of it.

Jewett gives his drowsy head a shake. He reads his watch. It's very early but he is falling asleep. He does not want to go into Susan's room. There's no help for it. He must try to reach Akmazian again. He has rung him three times since noon and left his name and Susan's number on the answering machine. But he's been out chasing around, and Akmazian may have tried to call back. He keeps his eyes on the phone. He doesn't want to look at the bed, neatly made up because Susan had told him the hemorrhage was only a temporary reversal, lying to herself, and she intended to come home. He turns his back to the bed and punches Akmazian's number. No answer but the tape recording of Akmazian's lilting voice. Jewett hangs up and leaves the room, closing the door. He has done his best. He has done all he could do in every thinkable direction for today. Except eat. He can't bear the thought.

He drops the old rubber plug on its chain into the drain and starts water running in the bathtub. He retrieves pajamas and bathrobe—the house is cold—from his room, and returns to the bathroom, where he shuts the door so the steam will warm it up.

He drops the lid on the toilet and sits on this, drinking, flicking ashes from a cigarette into the handbasin. The tub fills. He turns off the taps and undresses, coughing a little in the mixture of steam and smoke. He lets himself down into the hot water. He is no handyman and he can't afford a plumber. If Bill were here, he would fit up a shower over the tub. Jewett prefers showers. He doubts that he will ever have one again. But the warmth begins to soak into his bones and he thinks maybe a bath is not so bad. He slides down in the water, leans his head back against the cold, curved porcelain, sighs, and shuts his eyes.

The buzz of the doorbell sits him up straight. The water has grown tepid—he must have slept. He climbs out of the tub into air grown cold. He shivers, grabs a towel, dries himself hurriedly while the buzzer burrs from the kitchen. It was a clear sounding bell once, but years of paint have given it this snarl. He opens the bathroom door, shouts, "Coming—just a minute," and flaps into pajamas. He snatches his robe off the door hook, works his arms into the sleeves, and knots the sash as he trots for the front door. Who can it be? Susan never mentioned callers. Elizabeth Fairchild, the Humane Society woman, with more flowers? No. She always came by day.

He switches on the porch light, pulls open the heavy door, and is astonished. Bill stands there, wearing floppy army camouflage, the lower pants legs soaked, the jacket shoulders soaked. His hair is wet and plastered to his beautiful skull. "Jesus," he says, "this is a hard place to find. All the streets look alike. They said at Mar Vista you didn't leave a forwarding address, a phone number, anything. But I figured this was where you'd go. I couldn't remember her last name, though, so the phone book was no help. All I could remember was the look of the house."

"Her last name was Lambert," Jewett says.

"Was? She died, then? I'm sorry."

"She died this morning," Jewett says, "and you're not sorry. Come in. I didn't want anyone to know where I've gone. I didn't think you'd care. Any mail for me that's important goes to

Morry first anyway. I've told his office to hold it. Come in. You're soaked. It's cold." He starts to turn away. "I'll get you a drink."

"I can't stay." Bill pulls an envelope from inside the camouflage jacket and holds it out to Jewett. "I just came to return this. I can't accept it."

"It's yours." Jewett puts his hands behind his back. "The furniture was yours. I had the dealer who bought it make the check to you. You didn't want the furniture. I can't use it."

Bill shrugs and drops the envelope into the mailbox beside the door. "I have to get back to Cherry Lee."

"You're on speaking terms again?" Jewett is surprised.

"Trouble in River City," Bill says. "Larry shot Dolan. Dolan's in the hospital. Larry's locked up in the juvenile facility at Sylmar."

Jewett grabs the edge of the door to keep from falling. Bill steps in, catches his arm, steadies him. "Hey, what's the matter? Are you sick?"

Jewett tries to smile. He shakes his head. "I haven't eaten today, that's all. Wasn't time. Let's shut the door. I'm freezing and your clothes are wet. You'll get pneumonia."

Bill shuts the door. "Okay. I'll have that drink. You better have one too. You look awful." He heads toward the back of the house. "Kitchen's down here, right?" Paper towels are on a rack on the wall. He pulls off a handful and scrubs his hair with them. He finds a cheese glass for himself and fills it from the whiskey bottle on the drainboard. He fills Jewett's cheese glass, which has waited on the table. Jewett is afraid, but he makes himself ask, "Why did Larry shoot Dolan?"

"Because Dolan was stupid enough to leave a gun lying around." Bill doesn't sit down. He tastes the whiskey and his hands prowl his clothes, hunting a cigarette. Jewett's pack lies on the table. Bill points at it, raising his brows. Jewett nods. "If there'd been a gun in the place when I lived with him"—Bill takes a cigarette, picks up Jewett's lighter, lights the cigarette—"I'd sure as hell have shot the son of a bitch."

Jewett hasn't strength in his legs to go on standing. He sits. His hands shake when he lights a cigarette for himself. "But there had to be a reason. What did they fight about?"

"Dolan says he was drunk, which he probably was. Fooling with the gun. Larry was afraid he'd hurt himself and tried to get it away from him and it went off by accident." Bill laughs without humor. "He's lying, of course."

"What does—" Jewett begins, but he can't get the question out. Something is wrong with his throat. He gulps whiskey from the little glass. "What does Larry say?"

"He won't say anything. They interrogated him at the Van Nuys police station for hours and he never gave them squat. Same thing at the detention hearing at Sylmar. He won't even talk about it with his lawyer—public defender. But you know Dolan. He did some shitty thing, and Larry couldn't stand it."

Jewett nods. "Yes, I know Dolan. What's going to happen to Larry? I'm surprised. He seemed like a nice, gentle kid." Jewett's smile is wan. "Like you."

"They filed a petition against him. They don't like it when people shoot other people. But Larry's PD says they can't make a case." Bill taps cigarette ash into the sink. "Dolan insists it was an accident. There were no witnesses. Mom and the kids were at a movie. The DA knows Dolan is lying. Anybody with an IQ of ninety knows when Dolan is lying, but he's not going to change his story." Bill shakes his head and drinks. "If you ask me, he's scared. Probably of what Larry would say if he opened his mouth. But Larry looks scared to me too, acts scared. Whatever happened between them, nobody else is ever going to know." Bill runs tap water on his cigarette, opens the doors under the sink, tosses the cigarette into the trash basket there, shuts the doors again. "Anyway, it's this public defender's opinion that the thing won't go to trial. They'll have to turn Larry loose."

"When did this happen?" Jewett gets off the stiff chair to pour himself more whiskey, top off Bill's drink, recap the bottle. "Why wasn't he released to Cherry Lee?"

"Maybe assault with a deadly weapon is too serious for the parental-custody route. She's pissed off at him anyway. Dolan's all she cares about. Crazy broad." Bill wrinkles his forehead. "When? A week ago, ten days?"

Jewett counts back silently. Right. Ten days. He hadn't gone to find Larry after paying off Dolan. And it puzzled him when the boy didn't phone, didn't appear. But he was grateful. He dreaded seeing him. What could he say? Not the truth. Larry would do something crazy if he learned the truth. And he had learned it, hadn't he? Dolan wasn't able to stop himself bragging. And Larry had done something crazy. Jewett feels sick. If any gun Dolan owned could shoot straight, the man would be dead. Jewett asks Bill, "Is there anything I can do?"

"Listen"—Bill swallows his drink and sets the empty glass on the counter—"forget it. You've already done plenty for the Haycocks. Too much. They'll bleed you white. I told you that. That's why I cut them off a long time ago."

"Only you went back this time," Jewett says mildly.

"Yeah, well, the way Cherry Lee told it on the phone, Dolan was going to die. I wanted to see that." He passes Jewett at the table, touching his shoulder. "I have to go."

Jewett rises and follows him through the house to the front door. Bill looks at the stacked stereo equipment, the cartons of books and records.

"I thought you were going to move in over the bakery."

"The bakery fell through," Jewett says. "I couldn't swing it without the money from 'Timberlands.' "

Bill stops with his hand on the door knob. He blinks. "You're still on 'Timberlands.' I watch it."

"Keep watching. Just when T.J. discovers he desperately needs Uncle Julius alive, Uncle Julius is killed in circumstances that make it look as if T.J. did it, which he didn't—but he's going to have a hell of a time proving it."

"Jesus." Bill wags his head. "Your sister dies, you lose your job, you lose the bakery. What's the bad news?" He pulls the door open to the sound of rain.

"Don't tell anyone where I am, all right?"

Bill steps out on the porch. "You going to be a hermit here?" He frowns in the weak, watery porch light. "Why? You really are sick of acting, right?"

"I'm sick of a lot of things." Jewett pulls the envelope from the mailbox. "Don't make it worse, all right?" He tucks the envelope into the loose pocket of the camouflage jacket. "This is yours. I have no right to it. I don't want what I have no right to."

Bill looks at the white end of the envelope sticking out of the pocket. He looks at Jewett. Tears are in his eyes. He opens his mouth to say something. He starts to reach out, but his hand drops, and he turns abruptly and crosses the porch. The heels of his surplus army combat boots thump down the wooden porch steps. At their foot, almost out of the light, he turns back in the rain, says, "I'm sorry," and then is gone, splashing down the long waterfall stairs toward the street, whose wan lamps flicker through the dripping black branches of the deodars.

Akmazian is not pleased with St. Barnabas. He has laid his coat with the astrakhan collar across the back of a rear pew and left his black fedora there, and is pacing the church and looking cross at everything he sees. In his handsome black raw-silk suit, he begins edging his bulk along the pews and gathering up the green and yellow plastic buckets the rector set out to catch the rain. It has not rained since the day Jewett saw the rector, but there must not have been services since. Akmazian sets the buckets in the aisle and, when he has them all, pours from one into another. None of them holds more than an inch or two in its bottom. With two reasonably full buckets, he marches up the aisle. Jewett pushes the vestibule doors open for him, holds open the heavy outside door, watches Akmazian dump rainwater into the gutter. Both men study the sky. The clouds are dark and thick and hang low. Akmazian pushes back three inches of shirt cuff to read his gold-coin watch. He turns to Jewett with the empty buckets.

"It's going to be lovely—some of the most distinguished

figures in the world of art standing with their feet in plastic buckets." He comes back inside. Jewett lets the door fall shut. The sound of it echoes under the pitched and raftered roof. So does the loose flapping of the vestibule doors. Akmazian goes down the aisle, gathering up the buckets, dropping one into another. He carries these to the altar rail, unlatches the gate there, and goes up past the altar to the door from which the priest comes in at services. Jewett wonders whether this priest will show those grubby suede shoes under the hem of his cassock. Will he even wear a cassock? Akmazian opens the door. "I'll just stash these back here. If they're suddenly needed, we can all run around setting them out. It will make for a diversion." The buckets clatter out of sight, Akmazian emerges, closes the door behind him. "Susan would think it was funny." He looks out into the church and shakes his head. "But it really is too shabby, don't you think? Dear me, those window patches."

"It was her church," Jewett says.

Akmazian sighs windily on the altar steps and pulls his mouth into a gentle smile. "Of course. That's all that counts." He frowns again, wagging a fat finger at the pews, counting the house with nobody in it. "I hope there'll be enough room." In the short time Jewett has allowed him, he has done his best to see to it that the world knows its loss. Jewett judges he is exaggerating when he mentions mourners jetting in from Rome and Tokyo, Paris, London, Helsinki, and when with awe he drops names Jewett doesn't recognize but supposes must mean something. Would Susan be impressed? He wonders. Still, she thrived on that New York trip. Tears threaten him now when he thinks how short a time she had to enjoy her celebrity—if enjoy it she did. Akmazian may be right. A lot of flowers have come. They almost conceal the altar and the altar steps. And more are at Owens and Ewing, in the room where Susan's wasted body lies in the wooden coffin. Jewett ordered the coffin closed. She hated to be stared at in life. He wasn't going to subject her to the gaze of strangers now. As if she would know. Akmazian begins taking down flowers from the altar. "Let's brighten the whole place up." He turns, cradling baskets of flowers in his arms and, shedding fern fronds, comes toward Jewett. "We'll start with that bleak, bleak vestibule."

It doesn't rain, but the clouds still frown, and a cold southerly wind smells of rain. Jewett stands at the edge of the grave and watches workmen from the mortuary dismantle the canvas marquee that sheltered folding chairs. The chairs, which almost no one used, have been loaded into a shiny black pickup truck. The aluminum tubing of the marquee follows, then the rolled green-and-white-striped canvas. The doors of the truck slam in the cemetery silence, the engine of the truck thrashes into life, and the truck drives off down the curved lane between trees, flower beds, headstones.

Akmazian worried for nothing. The church was far from crowded. It did not rain, and no one had to stand with feet in a bucket. Maybe the mourners were famous. Most were strangers to Jewett—all except Young Joe Pfeffer in a suit and tie, and Elizabeth Fairchild, who hurried away afterward without speaking to him and did not come here to the cemetery. Busy, probably. Christmas is coming. Celebrants will wants pups and kittens to give to their kids. No old dogs. No tomcats.

A balding, red-bearded young man from the Los Angeles County Museum of Art spoke from the pulpit about Susan's remarkable legacy to the world. He sneezed, he coughed, his nose ran. Little balls of used Kleenex dribbled down the pulpit steps. Yet the service was over in no time. Its brevity bewildered Jewett. He followed the stately, stalwart old prayers and psalms in the book. The gawky boy rector—Jewett needn't have worried about his shoes, which were black and polished, not even worn over at the heel—omitted nothing. Yet Jewett was shocked to be so soon out of the church, so soon seated in the lush rear of a mortuary limousine, following the Cadillac hearse up here toward the mountains. He felt angry. Susan had been cheated. She had been hustled into the grave.

He reads the headstone on the grave. HAROLD LAMBERT 1915-1973. SUSAN JEWETT LAMBERT 1918–. Where does he find someone to carve the death date? A rattling noise makes him look up. Once more the workmen come, as at his father's funeral, from the gardener's stone shed, in blue coveralls this time, but wheeling the same metal barrow with the fat tire, shovels lying in the barrow. Jewett turns away. He turns back, steps closer to the grave, looks down at the flower-strewn coffin. He must say something, though he knows she is not there and cannot hear. "Sleep well," he says. She loved sleep. Maybe now she'll get enough. She has earned it.

The rattling of the barrow stops. A shovel gongs the barrow. A shovel grates into loose earth. Loose earth rattles down on the coffin. He walks away down the long slope among the graves. The old turf is springy underfoot. Here trees, not California trees, have scattered dead leaves, brown, almost black. He looks up at the bare branches of these trees, wondering where he is—and light rain touches his face. Down the slope, Akmazian in his beautifully draped gray coat, his fedora, leaves off chatting with a tiny, middle-aged Japanese woman in immense horn-rimmed spectacles and begins to wrestle with the black convertible top of his red Italian sports car. He has been waiting for Jewett, whom he brought to the church this morning from the house on Deodar Street and now means to drive back there. He does not manage the cloth and struts of the car top with the same grace as he arranged the flowers in the church vestibule and down the side aisles. He is like an elephant asked to put up too small a tent.

Another man, this one old and frail, the wind fluttering his white hair, stands in a clump of big, rough-barked, long-needled Japanese pines, and argues with the workings of one of those European umbrellas that folds up small. But he keeps glancing up from it at Jewett as Jewett nears. At last he gives up on the umbrella and steps out of the shelter of the trees to stand in Jewett's way. Something is familiar about the look of him, but Jewett cannot raise his name. The man holds a very clean hand, all knotty veins and arthritic knuckles. His smile is slight.

"Oliver," he says. "You probably don't remember me. Morgan Reeves. I succeeded to your father's law practice when he died."

Jewett is careful of that hand. It looks as if it must harbor pain. "Of course," he says. "It's good of you to come."

"Oh, Susan was my client," he says. "That would follow, wouldn't it? I'm sorry for your loss. She ought to have had more time."

"We're not a long-lived family," Jewett says.

Reeves doesn't offer to answer that. Since Jewett is the last relict, maybe any answer would be a mistake. He tries again to open the umbrella. But his crippled fingers lack the strength. The rain falls with more conviction now, and Jewett gently takes the umbrella from Reeves, opens it, hands it back. "Thank you," Reeves says, and holds the umbrella aloft so they can both shelter under it. The rain patters on the taut cloth. Reeves starts walking toward the lane, and Jewett falls in beside him. Reeves says, "I understand you're living in the Lambert house." His sidelong glance at Jewett is bird-sharp. "On Deodar Street?"

"Before it was the Lambert house, it was the Jewett house. Susan came there from the hospital aged two days. Five years later, so did I. I grew up there. Both of my parents lived there till they died. With the exception of a few years between my father's death and my mother's, so did Susan. Compared to all that, poor old Lambert's tenancy didn't amount to much, did it? Ten, twelve years? It's the Jewett house, Mr. Reeves."

"Yes, yes. Well—no." Reeves walks on, frowning, pursing his thin lips. "Not with your sister's death." He turns away, making for a stone bench. "Let's sit down." He sits down, back against carved words worn by wind and rain: IN LOVING MEM—. He looks up into Jewett's face. "It passes into other hands. You can't continue to live there."

Jewett stares. "What do you mean? Susan told me that I was to be—" He doesn't finish. The look on the old man's face tells him it is no use. He sits down. "All right," he says. "What happened?"

"In 1973 when Susan came to my office, I got the impression you two were estranged. She was terribly bereft at losing Lambert. And the way he was taken. Struck down that way." Reeves's keen bird's eyes reproach him. "You didn't come to his funeral."

"I was away on location with a film."

"She loved him deeply. They'd both lived lonely lives. They knew what that meant. They were attached to each other."

"What are you trying to say?" Jewett asks.

"That in Lambert's will, in the event that Susan should predecease him—which of course she did not—the estate should go to the Humane Society. He had a strong affection for those dogs of his. Ironic they should have been taken at the same moment as himself, wasn't it?"

"Susan was afraid of dogs," Jewett says. "In her mind she was a medieval cripple, hobbling along the village streets in rags, jeered at and pelted with stones by children. Barked and nipped at by dogs. She hated dogs."

Reeves, looking into his face, sadly shakes his head. "She had me draw up her own will after Lambert's death. I'm afraid it's going to be unwelcome news, but I can see no way to change it by postponing it. With the exception of one item, the entire estate goes to the Humane Society—in memory of Harold Lambert."

"We're not estranged," Jewett says hopelessly. "We were very close this year. She was dying. I was trying to make it easier for her. I was trying to make it easier."

"That was the only will she made," Reeves says. "She wanted you to have your father's clock." He waits for a reaction from Jewett. Jewett is too dazed. Reeves lays a hand briefly on his shoulder. "Perhaps you'll want to buy the house."

"I'm not able to do that. No money."

"Well, don't feel pressed about vacating the place. I expect there'll be all sorts of family papers and memorabilia to go through. There always is in a house like that, lived in by one family for so long. Take your time. The will has to be probated. The mechanisms for leaving such a large estate to a charity are complex."

"It's not large," Jewett says numbly. "Only three bedrooms, two of them small. One bath. It's not a large house, Mr. Reeves."

Reeves smiles tolerantly. "I meant that Susan was a wealthy woman. From the sales of her—tapestries."

Jewett gets up off the bench. He feels light, as if his bones were hollow, like a bird's. "They're called hangings," he says.

"But that's incredible," Akmazian says. He has managed to fasten down the roof of the little car, into whose leather bucket seat he has somehow fitted his bulk. Under his hands in driving gloves the little steering wheel is almost invisible. The tires of the car must be very hard or the springs no good: it jars Jewett's spine with every pebble it strikes on the rain-glazed streets. The windshield wipers bat the rain off the glass with the same testiness as is in Akmazian's voice. "She told me repeatedly that you were to have everything. You were the dearest person on earth to her, and you'd been so kind, so helpful. Never a thought for yourself. Nursing her, driving her to the hospital for those hideous treatments, staying overnight, cooking, cleaning. I heard all about it. That little old man must be mistaken. There has to be another will."

Jewett shakes his head. "She saw him only a few weeks ago. About her medical insurance. Not a word about a new will."

"Simply unbelievable," Akmazian says.

"Not really. She was sick. She was rushing to get her work done. She was never money-minded. None of us was, not me, not my father, not my mother, certainly not Susan. She was an artist. She just forgot. She didn't mean it. You say so."

"Indeed I do." Akmazian brakes the little car at a Main Street stoplight. Tinsel and colored bulbs hang in sad, wet loops above the street. Shop windows are painted with fir trees, Santa Clauses, snowmen. From bell-shaped loudspeakers attached to lampposts, Christmas songs blare into the rain. "The last time was in the hospital. I was speaking about your losing out on 'Timberlands.' Such a shame." He pats Jewett's knee. The traffic light changes to green, and he fumbles with the stubby stick shift. Behind them, a horn honks impatiently. The little car jerks ahead. "She told me not to worry, that as soon as she was gone, you'd be a wealthy man. Now, that's a fact. Only a week before she died."

"She wasn't always clear in her mind," Jewett says.

"That day she was," Akmazian snaps. "Dogs, indeed! I'd sue, if I were you. As her only living relative, you have every right. I'll be a witness. The courts will see it your way. Half a million dollars to a bunch of flea-bitten mongrels nobody wants? It's outrageous."

"I get the clock," Jewett says.

Reeves was right. Cartons brittle with age and thick with dust, tucked away on closet shelves, in the back corners of closets, on shelves on the back porch, on the workbench in the garage, under the workbench, on planks laid across the rafters of the garage—all of these are stuffed with papers, loose, in folders, in envelopes. Most are junk, canceled checks from decades past, bank records, receipts, tax statements, bills marked paid by hands long dead. To these he gives no more than a glance. Box after box he lugs to the front porch, to be hauled down the stairs to the curb on trash day and carted off to be burned. The bundles of old letters follow, mostly from his mother's sister in Denver, occasionally from his father's mother in Chula Vista, the dates in the early 1920s—Jewett never met her. Now and then, a snapshot falls out when he opens the crackly folds of a letter. The yellowing photos are of men, women, children he doubts he ever saw in the flesh.

He finds photograph albums, the pages black paper, inscriptions under the pictures in white ink that flakes away even as he turns the leaves. The Jewetts picnicking among bristly Joshua trees, squinting in the harsh desert light, the Model-A in the background, hung with canvas water bags. The Jewetts at the beach, amusement pier gaunt in the background, Susan in jeans, a beach blanket pulled over her head, Oliver in a knitted wool bathing suit with a white belt. He remembers the scratchiness of the suit. He thought himself handsome in it. He grins. How old was he? Fourteen? All hands and feet. Here is little Oliver holding a fishing rod in one of those leaky boats at the little mountain lake. Here are the muffled-up Jewetts in deep snow in the mountains under pines, Susan on skis and clutching tall ski poles, proudly smiling, forgetting in her triumph those crooked, squirrely teeth. He sets the albums aside. Someone may want to write a book about Susan someday. Akmazian will know what museum or university to give the albums to.

Jewett finds a thick manila envelope. *Oliver* is written on it in his mother's school-teacherish script, but he doesn't remember it. The seams are splitting. The flap is glued shut, not by intention, by the damp of winters past, winters like this one: it rains today, it rained yesterday, and the prediction is that it will rain tomorrow and into the foreseeable future. He pries open the flap. He remembers the photos—eight-by-tens. Oliver with the rest of the cast in his first play at Junipero Serra High School. Oliver, tuxedo, bow tie, in the Boy's Glee Club. His mother has pointed him out with a scratchy arrow in white ink. Next to him, Richie Cowan's face is a blur. Here, Oliver stands with a girl whose name he can't remember, flanking a poster for another high-school play. Here Oliver stands at a microphone, holding a script. The envelope also holds mimeographed programs for the plays and age-brown newspaper clippings, reviews from the Cordova *Courier*. "Talented, handsome, mature, wonderful future."

The discard carton is full, but he jams this stuff into it, rises stiffly from his cross-legged posture on the floor, and crushes down the overflow with a foot. Grunting, he picks up the box, carries it to the front door, props the box against the wall with a knee, pulls open the door, and, outside, piles the box with the rest that never will be missed. When he straightens up, his lower back warns him it is tired. Being the only survivor makes for hard work. He has been at his sorting and discarding and regretting since before daylight. He detests being here on sufferance, and is in a hurry to leave. But for today, he is out of steam.

He lights a cigarette, leans back against the rough shingles of the brown wall, and watches the fine rain sift down through the dark branches of the deodars, listens to the whisper of the rain. He is sore at Susan. "Sore" is the word he wants. Not about the money. About the house. It is full of ghosts and he can't get any sleep in it. He could never stay here. Yet he hates for the house to be lost to strangers. This is sentimentality, which he despises. This house, like every other, is lumber and nails, wires and pipes, bricks and beams. If it amounts to more than that, he can carry whatever it amounts to with him. With everything else? He grimaces. He had better forget it as quickly as he can. If he can.

Now he hears a scrape of shoes on the stairs up from the street. Scowling, he walks to the broad porch rail and peers down through the branches. If this is Elizabeth Fairchild, he will probably lose his temper with her. But it's no gaunt woman who comes into view. It's a fat man in a pale raincoat and canvas hat with its brim turned down. The effort of climbing the stairs makes him gasp and wheeze. The blubbery, blue-chinned face he turns upward pleads for there to be an end to this climbing. He sees Jewett and halts for a moment to raise a pillowy hand in greeting and to smile. He saves his breath, doesn't try to say hello.

"What the hell are you doing here?" Jewett says.

"The telephone's out of order," Morry pants, and lowers his head and heaves himself up the rest of the steps.

"You're supposed to be in Australia," Jewett says.

"Yeah. Well. I'll tell you. One thing." Morry stands at the foot of the porch steps, puffing. "The weather. Is a hell. Of a lot. Better there." He squints. "You growing a beard?"

"I plan to disappear behind it," Jewett says.

"You almost disappeared without it." Now Morry mounts the steps. He holds out his hand and Jewett shakes it. "I had a hell of a time tracking you down. Finally got the address here from Blackbird Productions." Morry looks at the open door into the house. "How is your sister? They said she was sick and you were looking after her. Said you left the number because you were here a lot."

"That was when I was working for them," Jewett says. "I forgot they knew about this place. Or maybe I didn't. Maybe that's why I unplugged the phone. My sister died."

"Aw." Morry's fat face sags. "I'm sorry."

"And now I'm cleaning up the family wreckage. And after that, I'm going away."

"Don't go away," Morry says. "I've got you commercials that'll keep you knee-deep in checks from here on out." This reminds him, and he unbuttons the raincoat and gropes inside his plaid jacket for an envelope that he hands to Jewett. "That's a couple residuals," he says. "Of course, you got all that bread from 'Timberlands.' But"—he shrugs and automatically smiles—"every little bit helps, right?" He wipes at the back of his fat neck with a hand, takes off the rain hat and shakes it. "Listen, you wouldn't have a cup of coffee or a drink or something, would you?"

"Sure thing, Morry. Sorry." Jewett leads him into the paper-littered living room, and shuts the door. The kitchen is the only room that stays a little warm these days. They sit at the kitchen table and drink coffee. It is all Jewett has put into his stomach today, and this mugful makes him dizzy. "I blew the 'Timberlands' money."

"You were going to buy a bakery," Morry says.

"I invested in a get-rich-quick scheme." Jewett twists out his cigarette and lights another. "One of those where it's the other fellow who gets rich quick."

"Listen," Morry says. "Not to worry. This is a great deal I got you. For a new spray cleaner, right? Zing? Zap? Something like that. Biggest ad campaign for any household product in history. Captain Bathroom—that's you. You'll be bigger than Katy the Cleaning Lady."

"No, thanks," Jewett says.

The antique dealer is a blithe, rosy-cheeked boy of forty, not quite five feet high. His bleached blond hair is almost gone on top, but he has let it grow long on one side, combed it across his bare scalp, and tacked it there with hair spray. Raindrops sparkle on it now. He wears a handsome Irish hand-knitted sweater whose bulk adds to the small-boy effect he obviously relishes. His jacket is a blue blazer with brass buttons. His trousers are gray flannel—Mr. Gray forever, Mr. Le Clerc—and his shoes gray suede, rain-spotted. He holds a glass of Susan's white wine and gazes up at the square face of the clock under its heavy cornice. The face is brass with a silver circle for the numerals.

"It's exactly as good as you said it was." He tightens the corners of his boy mouth in a brief smile. "And exactly as old. Well—within five years. Hepplewhite replaced that flat top with an arch in 1725." He turns his blue-eyed gaze on Jewett, sucks in his cheeks, sips his wine, cocks an eyebrow. "Must you sell so quickly? It's a shame to be in a hurry with such a splendid piece. You see, there's no market to speak of in California for tall clocks. If you were to sell it in, say, Washington, D.C.—they're wild for them there, and this one is very, very good. A dealer there would give you five thousand, perhaps five thousand five hundred for it. I can't offer you more than three thousand."

Jewett is drinking on an empty stomach. "Four."

"Thirty-five hundred," the dealer says.

"Done," Jewett says, and alarms the little chap by vigorously shaking his hand. That's what Andrew Jewett would have done. Except, of course, that Andrew Jewett would have died before he'd sell this clock. And that was precisely the order in which it happened.

The weather has cleared. *All is calm, all is bright.* Also cold. Jewett has opened the front door and stands in the living room with a suitcase in each hand, that luggage bought for Susan's New York trip. It doesn't belong to him. It belongs to the estate. On the other hand, he is leaving behind—oh, is he ever!—the television set. That he paid for. So perhaps he and the estate are square. He is leaving his stereo equipment, records, books, too. It is Christmas Eve, and he wishes he could think of a way to give them to Larry Haycock but he can't think of a way. So they must go to the dogs. He is drunk. His beard itches and he sets the suitcases down so he can scratch it and clumsily light a cigarette. Then he pats his pockets in search of the envelope with the keys to the house. There it is. He takes it out, stares at it, tucks it back into his sheepskin coat. He counts on his fingers. He has notified the gas company, the water and power companies, the newspaper. The windows and doors are closed and locked—except for this one in front of him, through which he sees stars in an ice-black sky. Among the endless junk, he found a silver whiskey flask his father used to take to football games as if it were snowy around here in football season. He has polished this flask and filled it. It is in his side jacket pocket now. He takes it out and drinks from it, screws the cap back on, slides it into the pocket again, hangs the cigarette from his mouth, and carries the luggage out onto the porch. He punches the latch buttons so the door will lock and pulls it shut. *For the last time,* says a cheap emotional voice in his head. He picks up the luggage and in the dim light thrown up from the streetlamps below makes his way down the long steps. He opens the trunk of the Toyota and sets the luggage inside and slams down the lid of the trunk. He gets into the car and drives it to the corner, where he stops it at a mailbox. Into the slot goes the envelope with the keys addressed to Morgan Reeves. As he drops down out of the foothills, he begins to hear faintly the Christmas carols from the loudspeakers on Main Street. He would like to avoid Main Street for this and other reasons, but it is the route he has to take to connect to the highway that will take him to the high mountains. He is going back to that ski town where he worked in the chain-saw movie. Maybe the fat man in the bad café meant it when he told Jewett that if he ever needed a job cooking he knew where to come. Jewett hopes he meant it. There will be residuals from the reruns of "Timberlands" for years. If he can't get a job cooking, he knows he need never starve. But he likes the idea of never touching that money, of Morry never being able to find him to give it to him. In the tree-dark of a street on which he used to deliver newspapers, he halts for a tin sign marked Stop. He gets out the whiskey flask and takes another drink. He puts the flask back and drives on past houses strung with little colored lights. There will be snow in the mountains. He hopes the roads are clear.

Fabulous Fiction From PLUME